"*You've been the* one good thing to come into my life from this damnable mess, Gus," he said. "If I have shamed myself so grievously by my boorish behavior that you no longer wish my acquaintance, then I will understand. If you decide to shed me as your sister has, then I will understand that as well. I'll never forgive myself for driving you away, but I'll understand. I won't—"

"No more, Harry, no *more*!" She flew from the chair like the little bird he'd first thought her, but instead of flying away, she flew straight to stand beside the bed. "You are good and kind and brave and generous and if my sister cast you off, then she was a fool, and—and—oh, no more!"

Swiftly she bent forward and seized his face in her hands, her palms warm against his cheeks, and kissed him. Last night might have been her first kiss, but she'd clearly learned from the experience. She slanted her lips over his, pressing so deliciously that he'd no choice but to kiss her in return.

Choice, hell. This wasn't about a choice. This was about wanting to kiss her more than he wanted anything else in his life at that moment. He'd been so sure that he'd lost her, that he'd driven her away, and he hadn't, which made this kiss as full of joy as it was passion. He forgot his well-prepared speech of contrition and apology, forgot his misgivings, forgot his worries, forgot his broken leg propped up on the pillow. All that mattered was kissing Gus.

By Isabella Bradford

When You Wish Upon a Duke
When the Duchess Said Yes
When the Duke Found Love
A Wicked Pursuit

A Wicked Pursuit

A BRECONRIDGE BROTHERS NOVEL

Isabella Bradford

BALLANTINE BOOKS • NEW YORK

A Wicked Pursuit is a work of fiction. Names, characters, places, and incidents are the products of the author's imagination or are used fictitiously. Any resemblance to actual events, locales, or persons, living or dead, is entirely coincidental.

A Ballantine Books Mass Market Original

Copyright © 2014 by Isabella Bradford
Excerpt from *A Sinful Deception* by Isabella Bradford copyright © 2014 by Isabella Bradford

All rights reserved.

Published in the United States by Ballantine Books, an imprint of Random House, a division of Random House LLC, a Penguin Random House Company, New York.

BALLANTINE and the HOUSE colophon are registered trademarks of Random House LLC.

This book contains an excerpt from the forthcoming book *A Sinful Deception* by Isabella Bradford. This excerpt has been set for this edition only and may not reflect the final content of the forthcoming edition.

ISBN 978-0-345-54812-2
eBook ISBN 978-0-345-54813-9

Printed in the United States of America

www.ballantinebooks.com

9 8 7 6 5 4 3 2 1

Ballantine mass market edition: March 2014

For Junessa,
whose wise suggestions, thoughtful editing, and
perpetual sense of humor helped me tell this story
the way that Gus and Harry deserved.

May this be only the first book of many!

Acknowledgments

This book would not be as true to its eighteenth century setting without my friends and acquaintances from the Historic Trades program of the Colonial Williamsburg Foundation. They have generously shared their knowledge and experience with me, and I can't begin to thank them enough.

From the Margaret Hunter Shop:
Janea Whitacre, Sarah Woodyard, and Abby Cox
Mark Hutter, Jay Howlett, and Michael McCarty

From the Apothecary Shop:
Robin Kipps and Sharon Cotner

From the Historic Foodways department:
Rob Brantley, Barbara Scherer, and Melissa Blank

A Wicked Pursuit

CHAPTER

1

Charles Neville Fitzroy, fourth Earl of Hargreave, was not by nature a moderate man. To him, if a thing was worth doing at all, it was worth doing completely, without hesitation or doubt, whether it was urging his hunter over the tallest fence or wagering the deepest stakes at cards.

There was no halfway with Harry—for so he was called by his family and closest acquaintances—not even when it came to love. He was nearly twenty-four, an earl in his own right, and heir to his father's dukedom as well. As everyone kept reminding him, it was time—past time—for him to marry and sire an heir of his own.

And so, with the same determination that he applied to everything else, he had decided on the most beautiful, most desired, and most perfectly suitable young lady available in Britain: the Honorable Miss Julia Wetherby. She had, of course, been in his orbit for most of the season in London—the beautiful young ladies always were with Harry—and she'd made it charmingly clear that if he chose to pursue her in earnest, she'd agree to be caught.

In the way of such matters, however, he'd only realized how perfect a wife Julia Wetherby would make after she had abandoned London for her father's distant country house. He had come to this decision yesterday morning over his coffee, and he had left town as soon as his cup was empty and his carriage ready, stopping on the road just long enough to change horses. Julia would be his countess; there was no question or doubt whatsoever in his mind.

All of which explained why he was now here in this benighted corner of Norfolk, and why, too, he was reduced to standing to one side of her father's drawing room while a small pack of country gentry paraded about before him. He didn't know any of them, and they didn't seem to want to know him, either, since it was obvious that he was tired and hungry and not particularly clean. He hadn't known when he had arrived at the house that there would be some sort of party in progress, in honor of Julia's older brother, the Honorable Andrew Wetherby, who was leaving soon for a tour of the Continent. While Harry was perfectly happy to wish Wetherby *bon voyage,* he hadn't wanted to be part of this boisterous country celebration, and he didn't want to have to pretend that he did. What he wanted was Julia.

"Where the devil is your sister hiding herself, Wetherby?" Harry said to the brother after the customary good wishes. The two were standing together, relegated to the area near the fireplace with the other unattached gentlemen. "She was told I was here at least a half hour ago."

The Honorable Andrew Wetherby sighed in sympathy and held his glass out for the passing servant to refill. "Julia will show herself according to her own time, not ours. You'd best become accustomed to that, my lord."

But Harry was not in such a jocular humor, not after his long ride on deplorable roads. He'd imagined this evening much differently. He'd pictured being welcomed warmly by Julia herself, and that she'd take him someplace where they could be alone together so he could surprise her with his proposal.

"I'd rather thought she'd be glad to see me," he said, not bothering to hide either his disappointment or his displeasure. Perhaps Julia hadn't been informed of his arrival; the young servant girl he'd told had been thoroughly flustered, a feminine response that he was so accustomed to inspiring, he hadn't given it much thought. "I'm nearly of a mind to go upstairs to her rooms and flush her out myself."

"If you do that, Lord Hargreave, then I can guarantee you will have a hairbrush hurled at your head for your trouble, or perhaps an entire vase of flowers," Wetherby said with brotherly resignation. "French coquettes may enjoy being interrupted as they dress, but Julia prefers—no, demands—that none should see her until she is in perfect readiness. She's always been like that, you know."

Harry didn't answer, because he didn't believe it, not of Julia. He'd seen demonstrations of a certain petulance from her, to be sure, but that was to be expected of all great beauties, which Julia most certainly was. Beauties were entitled to imperiousness. But he'd never observed any ill temper to the point of vase-hurling, and he was inclined to believe that this was more her brother's exaggeration than any worrisome hint for the future.

But Harry did wish she'd show a bit more of the eagerness he himself was feeling, and again he drew his enameled gold watch from his fob to calculate exactly how long he'd been waiting. Poets claimed that absence made the heart grow fonder, but he didn't want to be kept a minute longer from Julia than he must.

Forty minutes. He clicked the watch shut, tucked it back into his waistcoat pocket, and took a deep breath to calm himself. His sentimental father would call this time well spent, the price he must pay for the sake of love.

Harry supposed Father was right, just as he supposed that he was in love with Julia. After all, who else was he supposed to be in love with but the woman he meant to marry?

All he had to do now was propose, if only she'd appear. There was, he supposed, a distant chance that she was no longer interested in him, a niggling, unworthy doubt that he quickly shoved away. Not his Julia, his golden goddess. Still, there was little wonder he was in such a state of perfect misery.

He checked his watch yet again, as if the minutes weren't dragging by without her.

"Here's Julia, my lord," Wetherby said, smiling with more relief than pleasure as two footmen opened the doors for his sister. "She looks exceptionally fine, too."

Harry looked up and agreed. She did look fine, very fine. The one thing Julia could do supremely well was make an entrance. She seemed to sail into the room, her smile graciously including everyone fortunate enough to be in her presence. She hadn't powdered her hair, but had left its true color to gleam like spun gold, piled artfully high above a face as lovely as any goddess's.

What lay below that face belonged to a goddess, too, as long as that goddess was Venus. Only three features of Julia's gown registered in Harry's brain: that it was emerald green, fitted her very tightly, and was cut very, very low in front. Not that he objected. She wasn't his wife yet, and besides, no healthy young English male could gaze upon the bounteous display of her breasts above all that narrow-waisted corseting and wish it otherwise.

Naturally he forgot the long, uncomfortable journey and his impatience, and when she came smiling toward him with her hands outstretched and her breasts quivering, he could think of only one thing. Well, perhaps two things, as she sank into a curtsey, but he wasn't in a position to act upon one of them, not in her father's drawing room.

"Good evening, my lord," she said, her blue eyes sparkling up at him beneath her lashes. "My dear, dear Lord Hargreave! You cannot begin to know how much I've missed you!"

"Good evening, Miss Wetherby," he said, acutely aware that he was grinning like a fool. He kissed her offered hand and used it to draw her closer. "I must speak to you at once, on a most urgent matter."

She blushed and pulled back. "Not here, Harry, not with everyone watching."

Ordinarily he loved to tease her and make her blush, but he was too impatient for that now. "Then let us go where they can't see us."

"Oh, Harry," she said, her blush deepening. "You know I cannot do that, not with Father so near. Besides, it's Andrew's party, and I must be here for him. You—you should say something more proper to me, such as complimenting my gown."

"Your gown?" he asked, mystified.

"I'm so honored that you like my gown, my lord," she said, purposefully raising her voice for the benefit of the others around them, especially her father. She pulled her hand free so she could turn before him, spinning her skirts.

"Isn't it the most beautiful shade of green?" she continued. "My mantua maker says it's called *le vert de trèfles Irlandais*. That's 'the green of Irish shamrocks' in English. Don't you like it?"

"Yes, yes, it's nice enough," Harry said, refusing to be distracted from his purpose by green silk and Irish shamrocks. "But that's not why I've come all this distance."

She stopped before him, slowly opening her lace-trimmed fan one blade at a time, with a graceful precision that fascinated Harry.

"I suppose not," she said breathlessly, her eyes sparkling over the top of the fan. "But exactly why *are* you here, my lord? I only just bid farewell to you in London, not a week ago, and now you appear here, in the middle of Andrew's farewell dinner."

"Julia, please," said her brother Wetherby irritably. "Stop being so willfully dense. His lordship has come a great distance to converse with you, and the least you can do is step aside and listen."

"You know I can't do that, Andrew," she said. "I'm supposed to be Papa's hostess tonight, for *your* party. I can hardly vanish from the company."

Wetherby snorted. "I doubt they'll notice. You were already an hour late coming downstairs."

"They *would* so notice," Julia insisted, clearly wounded. "And who else would take my place? Gus?"

"Gus has too much sense to attend one of these infernal parties," Wetherby said. "When I saw her earlier, she hadn't even dressed for evening, the wise little creature. I wish I'd followed her lead and kept away, too. This whole party was your idea, anyway, not mine."

"Who's Gus?" Harry asked. He didn't particularly care, but he did want Julia to begin talking to him again instead of Wetherby.

"Gus is our sister," Julia said. "Half sister, to be more accurate. She's much more . . . *practical* than I am. She doesn't like pretty clothes or jewels or company at all, and I vow that she'd rather fuss about with the servants than enjoy the company of genteel people. You'd never know we were related."

"That's unkind, Julia," Wetherby said. "I'm sure there are plenty of days when Gus feels the same about you."

But Julia only shrugged and took Harry's arm, purposefully turning them both away from her brother.

"I'm so sorry I can't listen to you now, my lord," she said softly. "But I promised my father I'd spend the evening with his guests, and I can't disappoint him. I didn't know you'd be here, or else I would never have agreed. But you know how fathers can be."

"That is true," he said grudgingly. He did know how her father was: a bluff, blustering John Bull of a viscount that he would not want to cross.

She ran her jeweled fingers lightly along his sleeve, turning in such a way that she brushed those magnificent breasts against the side of his arm, as if by accident. It wasn't, of course, and they both knew it. It was calculated entirely to tantalize Harry all the more. It worked, too.

"But I will make it up to you, Harry, I promise," she said, lowering her voice again to a conspiratorial whisper. "Meet me tomorrow morning at the stables, and we shall ride out together, just the two of us."

He liked the sound of that. It wasn't quite as good as being able to take her away from the others this instant, but at least in the morning he'd be shaved and washed and fed, and generally more agreeable.

He covered her hand with his own, stilling her restless fingers. "What time shall I meet you?"

"Early," she said, dipping her chin a fraction in a way that was filled with promise. "Before anyone else is about. Shall we say eight?"

"Eight it shall be." He raised her hand to kiss the back of it, and she smiled. When Julia smiled like that, he could forget all the dithering country folk around them and think only of tomorrow, when he'd have her to himself at last.

At least he could until she pulled her hand away before his lips reached it, turning to wave merrily at two of her father's guests.

"Oh, Lady Frances, do come here!" she called. "Please bring Sir John with you as well. I wish to present you both to one of my favorite London acquaintances, His Lordship the Earl of Hargreave."

With that Harry felt himself toppling into the very

depths of country hell, with no chance of escape, and there he remained through the rest of the night. By the time he finally was permitted to crawl into his bed—a bed designated as the house's "best," yet still smelling of damp and disuse—he had drunk far too much of the viscount's indifferent claret for comfort. As a result, his sleep was not restful, and when he rose the next morning for his appointment with Julia, his humor was not nearly as felicitous as it should have been for such an important occasion.

Harry's manservant, Tewkes, did his best to see that he was shaved and combed and handsomely dressed, and prepared his special restorative with beaten raw eggs. Harry had dutifully swallowed this concoction, swearing mightily at the foul taste—which was part of its potency. He patted his chest to make sure that the plush box with his mother's betrothal ring was tucked deep into his waistcoat pocket, ready to be produced at the proper moment, and then two minutes later checked again to make sure it was still there. Finally he headed down the stairs through the still-sleeping house and out to the stables, his long-caped greatcoat billowing behind him.

The driving rain that had made yesterday's journey so unpleasant had stopped in the night, but puddles remained across the graveled stable yard, and water still dripped from the sodden eaves. Worse still, a thick fog had replaced the rain, a chill, wet mist that clung close to the ground, masking the tops of trees and the roofs of buildings.

The fog seemed to echo the thickness in Harry's head, and if Julia were not waiting as his prize, he would have gladly retreated to his bed. Instead he persevered, his polished boots sloshing through the puddles to the stable.

And there, at last, like a golden fairy in the mists, was Julia—soon to be *his* Julia—warming her hands before a small brazier that the grooms had lit for that express purpose. She was dressed in a soft gray habit trimmed with a lavish amount of silver lace that sparkled in the light of the hot coals, and a charmingly foolish black cocked hat with a single curling feather. Though the habit covered her to her chin, the soft wool was so closely tailored to her body that her waist looked impossibly small and her breasts high and full, and he thought again of how perfect a wife she would be.

"Good morning, my lord," she said, making a quick curtsey and deftly managing to keep her skirts from the puddles. The grooms and stablemen faded away, back into the shadows, giving them privacy. "And a fine morn it is, too, isn't it?"

"It's wretched," Harry said, smiling as he held his gloved hands over the brazier to warm them. "Don't pretend otherwise."

She laughed, and the warmth of her smile banished the remaining chill of the morning. It was cozy and intimate standing here with her, watching how her breath came out from her lips in little clouds. Her cheeks were rosy, and tiny blond wisps had escaped from beneath the foolish hat to dance around her face.

"You are looking quite handsome this morning, my lord," she said, eyeing him up and down, and from her smile she clearly approved of what she saw. "How fortunate I am to have such a manly squire to ride with me."

"I am entirely your servant, Miss Wetherby," he said, feeling as if the very air between them crackled with desire. If she'd been any other woman, he would have seized this opportunity and kissed her, but because she was going to be his wife, he was determined to be respectful. It wasn't going to be easy; he was much more accustomed to beautiful women obliging him however and whenever he wished. A future wife was different from a mistress, though, and he would force himself to wait until after she'd accepted his proposal, no matter how powerful a temptation she might be.

Likely she knew it, too, from the seductive way she turned to glance out beyond the dripping eaves.

"The weather's not so very bad, my lord," she said. "And it's a proper morn for Norfolk."

"That does little to recommend Norfolk to me," he said, resolving that, once they were wed, they'd never return to Norfolk again. "We don't have to go riding, you know. I can speak to you just as easily in your father's drawing room, and we'd both keep dry."

"I wouldn't dream of it, my lord," she said, adjusting her hat to dip a fraction lower over one eye. "You've told me yourself that you always begin your day by riding in the park, and I couldn't possibly disrupt your ordinary morning routine."

He smiled, liking how she peeked coyly from beneath the hat's brim. "Today is different, Miss Wetherby. There is nothing ordinary about it, because you are sharing it with me."

She smiled, too, and glanced over her shoulder to the grooms before she leaned forward over the brazier, lowering her voice to a husky whisper.

"That is exactly why I wish to ride, my lord," she confessed. "Because if this day is all I pray it shall be, then it must be perfection, and I don't wish us to be disturbed by Papa, or some busy parlor maid."

"Not at all," he murmured. So she did understand why he was here, the dear minx. God knows she should. Hadn't she been leading him along through an entire London season of well-chaperoned dinners and balls and operas?

"No, no, no," she said, licking her tongue daintily over her lower lip. "I have never been alone with a gentleman, my lord, but today, with you, I intend to do exactly—

exactly—that. Ahh, here are the grooms with our horses now."

He didn't give a damn about the horses, not after that. How could he? He knew an invitation when he heard one, especially from a lady.

"This is my dear Tansey," Julia was saying fondly, stroking the mare's nose beneath her bridle while the groom held her. "Papa has offered you Hercules, my lord. Hercules is his own special favorite, you know, and Papa's never trusted him with anyone else. Isn't he a splendid beast?"

"No question of that," Harry said, noting how the big black gelding required two grooms, one on each side, to bring him into the yard. It wasn't a good sign. The horse was obviously strong, restlessly pulling at the grooms who held his bridle. Depending on one's perspective, the horse was either very spirited or simply ill trained, and neither possibility was encouraging. But if her stout old father could master Hercules, then Harry was certain he could as well.

He followed Julia, the two horses, and the grooms out into the misty yard. He liked watching her walk. She had to pull her trailing skirts to one side to keep them from the puddles, and that tugged fabric gave her hips an enticing sway. She used the carriage steps to climb up onto her sidesaddle, letting him catch a glimpse of bright yellow stockings above her black riding boots. Still he watched as she arranged her skirts over the sidesaddle and across her legs. He'd seen her on horseback in Hyde Park, and knew she was an excellent rider, yet still he admired the effortless grace with which she sat on her mare, her breasts high and her back straight as any Amazon.

Really, was there anything more he could wish for in a wife?

"Forgive me for being impatient, my lord," she teased,

smiling down at him, "but I do believe Tansey is falling asleep beneath me while you dawdle."

"I wouldn't make a wager on that, Miss Wetherby." He seized the reins from the groom and swung himself up onto Hercules. "We'll soon enough see who dawdles."

She laughed merrily and gave her horse a quick tap of her crop to urge her on. At once the little mare jumped forward and trotted through the yard's gates. Harry gathered his reins and dug his heels into Hercules's sides, urging him to follow. But the big horse wanted none of it, turning restive and skittering backward with decidedly unherculean cowardice.

Chagrined, Harry tried to calm the nervous horse. He'd always prided himself on being able to ride any mount he was given, but usually that meant the most fiery of steeds, not this quivering equine milksop. By now Julia was out of sight, and he didn't have to look to know the grooms were all smirking around him. It was not an auspicious beginning to his proposal.

Swearing under his breath, he dug his heels into the horse's sides. Hercules whinnied, then launched himself forward as if he'd been shot from a cannon. Startled as he was, Harry held on as the horse raced through the same gate where Julia had disappeared. This wasn't what he'd expected from Hercules, but it was a sight better than moping about the stable yard. A spirited horse was much more to his taste, and one that would carry him closer to Julia, too.

While he'd no notion of where she'd gone, her horse's hoofprints in the wet, sandy soil showed her path as surely as a signboard. He realized now that she'd meant all this as a kind of game, that she'd wanted him to chase her all over creation before he finally proposed, and he had to admit he found the notion of hunting her down like a wily vixen more than a little exciting.

Swiftly he followed her tracks along a drive, through

an orchard, and across a mowed field; over a shallow creek and down into a small stand of trees. The fog had gathered here, betraying their nearness to the sea, and was so thick it completely hid the tops of the trees.

Harry reined in the horse and began to pick his way through the trees and underbrush with more care. The last thing he wished was to crack his skull open on a low branch. It was more difficult to tell her path here, and he had to search carefully for the broken foliage and hoof-prints that marked her way. Hercules didn't like the slower pace—or perhaps it was the fog that unsettled him. He kept making anxious little huffs, his ears swiveling uneasily at the slightest chirping bird or cracking twig.

"Miss Wetherby?" he called. He sensed she was nearby in the fog, watching him, and he'd chased her long enough. "Come, Miss Wetherby. Join me, please, so we may speak."

Still there was no response. The fog made the woods eerily silent.

"Miss Wetherby?" he called again, raising his voice. "Miss Wetherby! Where in blazes are you?"

"I'm here before you, my lord," Julia said, whooping and laughing with delight as she popped directly into his path from behind a thicket of bushes. She swept him a grand curtsey on the dry leaves, her mare's reins in one hand. "Aren't you surprised?"

Harry was surprised, yes, but not nearly as surprised as Hercules. The horse took one look at Julia's spread skirts and glittering silver lace and that twitching black plume on her hat, and jerked backward. His eyes rolled and his head thrashed and he snorted with distress, and the harder Harry tried to rein him back, the more the horse panicked. He danced backward two steps, and Harry thought he'd won back his control.

But suddenly Hercules reared up, lashing out with his front hooves. Harry had a single glimpse of Julia's terrified, upturned face before him as, with all his strength, he wrestled the horse's head away from her. Hercules twisted and lurched, bucking backward. Harry felt himself thrown from the saddle, and for an instant that seemed at once fleeting and interminable he hurtled through the air. Then he hit the ground hard, the uncivil shock of landing the last thing he remembered.

When he woke—was it after minutes or hours?—he was lying on his back in a pile of dried leaves and branches. Everything else was spinning crazily overhead, so fast that he quickly shut his eyes again. The spinning continued, as if his head weren't connected to his body. Yet if that were so, then his head wouldn't be so acutely aware of the driving pain in his left leg. He tried to move, hoping that might ease the pain, yet movement only increased it, so sharp that he could do nothing more than gasp and swear.

"Oh, my lord, thank God you're still alive!"

He forced himself to open his eyes again, squinting upward. Julia's face was in the center of the spinning trees as she leaned over him, or at least a version of her face with four eyes. She was crying, which was gratifying—perhaps the only gratifying thing about his present situation.

Manfully he tried to sit upright, but only managed to push himself up on one elbow. That was enough—more than enough—both to worsen the spinning in his head and to send a fresh bolt of pain from his leg. To his mortification, he felt the last of Tewkes's potion make a lurching, precipitous rise from his stomach, and he barely turned to his side before he vomited on the ground beside him.

"Oh, heavens, my lord," Julia exclaimed from somewhere nearby. Fortunately she wasn't hovering over him any longer, or he would have puked on her, too. "I don't suppose you can help me catch Hercules now, can you?"

He sank back to the ground, his eyes closed. So much for being manful.

"No," he rasped. "I cannot."

"No, I suppose you can't," she said. "I had better go back to the house for help. I'll return, I promise. And here—here is my handkerchief, my lord, if that will help."

She tucked her handkerchief into his fingers, fine linen with a profusion of lace and an even greater quantity of perfume. He smelled it even without lifting the handkerchief to his face, and a fresh wave of nausea roiled through him in protest.

"Thank you," he somehow said. "Thank you."

But Julia didn't hear it. She'd already turned, climbed back onto Tansey, and ridden away. He tried not to feel abandoned. He hoped her haste showed her concern, and not that he was such vastly unpleasant company— which, of course, he was. She should realize that none of this was the way he'd wanted the day to go, either, and he was thinking that still as the combination of the pain in his leg and that in his head claimed him again, drawing him back into the relief of unconsciousness.

The relief did not last, however, nor did his solitude.

"My lord Hargreave," the woman said. "Can you hear me?"

It didn't sound entirely like Julia. Not only was the timbre deeper, without her girlishness, but there was far more authority in this voice than Julia would ever be able to muster. Still, he dared hope it might be her, and he dragged his eyes open a fraction.

His disappointment was severe. This was not his golden-haired goddess, but some plain-faced young servant, her brown hair scraped back beneath a linen cap and a rough wool shawl wrapped around her shoulders. She seemed familiar, and then he remembered that she'd been the one he'd sent to Julia when he'd first arrived last night. He was vaguely aware of other servants around him, too, the same stablemen he'd left behind earlier, but no sign of Julia.

"There you are, my lord," the young woman said. She had pale gray eyes the same color as the fog, eyes that now showed much concern for him. "You're gravely hurt, I fear, but the fact that you've responded this much is a welcome sign. You're doubtless quite thirsty. Here, let me give you a sip of this."

He was thirsty, far thirstier than he'd realized. Gently she raised his still-spinning head, cradling it in the crook of her arm as she tipped a spoonful of water to his lips.

He'd never tasted anything so good. "More," he whispered hoarsely. "Please."

"I can't, my lord," she said. "Not if there's any risk of you falling unconscious again. I won't have you choke while you're in my care."

"I won't," he said, meaning that he didn't intend to choke or lose consciousness again. He'd lost his memory of how exactly he'd come to this state, too, with little before being thrown from his horse. He'd already been weakling enough, and his determination must see him through this. "Please."

"No, my lord," she said, smiling to soften her refusal. "I do not believe you are capable of making such assurances at present."

He grunted, from pain and irritation. Who was she to refuse him anything?

"I'm sorry, my lord," she said gently, hearing only the pain. "I fear things will grow worse before they're better. We're going to shift you onto a litter and carry you back to the house, where the surgeon will be waiting to tend to you properly."

"Send—send for Sir Randolph Peterson, in Harley Street," he managed to say. "The surgeon."

"We will," she said, her assurance comforting. He was vaguely aware of the men moving around him, making arrangements with the litter. He knew he could not lie here in the leaves forever, but he was not looking forward to being moved. The woman was right: as much pain as he felt now, he was sure to feel far more before he was done.

"Miss Wetherby?" he asked. In a way he hoped she wasn't there, and wouldn't see him like this. What a fetching picture he must make, covered with dirt and leaves and vomit!

"She'll be waiting at the house, my lord," the woman assured him. "The men are ready. They'll be as gentle as they can."

They might have thought they were being gentle, but Harry felt every jostle and bump with excruciating sharpness. His leg hurt more than he'd ever thought possible, hurting so much that he couldn't even swear. He was shaking with shock and clammy with sweat, and he could sense the dark cloud of unconsciousness coming to claim him again.

"You're a strong man, my lord," the woman said, tucking a woolen blanket around him as if he were a swaddling babe. "A brave one, too. Here, take my hand, and squeeze it whenever you feel the pain's too great to bear. I'll be walking beside you, and I promise I won't let go."

Her hand was surprisingly soft, her fingers warm and more comforting than he'd ever dreamed a woman's could be. She wouldn't let him go. He felt certain of that.

She wouldn't . . . let him . . . go . . .

CHAPTER

2

In a straight-backed chair, Miss Augusta Wetherby sat beside Lord Hargreave's bed, watching over the man who loved her sister.

The curtains were drawn and the room was dark except for the light from the fire in the grate, the way the doctor had ordered. There was just enough light for Miss Augusta—or Gus, as she was known within the family—to see the earl's pale, drawn face against the pillow, his eyes closed in the deep sleep that the laudanum had brought.

Sleep, but clearly no peace. Suffering shadowed his closed eyes, and pain had carved its mark on his handsome features. A day's growth of beard only emphasized his pallor, as did his dark hair tousled against the white linen. The counterpane covered his splinted and bandaged leg, raised and contained in a wood-and-leather contraption called a fracture-box. There was nothing more to be done for him now, and so Gus sat, her hands busy knitting a stocking as she tried not to think of the danger in which the earl so clearly remained.

She had been here most all of yesterday and through last night, and now this morning as well. It was hardly expected of her, nor was it necessary, either. Dr. Leslie had brought a hired nurse with him from Norwich, a grim-faced woman in a starched apron named Mrs. Patton. His lordship's distraught servant, Tewkes, was also more than willing to sit by his master's bed, and it really would have been more proper for him to take that role instead of one of the unwed daughters of the house.

But Gus was accustomed to this kind of responsibility. Since her mother had died six years ago, she had gradually taken over more and more of the running of the household for her widowed father, and now that she was nearly twenty, she was virtually the mistress of Wetherby Abbey. The Earl of Hargreave had been Papa's guest when he had suffered his grievous accident, and to Gus it was her duty to make certain his lordship received the best possible care as long as he remained beneath their roof.

He stirred a fraction and gave a sigh that was half groan. Quickly Gus put down her knitting and leaned close, ready to listen if he tried to speak or make some other sign. But he once again sank back to wherever he was deep in himself, his breathing so faint that the rise and fall of his chest was barely discernible.

Gently she lay her palm over his brow to feel for the fever the doctor had predicted would come. To her relief, his skin was still cool, and she smoothed his hair back from his forehead, marveling that a man so large and strong should have hair so soft.

Behind her the bedroom door opened, and she turned quickly, expecting Dr. Leslie's return. But instead of the surgeon, it was her father's portly silhouette that filled the doorway.

"How is his lordship, then?" he asked in a whisper, his expression solemn beneath his old-fashioned wig as he joined Gus at the earl's bedside. "He certainly doesn't have the look of a well man."

"No," Gus whispered back. "There's still no fever, which is good, but if it weren't for the laudanum, I fear he'd be in great pain."

"And why shouldn't he be, considering what a tangle

he made of his leg?" The earl shuddered. "I've seen my share of falls from horses in the field, but nothing like that."

It had been like nothing Gus had seen, either. She'd tended to the usual sprains and cuts that happened around the estate, the same as her mother had, but as soon as she'd seen the earl lying on the ground with his leg twisted and bent beneath him she'd known his injury was far beyond her limited experience.

It was also beyond the experience of Dr. Leslie, called in from Norwich. He had dutifully seen that the earl was both purged and bled according to best medical practices, and then he'd reduced, or set, the earl's broken leg as well as he could. But still a messenger had been sent racing to London, delivering news of the accident to his lordship's father, the Duke of Breconridge, and requesting assistance from his lordship's own surgeon as he'd requested, the celebrated Sir Randolph Peterson.

"Where's that nurse that Leslie brought?" Papa asked, glancing around the room. "The one who looked as puckered as a lemon?"

"Mrs. Patton has gone belowstairs to the kitchen to prepare her tea," Gus said. "She doubts our staff can make it properly, at least not to her satisfaction. I expect her to return soon enough."

Papa shuddered. "I doubt we do anything properly in this house, according to that termagant. She should be here tending his lordship now, not you."

"I don't mind," Gus said quickly. "Not at all."

"His lordship's not one of your weepy parlor maids with a scraped knee," Papa said gloomily. "Leslie says the earl's in a bad way. He's sure the flesh will putrefy around the break, and then the only way to save the man will be to—"

"I know what he said, Papa," Gus said. She'd kept her

word to the earl, and had been beside him, holding his hand while Dr. Leslie and his assistant had done their best to pull and settle the broken bones into place and secure them with a leather splint. She could not imagine the agony that his lordship must have endured, yet even as he'd drifted in and out of consciousness, he'd never cried out once—though he'd squeezed her hand so tightly that it was a marvel she hadn't needed Dr. Leslie's ministrations, too.

"His lordship's a powerfully strong gentleman in his prime," she continued, "and between Dr. Leslie and the London surgeon, I'm sure he'll recover."

But Papa shook his head. "You've always been my little optimist, Gus, but according to Leslie, his lordship may lose that leg before he's done."

"Don't even whisper such a thing, Papa," Gus protested, horrified. "We're not on board some man-o'-war in the middle of a sea battle, with surgeons sawing off limbs left and right!"

"No, but mortal man is made of flesh and blood, no matter if he's a sailor or a peer," Papa said, turning philosophical. "Pray the poor devil doesn't die under our roof, or before he can marry your sister."

Gus didn't answer. She knew this man loved Julia—so Julia herself had proclaimed, over and over—and everyone in the house knew he'd come here to ask for her hand. It would be a splendid match for her sister, especially after Julia had spent the past two seasons in London unable to make herself settle on a single eligible suitor. Lord Hargreave, however, would one day be a duke and Julia could be his duchess, and even she couldn't deny the merit in that.

And yet deep down, Gus couldn't help but feel that her flighty, self-centered sister wasn't worthy of a man as courageous as this one. He was not an ordinary gentleman; she'd seen that at once, the moment he'd entered the house. All he'd done then had been to smile and ask for her sister, yet that had been sufficient to reduce Gus to near incoherency. It wasn't just that he was blindingly handsome. There was something more, something that Gus couldn't define, but also couldn't ignore. Yet she also couldn't ignore that he belonged to her sister, who didn't quite seem to appreciate what she had. Julia had been too given over to hysterics since the accident to be able to explain exactly what had happened, but after a lifetime together Gus could guess—a guess that was making her thoroughly uneasy.

"Look at him," Papa said, mournfully regarding the earl. "Battered and broken, yet still as handsome as sin. No wonder he's so besotted with Julia, and she with him. The pretty faces always do pair off, don't they?"

Gus bowed her head, busying herself with smoothing the counterpane and tucking it more closely around the earl. Papa hadn't meant to wound her—he never did— but his words stung nonetheless. How could they not? What he'd said was only the truth. Gentlemen like the earl chose beautiful ladies like Julia as their wives. They'd never even notice ladies who looked like Gus.

"Where *is* Julia, Papa?" she asked. "Andrew visited with his lordship before he left this morning for Calais, and he's not the one who expects to marry the gentleman. Why hasn't Julia called upon him?"

Papa's shoulders bunched and shrugged, the way they always did when he was preparing to make excuses for his older daughter.

"She's in her rooms, I suppose," he said. "I don't believe she left her bed all yesterday. The shock, you know. She's such a sensitive creature, and yesterday's events disturbed her mightily. Dr. Leslie had to give her a special draft to calm her."

It seemed to Gus that the earl had suffered far more

than Julia had. Yet all Gus did was nod in agreement, for there was nothing to be gained by questioning her sister's sensitivity.

"Is she better today?" she asked. "If she is, you could bring her here yourself."

Papa frowned and puffed out his cheeks. "I don't see the purpose to that," he said. "I doubt his lordship would know if Julia was here or not, and it would only distress her to see him like this. Best not to interfere between them, Gus. I don't want their match broken before it's fairly made. Has Julia told you the earl has royal blood in his veins? That his great-great-grandfather was the king himself?"

"And that his great-great-grandmother was a French trollop, made into a duchess for services rendered," Gus said. "Of course I know. But that has nothing to do with the fact that he was asking for her the moment I found him in the woods, and she has yet to visit him."

"I'm sure she'll come in time, Gus, as soon as she feels able." Awkwardly Papa put his hand on Gus's shoulder, trying to soothe her when she was in no humor to be soothed. "What of you, duck? It's been very good of you to sit with his lordship, but I don't want you falling ill, too."

"I won't fall ill, Papa," she protested. "His lordship's injured, not sick."

"Still, if you exhaust yourself, you'll take ill fast enough," Papa said, his broad face softening. "It's times like this that you remind me so much of your mother, Gus. She'd be so intent on helping everyone else that she'd refuse to think of herself, too."

Gus's smile was wobbly with emotion. Papa seldom spoke of her mother, not like this. Possessing freckles and pale brown hair, Gus knew she resembled her mother—she'd only to look at her mother's portrait in the library to see it—but she'd rather be like her mother in this, the ways that would have made her most proud.

"I try, Papa," she said simply.

"And you succeed, duck," he said, awkwardly patting her shoulder. "Don't know what I'll do without you, when it's your turn to go to London and find a husband."

She blushed and ducked her chin. "Oh, Papa," she said. "It won't be anytime soon."

"It will," he said, "as soon as Julia settles her own affairs. You're nearly twenty. With her to help you, maybe you'll snare a duke for yourself, too. That's why I want you to come away from this poor fellow with me now."

"Papa, please, I don't—"

"You'll listen to me, Gus," he said firmly. "There's an unhealthy miasma around every invalid, no matter the cause. As soon as that nurse returns, I want you to retire to your rooms and rest, and then come down to dine with the rest of us this evening. I don't want you hiding yourself up here any longer."

"I haven't been hiding here," Gus said with equal firmness; she was, after all, his daughter, too. "I have been giving his lordship the best possible care, and it's fortunate that one of us has. I needn't remind you that he was riding your Hercules—a horse that never respects any rider but you, Papa—at the time of his fall, and who knows what manner of foolishness Julia was doing when—"

"No more argument, Gus," Papa said gruffly, his hand like a bear's paw on her shoulder. "For you to speak like that of your sister and of me only proves exactly how weary you have let yourself become. You have done an exemplary job treating his lordship, but now it is time to stand aside for Mrs. Patton."

Tears stung her eyes, more proof, really, of how very tired she was. She didn't bother with her handkerchief, dashing the heel of her hand at the corners of her eyes.

"But I promised his lordship I would stay with him," she said. "I promised I'd be here if he needed me."

Papa sighed. "Gus, the poor man likely won't recall having so much as met you, let alone what you promised him."

It was true, all true. Just because she wouldn't forget him didn't mean he'd feel the same. She'd held the hands of many people through their suffering, and while a comfort at the time, it seldom amounted to anything of lasting substance. It wouldn't now, either. She swallowed hard and blindly gathered up her knitting, tightly wrapping the half-knit stocking around her needles and wool.

Misreading her silence as acquiescence, Papa greeted the nurse with hearty relief. "Ah, here's Mrs. Patton. You've nothing more to concern yourself with, Gus. Everything here will be looked after."

Mrs. Patton curtseyed grandly to Papa and began to bustle importantly about the room with a show of efficiency, or so it seemed to Gus.

"Come now, duck," Papa said gently, once again taking Gus by the arm. "If there is any change in his lordship's condition, I'll be sure you are notified."

She stole one last glance at the unconscious earl, his elegantly chiseled profile and dark waving hair, his unshaven jaw and the way his lashes feathered over his closed eyes. She willed him to be well, to heal and recover. Then with her head bowed, she turned and left, and did not stop until she'd reached her own rooms.

She was washing her hands and face when her lady's maid, Mary, entered behind her.

"Do you wish to bathe, Miss Augusta?" she asked, curtseying. "At this time of the morning, it won't take long for them to fetch the hot water from the kitchen."

"Thank you, no," Gus said, blotting her face dry. "I'm going to lie down for a bit, that's all. I don't wish to undress, but be ready when the London doctor arrives."

She sank onto the edge of the bed. She'd known she was tired, but until that moment she hadn't realized how truly exhausted she was. She could scarcely keep her eyes open as she held up each foot for Mary to unbuckle her shoes.

"Begging pardon, miss," Mary said with unabashed disapproval, "but there's leaves and muck on your petticoat from traipsing through the woods. Let me find you a clean one."

"Very well," Gus said, standing just long enough for Mary to untie her petticoat and slip it over her underskirt. She sank back down onto the bed, drawing her feet up to curl on her side.

"At least permit me to untie your pocket, miss," Mary said as she brought a light quilt to cover Gus. "You can't rest properly with that heavy thing on your side."

Gus wore an embroidered linen pocket tied around her waist as every woman did, but while Julia's contained little vanities like a pocket glass, rouge box, and comb, Gus's was lumpy with practical things such as keys, a thimble, and a needle case. "It will be fine, Mary," Gus mumbled, already half asleep as she shoved her pocket up on her hip. "I'm only going to lie down for a few minutes."

"Very well, Miss Augusta," Mary said, drawing the quilt up over Gus. "Sleep well."

She gently closed the door, and with a sigh Gus burrowed her face into the pillow. As she settled, her pocket slipped from her hip and fell forward, and drowsily she shoved it back out of the way. Her fingers brushed over an unfamiliar lump in the pocket, and suddenly she was awake. She reached inside it and pulled out a small, hinged box, domed on the lid and covered in red leather.

The box had fallen from Lord Hargreave's clothes as the servants had carried him up the stairs, and at the time she'd tucked it away in her pocket for safekeeping. She'd forgotten about it until now, but as she saw it again in her palm, she'd no doubt what it was.

She didn't need to have Julia's obsessive fascination with costly jewels to recognize a ring box when she saw one, and there was only one reason that the earl had been carrying a lady's ring with him when he'd gone out riding with her sister. When Julia had returned home to Wetherby last week, she'd predicted gleefully that the earl would soon follow her, and when he did, he'd ask for her hand. Apparently she'd been right.

Gus knew she shouldn't open the box, that the ring inside was no affair of hers, and yet she could not help herself. Slowly—as if slowness would somehow mitigate the sin of peeking at something that wasn't hers—she unfastened the little brass catch and opened the box.

She gasped. She couldn't help that, either. The ring was like an extravagant flower of diamonds, with one large stone centering a dozen smaller ones, flashing brilliantly in its velvet nest. She stared at it, turning it this way and that to catch the light, and wistfully imagined what it would be like to be given such a ring by such a gentleman. Julia would know, of course; she herself wouldn't.

At last she closed the box and slipped it back into her pocket, intending to give it to the earl's servant as soon as she could. She wasn't sure she'd sleep now, not after seeing the ring, but soon the exhaustion claimed her, and she fell soundly, deeply asleep.

It was the sound of a carriage in the drive below her room that woke Gus. Disoriented by the unfamiliar hour, she didn't wake easily, squinting at the late-afternoon sun that slanted in through the front window.

Late afternoon: Oh, saints deliver her, she'd slept through the entire day! Swiftly she slid from the bed and hurried to the window. The carriage she'd heard on the gravel drive belonged to Dr. Leslie, and it was now heading for the front gate. If he was leaving, then the London surgeon must be here now with the earl—or he might already have finished his consultation and be gone as well. Why hadn't Papa remembered to send someone to wake her?

"Mary! *Mary!*" she called impatiently, and the maid appeared. "Where is that fresh petticoat you promised? I must go down to his lordship's room at once. Hurry, Mary, hurry, else I'll go down without it!"

She fidgeted while Mary helped her into a clean petticoat of dark red silk, then smoothed her neckerchief and repinned her blue woolen bodice for her. Ten years older than Gus, Mary had been her lady's maid since Gus had been a young girl, and because of it often took more well-intentioned freedom than was customary—freedom that Gus usually did not mind.

But not now, not when she must return to the earl. "I'm not going to be presented to the queen, Mary," she said. "I needn't be perfect."

"So long as you're my lady, it's my duty to turn you out as best I can," Mary insisted, tucking stray strands of Gus's hair back beneath her cap. "Forgive me, Miss Augusta, but you worry that you can't compare to Miss Wetherby, yet much of that's your own doing, with not taking care to look your best."

Over Mary's shoulder, Gus caught her reflection in the looking glass on her dressing table. She had inherited the most humble characteristics from each of her parents: her father's round face and dusty brown hair, her mother's freckles and slight stature. There was nothing really wrong with her appearance, but there was also nothing to it that made her memorable, either, and all of Mary's fussing wasn't going to change that.

"I must go, Mary," she said, slipping free of the maid's ministrations. "Everything's well enough as it is."

She hurried back to Lord Hargreave's bedchamber. She might not be beautiful, but she was determined to be useful, and she briskly marched past the footman holding the door for her.

Nothing much had changed since she'd left earlier. The room remained full of shadows, with the exception of a single candlestick being held close to the bed by his lordship's servant Tewkes. The earl continued to be still and pale in the bed, with her father standing solemnly to one side, his hands clasped behind his waist.

At the foot of the bed, putting his instruments back into a leather case, was a tall, angular gentleman in an impressive wig and a costly black suit, his sleeves rolled up to the elbow, whom she guessed must be the surgeon from London. Beside him Mrs. Patton held a basin with the soiled dressings that the surgeon had evidently just changed. He turned as Gus entered, and quickly Papa stepped forward to introduce her.

"My dear, this is Sir Randolph Peterson, here from London to look after Lord Hargreave, as the earl requested," he said, unable to keep back his excitement even in a low voice. "Sir Randolph, my daughter, Miss Augusta."

"Good day, Sir Randolph, and welcome to Wetherby," Gus said, automatically falling into her customary role as hostess. "Though I wish the circumstances were not so grievous."

Sir Randolph rolled down his sleeves and bowed. "I am honored, Miss Wetherby," he said, his voice low and serious. "His Grace has often spoken of how pleased he is by his son's admiration for you."

"No, no, Sir Randolph, not Augusta," Papa said. "It's my older daughter, Julia, who caught Lord Hargreave's eye."

Sir Randolph bowed again. "Forgive me my error, Miss

Augusta," he said, clearly chagrined. "I was so eager to praise Lord Wetherby's daughter for the thoughtful care and solicitude she has shown his lordship that it seems I confused ladies."

"It is not often we are confused, Sir Randolph," Gus began, but again Papa jumped in.

"You can still praise Gus, Sir Randolph," he said proudly. "She's the one who had his lordship brought back here, and looked after him until Dr. Leslie came. No one's as capable as my Gus."

Sir Randolph's smile faded, clearly more perplexed, not less. "Yet he was riding with Miss Wetherby when the accident occurred, wasn't he?"

"My sister sought my help," Gus said quickly. It was one thing for her to know how Julia had shamefully abandoned Lord Hargreave in his distress, but she'd no wish for her sister's weakness to be repeated outside the family. "But tell me, please, Sir Randolph: How does his lordship fare? What is his condition?"

He sighed, the way doctors often did when delivering unwelcome news. "He remains in a very grave state, Miss Augusta. There are not only breaks to both tibia and fibula, but possible damage to the ligaments, muscles, and tissues surrounding them. I can make no predictions yet as to the extent or length of his recovery."

"But he will recover," Gus said, a statement and not a question. "He will not perish."

There was that forbidding physician's sigh again.

"I am sorry, miss, but it is too early in the process to tell for sure," he said. "Cases such as this one can turn so quickly if there is any onset of putrefaction to the wound, or a fever brought on from lying upon the chill ground. I have purged and bled him to relieve the foul humors, and also applied leeches to the source of the inflammation. I have examined him as closely as I can for the presence of any smaller, dangerous fragments of shattered bone, and though it is nearly impossible to know for certain, I do not believe there are any. All that can be done now is to keep his lordship as easy as we can to help promote an agreeable healing. That, and to wait."

Until that moment, Gus hadn't realized how much she'd been counting on Sir Randolph, the great learned physician from London, to bring an instant cure, a miraculous turnaround. Instead he'd offered no more efficient remedy than Dr. Leslie from Norwich, and no more hope, either. To hear him speak so frankly both worried and shocked her. She glanced back at the earl's pale, expressionless face, thinking of how abruptly his privileged life as a peer had come to this.

"It will be best to continue the laudanum for another day or two, as Dr. Leslie prescribed," Sir Randolph continued. "By then we should know what course to take next. We must be vigilant for any signs of a mortification or a gangrene, in which case amputation will, I fear, be inevitable to preserve his lordship's life."

"Amputation!" repeated Papa. "The poor devil. I thought we were past that possibility."

"Not yet, Lord Wetherby," Sir Randolph cautioned. "I have dressed the splinted limb liberally with an application of oxycrate—that is, vinegar, water, and spirits of wine—as a preventive, but from this point onward he is more in God's hands than mine. Nurse, you may take that away."

Mrs. Patton curtseyed and left with the basin in her arms. Sir Randolph gathered up his leather satchel, also preparing to leave.

"You'll stay as our guest, won't you, Sir Randolph?" Papa asked. "I won't hear a refusal."

Sir Randolph nodded. "You are generous, my lord. I

have sent word to His Grace that I will remain with his son until the danger has passed."

"I'm glad of it," Papa said. "Between you and Leslie, you'll have Hargreave patched back together in no time. Now come, pray, join me in drinking to his lordship's recovery."

Sir Randolph placed his hand over his heart and bowed. "I should be honored, my lord. I'd like nothing better."

"To my library, Sir Randolph, my little retreat from the world's troubles," Father said, leading the other man from the room. "Gus, you'll make arrangements for Sir Randolph's rooms?"

"Yes, Papa, of course," she said. She must speak to the housekeeper about opening another guest room, lighting the fire and freshening the linens, and she'd also need to review the dinner menu with their cook, Mrs. Buchanan, to make the meal a bit grander in honor of their guest. "I'll come in a moment."

She waited until the two men had left before she turned to Tewkes, still standing patiently beside her at his master's bedside. He was a slight man with deep-set brown eyes and an air of quiet calm that likely made him an excellent servant, and she wondered if he'd been with the earl as long as Mary had been with her.

She took the ring box from her pocket and held it out to him. "This fell from his lordship's coat while he was being carried. I'm sure he'd want it back."

"Miss Augusta, I thank you." Tewkes set the candlestick on a nearby table and took the box, cupping his other hand over it as if fearing it would somehow fall again. "This ring belonged to his lordship's mother, the late duchess, and he'd be most distraught if it were lost."

Gus smiled wistfully, remembering the ring's rare beauty. Of course it had been his mother's, intended to be passed from one duchess to the next.

"I'm certain you'll put it someplace safe, Tewkes," she said softly. "But before you go, I've a small favor."

"Anything, Miss Augusta," Tewkes said, the ring still clutched between his hands for safekeeping.

"I wish to know your opinion, Tewkes," she said. Doctors—especially the more important ones—tended to ignore the opinions of servants, while in her experience they were often of great help. "You know your master and his habits far better than we do. Is there any change to him, however small, that the doctors might have missed?"

"No, miss," Tewkes said, unable to keep the sadness from his voice. Though he stood straight while he addressed her as a good servant should, his gaze kept drifting back to the earl. "All he has done is sleep. They have given his lordship so much physic that I wonder if he'll ever wake again."

"It's to keep the pain away," Gus said. "I don't wish to imagine how he would suffer without it."

"I can't imagine any of this, miss," Tewkes said with genuine anguish. "I hear the surgeons speak of 'taking' his leg, as if it were some useless rubbish to be hauled away. If his lordship was to wake and discover he was no longer a whole man, that he was a cripple—why, Miss Augusta, it would break his heart, and his spirit, too, and I wouldn't—"

"Gus?" Julia hovered in the room's doorway, uncertainly pushing the door farther open. "Gus, are you still here?"

"One moment," Gus said. "Thank you, Tewkes. You are a credit to your master."

The servant bowed, and she hurried across the room to join her sister. "Julia, I'm so glad you've come at last to visit his lordship."

"Papa told me I must," Julia said, hanging back in the hallway. She was already dressed for dinner in a gown of pale blue changeable silk that shimmered beneath the candlelight. "How is he?"

Gus took her hand to lead her into the room. "Come, you can see for yourself."

But Julia pulled back. "I don't do well with sick people, Gus," she said. "You know that. I'm not like you. It's difficult for me."

"He's not sick, Julia, he's injured," Gus said, "and it happened while you were with him. You were ready to accept his offer of marriage, and to be his wife. Doesn't that mean you love him?"

Julia twisted her fingers around a lock of her hair. "What would *you* understand about love?"

Gus flushed. It was not so much that Julia was right about her having no experience of her own, but that her sister was being so careless about the love that the earl bore for her.

"What I understand, Julia," she said, "is that if you love his lordship sufficiently to wed him, then the least you can do is see him now."

Julia shook her head, her pearl earrings swinging against her cheeks. "I don't believe I wish to, Gus."

"It's not a matter of what you *wish*," Gus said firmly, and not for the first time she felt like the older—much older—sister, not the younger. "It's what you must *do*. Julia, I have no notion of what occurred between you and his lordship while you were riding in the woods."

"Nor shall you," Julia said quickly, "because it's none of your affair."

That was all that Gus needed to be certain that, in some way, Julia had caused the earl's accident—not that she could ever say so to Julia. The more guilty Julia felt, the more she'd deny that she'd done anything wrong, and deny it so vehemently that no one could ever doubt her. It was always that way with her.

"What I do know," Gus said instead, "is that when I found his lordship, the first words he spoke were to ask for you."

Julia ducked her chin. "Has he asked for me again since the doctors have come?"

"No," Gus said, wondering again exactly what had happened in the woods. "But only because he can't, since they've given him drafts against the pain, which make him sleep."

"Then why must I see him?" Julia asked, clearly seizing on this as a logical reason for her to escape. "If he's sleeping, then he won't know if I have come or not."

"Because in some fashion, he *will* know, Julia," Gus said. "Now, you will come to his bedside, if only for a minute. It's your duty, not only to his lordship but to our family."

She tugged hard on Julia's hand, giving her no choice but to follow Gus into the bedchamber. Side by side, they stood at the earl's bed.

"He—he looks quite dreadful, Gus," Julia whispered, shocked. "I do not believe I would recognize him. Oh, Gus, this is exactly why I didn't want to see him like this!"

"Hush," Gus said firmly. "I'll go back by the door, so you may say something sweet and encouraging to him."

But now it was Julia who grabbed Gus's arm. "Don't leave me, Gus, please," she pleaded, her voice squeaking upward. "I—I don't want to be alone with him. What should I say? What should I do?"

Gus sighed. "You must do what feels appropriate, Julia. I can't tell you more than that."

Julia clutched tightly to Gus's arm, her eyes wide with dread. "I heard what that servant was telling you, about how Sir Randolph and Dr. Leslie want to cut off his leg. Is that true, Gus? Will they do that to him?"

"Only if they must, to save his life," Gus said gently,

gazing down at the man before them. The flickering light of the single candlestick cast dancing shadows over his face, suggesting an animation to his handsome features that wasn't there.

"Oh, Gus, this is so, so unfair!" Julia cried softly. "I was so close to having everything I'd wished, everything I dreamed!"

Gus put her arm around her sister's shoulder. "His lordship is a young man, Julia, and in good health, too. All is being done for him that can be."

"But what if he survives with only one leg?" Julia said, tears beginning to trickle down her cheeks. "I'm not strong like you, Gus. I fear I wouldn't be a good wife to a—a crippled gentleman."

"He's not crippled yet," Gus said, defensive on his behalf. "Mama said that love, true love, would always find a way past all adversities. If you and his lordship love each other, then—"

"I cannot speak of this any longer," Julia said, a catch in her voice. "It is too—too tragic."

Gus shook her head. "It's not as tragic for you as it is for him," she said firmly. "Unless you accidentally did something foolish to make him fall from the horse. Is that the truth, Julia? Is it guilt that makes you shy from him now?"

Julia gasped. "How dare you speak such a thing to me, Gus? How can you be so—so *cruel* to me?"

Abruptly she pulled free of Gus's arm and bolted for the door, her skirts flying.

"Wait, Julia, please," Gus called after her in as loud a whisper as she dared. "Don't leave now, I beg you!"

"Don't leave," Hargreave said, his voice a rusty croak from disuse.

Stunned, Gus looked at him. His eyes were heavy-lidded with the drug-induced sleep, but he was awake, and he was watching her.

How had she forgotten the startling blue of his eyes?

"My lord," she said, more flustered than she'd any right to be. Clearly Julia's voice had roused him, and it must be her that he wanted to stay. Gus only hoped he hadn't understood all that they'd said. "Pray excuse me, and I'll go after—"

"Don't," he said. "You're here now. Don't leave."

Gus hesitated, unsure of why he'd wish for her, not Julia.

"Don't leave," he repeated. "Stay. Sit."

"I'm not your dog, my lord," she said, pulling the chair beside the bed. "I don't need orders. I won't leave you."

"Good." His eyes fluttered closed again, as if the effort to speak even that small amount had taxed him. "Thank you."

She grinned foolishly, from surprise and relief, and was thankful that he hadn't seen it. "Is there anything you require, my lord?"

"Your hand," he said. "You gave it to me once. I trust you will share it again."

At once she slipped her fingers into his as his hand lay on the counterpane, pressing against his gold ring with the onyx intaglio. She squeezed gently, so he'd know she'd done what he asked.

He did. He smiled wearily, and she smiled, too.

"What's been done to me, eh?" His voice was thick with the effects of the draft, but he was still coherent. "Can you tell me that, sweetheart?"

She blushed at the casual endearment, reminding herself that he'd still no notion of who she was. "You fell from your horse—"

"I was thrown," he corrected, "thrown by a four-legged devil straight from the jaws of Hell."

"You were thrown, then," she said. "When you landed,

you struck your head, and you broke your lower leg in two places."

"Ahh," he said, and fell silent, perhaps connecting what she'd told him with how he felt.

"Do you remember being thrown?" she asked cautiously, not wanting to pressure him, but fearing that a loss of memory could signal a more grievous wound to the head.

"I remember that, yes," he said. "And the devil-horse. But how or why he threw me—no. No."

She didn't press, not wanting to tax him further. "Would you like me to send for the surgeon to explain your injuries more completely? As you requested, your physician, Sir Randolph Peterson, has come up from London to assume your case, and he will be a guest of this house until he deems you out of danger."

"Oh, old Peterson," he said, smiling faintly once again. "A gaming acquaintance of my father's, and much esteemed because he tends the scrapes and bruises of the royal princesses."

"You have apparently proved more of a challenge," she replied. She carefully said nothing of having also sent for his father, the Duke of Breconridge; to Gus's surprise, there had been not a word from His Grace regarding his eldest son's condition. It shocked her that no one in his lordship's own family had come to him when he was in such peril, and she feared that by now he must have noticed their absence as well.

"Do you wish to speak with Sir Randolph now?" she asked. "He will talk to you of your injuries, and his treatment."

"All I wish is to have you here with me, sweetheart," he said. He shifted restlessly and grimaced, squeezing her hand hard as he did.

"You're in pain," she said softly. "Are you certain you don't want me to fetch Sir Randolph?"

"No." With a clearly conscious effort he opened his eyes and tried to smile. "Just . . . stay."

"I will, my lord." She should excuse herself to make arrangements for dinner and Sir Randolph's rooms, but all of that could wait a little longer. The earl needed her more.

"Silk," he said suddenly, surprising her again. "Your skirts."

She nodded, wondering at the significance.

"I noticed," he said, almost proudly. "Wetherby must pay his serving maids well."

"His serving maids?" she repeated. It was, she realized, an obvious mistake to make. From habit she dressed for comfort and practicality, not for style, and she'd none of Julia's inborn elegance to betray her rank. "Oh, my lord, I'm not a serving maid."

"The viscount's housekeeper, then," he said. "You're young for the role, but I've no doubt you're very accomplished at it. I've seen what you've done for me. You're a prize."

"Oh, my lord," she murmured with a mixture of pleasure and dismay.

"No, not merely a prize," he said, smiling as saw her discomfiture. "An angel. A *lucky* angel. Where's Tewkes?"

"Here, my lord," Tewkes said, instantly appearing beside her.

"Tewkes, I wish to reward this young woman," he said. "She has saved my life. Give her five guineas directly."

Tewkes's eyes widened with astonishment. "To *her*, my lord?"

"Yes, you rascal," he said. "Five guineas, and don't let old Wetherby interfere and say she doesn't deserve it."

Gus caught her breath with dismay. "Five guineas! Oh, my lord, you cannot—"

"I can, and I will," he said, clearly pleased by her reaction, even though he'd misunderstood it entirely. "You deserve it. You're worth ten of Sir Randolph and his leeches and mumbo jumbo."

"No, my lord," she said firmly. She could overlook being mistaken for a servant, but having him offer her five guineas for doing what amounted to her duty was unforgivable. Five guineas was more than any female servant earned in a year, and for him to toss gold about to the house's servants like this could send the entire staff into an uproar of envy, jealousy, and general unhappiness. "You cannot, and I cannot—"

"My lord!" Mrs. Patton bustled into the room, carrying a tray with a decanter and a spouted invalid's cup. "It is a welcome sign that you are feeling sufficiently improved to speak, but pray do not exhaust yourself with unnecessary conversation."

"It was hardly unnecessary, Mrs. Patton," Gus said, self-consciously slipping her hand free of the earl's. "His lordship and I were discussing important matters."

"Indeed we were," he said, his gaze never leaving Gus's face. "Most important."

Gus would not have thought it possible for a man who was as grievously injured as the earl to look as if he was trying very hard not to laugh. But so it was: and swiftly she forced herself to look away from him, and back at Mrs. Patton.

"Forgive me, my lord," Mrs. Patton said briskly. "But no conversation with a lady can be as important as his lordship's health."

"'A lady'?" he repeated. "A lady who?"

"Why, Miss Augusta, of course," Mrs. Patton said, pouring the wine from the decanter into the cup. "There is no other lady here at present. Now, here, my lord, you must drink this, on Sir Randolph's orders. To be taken as soon as you awakened."

She came around to the other side of the bed, tucking another pillow beneath his head to help him sit to drink. He, in turn, ignored Mrs. Patton completely, his gaze intent on Gus, who felt her cheeks grow hot for what seemed like the hundredth time this afternoon in his company.

"You're Miss Wetherby's sister," he said, incredulous. "You're not a servant at all."

"I never pretended I was," she said defensively. "Not once."

"I must insist, my lord," Mrs. Patton said, holding the cup before him.

He didn't let her put the spout to his lips to sip, but instead grabbed the cup from her hand and emptied it from the side, in a single long gulp.

"Oh, my lord," Mrs. Patton said, shocked, as she took back the glass. "That was rash. That was canary, with twenty drops of laudanum. For you to ingest it in such haste—"

"I am often rash," he said, even as he sank back against the pillows, breathing hard from that small exertion. "Did you enjoy your little ruse, Miss Augusta? Did it please you to make a fool of me?"

"I never made a fool of you," Gus said, striving to remain calm even as she defended herself. No matter how irrational he was being, he remained a very unwell man, one who should not be unnecessarily excited. "There was no harm intended, my lord, nor any done. If you are feeling foolish, then it was of your own doing, not mine."

He was already fighting against the laudanum, his eyes closing and his words slowing and slurring. "You should have told me, Miss Augusta. Told me who—who you are."

"I'm sorry, my lord," she said, "but I do not see how it would have mattered under the circumstances."

"Miss Augusta, please," Mrs. Patton said sternly. "It is much better for his lordship that we let the draft take its course."

To Gus, he looked as if the laudanum had already taken effect. His eyes had closed and his features had relaxed, his head sinking more deeply into the pillows. She doubted he'd even heard what she'd last said.

But he had.

"It—it matters," he said, no more than a rough whisper. "Because it—it was you."

CHAPTER
3

⁂

Harry didn't need the high-flown advice of Sir Randolph or even the more modest Dr. Leslie to know when the fever they'd feared finally began to take hold later that night. Not even the laudanum could spare him from the fire that consumed his body, or the sweating and restlessness and confusion that followed. Worst of all were the dreams, dreams that plagued him with a relentless fury each time he closed his eyes.

They all began the same way. He was once again riding in the misty woods looking for Julia, following her teasing laughter. That was the best part of the dream, and unfortunately the part that passed the fastest.

Because before he could stop it, he was being thrown from his horse again, unable to save himself as he flew through the air. Sometimes he fell on the hard, leaf-covered ground. More often he landed in an unexpected place, like the patterned carpet of the dining room at White's, with all his fellow club members clustered to stare down at him, or the floor in the center of the House of Lords. In one of the dreams—or the nightmares, really, for that was what they were—he was hurled into the muddy track at Epsom, with a score of horses and jockeys thundering down upon him, and in another he was tossed into the lion cage at the Tower of London, a place he hadn't visited since he was a boy.

In every dream, he was trapped, doomed, unable to move or save himself because of his broken leg. Yet in every dream, too, there was another constant, and that was Miss Augusta, the gray-eyed sister her family called Gus. Each time when he'd despaired of rescue and the pain had become almost unbearable, she appeared to join him exactly as she had in reality. She came, and she took his hand. She murmured ordinary things to him in an extraordinary voice, and promised she would not leave him alone.

But in his nightmares, she did not stay. She vanished like the mist itself, leaving his hand to close, empty, over where hers had been. Each time as he struggled to reclaim her, he woke, covered in sweat and gasping as he fought against the tangled sheets and pillows and the leather splint bound around his leg.

"Be easy, my lord, be easy," murmured Sir Randolph as he pressed him back down onto the bed. He was wearing a blue apron over his waistcoat, an apron marked with fresh blood.

"Damn you, what have you done?" Harry demanded hoarsely, trying to shove the other man's hands aside. He'd overheard them speak cavalierly of amputation when they'd thought he was asleep. Surgeons were always ready with the knife, ready to cut a man in the name of healing. He'd an old acquaintance from school, an officer, who'd lost his leg fighting in the American colonies, and he'd seemed half a man ever since, hobbled like a graybeard. "If you've maimed me—"

"You've been bled, my lord, that is all," Sir Randolph said with maddening calm. He held Harry's arm before him so he could see the fresh wound from the knife and the bloodstained linen wrapped over it. "We wish to bring the fever down."

"That is all, that is all," Harry repeated darkly. "What of my leg, eh? What have you done to it?"

"Your leg remains in a perilous state, my lord," Sir Randolph said, "though it is my every intention to preserve it, despite the increase of morbid matter around the break, which has brought on your fever. It is my belief that a course of bleeding will serve to correct the humors and restore you to health."

"Mumbo jumbo, mumbo jumbo," Harry muttered, shifting restlessly. The motion made his leg throb with pain, trapped as it was in the vise-like splint combined with the fracture-box: a good sign, for at least it meant his leg was still there, and the doctor wasn't lying.

"I assure you, my lord, that what sounds like nonsense to you is the very key to your restoration," Sir Randolph said. "You must trust me to do what is best for you."

"Then open a window, Peterson, so I might breathe," Harry said, impatiently shoving at the sheets and counterpane. "It's hot as blazes in this room."

"That is the fever, my lord," Sir Randolph said as the nurse pulled the covers back over him. "The air from an open window could be fatal to you in your present state."

Exhausted and frustrated, Harry stared up at the bed's pleated canopy overhead, watching it spin before his eyes like a Catherine wheel. It made his head ache, yet he couldn't force himself to look away.

Where the devil was Miss Augusta, anyway? She could make this infernal bed stop spinning. Why wasn't she here?

"Here, my lord, this will help ease your discomfort," Mrs. Patton said, pressing a warm, damp cloth over his eyes.

"The hell it will." He reached up and snatched the cloth away. "Where's Miss Augusta?"

Sir Randolph and the nurse exchanged glances in a way that did nothing to reassure Harry.

"Miss Augusta is not here, my lord," Sir Randolph said carefully. "I've told you before that this is not the proper place for an unmarried lady—"

"When have you told me?" Harry demanded.

"Several times, my lord," Sir Randolph said. "While this is the fourth day since your fall, the delirium of the fever may have disturbed your, ah, judgment."

Four days, thought Harry with increasing despair. That shocked him. It was bad enough that he felt weak as a puling baby and as helpless as one, too. His leg throbbed and his head ached and his entire body felt on fire. Could his life truly be in the danger that Peterson and the others claimed?

"Send for her," he said wearily. "Now."

"Perhaps it is rather Miss Wetherby you wish to see, my lord?" Sir Randolph ask.¹ delicately, as if Harry were too stupid to know the difference between the sisters.

"No," he said bluntly. The last thing he wished was for Julia to see him in this ruinous state. It wouldn't matter to Augusta, and he wouldn't care even if it did. She was his lucky angel, her touch like soothing magic, and if he ever needed luck, good luck, it was now. "Miss Augusta."

Again there was that ominous exchange of glances among Sir Randolph, his assistant, and Mrs. Patton. Did they think he was blind as well as ill?

"My lord," Sir Randolph began again. "I do not believe it is appropriate for—"

"*Now,*" Harry ordered, mustering what little strength he still possessed to sound like his customary, forceful self.

Sir Randolph hesitated, his lips pressed tightly together to show his disapproval. Then he nodded.

"Very well, my lord," he said, gesturing to a footman near the door. "I shall respectfully request that Miss Augusta join us, although I cannot guarantee that she will come."

Harry sank back against the pillows and closed his eyes. She'd come to him. He didn't doubt that for an instant. If it had been up to her alone, he felt certain she would have been here all along. All those nightmares where she'd left him—they were because Peterson and the others had kept her away.

He must have drifted off again, because he awoke to the sound of her voice, and then she was sitting in the chair beside his bed, exactly where she belonged.

"Good day, my lord," she said, leaning close with a rustling *shush* of silk. "How are you?"

She had newly returned from somewhere, and it gratified him to realize she'd come directly to him. She wore a silk gown splashed with flowers beneath a gauzy white perline, and a wide-brimmed straw hat with silk flowers. It was all pretty and fresh and somehow rather innocent, and while she didn't dress with the same provocative French flair that her sister did, he would never have mistaken her for a servant if she'd dressed like this in the first place.

He ignored her question regarding his health, which he thought was patently obvious. Instead he asked one of his own, and one he wished the answer to. "Where have you been?"

She hesitated just long enough for him to know for certain that she hadn't stayed away from choice, but had been excluded.

"I've been to church, my lord," she said, pulling off her kidskin gloves. "We all have. It's Sunday."

She smelled of new-cut grass and sunshine and green meadows, and at once he'd a pleasing image of her walking purposefully across a field in her flowered gown, her Book of Common Prayer clasped in her hand.

"Did you pray for me, Miss Augusta?" he asked, unable to keep from teasing her, no matter how ill he might be. "For my wicked old soul?"

"You were included in the minister's list of those who were ill or infirm and in need of the congregation's prayers, yes," she said, deftly avoiding any reference to his wickedness. She lay her palm across his forehead, her hand refreshingly cool. "Oh, my, you are very warm."

"It is as I said, Miss Augusta," Sir Randolph intoned. "The fever has taken his lordship firmly into its grip, and we are taking the most aggressive course to combat it."

"You've carved his lordship's arms to bits with bleeding, I see," she said, more tartly than Harry would have expected. "It's a wonder he has any blood left in him to be feverish."

"Miss Augusta," Sir Randolph said sternly. "I assure you that I am treating his lordship according to the latest and most considered beliefs of the learned medical profession."

"I've no doubt that you are, Sir Randolph," she said, smiling sweetly as she turned back to Harry.

"Are you thirsty, my lord?" she asked softly. "Your lips are so dry."

Automatically Harry licked his lips, which were in fact parched and cracked, most likely from the fever, and tried to swallow. "I am wickedly thirsty, yes."

"If you are thirsty, then you must drink," she said firmly, rising to go for the water herself.

"I must object, Miss Augusta," Sir Randolph said sternly. "It is my belief that the sure way to deplete a fever is through vigorous bleeding and withholding excessive liquids, the better to draw away the morbid humors. The canary in which the laudanum is mixed is more than sufficient to supply his lordship's base needs, and more fortifying than mere water as well."

"Yet surely a patient's comfort must be paramount to his recovery, Sir Randolph, mustn't it?" she asked, pouring a glass of water from the pitcher on the near table.

"The ancient monks who built their abbey here chose this spot for the purity of the water rising from a deep spring, and our water continues to this day to be famously restorative. I cannot help but think that his lordship might benefit from it as well."

Harry agreed. The more she spoke of this miraculous water, the more thirsty he became, and he longingly watched the water splashing into the glass in her hand.

But Sir Randolph was not happy with her, not at all. "Miss Augusta," he began irritably. "Miss Augusta, I must ask you not to interfere with the treatment of my patient, and I—"

"Damnation, Peterson, I am dry as the Sahara," Harry interrupted, "and I want the water."

Sir Randolph shook his head. "My lord, I cannot condone this, not when you are in such a delicate and perilous state."

"I can," Harry said. "And I will have the water."

"My lord," Sir Randolph said. "I have undertaken your care because of the acquaintance I have for His Grace your father, and if anything should go awry because of—"

"I'll answer for my father," Harry said, "and explain to him, too, if necessary. Miss Augusta, the water."

Sir Randolph nodded curtly, admitting defeat, or at least admitting that the Duke of Breconridge would be more inclined to take the word of his son than that of his physician.

Gus didn't gloat, but simply brought the glass around the bed to Harry. He struggled to sit up, mortified that he was too weak to do so. Without hesitation she slipped her arm around his shoulders to help him upright, then tipped the glass against his lips.

"There, my lord," she murmured. "Slowly, now. I won't have you drown and prove me wrong."

She didn't need to caution him. As thirsty as he was, he

meant to take his time so that he had could have her close like this, her arm so gentle around his shoulders that he could almost pretend it was an embrace rather than a necessary support. Beneath the slanting brim of her flowered hat, her round face was solemn, concentrating on his swallowing.

The sheer foolishness of that hat with its jaunty pink silk blossoms cheered him enormously, a bit of frivolity in his present grim circumstances. He could see her freckles, too, scattered across her full cheeks and over the bridge of her nose like dappled sunshine. He'd never thought of grown women having freckles; he supposed other ladies must cover them with powder, yet apparently Miss Augusta didn't bother, or care. He was glad she didn't.

He held her gaze after he was done, long enough that her cheeks pinked and she quickly looked away.

"That's enough for now," she said, beginning to lower him back against the pillows.

"Excuse me, Miss Augusta," Mrs. Patton said with the usual medical sternness, "but it's time for his lordship's draft."

She stepped forward with the now-familiar invalid's dose of canary ready in her hand. She'd thoroughly ruined canary for him forever. It wasn't just the association with pain and laudanum, but her officious manner as she loomed over him, like some overbearing female raptor in an apron swooping down upon him. Having her appear now in place of Miss Augusta was worse still, and he realized he'd had enough. He'd spoken up against Sir Randolph. Now it was Mrs. Patton's turn.

"Give the glass to Miss Augusta," he said. "I'd rather take it from her."

Mrs. Patton scowled and looked to Sir Randolph for reinforcement—reinforcement that did not come.

"Please, if Miss Augusta would be so kind as to assist," Sir Randolph said, swallowing his pride for the sake of his fashionable practice. "While my first concern is for his lordship's health, I wouldn't wish to offend either his lordship or His Grace. I desire only to be amenable to his lordship's wishes."

Reluctantly Mrs. Patton handed the cup with the draft to Gus. Harry had won again, but even this minor drama had exhausted him, and laudanum or not, he was already struggling to stay awake.

"Wait," he said, shaking his head as Gus held the draft for him. He reached for her free hand, linking his fingers into hers so she couldn't escape.

"I—I want you to know that I am happy you are here," he said, exhaustion turning the words clumsy on his tongue. Damnation, why did this keep happening when he'd important things to tell her? Why couldn't he focus? "I'm—I'm glad you came back, and I do not wish you to leave. *There*."

She smiled, a quirky, tight-lipped little smile. "There, my lord?"

Could she really be teasing him as he'd teased her earlier, or were his fever-addled wits playing tricks on him?

"Here," he said as firmly as he could. "Stay here. You bring me luck, and I—I need luck."

"Then luck you shall have," she said softly, holding the glass to his lips. "Because when you wake again, I'll be here still."

"Miss Augusta?"

Gus hung on the edge of her dreams, not yet ready to wake, and burrowed back against the pillow and away from the gentleman's voice that was rudely trying to wake her.

"Miss Augusta, if you please," the gentleman said again, and reluctantly Gus turned toward him and opened her eyes. It took her a moment to remember that she wasn't in her own bed, but sleeping curled beneath a shawl in an old-fashioned wing chair that had been pulled beside Lord Hargreave's bed. The gentleman's voice belonged to his lordship's surgeon, and when she opened her eyes Sir Randolph's long, serious face beneath his elaborate wig was gazing directly at her.

"Miss Augusta," he said softly as soon as he was certain she was awake. "There has been a change in Lord Hargreave's condition, and I thought you would wish to know of it."

Her heart racing, Gus threw off the shawl at once and rushed to the side of the bed. He'd been so sick already that she dreaded the thought of him having worsened.

But as soon as she leaned over him, she saw that the change was only for the good. His face was relaxed, his forehead dry and no longer sheened with sweat, his breathing deep and regular.

"His lordship's fever broke during the night," Sir Randolph said, keeping his voice low. "I believe when he wakes and we dress his leg, we shall see an improvement there as well."

"Do you believe him out of danger?" she asked anxiously.

Sir Randolph smiled. "If his lordship continues in this state through this evening, then I will be willing to pronounce him so, Miss Augusta."

Gus pressed her hands to her cheeks, overwhelmed. She hadn't realized how much she'd been fearing the worst until this moment. The earl wasn't out of danger yet, and he'd have a long recovery before he could hope to regain even a fraction of the use of his leg. He'd lost a great deal of weight while he'd been ill, and his face beneath his dark beard was gaunt, his cheeks hollowed. Gus suspected he'd lost much of his strength with it, more than he likely realized. In her experience, gentlemen made particularly poor convalescents, and she pitied whomever would be overseeing the earl for the next months.

"If he progresses today as I expect," Sir Randolph continued, "then I shall cease my imposition on your hospitality, Miss Augusta, and return to London. Mr. Leslie can look after him from here on, and I've already summoned him for a final consultation before I leave. I've other patients clamoring for my return."

"I would imagine so," Gus said, still watching the sleeping earl. "Will you be taking his lordship back with you?"

"Oh, good heavens, no," the surgeon said, drawing back a fraction as if from something distasteful. "I would not recommend moving his lordship for some weeks, even months to come. A long journey by carriage would quite kill him at present. There is no question of that. No, Miss Augusta, I fear he must be your father's guest for some time longer."

"We shall welcome his company," Gus said, her thoughts racing ahead to the basic logistics of such a grand houseguest for a lengthy stay.

"I should imagine your sister will enjoy it," Sir Randolph said, smiling slyly. "There's no better way for a pretty lady to win a gentleman's heart than to nurse him winsomely back to health."

Gus smiled, too, only because it was expected. But then, she knew what Sir Randolph didn't: that after the single disastrous visit to Lord Hargreave's bedside, Julia had refused to return. Nor had she shown any wish to discuss his health or circumstances, no matter how Papa had pressed her.

To be sure, Gus herself had spent so much time at Lord Hargreave's bedside over the last days that she wasn't exactly sure what Julia had been doing or saying, but from Papa's ill humor on the subject, it had been easy enough for Gus to guess. Privately she felt sorry for his lordship for having Julia turn so skittish and squeamish and ignoring him as she had. Julia was her sister, but to Gus her actions just didn't seem right.

Still, there was no real reason for Gus to think of his lordship as anything other than her sister's future husband. Everyone else did. Nothing had changed. His lordship might babble in his fever-dreams about how Gus was his lucky angel, but his heart still belonged to her beautiful sister.

All of which was why, when Sir Randolph began speaking of how Julia would be so pleased to look after the earl, Gus realized that her sister should also be informed of his lordship's improvement.

"Excuse me, Sir Randolph," she said, "but I'm going to share this excellent news with my sister and my father now."

With a final look at the sleeping earl, she left the room and hurried down the long hall to the wing with the family's bedchambers. She wouldn't be gone long, intending to return before he woke.

It was still early in the morning, and the house was just starting to rouse for the day. The parlor maids were beginning to open the curtains and sweep the hearths, and the aroma of Papa's black coffee came drifting from his bedchamber. Gus expected to find Julia still in bed and dawdling over her breakfast tray, or perhaps sitting at her dressing table to have her hair brushed and arranged for the day.

What she didn't expect, however, was to find Papa raging and swearing and crashing about like a caged bull in Julia's pink-and-white bedchamber. The bed was unmade, and clothes and hats and stockings and shoes were strewn about the room, as if tossed aside in great haste. An open trunk stood near the wardrobe, half packed with more clothes; none of the disarray made sense.

"Gus!" Papa exclaimed as soon as she appeared in the doorway. "Thank God you're here. What do you know of this? What has your fool of a sister done now?"

He was standing in the center of the room, red-faced and waving a letter in his hand. He was still wearing his paisley dressing gown, his nightcap shoved back on the crown of his head. Footmen and maidservants stood guiltily around him, as if they were somehow to blame for whatever had happened.

"I don't know anything yet, Papa," Gus said, using her calmest voice to try to settle him. "You must tell me first. Where is Julia?"

"She's bolted," he said. "Run back to London like the cowardly brat that she is. Look, she even admits it."

Gus plucked the letter from his waving hand. It was indeed from Julia, written in her loopy, schoolgirl's hand. She'd done exactly as Papa had said, and fled to London.

The letter was very long, and filled with the overwrought phrases that Julia had doubtless borrowed from one of her favorite romantic novels: She was *racked with Purest Agony, her Tender & Fluttering heart Tormented* because of the *unspeakable & cruel suffering of her Noble Beloved,* until she could bear *this Terrible Tedium No Longer, & must seek Succor & Relief* elsewhere to *preserve & restore Herself.* Her sanctuary from all this dreadful *Agony* would be Aunt Abigail's luxurious house on Portman Square, from which she likely intended to soothe herself with a fresh round of balls and parties.

"Do you know when she left?" Gus asked as she scanned the letter.

"Hours ago," Papa said with gloomy imprecision. "That damned rogue Tom was her accomplice, taking her and her maid in the chaise, and it's the last time he'll ever show his face in my stable. I'll see him charged with stealing my daughter and my horse—"

"You'll do nothing of the sort, Papa," Gus said firmly. "You know poor Tom had no choice, not with Julia. She can be very persuasive."

"She can be very wicked, the little baggage." Papa dropped heavily into a nearby armchair and pulled off his nightcap in disgust. "Wicked and faithless! Look at that driveling letter she left. All she considers is herself, and scarce a word about Hargreave."

Gus sighed. Everything he said was true, but what mattered more was trying to salvage the situation before it was too late.

"Did Julia leave his lordship a letter, too?" she asked, praying her sister hadn't.

"Not that I've found," Papa said, "and thank the Heavens she didn't. Think of it, Gus, think of it. Here she has her chance at a dukedom, and what does she do? She throws it to the winds because she's too damned impatient to wait for Hargreave to recover! What man would want her after that?"

"You must go after her, Papa," Gus said, striving to remain calm herself. As he said, this could be disastrous for Julia. It would be bad enough if fashionable London learned that she'd simply refused an offer of marriage from Lord Hargreave. But to have her abandon him, broken and unconscious and injured in the process of proposing, would be far worse, and make her the talk of the town for all the wrong reasons. "You must catch her before she reaches London."

"Oh, I'll catch her, I will," Papa said, rising to his feet with fresh determination. "I'll catch her, and she'll be sorry I did, the selfish little wretch, and then I'll—"

"Go dress now, Papa," she said firmly, taking him by the arm and steering him through the door. "Don't squander any more time talking. I'll ask William to go with you, and to have the horses ready."

Papa nodded. "William's a steady lad, not like that black dog Tom, stealing my daughter—"

"Papa, now," Gus urged. "You must go after her *now*."

"I'm going, Gus," Papa said, charging off in a fury of fresh outrage. "You'll see. I'll have your sister back home by supper."

Gus turned back to the little circle of servants, still waiting expectantly for her to address them. Papa so trusted the staff that he thought nothing of speaking freely—even rashly—before them, leaving it to Gus to offer the words of caution.

"You've all heard what my sister has done," she said, her hands clasped before her, "and how the viscount is doing his best to rectify her impetuous actions. In the meantime, I trust you will not share this—this confidence with any outside the abbey, especially the attendants or servants of Sir Randolph Peterson and Mr. Leslie. My sister's future happiness, and therefore the happiness of this entire household, rest upon your discretion. Is that clear?"

They murmured their agreement in unison, and Gus could only hope they meant it, and—better—that they could do it. Julia's impulsiveness was so scandalous that even the most loyal servants would be hard-pressed to keep it to themselves. Quickly she gave orders to have her sister's rooms put to rights, and for horses to be readied for her father and the head groom William. Then, at last, she hurried back to the other end of the house where, with any luck, Lord Hargreave would still be blissfully asleep and unaware.

But any luck of the favorable kind seemed to have fled from her. Even before she reached the earl's room, she could hear that for the second time this morning she would have to confront an angry male.

For the first morning in a week, the curtains at the windows were drawn and the large corner room was filled with sunlight. It was the abbey's best bedchamber, the one reserved for visitors of rank, with yellow dragon-patterned silk hangings and coverings on the mahogany chairs, and well-polished brasses on the tallboy that gleamed in the sun. In the center of the room was the large mahogany bedstead, also hung in yellow Chinese silk, and sitting beneath the elaborate cornice and canopy like some exotic potentate was Lord Hargreave.

No, not like an exotic potentate, but an angry one. He was leaning against the mounded pillows, his black hair wild and tousled above his equally black beard, and his blue eyes clear and sharp. Standing beside his bed were Sir Randolph and his assistant, the unhappy targets of his wrath; if he truly had been an exotic potentate, it was clear he would have ordered both of them executed on the spot.

"Where the devil have you been?" Lord Hargreave demanded, glaring at Gus. "You promised you would stay with me, Miss Augusta. Obviously, you did not."

She stopped abruptly, drawing herself up straight and clasping her hands before her waist.

"Good morning, my lord," she said with as much serenity as she could marshal. "I had another matter of importance requiring my attention."

He raised his dark brows with surprise at her explanation. "How in blazes could anything else be more important than keeping your word to me?"

"It was, my lord," she said, with no intention of explaining further. Thanks to her father, she'd an entire lifetime's practice of dealing with irascible, illogical males. Although the earl was an astonishingly handsome example, he really wasn't that different. She knew better than to lapse into a quarrel with him, a quarrel that would accomplish nothing. Distraction, plus a touch of flattery, would work much better.

She smiled. "I am so glad to see how much improved you are, my lord. You are looking much more like your old self on this sunny day."

He glanced impatiently at the windows, as if to remind himself of what exactly a sunny day might be.

"You did not know my old self, Miss Augusta, if you can find any such a resemblance," he said. "I am weak and wasted, a husk of what I once was. Here, see for yourself."

He thrust his arm out toward her and shoved up the sleeve of his nightshirt to above the elbow. To Gus's eyes, his bare arm looked well muscled and manly—exceptionally manly, if she was honest, and quite manly enough to make her cheeks grow warm at the display of it like this.

"Look at this," he said with disgust, making a fist to flex the muscles against the small linen bandage that marked his last bloodletting. "I've lost so much flesh, I'm weak as a kitten."

"You exaggerate, my lord," she said, refusing to commiserate the way he so obviously wanted. "You must still possess the strength of a full-grown cat."

He smiled quickly at that, clearly not expecting it from her.

"Make that at least a tom," he said, dropping his arm. "And a cantankerous stable-variety tom at that."

"I would not argue, my lord," she said seriously. "A tomcat seems most appropriate."

"Yes," he said, his eyes gleaming in an appropriately predatory way. "But if I am ever to recover to a full tigerish strength, I must eat, and yet these imbeciles here refuse to send to the kitchens for a fit meal."

"I am not refusing you sustenance, my lord," Sir Randolph said. His expression was so pained that Gus suspected he could not wait to be on his way to London and those other, less challenging patients. "I am simply urging caution in it. You must eat lightly for the next few days, or risk inflaming the humors and causing the fever to return. A broth made of beef or poultry, a plain panada—"

"A panada?" his lordship asked suspiciously. "What in blazes is that?"

"It's a simple, restorative dish," Gus said, even as she knew there'd be no way to make panada sound appetizing. "Plain bread is boiled together with milk until it becomes a kind of pudding. With a little honey or sugar for sweetening, it's—"

"It's wretched pap meant for infants, not grown men," the earl declared. "Do you want me to remain an invalid, Peterson, so you might claim a bigger fee? Is that why you'll only give me invalid's food?"

"I wish nothing of the sort, my lord," Sir Randolph exclaimed. "My sole aim is to see you restored to health and purpose. You have already shown remarkable improvement, sufficient for me to return to London."

"I'll be following you soon enough," Lord Hargreave said. "I cannot remain buried here in Norfolk for much longer, or I'll expire from boredom."

"No, you will not, my lord," the surgeon said firmly. "You must remain here in this bed for at least another five weeks in order for the bones to heal themselves. Travel is absolutely out of the question. You would risk dislodging the setting bones, and putting yourself in danger again of losing the leg."

The earl swore, long, loudly, and colorfully. "But I cannot stay here, Peterson! Not for five more weeks!"

"You will, my lord," Sir Randolph said, righteous and stern. "Instead of using such oaths before this lady, you would do far better to throw yourself on her mercy and her hospitality, for you will have need of both for your recovery."

The earl glared at Gus as if all of this were somehow her fault. "Is this true, Miss Augusta? Must I remain here as a prisoner in this wretched room for five more weeks?"

Gus frowned; she could not help it, despite her best intentions. Hearing him dismiss the abbey's finest guest room as wretched hurt both her family pride and the pride she took in running the household.

"If you care for your leg, my lord, you'll follow Sir Randolph's orders," she said tartly. "Of course you may continue as my family's guest as long as you wish, and as our guest, I'll see that you receive every comfort."

"Panada is not a comfort, Miss Augusta," he said sharply. "Nor am I a guest here. I'm a prisoner."

"I assure you, my lord, that you are not a prisoner," she said, her temper rising. "You may leave at any time, and you and your leg may go straight to the devil. I'd prefer that to the shame of having you perish beneath our roof simply because you were too willful to obey your surgeon."

He glowered at her, his cheeks flushed above the dark beard. "Peterson, leave. I wish to speak to this . . . *lady* alone."

"My lord, I implore you to consider the dangers of such a private conversation," Sir Randolph urged. "If you grow intemperate in your passions and succumb to a forceful anger, then you risk unbalancing your humors once again, and—"

"I can guarantee that they'll be unbalanced if I do not say what I must to Miss Augusta," the earl said. "Leave us. Now."

Reluctantly Sir Randolph bowed and withdrew, with his assistant and Mrs. Patton following. The door closed shut with a decisive thump, and Gus was left to confront the earl by herself. She'd been alone with him before, of course, and thought nothing of it. But that had been while he'd been drifting in and out of consciousness, so weak that he'd barely been able to raise his head. This Lord Hargreave, sitting up in his bed with his handsome face animated and his blue eyes full of fire and quite possibly brimstone, was a far different proposition.

Yet he did not speak, and neither did she, the silence stretching longer and longer as they each waited for the other to begin. *Sizing him up:* That's what Papa would have called it, and Gus was certain the earl was apprais- ing her as surely as she was him. At least the angry flush was fading from his face; as irritating as he'd been, she didn't wish to be the cause of a relapse.

"Miss Augusta," he said at last. "Dare I trouble you for a glass of your famous Wetherby water?"

With guilty haste, she flew to the table where the pitcher stood, filled a glass, and returned to hand it to him. He drank it slowly in long swallows, clearly savor- ing it, which made her feel all the more guilty for him having to ask her for it.

He handed the glass back to her, watching her closely.

"Well now, Miss Augusta," he said. "Here we are."

"Indeed, Lord Hargreave," she said warily. She didn't know why she felt so disconcerted, so off-balance, in his presence; it made no sense, really. "We are here."

He sighed and waved toward the armchair beside the bed, the same one in which she'd sat for so many hours watching over him. "Sit, Miss Augusta, please."

She perched on the very edge of the chair like a small bird, her back straight and her hands folded in her lap.

"That is better." He leaned his head back against the pillows and winced a bit as he must have shifted his splinted leg, and with a twinge of guilt Gus thought of how he was still an unwell man.

"It is, my lord," she agreed, resolving to put aside her

earlier stridency. "I am glad you seem so much improved."

"If this is an improvement, then I can only marvel at the depths to which I had sunk," he said, and sighed with more resignation than she'd expected. "I have but the vaguest recollections of this past week, Miss Augusta, though I can recall you showed me considerable kindness. Kindness that I most likely did not deserve, for I've recollections of my own ill humor as well."

"I did what was necessary, my lord," she said, acutely aware of how awkward that must sound. In a way, she wished he'd no memory of what she'd done for him. He was almost Julia's betrothed, and one day he likely would be her brother-in-law. No matter what the circumstances had been, it now made her uncomfortable to think of how she'd held his hand, and how, in his fever, he'd called her his angel.

"Necessary or not, it gives me hope that we can attempt a certain rapprochement between us," he said drily, taking note of her reluctance. "It seems I have no choice but to be your guest here for some time to come, and a degree of civility will make it less of an ordeal for us both."

"It will be my duty to look after you, my lord," she said, drawing herself even straighter, as if to take the burden of his care literally onto her shoulders, "not an ordeal."

"Well, now, that sounds so much better, doesn't it?" he said, not bothering to hide his chagrin. "My God. I never thought I'd ever become some young woman's *duty*."

"I did not intend it like that, my lord," she said swiftly. "Not at all."

"Oh, you needn't explain further, Miss Augusta," he said with an exasperated wave of his hand. "I should not be surprised. Your sister warned me the two of you were as different as the proverbial night and day, and you are. I've only to look at you to see that."

She knew she'd never be as beautiful as Julia. She'd known it nearly all her life. But the casual conviction of his words stung, stung hard, and swiftly she looked down at her clasped hands, not wanting him to see the unhappiness that must surely show in her eyes.

Unhappiness, and confusion, too. Why should she care if he thought her plain? What did it matter if he preferred Julia to her? They weren't rivals for his attention. Just as Papa had said, the pretty faces always paired off, and she was not pretty, especially not to a gentleman as handsome as the earl.

"Julia and I are half sisters," she said. "We each favor our mothers, not each other."

"I guessed as much," he said absently, his thoughts shifting to something else. "Listen to me, Miss Augusta. It is no secret that I came here intending to ask for your sister's hand in marriage, and I still mean to do so. I have every reason to believe she will accept."

Still Gus looked down, troubled by what she knew about Julia and her present whereabouts that he didn't.

"I hope to wed your sister as soon as possible," he continued. "I do, however, have one question. Where exactly is Miss Wetherby at present?"

Gus had prepared herself for this, and was ready with an answer that was truthful, yet unspecific.

"Julia is not at home, my lord," she said briskly. "She has ridden out to visit our aunt."

"When do you expect her to return?"

"I do not know," she said, again truthfully. "She can be unpredictable in her habits."

He smiled, the same sort of maddeningly indulgent male smile that Papa often smiled where Julia was concerned.

"You know, I have no memory of her visiting me while

I was ill," he admitted sheepishly. "Not one. Though I beg you not to tell her, Lady Augusta."

"Oh, no," she quickly agreed, thinking of how very lucky Julia was. "Your secret will be safe with me."

"Then I must beg one more indulgence," he said, rubbing his palm across his bearded jaw. "I do not wish the dear creature to see me in my present state, like some wretched, wasted castaway. Could you possibly contrive to keep her from this room until I am more agreeable?"

"You wish me to keep her from you?" she asked with astonishment. This was beyond mere luck: this was the best possible good fortune with a blessing or two thrown in besides, and—though she felt disloyal even thinking it—was far more than Julia deserved.

"Only for a few days," he said, misinterpreting her surprise. "I can do nothing about this infernal leg, not for a good long while, but I trust that with a razor and a bit of food I'll begin to look more civilized."

He tried to smile, but winced again, and closed his eyes against the pain.

She rose quickly. "I'll fetch Sir Randolph," she said. "This is my fault for tiring you with so much talking. He'll prescribe a fresh draft, so that—"

"No," he said raggedly, his eyes still squeezed shut. "I want no more drafts, no more laudanum. I'd rather feel the pain than be numbed into nothingness like that again."

"But Sir Randolph—"

"Peterson can go to the devil for all I care," he said, and slowly opened his eyes halfway. "He can join me there. I'm told it's much more agreeable with company."

She flushed, wishing he'd forgotten her earlier outburst along with Julia's nonexistent visits. "I'll fetch him."

"No." He caught her hand, holding her there. "I am serious, Miss Augusta. You do me infinitely more good than that man ever will. If you care for my welfare, you'll bring me a bowl of your cook's finest panada, and speak nothing more of Peterson."

She looked down at his hand holding hers, and tried not to think of how warm and familiar it was.

"I'll fetch the panada, my lord," she said firmly, pulling her fingers free of his. "Mind you, if I bring it, you must eat every morsel."

"I vow to devour it." His eyes were still half closed, his slow smile shockingly disarming. "So long as you, Miss Augusta, agree to sit beside me as I do."

She pressed her lips tightly together, trying to be stern. "I will return with the panada."

She was nearly at the door when he called her name again. She turned expectantly, her hand already on the latch.

"Miss Augusta," he said, still smiling. "Please. Say you'll sit beside me. You must agree, for the sake of your fair panada."

She took a deep breath, suspecting that none of this had anything to do with the panada. She guessed he was teasing her. To be sure, she'd very little experience with gentlemen—especially handsome gentlemen, and most especially handsome gentlemen who were supposed to be in love with her sister—teasing her, but her older brother, Andrew, often teased her when he was home, and this was suspiciously similar. Except it wasn't, because the teaser wasn't her brother, but Lord Hargreave.

"I'll promise," she said finally, "on the condition that you *will* eat it."

"Oh, I will," he said easily. "So long as it contains a sufficient amount of honey, as you earlier described. You should know, Miss Augusta, that I have the most wicked desire for . . . sweets."

Blushing furiously, she did not deign to answer but

hurried through the door, his laughter following her down the hall.

She paused on the stairs, pressing her hands to her cheeks to compose herself before she faced Mrs. Buchanan and the rest of the kitchen staff. This was going to be a very, very long and taxing convalescence. That length would have nothing to do with how fast his lordship's leg healed, but everything to do with *him*.

CHAPTER
4

Five days later, Harry sat in the bed with his eyes closed, relishing the familiar pull and scrape of a razor across his jaw as Tewkes shaved away his nearly fortnight-old beard. With his eyes shut like this, he could almost pretend that his life was the same as it always had been, and that nothing had changed from its pleasantly predictable course.

But his life wasn't that way any longer, and if the pair of grim-faced physicians were telling him the truth, then the pleasantly predictable days might be forever gone. His leg had been preserved, and his life with it. He had not died of a fever, or mortification, or gangrene, or putrefaction, or any of the other gruesome possibilities that had apparently hovered about him while he'd been dosed into insensibility. For that much he was supposed to be grateful, or so Sir Randolph and Dr. Leslie had informed him, almost in unison.

But Harry wasn't grateful. Not at all. Because according to these same two rascals who dared to preach gratitude, the leg that had been salvaged was never again going to be a match for the one beside it. The best hope they offered was that this sorry excuse for a leg might support his weight when he stood, a kind of prop for stability, not locomotion. There had been too much damage, too much displacement, to expect any more.

They told him if he was fortunate, he would be able to learn to walk with the aid of a cane or a stick. If he was not, he would require crutches or, even worse, an invalid's wheeled chair. His days for running, dancing, riding, hunting, fighting with swords or fists were now all in the past. In the handful of seconds that it had taken him to be thrown from that damned horse, he had gone from being a young man of twenty-four with all the world's possibilities stretching before him to one now confounded by limitations and restrictions.

Instead of being the dashing Earl of Hargreave, he'd become an object of whispered pity, and those less kind would give him some heartless nickname like Halting Harry.

No wonder there seemed to be precious little to be grateful for. But during the long hours he lay in this bed staring up at the hideous yellow silk hangings, he kept returning to the only positive that he could find in this entire wretched mess, and that, of course, was Julia.

How thankful he was that he'd already won her! He still had to make his actual proposal, but he was certain she'd accept. Although she'd led him on a coquettish chase this entire season, she'd made her affection clear enough. His life might not be what he'd planned, but at least there'd be some pleasure in it with a wife to love and support him, and to warm his bed, too. Thank God that part of him hadn't been damaged, and he could not wait to prove it to her. Just the thought of her lovely face—and even lovelier person—was enough to make him smile.

"If you please, my lord, no smiling," Tewkes said sternly, drawing back. "I cannot answer for what may happen with a razor in my hand."

"So you've been telling me for as long as I've had whiskers," Harry said mildly. He reached up to feel his now-bare jaw. "It feels as if you're done anyway."

"Nearly, my lord." His face screwed up with concentration, Tewkes leaned forward to flick the last bits of soap and whisker from Harry's cheek. "Forgive me for speaking plainly, my lord, but I have never before had to scrape such a growth of beard from your face."

"That's because I've never let it reach such an ungentlemanly state," Harry said, scarcely moving his lips, in the Tewkes-approved method. "There must be savages in the wilderness with less of a beard than I possess."

"There is no shame in your beard, my lord," Tewkes said, almost scolding. "It is a mark of your royal lineage, displaying your Italianate blood from the De'Medicis."

"It's a mark of me being furry as a bear," Harry said. "Apparently an Italian bear, too, not even an English one."

Tewkes was far prouder of his master's royal antecedents than Harry was himself. To him, there wasn't much romance in having had his family's fortunes and titles given as a reward to the French mistress of an English king a hundred or so years before. It was all dependent on how skilled his great-great-grandmother had been at pleasing the king, and at how she'd conveniently produced a royal bastard who'd required legitimizing and ennobling, unsavory facts that Tewkes—and most everyone else—preferred to forget. Still, it was better to be the oldest son of a duke than not, and since he'd inherited a share of his royal ancestor's legendary prowess with women along with his thick black hair, Harry wasn't about to complain.

Nor was Tewkes so indelicate as to offer an opinion on his master's likeness to an Italian bear. Instead he gently swabbed Harry's face clean with a warm, damp linen cloth, and then, in the final step of the ritual, he presented Harry with a large silver-framed hand mirror.

Usually Harry gave his reflection only the most cursory glance. He knew what he looked like, and he wasn't some vain macaroni beguiled by his own appearance. But this morning he not only looked: He stared, shocked.

This was not the usual face he saw in the looking glass. He was pale, without his customary ruddy tan from being out-of-doors. His cheeks were hollowed and lean, and exhaustion and illness had stolen the life from his eyes. Although he'd known he'd lost flesh and muscle, lying here in bed without eating anything of substance, he hadn't been prepared for this.

"Did I miss a spot, my lord?" asked Tewkes, misinterpreting Harry's silence.

"No, Tewkes, it's fine," Harry said. He was stunned by the change in himself, and if he'd met this new version on a London street, he wasn't sure he'd recognize himself. "But tell me, and for once don't lie. Did I look worse than this when they pouring the laudanum down my throat?"

"Oh, yes, my lord," Tewkes said, packing the shaving things away in Harry's dressing case. "You're much improved over how you were."

"Was it that bad?" Harry asked uneasily, wondering how it was possible to look worse than he did now.

"Yes, my lord," Tewkes said, so quickly that he left no doubt. "You had the very look of death itself."

Shaken, Harry took one last look at his face and thrust the mirror back at Tewkes. He'd thought he might finally be ready to see Julia again, but he couldn't, not unless he wished to terrify her.

"In your ramblings around this house, have you seen Miss Wetherby these last days?" he asked, not quite sure if he hoped the manservant had, or hadn't.

Tewkes took the mirror and tucked it away, too. "No, my lord. But since I have only gone up and down the back stairs to the kitchen, I would not have necessarily seen the lady."

"True, true." Ordinarily Harry didn't believe in using servants as spies, particularly when visiting, but he was so desperate for any news of Julia that he pressed Tewkes a bit further. "Do they speak of her belowstairs?"

"Of Miss Wetherby, my lord?" Tewkes paused and tipped his head to one side, thinking. "I don't believe I've heard a single word of Miss Wetherby. She might not even be in residence for all I've heard of her."

"Then Miss Augusta is doing exactly as she promised," Harry said, relieved. "As a favor, I asked her to keep her sister away until I was, ah, more fit for company."

Tewkes nodded. "Miss Augusta is a very reliable and capable lady, my lord," he said with obvious approval, and just as obviously more approval than when he'd spoken of Julia. "As young as she is, she acts as the mistress of this house, and is much liked by the entire staff for her kindness."

Harry sighed, leaning back against the pillows as he thought of Gus. He understood why the staff would like her, for he liked her, too, very much. She *was* kind, and generous, and reliable, exactly as Tewkes had said, all good reasons for why Gus was the sister he remembered through the pain and fever.

He didn't need to hide himself away from her, either, because she had been with him through the worst of it, and she'd comforted him in a way that was difficult to explain. He looked forward to the time she spent here with him, and missed her when she was gone. She wasn't beautiful, not like Julia, and she was such an unassuming little wren that she'd be lost entirely in a crowded assembly or ball. Yet there was a certain beguiling charm to her wide gray eyes and the freckles on her nose, and the delightful way she tried to turn serious and stern whenever he teased her.

It was so delightful, in fact, and he was in such need of amusement to stave off his boredom and frustration, that he teased her nearly every time she came to his room. Not hard, and with no mean intention, but he couldn't help it.

He smiled, thinking of that, and thinking of Gus in general. If asking Julia to be his wife was the best thing that came from this disastrous visit, then meeting her sister would have to be a close second. Having only brothers himself, he liked the prospect of gaining Gus as his little sister through marriage, knowing she'd always be part of his life, too.

"The surgeons say Miss Augusta saved your life, my lord," Tewkes continued, breaking into Harry's reverie. "They say that if she hadn't acted as she did when she found you, you would have died, or at least lost your leg."

"She didn't find me on her own," Harry said. "Her sister brought her to the place where I'd fallen."

"As you say, my lord," Tewkes said with a small nod of concession. "But as I've heard it told in the kitchen, Miss Wetherby was too distraught by your accident to offer any assistance. It was Miss Augusta who guessed where you must have fallen and, with several men from the stables, followed the horses' tracks to find you where you lay. She kept you calm and warm, and made certain the men used the greatest care in transporting you."

"She did?" Harry asked uneasily. He did not want to give up the pretty picture of Julia loyally returning to bring help to him in the woods. Yet it was only Gus that he remembered being there, holding his hand and telling him how brave he was. "You are certain this is true?"

"It is what was said by several individuals, my lord," Tewkes said. "All I can say for myself is that Miss Wetherby was not a member of the party that brought you back to the house."

Tewkes was not a man given to inventions. If he said Julia had not been there, then Harry had no choice but to believe it.

"Why didn't you tell me this before?" he asked.

Tewkes bowed his head, just a fraction. "You did not ask me, my lord."

Harry sighed impatiently. "Are there any other great secrets I should know, Tewkes?"

"No, my lord," he said, hesitating a moment to choose his words. "It was not my intention to fault Miss Wetherby in any fashion. I only wished Miss Augusta to receive the credit that she deserved."

"They are different ladies, Tewkes," Harry said, carefully choosing his own words as well. "Miss Wetherby is a lady of great delicacy, while Miss Augusta is not."

As soon as he'd spoken, he realized how disparaging to Gus it must have sounded. "That is, Miss Augusta is delicate, too, the way a lady should be, but she's more practical about it."

"Yes, my lord," Tewkes said, deliberately, blandly noncommittal as he gathered up the dressing case. "Will that be all, my lord?"

As if on cue, there was a knock at the door, and Gus's voice on the other side. Hurriedly Harry raked his fingers back through his hair and pushed himself up against the pillows as he motioned for Tewkes to open the door.

"Good day, my lord," Gus said, entering with her usual brisk purpose. She wore a gown of currant-colored calico, dotted with tiny green leaves, with lacy white sleeve ruffles, a sheer kerchief and ruffled cap, and a snowy white apron around her waist with her household keys clipped to a plain silver chatelaine at her waist. Harry liked her waist; she wasn't as curvaceous as Julia, but her waist was small and neat, much like the rest of her, and exactly the kind of waist that a man liked to settle his arm around. She made a quick curtsey and came to stand beside the bed, a well-read magazine or journal in her hand.

"Good day to you, too, Miss Augusta," he said. She looked crisp and fresh, her hair sleeked back beneath her small white ruffled cap, but he wished she were smiling. "What have you brought me?"

"In a moment, my lord," she said sternly. "First I must have a word with you."

Damnation, he hoped she hadn't overheard that last bit about her being practical. He tried to look innocent.

"Any word from you is welcome," he said as winningly as he could.

She'd have none of it. "Is it true that you've dismissed Mrs. Patton?"

He frowned, feeling defensive. "I did," he said. "Earlier this morning. She did not please me."

"Pleasing you was not her purpose," she said warmly. "She was employed to nurse you to health, not to be your mistress."

He wrinkled his nose at the thought. "She was disagreeable. With that face, she made me feel worse, not better."

"Mrs. Patton was an excellent nurse, and highly recommended by Dr. Leslie," she said. "I do not know how I shall replace her."

"Don't," he said. "There, that's easily solved."

"No, it is not," she said, her cheeks flushed with indignation. "You are barely a fortnight removed from your accident. You are still weeks away from being able to leave this bed. You need a nurse to—"

"To do exactly what?" he asked. He wasn't teasing any longer. He was serious, or he wouldn't have sent Mrs. Patton away. "Leslie comes every other day to unwrap my leg and peer at it, then swaddle it up again. That is the extent of my care. My bones will rejoin together in their own time, at their own pace. Until then, there's nothing more that a score of Mrs. Pattons could do to urge the process along."

"But who will change your bedding, and wash you, and—and tend to your personal affairs for you?" Her cheeks were pink now, not with an angry flush but with an embarrassed one, no doubt brought on by thinking of his Personal Affairs.

"Tewkes can manage," he said. "And there's always you as well. You said you would, you know."

"I, my lord?" She stared at him, her eyes round with surprise, and probably also from misgivings regarding those same Personal Affairs of his. "I am not your servant, my lord, and I am not your nurse, and I will not—"

"But you act as the mistress of this house," he interrupted, "and you did promise you'd look after me as your guest. I do not require much, really. You and Tewkes together should have no trouble accommodating me."

"But that was when you were in such a dire situation!" she exclaimed. "Now that you are so much improved, there is not the same urgency."

"You mean there is no longer a need to oblige your father's guest." He was not accustomed to being refused like this. She had offered; he had accepted. It was perfectly logical to him, and he couldn't understand why she was balking now.

"I mean that it's not proper for me to spend so much time in your company when I've other things—"

"Other things more important than I?" Glowering, he folded his arms over his chest. He hadn't intended to be so overbearing, not with her, but he didn't want her to replace her own charming self with another wretched Mrs. Patton. "You're being willful in this matter, Miss Augusta. Willful and stubborn."

"'Willful and stubborn'?" she repeated, incredulous. "Oh, my lord, I cannot agree with that, not after all I have done for you!"

"Then where is the harm in doing more?" he demanded, turning as imperious as if he were in his own house, not a guest in hers. "Especially since I am the one asking?"

"You are misconstruing my objections, my lord," she

said furiously, clipping every syllable. She was so agitated now that the keys dangling from her chatelaine were all trembling and jingling against her skirts. "I meant that now that you are no longer in peril, I cannot devote as much time to you as a hired nurse would. I have many other responsibilities in this house, and I cannot neglect them."

"Other, grander responsibilities than I, no doubt," he said, allowing a certain amount of contempt to creep into his tone. He waved a hand grandly through the air, as if to dismiss every possible objection.

"And what could those responsibilities possibly be?" he continued. "Gathering up old candle stubs? Marking the linen? Checking the padlock on the meat safe against servants' temptation? Making sure the broken victuals are collected to make broth for the deserving poor?"

"I see that this house is well run and managed, my lord," she said stiffly, "exactly as my father desires."

He hadn't really thought that any of those gibes were that close to the mark—after all, she was a lady and a daughter of the house, not a housekeeper—but he realized from the stricken expression in her eyes that her vaunted responsibilities must indeed include at least one of those mundane tasks. That expression made him uneasy and uncomfortable, and made him fear he might have pushed her too far, which of course only made him belligerently defensive.

"I never said I'd want to counter your father," he said. "Not in his own house. Don't put your words in my mouth."

"*I* didn't do anything of the sort," she said, rolling the magazine into a tight tube in her hands. "My words are my own, thank you, and I intend to keep them far, far from your mouth."

Realizing that this would not be a profitable path for discussion—and fearing she might strike him with the rolled-up magazine if he pursued it—he returned to the safer topic of her father.

"Where is your father, anyway?" he demanded. "I have not seen him since I awoke. I told you I wasn't ready to see your sister yet, but not your father. Why don't we send for him now, and ask his opinion on your responsibilities? Tewkes, tell the footman in the hall to summon the viscount."

She caught her breath with obvious dismay, replacing anything that might have been stubbornness.

"Please, my lord, you cannot," she said quickly. "That is, he is not here, but has—has gone to Norwich on business, but if he were here, I know he would agree with you in this, and so I—I will defer to you, my lord. Yes. That is what we shall do."

The speed of her capitulation surprised him, and he frowned, studying her closely. He knew an untruth when he heard one, though this particular untruth was so badly told that any child would have perceived it for what it was. Worse yet, she appeared almost on the verge of tears, her wide gray eyes so unhappy that he felt small and mean and very, very sorry.

But why should she not wish her father involved? Had they already had words about him?

"Very well, Miss Augusta," he said gruffly. He didn't want to disturb her any further, whatever the reason, but he couldn't quite bring himself to apologize when he wasn't sure what he'd done. "I am glad we are in agreement."

She sniffed, and patted blindly at her nose with her handkerchief.

"Yes, we are," he said hastily, supplying the answer when she didn't. "Now, why don't we begin with you sharing that magazine in your hand?"

She took a deep breath to recover herself, and looked down at the magazine as if seeing it for the first time.

"You said you were bored, my lord, and wished diversion," she said, her voice wavering a fraction as she held the cover up so he could see the title for himself. "I fear my father is not much of a reader, but I did find this in his library, and thought it might be sufficiently amusing to you."

He was oddly touched that she would take his earlier grumblings about boredom and ennui so seriously, even if it meant her finding a dog-eared copy of *The Gentleman's Magazine and Historical Chronicle*, six months out of date and dry reading even when it was new. He hadn't the heart to tell her that he'd already addressed his lack of reading material by sending to his London bookseller for a selection of the newest books, journals, and newspapers.

He also wouldn't tell her just yet that this morning he'd sent for a few other things, as well as people, to help him pass the time. It didn't seem right, given her present humor, and besides, she'd learn of it soon enough when the arrivals and deliveries from London began.

But right now she was staring at him.

"You're shaven, my lord," she said. "Your beard is quite gone. How did I not notice that?"

"It had overstayed its welcome," he said, rubbing his hand along his clean-shaven jaw for emphasis. "Do you regret that it is gone?"

"I do not," she said primly. "Your visage is much improved, my lord. You no longer resemble a pirate."

Thank God she'd stopped looking like she was going to blubber and weep. From relief, he laughed, something he had done far too little of lately. "What do you know of pirates, Miss Augusta?"

"Enough to know that you looked like one, my lord," she said succinctly. "Would you like to read now?"

"I want you to read to me," he said, settling back against the pillows. "I find I am still too weak to hold a page before me."

Skeptically she glanced at his forearms, which, though diminished by illness, were still impressive. "Are you certain of that, my lord?"

"I am," he said, folding his supposedly weak arms comfortably over the coverlet. "Reading aloud will be an important part of your new duties. The Patton woman couldn't read worth a tinker's damn. You're bound to surpass her. Now sit there, in the armchair, so I'll have no trouble hearing you."

"Very well, my lord," she said, unrolling the magazine. "Might I turn the chair toward the window, my lord, to improve the light for reading?"

Did he detect a slight whiff of mockery in her obedience, a hint of obsequious sarcasm in the way she tipped her head?

"You may move the chair however you please, of course," he said warily. "Forgive me for not assisting you myself."

She smiled sweetly. "I had no such expectations from you, my lord."

He smiled uneasily, wondering if she was now the one teasing him. With Julia, he always knew where he stood; she was charmingly uncomplicated, her thoughts and moods writ clear across her lovely face. But Gus was much more of a challenge to decipher, and he was quickly coming to realize that he needed to pay close attention to what she said when he was with her.

He watched her as she first pulled the window's curtain more fully open, and then arranged the chair so the sunlight would fall over her shoulder. Although he hated being restricted to a single room, he'd grudgingly come to realize that the bedchamber had its merits here on the corner of the house, with tall windows that let in the sun throughout most of the day. Hungry for the outside world, he'd had Tewkes leave the curtains drawn day and night so he could see the trees and fields, the sky and changing skies.

Now the dark wood of the nearest window's sash framed Gus as well as the landscape behind her. While Julia had a classically styled profile, her sister's cheeks were full and her freckled nose snubbed. But her brows were delicate and elegantly arched, and the sweep of her long lashes over those rounded cheeks as she looked down at the magazine in her lap was pleasing indeed.

He'd dismissed her hair as ordinary, a pale brown of no distinction, but here the sunlight discovered a fascinating variety of light copper and gold strands mingled together. Little wisping curls had slipped free from beneath the ruffled cap, swaying around her face in the breeze through the open window. As she spread the magazine on her lap, she licked her lips in preparation for reading, a delicious little flick of her tongue that intrigued him no end.

"There certainly are a great many articles in this issue," she said, frowning a bit as she surveyed the contents. "What would you like me to read to you?"

"Read me the titles that interest you," he suggested, "and I'll choose one."

"Very well, my lord," she said, and cleared her throat. "'A description of the emblematical design on the gold box in which the freedom of the city of London was presented to His Royal Highness the Prince of Brunswick.' Goodness, I wouldn't think he'd need to be given the freedom. Being a royal prince, I'd rather assume he could go wherever he pleased in London."

"He's not an English prince," Harry said. "He's a German-Prussian one, and a soldier, too, responsible for heroic feats in the last war. Duke Ferdinand of Brunswick-Wolfen-something. I expect he's been given the freedom of the city because he's some distant Hanoverian cousin of our own king. His Majesty does like to keep his family about."

She looked up, curious. "Have you been presented to His Majesty?"

"Of course." Being a duke and one with royal blood as well, his father was often at court, serving as one of the king's Gentlemen of the Bedchamber. "That is, I don't recall being formally presented to His Majesty. My father spends much time at court, and frequently took me with him when I was a boy. The palace is much like any other London town house, only larger and grander, and filled with odd folk."

"Truly?" she asked, her eyes wide. "Julia said it was a very grand place, the grandest she'd ever seen. She said being presented was the most magnificent moment of her life."

"It can also be the most tedious moment, given the size of the crowd," he said from the experience of one who generally avoided the royal drawing rooms. "But I expect one day they'll stick white feathers on your head and make you curtsey low, just like all the other noble daughters."

"I suppose so," she said faintly. "Do you wish to hear about the prince's gold box or not?"

"Not particularly," he said. "What else is there?"

She cleared her throat, and returned to reading. "'A Description of the Duke of Bridgewater's navigable canal.'"

"I've seen the canal for myself," he said, "and a modern marvel it is. But why should I now wish to hear of some scribe's impressions? The next article, if you please."

"'Doctor Watson's improvements to prevent the ill effects of lightning to buildings.'"

"That is supposed to keep me from boredom?" he asked. "Next."

"'The Oracle,'" she read. "'A most extraordinary tale drawn from the Greek.'"

He mimicked a long, loud, ill-bred snore. "Next."

"Does politics interest you, my lord?" she said. "Here's an article: 'On the use which the fallen ministry makes of the name of Mr. Pitt.'"

"No politics," he said with a sigh of resignation, "especially not old and dusty politics. Perhaps this is all quite futile, Miss Augusta. Instead of reading aloud, we would do better with conversation."

"Conversation?" she repeated, smoothing the cover of the rejected magazine with her palm. "Whatever subject should we discuss?"

"We could be blandly predictable, and try the weather," he suggested. "Or we could embark on a topic that I'm sure I'd find fascinating, such as why you have no desire to follow your sister to court."

"You are inventing again, my lord," she protested. "I didn't say that."

"You didn't have to," he said easily. "I determined it for myself. And here I thought every young lady dreamed of the day she'd be unleashed upon the world of unsuspecting bachelors."

"I don't," she said, with such emphasis that there'd be no question. "From Julia's telling, it all sounded quite dreadful, and nothing I would enjoy. I do not shine at balls and routs, my lord, nor would I—yes, what is it, Price?"

The footman bowed and leaned close to deliver his message in a discreet murmur.

"William has returned, Miss Augusta," he said. "He is waiting to speak with you."

She looked up with surprise. "He is alone, Price?"

"He is, ma'am," the footman said.

"Then I must go to him directly," she said, rising. "My lord, I am sorry, but I must attend to this—this matter at once."

"You're leaving?" Harry asked, though it was obvious that she was. He was more disappointed than he'd expected, sorry—very sorry—to have their conversation interrupted exactly when it had begun to be interesting. "Is this one of your other, more pressing responsibilities?"

"I fear so, my lord," she said absently, her thoughts already far from him as she left the magazine on the table beside his bed. "I am sorry, but this cannot be helped."

"You will return?" he said, sitting upright and trying not to beg, though beg he would if it might keep her here. "When you're done doing whatever you must do, you'll come back?"

She was nearly to the door when she remembered to turn toward him and dip a belated curtsey. "Forgive me my haste, my lord," she said, "but I shall return when it is possible."

He didn't want to be left behind. He wanted to follow her, join her, see exactly what was drawing her in such haste. He felt hopelessly trapped on the bed, as mired by the leather splints bound to his leg as if they'd been iron bands chaining him in place.

"Miss Augusta, wait!" he called out in desperation.

With obvious reluctance she paused and turned.

"Miss Augusta," he said again. He'd have to say something of more importance than just repeating her name, and he did. "Miss Augusta. I've heard that I owe my life to you. Is that true?"

That stopped her. "Who told you that?"

"Tewkes said the surgeons told him it was so," he said. "That your care and quick thinking saved my leg, and my life as well. Is it true?"

"I could not have done such a thing alone, my lord, not if—"

"But you were the one who followed my horse's trail to find me," he persisted. "You saw that the servants carried me safely, and all the rest that was done before the surgeons arrived. I know you did, because I remember it."

"You cannot remember everything, my lord."

"I remember that it was you, and not Julia," he said. "I remember how you gave me your hand to hold. Is that not so?"

"Julia couldn't," she said, stunningly loyal to her sister. "She was too distraught by what had happened. Otherwise she would have been there with you in place of me."

"But she wasn't," he said, a finality that she couldn't deny. He hadn't really planned to say all this, but now that he'd begun, he was glad he had.

"No," she said slowly. "She wasn't."

"Then I thank you, Miss Augusta," he said softly. "With all my heart. Thank you."

Gratitude, that was all he'd intended it to be, simple thanks for what she'd selflessly done on his behalf. But her eyes widened and her cheeks grew pink, and she pressed her palm over her mouth as if fearing whatever words might slip out. Then she turned and fled.

Gus sat in the parlor to read the letter that William had brought, with him waiting before her to answer questions. She read the letter twice through to make sure she understood its contents, then again in the empty hope that she hadn't.

The letter rambled on as Papa's letters always did, but there was no way to mistake or misconstrue its message.

> *Portman Square*
> LONDON

To my devoted Daughter Gus,

As you can tell, your sister & I have not returned to the Abbey. Upon overcoming Julia & that rogue Tom, we stayed a Night together at the Royal George & dined upon turtle soup & a fine goose, with every intention of Returning Home. Upon rising the next Morn,

Julia threw herself at me in a state of Perfect Hysteria, crying out that to see Lord Hargreave again in Pain & Imperfection would Destroy Her, & to continue to Aunt's house in Portman Square would be her only relief.

I had not realized the Degree of her suffering until that Moment, & so Piteous were her Tears that I feared for the Very Life & sanity of my Darling Child. As her dutiful Parent, wishing only the Best for her, I saw no choice but to Convey her to Aunt's house, as she desired. I remain there with her now, protecting her like a Hawk with a Dear Chick, in the hope that her Desperate Spirits will lighten & improve with the Diversions of the Town.

Please advise me at once, Dear Gus, regarding the state of His Lordship's wound. I trust you are doing whatever is Necessary to ease his suffering. I fear your sister's Affection for His Lordship may depend upon his Recovery, so I beg you, do what you can to Restore Him for the sake of your sister's Poor Heart & the successful completion of this Most Advantageous Match. I know you will understand It All.

Take Care, my own Gus, & may Heaven Preserve you in all things,

> *With much Affection from*
> *Your Loving Papa*

Gus sighed with frustration. Of course she understood it all: She understood that once again, Julia had wheedled and whined and wept into getting her own way. She understood, too, that Papa—again—had forgotten every last one of his bold declarations and promises of punishment, and caved in to Julia's demands like a sand castle before a watery wave, or at least a wave of piteous tears.

Most of all, she understood that unless Lord Hargreave were to be miraculously restored—which she doubted very much would happen—to the same perfect health that he'd enjoyed before the accident, the match between him and Julia was done. Her fickle sister would dance off into the arms of some other handsome, wealthy gentleman with a title, and though there would be a certain taint of scandal around her, her beauty would likely carry the day.

Again.

Gus should not be surprised. Hadn't this been happening their entire lives together? She carefully refolded the letter and looked up at William, standing before her with the dust of the road still on his boots.

"Did my father give you any indication of when he'd be returning home?" she asked.

"No, miss," he said. "His lordship said for me to go on back to the abbey and to give you his letter, and not to worry over him or Miss Wetherby. He said they'd both be along in time, when Miss Wetherby was ready."

"That was all, Tom?" she asked, though she wasn't sure what else there could be.

"Yes, miss," he said, then with a sheepish look on his face he pulled another, smaller note from his pocket. "Except for this, miss. It's for you from Miss Wetherby."

Eagerly Gus cracked the seal. She hoped Julia would show some remorse, or at least inquire after Lord Hargreave's condition, and send an enclosed note for him. But as soon as she scanned the sheet, she saw it wasn't a letter at all, but a hastily written list of gowns and other scraps of clothing that Julia wished to have gathered up and sent to her in town.

Gus stared at the list in disbelief. For the past five days, she'd tried to pretend that this would not happen. She'd told herself that for once—and for the sake of a dukedom—Papa would be strong, and bring Julia back home, the way he'd promised. She didn't care if Julia felt guilty, or had simply changed her mind about marrying the earl. Her sister was behaving horribly dishonorably toward him, and it was not only cowardly, but . . . *shameful.*

For five days, Gus had kept up the difficult ruse with Lord Hargreave that both her sister and father were in other parts of the house. Now she'd no choice but to tell the earl the truth, and soon, too. He'd already begun receiving letters addressed to the abbey. If she put off telling him much longer, she'd risk having him hear from someone else that Julia was dancing with other gentlemen in London.

But how exactly was she supposed to tell him? He seemed to be improving so rapidly, both in his health and his spirits, and despite herself she smiled as she thought of how earnestly—even sweetly—he had thanked her earlier. She hated to douse all that with such bad news, and she feared it might even cause a setback to his recovery. She'd come to realize he was at heart a good man, if an occasionally arrogant one; he certainly didn't deserve the misfortune that had already befallen him. How was she now to tell him that the woman he'd expected to marry had changed her mind because of an accident that she might have caused?

She tucked the letters into her pocket for safekeeping, and turned back to the servant standing before her.

"Thank you, William," she said. "For both your service to my father, and the speed with which you returned. Now take yourself down to the kitchen, and tell Mrs. Buchanan I said you are to have whatever you please for your supper."

He grinned and bowed and tugged on the front of his cap, backing from the room. But before he'd reached the open door, Royce, the house's butler, appeared behind him.

"Miss Augusta," he said, his expression perplexed. "May I have a word with you on a matter of some urgency?"

Her first thought was that she didn't need another urgent matter, not today. But her sister's follies were not the butler's fault, and so she smiled and gestured for him to enter and join her.

"What has happened, Royce?" she asked as he bowed.

"The new visitors have arrived, miss," he said. "Lord Hargreave's musicians. Where should I put them, miss?"

She frowned, instantly fearing the worst. "Lord Hargreave's musicians? What musicians?"

"There are three of them, miss," Royce said, not trying to lessen his disdain. "They're foreign gentlemen, very brown. I should guess them to be Italians, miss."

Now Gus could hear some sort of cacophony of raised voices from the front hall, her own people mixing unhappily and loudly with others, who had foreign accents.

"They have brought their instruments and their trunks and goodness only knows what else, miss," Royce continued, his indignation rising with each word, "and they are insisting that they are to be your guests."

Gus didn't need to hear more. At once she headed toward the front hall, determined to sort out this misunderstanding, for of course that is what it must be.

But as accustomed as she was to general sorting out of misunderstandings, she was not prepared for the sight that met her. The abbey's front hall was a grand space with high, arched ceilings and large, faded tapestries alternating with life-sized paintings of long-gone Wetherbys along the dark paneled walls.

Camped in the middle of the black-and-white-patterned floor were three men and a great deal of luggage, including fitted cases for instruments as well as trunks for belongings, which all indicated a lengthy stay. The men were flamboyantly dressed in tight, striped jackets with laced hats perched on elaborate wigs. All three were speaking forcefully and at once, determined to drown out her own three footmen and two maidservants, who were hovering uncertainly around them as if they were ferocious wild beasts. As if their voices weren't sufficiently loud, one of the newcomers kept thumping the side of a trunk like a drum with the head of his walking stick for extra emphasis. Standing at the door was a coachman, his whip in one hand and his other outstretched, palm up, who was demanding in an equally loud voice that he be paid for the passage and carrying from London.

It was all like nothing that Gus had ever seen, and likely like nothing ever seen in the hall by her solemn painted ancestors on the walls, either. She took a deep breath and charged into the fray, taking her place on the second step of the staircase so at least all these jabbering men could see her. Then she clapped her hands briskly before her to draw their attention.

To her relief, they fell silent, every face turned expectantly toward her.

"Good day, sirs," she said, conscious of how her voice echoed. "I am Miss Augusta Wetherby, of this house. Might I ask who you are?"

The three men instantly began speaking over one another again, forcing Gus to clap her hands again.

"One at a time, if you please," she said, feeling like a nursemaid overseeing a pack of unruly charges.

The three consulted briefly among themselves, and finally the tallest of the men stepped forward. He bowed extravagantly over his bended knee, whipping his hat from his head with a flourish.

"I am Mr. Giovanni Vilotti," he said, rolling the syllables on his tongue. "This is Mr. Arnoldo Bernadino, and Mr. Salvatore Riccio. We remain your most obedient servants, Miss Augusta Wetherby."

He bowed again, and Gus nodded: the most appropriate reply, but one that felt woefully inadequate compared with his salute.

Gallantly Mr. Vilotti held his hat over his heart. "My friends and I come to your beautiful house at the exact request of our dear patron the Earl of Hargreave. What a disaster he has suffered! What a miracle that he has been delivered! We came the instant we received his letter, to offer him the healing delights of our music."

Behind him the other two nodded solemnly, as if all of this made perfect sense. Apparently it did to them, but not to Gus.

"So his lordship invited you here?" she asked.

Vilotti nodded vigorously. "He requires us, Miss Augusta Wetherby, and we came. We would never deny his lordship."

Gus sighed deeply, already guessing the answer to her next question. "Did his lordship's request explain where you would be lodged?"

Vilotti waved his hat in a wide circle, encompassing the entire hall as well as every Wetherby ancestor. "He said you were delighted to accommodate us, for as long as was necessary for his recovery."

This was too much, thought Gus, even for Lord Hargreave. How could he presume to invite such guests to her father's house without consulting her?

"I am very sorry, Mr. Vilotti," Gus began, "but I fear I must first speak with his lordship before I can—"

"Signore Villoti!" exclaimed Tewkes, coming down the stairs behind her. *"Buongiorno miei cari amici!"*

"Mr. Tewkes!" Vilotti exclaimed, laughing with happiness. "How blessed are we to see you!"

"His lordship could scarce wait for you to arrive," Tewkes said. "This way, this way, you must come to him directly."

Gus turned to face Tewkes as the three musicians grabbed their instrument cases. "Tewkes, please. Permit me to speak with his lordship before these men intrude."

"It is no intrusion, Miss Augusta," Tewkes said, beaming as the three musicians hurried past Gus and up the stairs to him. "His lordship is expecting these gentlemen, by his express invitation. This way, my friends, this way."

"No, Tewkes, that is not what I meant," Gus said, but the men had already trooped up the stairs toward the earl's bedchamber. She looked back down at the remaining piles of trunks and bags, with her servants staring at her and the coachman still standing with his hand out.

"I needs to be paid, ma'am," he said, belatedly pulling off his leather hat. "Three fares from London."

If Gus had been a man, she would have sworn. Instead all she could do was give orders, which she promptly did.

"Royce, see that this man is paid what is owed him," she said. "And keep a tally of the reckoning, to be presented to his lordship. The rest of you move these—these things from the hall to the rear gallery until we decide what his lordship will want done."

She gathered her skirts in one hand and raced up the stairs after the men. She could already hear the sounds of violins being tuned in the corner bedchamber, and Lord Hargreave's booming laughter as he played the host, as if this truly were his own house, and he the master. Not an hour before, she'd felt so sorry for him, but now—now what she was feeling was much closer to murderous intent than sympathy.

She didn't care who he was, or what he'd suffered, or even that his great-great-grandfather had been the king of England: As far as she was concerned, this little frolic of his was about to end.

Now.

CHAPTER
5

"Here you are, Miss Augusta!" Harry exclaimed. "I was just going to send for you to join us."

He beckoned eagerly, motioning for her to sit beside him in the armchair that he now thought of as hers. The three musicians had taken possession of the corner near the windows, and were now sipping at the wine that Tewkes had poured for them as they tuned their instruments—a violin, viola, and a cello.

Harry was delighted that Vilotti, Bernadino, and Riccio had accepted his invitation, and so swiftly, too. Having music to help pass his hours here would be a welcome luxury. It was also something he'd hoped to share with Gus, as well as with Julia and the viscount in time; he doubted Wetherby Abbey had ever had music of this caliber in this corner of Norfolk, a small gift to begin to repay all their hospitality.

Gus, however, did not appear to share his appreciation. She stormed into his room, her skirts flying and her hands in fists at her sides—hands that, as soon as she stood beside his bed, she composed into a tightly clasped knot at her waist.

"My lord," she said, her voice clipped. "My lord, I must speak to you directly."

"You already are speaking to me, Miss Augusta," he

said, smiling warmly. He couldn't fathom exactly why she'd be so upset, but he was determined to disarm her. "Unless there is some special Norfolk-ian nuance that I am overlooking."

"Don't," she said crossly. "I'm in no humor for your raillery, my lord. How could you do this to me?"

"*To* you?" he asked, raising his brows with genuine surprise. "You make no sense, my dear."

She drew in her breath with sharp indignation. "I am not your dear, my lord. What I am is astonished by your condescension, your boldness, your sheer *presumption,* to invite these men to come and—and *lodge* at my father's house as if it were some low tavern, without saying so much as a whisper of it to me in advance."

"They're here now," he said in a loud whisper. "And yes, by my invitation, too."

He knew it was wicked of him to whisper like that, but he'd been unable to resist such a splendid opportunity—especially when he saw how her eyes widened with something very close to outrage.

"My lord," she said, speaking in a low, fierce whisper of her own. "If it were up to me, they would be deposited outside the gates now, and you with them."

He widened his smile, knowing the devastating effect that generally had on women. "Oh, Miss Augusta. You don't really mean that."

"I do." The clasped hands unclasped, and became arms crossed over her chest, a clear sign that she was too angry to succumb even to his smile. "I will not have this house turned into some low fiddlers' hall simply for your amusement."

"They're not low fiddlers," he said, turning a bit defensive himself. "They're *maestros,* Miss Augusta. They've performed at court, and for the French court as well. I have been honored to be among their patrons for several years, and even more honored that they've deigned to come to me here."

She pressed her lips tightly together as she listened, but at least she *was* listening, even if she still had refused to sit in the chair he'd offered.

"But why didn't you tell me you'd invited them, my lord?" she asked finally. "Why did you let me be surprised like this?"

So that was her real objection: He'd overruled her power as mistress of the house. He could understand that, especially since his convalescence was making him feel pretty near powerless himself.

"Forgive me," he said as contritely as he could. "I should have warned you. But your father's house is very large, and at present I appear to be your only guest. Considering how skilled as you are at managing, Miss Augusta, surely you could find one room for these fine fellows?"

She bowed her head, considering. But the fact that she was considering at all showed that he'd been right to praise her management skills. It wasn't empty flattery, either; he'd been impressed by what he'd seen of how well she ran such a sizable estate. Some married ladies never could figure out how to balance their staff, family, and guests with thrift and finances to make for a smooth-running household, and with disastrous results, too. Yet as young as Gus was, she seemed to have a genuine gift for it.

Somehow he doubted Julia had the same abilities or inclinations, which was worrisome. As his duchess, she'd be responsible for several different houses and estates and dozens of servants. Perhaps when the time came, he could beg Gus to come instruct her sister in some of the finer points of management—though as soon as the thought rose up in his mind, he discarded it as a pointless, empty experiment doomed to fail.

Which brought him back to the present, with Gus standing before him with a furrowed brow. Slowly the tightly clasped arms had relaxed to her sides, and they now rested akimbo with hands on her hips.

"How does one characterize foreign musicians, my lord?" she asked at last. "The only hired musicians we've had in the house for balls or parties came here from Norwich in an open wagon, and they left at the end of the evening. We've never had any stay with us."

It hadn't occurred to Harry that she would have no experience with musicians, let alone Italian musicians. Buried away in this provincial backwater, she'd likely never tasted Italian food, either, or seen Italian paintings, or a score of other wonderful Italian delights that he rather took for granted from traveling on the Continent.

"I suppose they must be like hired tradesmen," she continued, still struggling to sort out the typology of musicians in relation to Wetherby Abbey. "Not that we've ever had a tradesman stay the night, either. Or would they be considered a manner of visiting servant, or guests?"

"They should be treated as guests, Miss Augusta," Harry said, relieved and pleased that she'd asked. "Any one of your lesser rooms will do admirably."

"How long do you expect them to be here as our, ah, guests?"

"I believe they can only stay for two months or so," he said. "They've other engagements after that in the fall."

"Two *months*!" she repeated with dismay.

"I believe so, yes," he said. "They will not, however, expect the honor of taking meals with the family, but be content to dine with one another, separate from your other guests."

She sighed. "I can do that, yes," she said. "That is most helpful. I do not wish to give inadvertent offense, you see."

Harry glanced at the three men, who were already lost in their preparation. They had pulled three chairs in a semicircle before the window, each with his laced cocked hat sitting on the floor before him.

"You should also warn your younger maidservants to be on their guard," he said. "Bernadino is the very devil with women, a fox among the serving-hens if you do not take care."

Her expression grew very solemn, not at all in keeping with the light manner he'd adopted.

"Oh, yes, my lord, we have had that problem here at the abbey before," she said seriously. "We had one particularly, ah, amorous groom who was capable of inspiring love in every female servant who met him. I will be sure to take care with Mr. Bernadino, and caution all my staff to be vigilant around him, too."

She was so serious and innocent at the same time, standing there in her white apron and ruffled cap, ready to protect the virtue of the scullery maids from the amorous grooms, that Harry had to try very hard not to laugh. It was all very charming, and all the more so because he related to that amorous fox, with her being the delectable little hen.

He stopped himself abruptly, stopped himself cold. What the devil was he thinking? Gus was going to be his sister-in-law, and not even the most roguish of foxes would make the mistake of dallying with his wife's sister. But the vulpine side of him argued that Julia was not yet his wife, nor was Gus his sister. She was simply a young lady from Norwich who was miraculously becoming more and more attractive to him with each passing day.

Not that that was an excuse for anything. Far from it. But it was an . . . explanation.

Of sorts.

Damnation.

Vilotti stepped forward to the bed, bowing low before Harry with his violin already tucked beneath his chin.

"Whenever it pleases you, my lord," he said, "we are in readiness. Is there a piece that would please you above others?"

Harry smiled with anticipation. "You know my tastes better than I do myself, Vilotti," he said. "Surprise me."

Gus leaned forward. "I must go, my lord," she said. "I must make arrangements for the gentlemen's rooms, and tell Mrs. Buchanan they will be here for supper."

"Stay," he said, again motioning to the armchair. He wanted to share his own pleasure in the music with her. "Please. You'll enjoy it."

She shook her head. "I really should go, my lord."

"Why are you always so eager to leave?" he asked, disappointment making him sound moody. "Am I that odious in your eyes? Or is it because you know I can't follow you?"

He caught the little wave of sympathy in her eyes, a sympathy so close to pity that he did not want it. Yet it accomplished what his charm had not: She turned the chair to face the musicians and sat, gracefully sweeping her skirts around her legs as she did.

"One song," she said, a quick conspirator's smile, as if she'd been caught doing something she shouldn't. "Then I must go."

"Don't think of where you must go, or what you must do," he urged. "For once, don't think, but listen."

She smiled again, settling more deeply into the chair. Vilotti softly counted down in Italian, and with a light, dancing opening the music began.

Harry recognized it at once from the first notes, a cheerfully complex Vivaldi trio that was in fact one of his favorite pieces. He smiled as the familiar music filled the room, his spirits rising with every note. It was, he realized, the first time he'd ever listened to music in bed.

Granted, the novelty was small compensation for a broken leg, but it was much more pleasurable than sitting in a crowded music room or a stuffy box in a theater.

His smile widened as he glanced at Gus. She was enraptured, completely captivated by the music, her lips curved in an unconscious smile and her whole face radiating the pleasure and delight that she was feeling—exactly the response he'd hoped she'd have. He wondered if she'd ever attended a proper concert, something more substantial than those Norwich musicians in the open wagon. He couldn't recall having ever seen her in London with Julia or her father, and from what she'd told him, he suspected she might never have come there at all.

How entertaining it would be to show her about town, to be the first to take her to plays and concerts, Ranelagh and Covent Garden! He had, of course, done exactly that with several milliners and mantua makers' apprentices, pretty young women who had amused him as his mistresses for a short time, but never with a lady. It wouldn't happen with Julia, either, who already enjoyed the playhouse well enough, but mainly as a place to be admired as the gorgeous, golden creature she was. Not that he objected to that, of course—every man enjoyed a prize like her on his arm—but it wouldn't be the same.

He smiled to see Gus moving her head in time to the music, just a fraction, but enough to make the stray curls around her face skip lightly against her cheek. From the way she'd angled the chair to face the musicians, she wasn't directly facing him any longer, but leaning to one side with her hand resting on the arm of the chair.

Below the white ruffles at her elbow, her arm was as white as ivory, the veins in her wrist pale and blue. Her hand rested at ease and her palm turned up with her fingers lightly curled, almost like some kind of rare blossom. She wore neither rings nor bracelets, and there was something perfectly pure about her hand that stirred him. Perhaps it was the memory of the strength and comfort that same little hand had given him through his suffering, or perhaps, more simply, because it was a part of Gus herself.

All of which could be the reason for what he did next, more of that infernally complicated explanation.

When she'd turned her chair to face the musicians, she'd also brought the chair much closer to Harry, sitting against the pillows in the bed. As she lost herself in the music, he slowly reached out and trailed the pads of his fingers along her upturned wrist.

She started at his touch, jerking her head around to look first at his fingers on her arm, then at him, her eyes filled with question and doubt. But she didn't pull away, and he didn't stop, his gaze holding fast to hers.

Her skin was impossibly soft beneath his fingertips, and as he crossed the veins on her wrist he could feel the subtle beating of her heart. He turned his hand to rub his thumb over that pulse, just enough to make it quicken. He saw the awareness in her eyes, and the way her lips parted with the little catch in her breath.

From there it was easy enough to slip his fingers into hers, easy enough to tighten and close them together into one. At first she did not respond, keeping her fingers stiff and unyielding, but as he gently increased the pressure around them, she succumbed and curled her fingers into his. Then she blushed and hastily looked back to the musicians.

But their hands remained clasped, linking them together. She did not pull away, and neither did he, and what he felt this time was not mere comfort, either.

He'd never enjoyed Vivaldi more.

With a flourish, the musicians ended the piece. Vilotti looked to Harry, seeking direction.

"Continue, if you please," Harry said. "Pray, do not stop."

Effortlessly the Italians began another piece, a sweeter composition, filled with the quivering strings of romantic passion. Harry smiled, amused. So Vilotti had taken notice of how he held Gus's hand, and how she'd responded. Trust a Neapolitan to spot a blushing lady, even clear on the other side of the room.

But the spell had been cracked, if not broken outright, when the music had paused.

"We must talk, my lord," Gus said softly, clearly troubled as she gazed down at their hands linked together. "I fear I have something of grave importance to tell you."

"No more pompous formality," Harry said, "and no more 'my lord'ing me at every instant. That's what I must tell you. Call me Harry, as my friends do."

The trouble in her expression deepened. "Oh, my lord, I do not know if we are friends enough for that."

"We are," he said firmly. "You have visited me in my bedchamber. You have seen me in my nightshirt. And you have held my hand, oh, any number of times."

But as soon as he mentioned their linked hands, she skittishly pulled hers free. He was sorry for that, very sorry. Yet he also knew better than to pursue her again, and besides, what he really wanted was for her to call him Harry.

"You should not say such things," she said. "It does not seem quite right. Besides, once I tell you what I must, you might not feel the same about our—our acquaintance."

"What could you possibly say to change my regard?" He hadn't missed how for the first time she had let his honorific drop away. "If all that has passed these last weeks does not make us sufficient friends to dispense with titles, then I do not know what will."

She sighed, shaking her head.

"Harry," he said. "It's an easy enough name, and a good deal less of a mouthful than all my given ones strung out together. Harry. Try it."

Still she didn't speak, but he'd another tactic to try.

"You'll have no choice," he said. "You must call me Harry, because I have every intention of calling you Gus."

She looked up sharply, and he knew he had her attention.

"'Miss Augusta' must be a dreadful burden to bear," he continued softly. "It's a name for elderly maiden aunts with small, noisy dogs and barley-sugar twists tucked in their pockets. But Gus—Gus is spritely and charming and most excellent company. Gus likes Vivaldi, although she didn't know it until a quarter hour ago. Gus has freckles across her nose like a dusting of nutmeg, and hair with more colors in it than Welsh gold, and the softest, most innocent hands in the—"

"Dr. Leslie, my lord," announced the footman at the doorway, shouting the name to be heard over the music.

Gus almost catapulted from the chair in her haste to separate from him, and to greet the doctor as he came bustling into the room.

"Dr. Leslie, good day," she said breathlessly. To Harry's eyes, she looked rumpled and flustered and desirable, while Harry knew he must appear so frustrated that he expected the doctor to want to start bleeding him again.

"Good day, my lord, Miss Augusta," Dr. Leslie said, fortunately so stunned to see the musicians that he took no notice of either Gus's fluster or Harry's frustration. "Heavens! I did not expect to find a *musicale* in progress here in your bedchamber, my lord."

"It's done," Harry said curtly, growing more and more irritated. Blast Leslie! If he hadn't interrupted, Harry would have had Gus sweetly calling him by his name, and maybe even—well, he wasn't sure how far he would have taken things with her, considering he shouldn't have been doing any of it, but it would have been far better than what had just happened.

He nodded to Vilotti, and the three musicians abruptly stopped playing. "My apologies, my friends," he said, "but I'm afraid Leslie here is determined to poke and prod at my leg."

"If you will please come with me, gentlemen," Gus said quickly, falling back into her customary efficiency as she regained her composure. "I'll have a light refreshment arranged for you while your rooms are being readied."

Harry watched her go, the musicians happily following her with more bowing and complimenting at the prospect of food and drink.

Not once did she look back at him.

He hated being chained in one place like this, unable to leave this bed or go after her to explain. For a few precious moments, he'd forgotten he was a prisoner, forgotten he was a broken cripple, forgotten he was anything other than his old familiar self, flirting with a winsome girl.

The self that was gone forever, with a girl who would never be his.

Blast, blast, *blast*.

She was a coward. There was no other way to look at it. A bumbling, babbling, incompetent *coward*.

Gus stared up at the pleated silk canopy of her bed, her head too full of guilt and recriminations for sleep. Soon it wouldn't matter if she slept or not, for by her last count, the tall clock in the hall had chimed four times. Soon the birds would begin to sing in the trees outside her window, the roosters would crow beyond the kitchen garden, the sun would slowly appear over the fields to the east. The house would begin to wake, too, with the scullery maids starting the kitchen fires under Mrs. Buchanan's direction and the parlor maids opening blinds and sweeping out grates, and by then Gus should be up and beginning her own day.

But none of that changed the fact that she was an abject and absolute coward.

She groaned and buried her face in her pillow. Why hadn't she told him about Julia when she'd had the chance? Why had she let him be so—so forward with her? Holding his hand while he'd been suffering was one thing, but what he'd done last night was entirely, *entirely* another. And what he'd said as he'd toyed with her hand, all those pretty, meaningless words that no man had ever said to her before, words that she'd had no business listening to.

He was the Earl of Hargreave. He was going to marry her sister. He was going to be her brother-in-law.

Or much worse, he wasn't.

When she told him that Julia had fled, it was going to come out all wrong. How could it not? He'd know that she'd known, and hadn't told him, but because she hadn't pulled her hand away when she should have, he'd think she was encouraging him because Julia wasn't. Which she wasn't, but he couldn't know that, and neither of them knew what Julia would know if she were here. The more she tried to figure it out, the more muddled she became, and the worse she felt about how she'd behaved.

She shouldn't have left the way she had. She did run away, which was why she was such a coward. Talking to him had been easy because he was bed-bound, and by leaving she could control when to end a conversation. There'd been a cowardly comfort in that, too, especially as he'd begun to recover and had become less of a patient and more of a man.

Which would be bad enough if he'd been an ordinary man. But there was nothing ordinary about Harry. He was instead the most sinfully handsome man she'd ever seen. She thought of him sitting in the middle of the bed with his dark hair tousled and the throat of his nightshirt falling open and his sleeves pushed up over his forearms, his slow smile with the dimples—*dimples,* on a man who was otherwise so hard and lean—lighting his extraordinarily blue eyes as he watched her move around the room and—

No, she must not think of him, not like that. She mustn't think of him at all, and she thumped her fist into the pillow with the sheer misery of her life at present.

It was at some point in this early-morning despair that Gus first heard the dogs.

Dogs, barking furiously, and in the house. Her father's house, where dogs were not permitted. Because dogs had made her older brother sneeze and weep when he'd been a boy, Mama had banished them from the house, and from habit her father had maintained the banishment even after Andrew outgrew his difficulties.

Thus there was no reason for dogs to be inside the house, and especially not at this hour. The first light of dawn was filtering through the house, so at least she wouldn't need a candlestick. She slid from her bed, swiftly tied her robe over her night shift, and hurried out into the hall and down the stairs, following the sound of the barking dogs.

She didn't have far to look. For the second day in a row, there were unexpected strangers causing a commotion in her front hall by the wavering light of the night-lantern. A very sleepy-looking Mr. Royce and a footman without stockings and his shirt still untucked from his breeches were standing before two travelers. The first man was obviously some form of gentleman, dressed in sober clothes and with a large leather portfolio beneath his arm. The second, shorter man accompanying him was definitely not a gentleman, but a groom or other stable servant, in a heavy woolen jacket, a neat cap, and boots.

But more noteworthy than this man's dress was the pair of large spotted dogs that he held on leashes—or rather, the dogs appeared to be holding him, straining against their collars as they leaned eagerly toward the butler and the footman. The dogs weren't menacing, not with their feathered tails whipping furiously in unison, but they were noisy, and cheerfully determined to raise the rest of the house with their barking. Mr. Royce and the first man were both attempting to speak over the dogs, with the result that they were shouting against each other, and no one was hearing anything.

Gus flipped her long braid back over her shoulder and marched into the fray. The two men stopped speaking as soon as they saw her, but the dogs were not so easily intimidated.

"Hush," she said sharply, scowling down at them. "Hush, if you please."

To the surprise of the four men, the dogs immediately stopped barking, contritely sitting and hanging their heads with remorseful guilt.

"Hah, ma'am, I've never seen that before," marveled their handler. "Mostly they only obey his lordship."

" 'His lordship'?" Gus repeated. She should have known. Really, she should have. "Tell me, please. Are these Lord Hargreave's dogs?"

The other man stepped forward and raised his hat.

"Good day, ma'am, and pray forgive our intrusion at this unseemly hour," he said. "I believe I can explain. I am Mr. Arnold, ma'am, agent to the Earl of Hargreave, and I have come at his request."

The butler could bear this informality no longer; even if Gus was standing barefoot in her night shift, proper introductions should be made.

"Miss Augusta, Mr. Arnold," he intoned, as if Arnold had not just introduced himself. "Mr. Arnold, Miss Augusta Wetherby, the lady of this house. Mr. Arnold is his lordship's agent."

"Good day, Mr. Arnold," Gus said. "Though it is just barely day. Is it his lordship's usual practice to summon his people in the middle of the night?"

Arnold bowed, clearly embarrassed. "Forgive me, Miss Augusta. We would have arrived last evening at a more reasonable hour, if not for a broken axle on our conveyance. But yes, his lordship did express some urgency. His affairs have been unaddressed since his accident, and I have numerous papers that require his immediate attention."

"I can imagine," Gus said drily. She was sure Harry did in fact have business matters that needed his attention; a gentleman of his wealth and property would. But it would have been generous of him to have warned her that he'd invited yet more visitors to the abbey, visitors that she would be expected to house and feed.

And the dogs. She looked pointedly at them again, so pointedly that one of them whimpered and lay down. It was not that she didn't like dogs, because she did. What she didn't like was having them appear unbidden in the front hall before dawn, and against her father's wishes, too.

She sighed. "Did his lordship request the dogs as well?"

"Oh, yes, Miss Augusta," said Arnold hastily. "It was entirely his lordship's idea that his two favorite dogs be brought here, to help lighten his spirits. This is Hollick, from his lordship's household in town, who will be keeping the dogs. The dogs are Patch and Potch."

Hollick made a kind of ducking bow, as much as he dared while holding on to the leashes.

Gus sighed again, this time with resignation as she considered how she'd explain to Mrs. Buchanan that she'd have two more men to feed.

"I'm sure you'd both like breakfast after your journey," she said. "It will be some time before his lordship is awake and ready to receive visitors. Royce, please show Mr. Arnold to the green parlor. John, show Hollick and the dogs to the servants' hall for now. They'll have to stay in the stables, of course."

Hollick looked stricken. "The stables, miss? His lordship won't like that, miss. His lordship'll want his pups with him, same as home."

"I'm sorry, Hollick," Gus said, "but in this house, dogs live in the stable, not—"

"Mr. Arnold, good day!" Just as he had yesterday, Tewkes appeared at the top of the stairs, making a dramatic entrance like a character in a play.

But today it wasn't the newly arrived men who charged up the stairs to him. It was the dogs. Patch and Potch immediately recognized him—or at least recognized him as a sign their master was near—and lunged forward, pulling their leashes free from Hollick's hand. Barking with excitement, they raced up the stairs with their leashes trailing behind them, lingering only a moment before they disappeared down the hallway with Tewkes in pursuit.

"*No!*" Gus wailed, gathering her skirts to run up the stairs, too. As unhappy as she was with the dogs breaking her father's orders, what concerned her much more now was the thought of them leaping up onto their master's bed in a frantically joyous reunion. Although Dr. Leslie had kept Harry's broken leg tightly bound in the splints and resting on the leather sling inside the breakbox, he'd also warned that any sudden movement could dislodge the healing bones, in effect breaking them all over again. Patch and Potch practically defined sudden movement, combined with sizable weight, too.

It would, in short, be disastrous.

Likely Tewkes had the same fear, for Gus could see him ahead of her at the far end of the hall, moving faster than she'd ever thought possible, toward Harry's bed-chamber.

But when she reached the doorway, there was no sign of the boisterous mayhem she'd dreaded finding. Instead the two dogs were sitting quietly with their front paws on the edge of the bed, their eyes blissfully closed as Harry stroked their heads and rubbed their silky ears. If the dogs looked happy, then Harry looked ecstatic, softly crooning nonsense to them.

He glanced up when Gus appeared. "Have you met my boys?"

"I thought they'd jump on the bed," she said. "I thought they'd hurt your leg."

"What, my fine boys?" he said. "They'd never hurt any-one, especially not me. They're the best-mannered pups in Christendom. Isn't that right, my pretty fellows? Isn't that right?"

What was right was the sight of Harry with his two dogs. She'd never expected to see him display this kind of tender affection, and it made her smile happily, too, even as she realized it spelled the end of Papa's no-dogs policy.

"Papa says dogs belong in the stable, not in the house," she said halfheartedly to appease her conscience. "They shouldn't stay here."

"Then send your father to me if he objects," he said. "I'll show him what perfect gentlemen my boys are."

Almost too late, Gus remembered that Harry still didn't know Papa was in London with Julia.

"I suppose he'll make an exception," she said. "It wouldn't be fair, considering how you couldn't go down to the stables to visit them."

But Harry wasn't listening. "Why, Gus," he said, his smile turning rakish. "How agreeable of you to come visit me in your nightclothes."

The way he was looking at her, his gaze sliding all over everything below her chin, made her feel as if she were standing there naked. What was worse was that she realized she didn't dislike his scrutiny. In fact, to her dismay, her heart was quickening and she was breathing a little faster from it, the same as she had last night when he'd run his fingers along her wrist. Self-consciously she tugged the sash of her robe more tightly around her.

"I had no choice," she said. "Your dogs roused me from my bed with their barking."

His smile widened to a sly grin. "I told you they were perfect gentlemen."

"You needn't look at me like that," she said, her cheeks warming. "I'm thoroughly covered and decent."

"You're dressed for bed," he said. "Exactly as I am."

He didn't have to remind her. When he leaned forward to pet the dogs, the neck of his nightshirt had fallen more widely open, offering her an unexpectedly heady glimpse of his bare chest and the curling dark hair upon it.

"There's nothing wrong with how I'm dressed," she insisted. "For the hour and the circumstances, it's entirely appropriate and modest."

"Your feet are bare," he said, lowering his voice to a rough whisper. "And you're not wearing stays. I can see that your waist is still small without them, and your—"

"Harry, please," she said, turning flustered and stern at the same time. "That is quite enough."

"Hah, I heard that, Gus," he said, shaking his finger at her. "You can't deny it. You called me Harry."

She raised her chin in defiance, or more accurately defense. "You called me Gus first."

"*I* will not deny it," he said cheerfully. "Ah, more company. Good morning, Arnold! How very glad I am to see you. I trust you have brought me newspapers from London as well as all those letters I must read and accounts I must sign. I'm famished for news. Come, will you join me for breakfast before we set down to work? Gus, might I beg you to arrange that?"

"You may," Gus said, relieved to have something more to do than be stared at. "I'll go speak with Mrs. Buchanan now. But mind you, I am not running away. I am leaving because you asked me to."

"Agreed," he said, and smiled. "My next request is that you do not stay away."

Purposefully she didn't reply. "Do the dogs wish breakfast, too?"

"Of course," he said, clearly surprised she'd even ask. "It is not complicated. A mixture of minced beef hearts and livers, egg yolks, and a bit of bran. Hollick can tell your cook what's required."

She nodded, promising nothing, and left the men and the dogs. She could imagine all too well what Mrs. Buchanan was going to say when told she was now to be catering to his lordship's dogs, especially at the direction of Hollick. Gus personally oversaw all the bills from the butcher and other purveyors, and she knew for a certainty that there were no beef hearts in the larder at present, nor had there ever been, not in her memory.

She stopped in her rooms long enough to find a pair of mules for her bare feet and a shawl to wrap over her robe—if Harry claimed he could see so much of her person, then the last thing she wished was to reveal the same to her staff, or at least the rest of the staff that hadn't seen her yet today. Then she hurried down the twisting back stairs to the kitchen.

Yet as she did, she'd far more on her mind than the minced beef hearts for Patch and Potch. She was much more concerned with their master, and the news from London that he was so "famished" for. She had no idea of how much of the news that Mr. Arnold, as his agent, would share with him would be strictly of a business variety, of how his various properties and investments were faring, and how much might include the town's latest gossip.

She hoped against hope that all Mr. Arnold would confide were rents and improvements. Because if he included news of parties, balls, and sundry doings at court, then he was sure to mention the curious fact that Miss Wetherby was there, and not here.

It wasn't only that Harry would learn the truth about Julia's faithlessness. He'd send Gus's entire house of cards of well-intentioned half-truths and deceits tumbling down. He wouldn't be able to trust her again, and likely that would be the end of the teasing banter, the charming compliments that she'd never heard from any other man, the rakish smiles that made her heart beat a little faster, the delicious amusement of being Gus and Harry. They'd return to being Miss Augusta and Lord Hargreave, and then in four or so weeks, when at last his leg was healed enough for travel, he would be gone forever, both from the abbey and from her life.

Oh, why, why hadn't she told him the truth when she'd had the chance?

Harry lay in bed, as comfortable as he could be. Though he hated to admit it, he was tired, exactly as the surgeons kept telling him he should be. It was still some time until supper, and though through the windows he could see the sun was slipping lower in the sky, the day was not done, more afternoon than evening. Yet Arnold was finally on his way back to London with all the necessary decisions and signatures tucked in that voluminous leather bag, and Harry welcomed the peace of once again having his bedchamber empty of guests. On the carpet beside his bed Patch and Potch lay curled together, snoring with voluptuous canine abandon, and Harry suspected he'd soon be snoring along with them.

To help ease himself into that nap, he had in his hands one of the magazines that Arnold had brought from London. Titled *The London Observer,* this one was new to him, and he could already tell that it would be juicy with scandal, the leering antithesis of the dry old *Gentleman's Magazine* that Gus had so gamely tried to read to him.

He smiled, thinking how even the frontispiece would make her blush: a drawing of a bare-breasted goddess in a helmet, a goatish satyr lurking to one side, and several other clumsily drawn figures in ancient garb that looked more like bedsheets. Even he needed the caption to make sense of the picture: "A beautiful Frontispiece, representing Minerva, the Patroness of Learning, inspiring the Genius of This Magazine; while, in the Back-Ground, a Satyr exposes the Genius of Illicit Love."

He snorted with amusement at that, and idly wondered if Gus was worldly enough to know about satyrs, whose main occupation was ravishing nymphs. How would he explain that to her, he thought sleepily, flipping through the pages. The rest of the magazine was much as he expected, filled with bad poetry, inane observations, and articles with enticing titles such as "The Man of Pleasure" and "A Portrait of a Buck." Yawning, he finally settled on "Notes of the Town," wondering how many of his friends and acquaintances he could recognize in the scandalous exploits, their names reduced to decorous initials to protect the Genius of this Magazine from libel.

The words were swimming before him and his eyes nearly closed when, abruptly, a short passage jumped out from the others.

All regret the absence of Lord H—g—e from the Recent Divertissements; His Lordship is said to be re-

covering well from Wounds suffered in the Hunting-Field, & we wish Every Speed to his Return. Miss W—y, who was widely believed to be in Possession of His Lordship's Heart, has lately showed this to be an Exaggeration, & that no Hymeneal Union is imminent, by being seen much this last fortnight in the Exclusive Company of Lord S—l—d. Ah, Cupid! How sweet are his darts to the bosom of a Willing Beauty!

What in blazes was this? He'd begun by being mildly irritated to see his name included and his accident blamed on a hunting accident. But then he'd come to the part about Julia, and how she'd not only severed ties with him but was in London, and had taken up with that idiot Lord Southland. Lies, it had to be lies, all of it no more than another invention of this damnable rag.

Yet he had not seen her once that he could recall since his fall, nor so much as heard her voice in the house. He'd praised Gus for keeping her sister away, but what if he was the one who was being fooled instead?

He thought of all the little clues that he'd willfully ignored, clues that now made sense: how there'd been no sign of Julia or the viscount, how Tewkes had told him none of the servants ever mentioned Julia, how he'd not had so much as a scribbled note of cheer or endearment from her. He thought of how today, even Arnold had quickly tried to change the subject when he'd mentioned Julia and his intentions to marry her. Clearly he'd known the truth. The whole world did, except for him.

There was only one person who knew everything, the one person he'd felt sure he could trust above all others.

"Tewkes, here!" he roared, and the manservant came running from the next room. "Tewkes, send for Miss Augusta, and tell her I wish to speak to her directly. Here, now, and no excuses. I must speak to her at once."

He sank back against the pillows, his heart beating painfully in his breast. He felt furious and betrayed and scorned, rejected and humiliated and pitied. But most of all, he felt hurt, wounded in ways he hadn't expected.

And all he could hope for now was the truth.

CHAPTER
6

Gus was working in her mother's rose garden, clipping away the wilted blooms, when Mary came to find her, her footsteps crunching on the crushed-shell path.

"Oh, Miss Augusta, here you are!" she said, out of breath from her haste. "We've been searching everywhere for you. You're wanted at once in the house."

Gus immediately tucked her pruning scissors into her basket and began to walk briskly. "What has happened, Mary?"

"It's his lordship, miss," Mary said, hurrying alongside Gus. "Mr. Tewkes says he's in a terrible way."

At once Gus thought the worst. "Has one of his wretched dogs jumped onto his leg? If it has to be set again because—"

"Oh, no, miss, it's not that," Mary said. "Mr. Tewkes says his lordship's in a righteous fury over something, and wants to speak to you about it at once."

And without doubt, Gus knew. She'd dared to think when Mr. Arnold had left that she'd been spared, that he hadn't mentioned her sister. But clearly that had only been a false respite, and now she'd have to face the full force of Harry's unhappiness.

It was going to be full-force, too. She could see that from his black expression as soon as she entered his room.

"Miss Augusta," he said curtly. "I trust you have not seen this."

He tossed an open magazine across the bed in her direction, not even deigning to hand it to her.

"The first item at the top, under 'Notes of the Town,'" he said as she picked up the magazine. "Read it. I would very much like to hear your opinion."

Her heart sank as she read it. Only a few sentences, but she could see her sister's frivolity in nearly every word. Julia's greatest challenge was the sheer number of darts that Cupid had shot her way, making her seem fickle and perpetually looking for another conquest. There was good reason for why, with her beauty and charm, she was twenty-two and still not wed. But this was the first time that Gus would have to face the consequences of her sister's actions, and it wasn't going to be either pleasant or easy.

The only defense she'd have would be the truth. She could only pray that it would be enough.

"Am I correct in assuming that, for once, a scandal sheet is telling the truth?" he asked. "That Miss Wetherby is not in residence here, but in London?"

Reluctantly Gus nodded. "She is in London," she said. "She's not here."

His expression did not change. "When did she leave?"

"Soon after your fall," she admitted. "I don't recall which day exactly."

"Yet all that time you've covered for her," he said. "Did she ever visit me? The truth, Miss Augusta."

She hated having him call her that again, almost as much as she hated this horrible interrogation.

"She did," she said. "But you were not—not yourself. You wouldn't remember."

"Yet she judged that to be sufficient," he said bitterly. "Did she give you a reason for leaving me?"

"No," she said. "But I don't believe she left you so much as she left the, ah, the situation. The surgeons were saying you might die, and that frightened her."

"I didn't," he said. "She must be disappointed."

"I wouldn't say that of her, my lord," Gus said quickly. "Julia has never been good in the face of challenges, which is why Papa went after her, to make certain she was well."

His scowl deepened. "You father. Is he part of this deception, too?"

"Julia went back to London with a single servant in the night," she said, wishing Julia's antics did not sound so sordid in the telling. "Papa followed her from concern, as any honorable parent would."

"Any parent with a spoiled, selfish child," he said with disgust. "She's certainly consoled herself fast enough, and with one of my friends, too, if the gossip is to be believed."

His vehemence shocked her. "If she were to see you now, my lord," she said, trying to coax him into thinking better of Julia, "to see for herself how much you have already recovered—"

"But she won't, Miss Augusta, because I have no intention of seeing *her* again," he said. His words were sharp with anger, but it was the undercurrent of pain and rejection that told Gus he would keep his word. "I will write to her tomorrow, and that will be an end to it. Thank God I did not ask her to be my wife! If such salvation has cost me the use of a leg, then it's a small price to pay for not being shackled to a faithless slattern like her for the rest of my life."

Beside the bed, the two dogs had wakened, made uneasy by the tension in Harry's voice, and one of them let out a low, mournful whimper of distress.

Not that Gus was heeding the dogs. "My sister is not

a slattern," she protested, with more anger of her own than she'd intended. "Not at all."

"Her actions say otherwise," he said. "Friends warned me of her, of how she fluttered from one man to another. I should have believed them and seen what she was."

Gus came closer to the bed, her hands unconsciously bunching into fists at her side.

"What she is, my lord, is my sister," she said curtly. "And I'll thank you not to speak of her so—so—"

"So honestly?" he said, his blue eyes full of fire. "The truth isn't always pretty, Miss Augusta. Is this how you justified lying to me? That you were only protecting your sister?"

"I was also protecting *you*!" she exclaimed. "You were in pain and in danger of dying, and your wits were thick with laudanum and suffering. How could I have told you the truth then? What would I have accomplished?"

He folded his arms over his chest. "You would have told me the truth."

"I might have, yes," she said. "But it was a truth that might have made you despair so deeply that you could have died. You have no notion of how ill you were, my lord."

"You could have told me a score of other times since then," he said. "You chose not to."

"And I tried, at least a score of times," she said. "But you wouldn't let me, and you wouldn't listen, and I— and I—"

She broke off abruptly, realizing that she'd almost told him more truth than she wished to.

He jumped on the tantalizing fragment. "And you what, Miss Augusta? You didn't have time to concoct another lie for me?"

"I didn't want you to hate me, just as you do now!" she blurted out. "As provoking as you can be, my lord, I—I enjoyed the time I spent in your company, as friends would, and I did not wish it to end. Now it has, and exactly as I'd dreaded it would, too."

His frown deepened with disbelief. "You enjoyed my company?"

"I did," she said, her words tumbling faster now, "though I do not know if I should regret it or not. A man who cannot understand the virtue in being loyal to one's family may not be a man that I wish to know."

He shook his head, and shoved his hair back with one hand. "You're a fine one to preach to me of loyalty. Considering you belong to this family."

"My sister may not be loyal, my lord, or faithful, or whatever you wish to call it," she said. "But I am, else I wouldn't be standing here whilst you—you berate me in a fashion that I do not deserve."

Her voice was trembling now, with emotion as well as with the power of the truth. She *would* finish, no matter what it cost her.

"Despite what you may think, my lord, I never lied to you, not once," she said fervently. "For the sake of my sister, I may not have told you everything, but I did not lie."

With a final, emphatic shake of her head, she placed the offending magazine on the bed beside him and took two steps back. She stood very straight, with her hands clasped over the front of her apron, and waited.

He made a grumbling, wordless growl deep in his throat. Then he seized the magazine and hurled it as hard as he could across the room, where it dropped with a fluttering of pages to the floor.

She didn't flinch.

"Why the devil don't you leave?" he demanded. "If I'm so damned offensive to you, why don't you leave now like you always do? Go, leave me, and be like your sister."

"Because I'm not my sister," she said. "That's why."

He didn't answer. She didn't say anything more, for she hadn't anything left to say. Perhaps he felt the same way, too. All he did was glower at her for what seemed like an eternity, until, finally, he buried his face in his hands with a groan.

Still she did not leave him.

When at last he lifted his face and lowered his hands, he frowned, clearly surprised to see her there still. He took a deep breath, once again raking his hair back with his fingers.

"Miss Augusta," he said, struggling to find his way through this—this mess. "Gus. You *are* different from your sister. I must take care to remember that."

"Yes, my lord," she agreed warily. "You should."

He nodded and cleared his throat. "Will you dine with me this evening, Miss Augusta, the better to remind me further?"

"Here?" She gave a little shake of her head, surprised he'd ask.

"I fear I have no choice," he said ruefully. "It seems that you have been dining alone, as have I. Wouldn't it be more convenient for your staff if they were to serve us together?"

"It would," she said. "It would also be most . . . agreeable. As acquaintances, of course."

"Oh, of course." He smiled. "You don't have to remain here now, if you're wanted elsewhere. You needn't stay on my account. You've made your point."

"I thought I might offer to read to you, if you wished it." She crossed the room to retrieve the magazine he'd thrown, smoothing the pages as she walked back to him. She looked at the illustration on the frontispiece, and her eyes widened. "Goodness, Harry. What manner of magazine is this?"

"Ah, Gus." He grinned wickedly, motioning for her to

sit in the chair beside the bed. "I was hoping you'd ask me to explain."

Harry held his head still as Tewkes tied the black silk ribbon around his queue, taking care that the hair was neatly curled under. It was the first time since Harry had been hurt that he'd bothered with tying his hair back like this, but he wanted to show Gus at least a modicum of respectable formal dress for evening when she joined him to dine. He'd had Tewkes shave him again, too, and if he hadn't been able to put on a full suit of clothes, at least he wore a freshly washed and pressed nightshirt.

He'd taken extra care with the preparations for the dinner as well. It hadn't been easy to make anything a secret, given how the cook and the rest of the staff reported to Gus. But Tewkes had managed to work his usual magic, and had somehow gained entrance to the viscount's small cellar to produce several respectable—if likely smuggled, this being Norfolk—bottles of French and Spanish wines. Tewkes had pulled a small table close to the bed, and coaxed a damask cloth and silver candlesticks from elsewhere in the house. He'd even contrived a respectable bouquet of red roses and white phlox for the table, thanks to the garden. He'd spoken to Vilotti and arranged for the musicians to play for them after they'd dined, and he'd asked for more Vivaldi, Gus's newly discovered favorite composer.

He had summoned her cook to his bedside, a formidable woman named Mrs. Buchanan, and together they had planned a small supper that included Gus's favorite dishes. At least that was what Mrs. Buchanan had claimed, and Harry could only hope she was right.

In fact, he had hopes for a number of things regarding this evening. Would Gus make the same extra effort that he had? Would she put aside her usual apron and cap for something silk? Would she accept the role of his guest, or insist on being the mistress of the house? Most of all, was she anticipating their supper together as much as he was?

And he was. He tried to tell himself that it was only because he'd been as good as a hermit here in this room, that he was so starved for society that this little supper with Gus now loomed far larger than it ordinarily would. In London, he dined *tête-à-tête* with young women all the time, didn't he? So why now, when there was still over an hour before Gus would join him, was he looking at his watch every two minutes?

Tewkes held the silver hand mirror before him so he could survey his reflection. He was finally beginning to look like his old self, his clean-shaven cheeks not so hollowed. Best of all, the familiar spark was back in his eyes, and he couldn't help but smile.

But on the other side of the mirror, Tewkes made the tiniest *tut-tut*, an editorial sound of disapproval that was his prerogative as a longtime servant and, though rare, one that Harry recognized all too well.

"What is it, Tewkes?" he asked with a sigh. "What have I done now?"

"Nothing, my lord," Tewkes said, his nose so high that he offered Harry an unappealing look up his nostrils.

"Nothing, my foot," Harry said. "Out with it. That's your way of scolding me like an old biddy-hen. Do you judge it unseemly for me to wear a black ribbon around my hair when I'm still in bed? Is the collar on my nightshirt not falling the exact way you think proper for a gentleman?"

"No, my lord," Tewkes said, taking away the mirror. "It's Miss Augusta."

"Gus?" Harry was surprised; this was remarkably outspoken for Tewkes. "What about her?"

"I only wish that it be remembered that Miss Augusta is a lady, my lord, and not a common actress or milliner's apprentice," Tewkes said. "That is all, my lord."

"No, it's not," Harry insisted. "You don't approve of this supper, do you?"

Tewkes sniffed. "It's not my place to approve or not, my lord."

"That's never stopped you before," Harry said. "It doesn't matter that Gus has been in this room with me every day since I broke my leg, or that when I was sick, she likely saw a good deal more of my person than her sister ever did. You still think she needs protecting from me, don't you?"

"Miss Augusta has no knowledge of town wiles, my lord," Tewkes said severely. "She is a country lady, and may misconstrue your attentions."

Harry sighed. Tewkes was right about Gus: He could tell she was a true innocent, with next to no experience with men. For all her brisk efficiency in other areas, she was achingly vulnerable. He'd only to recall how she'd responded when all he'd done was touch her hand.

What Tewkes wasn't considering, however, was that those infamous "wiles" of Harry's weren't exactly at their best. While he realized now that Julia was not the prize he'd once thought, her rejection had stung his pride and shaken his confidence. He'd never before had a woman break with him, especially not in so dramatic and public a fashion, and he didn't like the feeling. Still, he wasn't a heartless rake, and he'd more scruples than to seduce Gus simply for the sake of restoring his male sense of omnipotence. Gus didn't deserve that, and frankly, neither did he. He had asked her to join him as a friend, and he meant to keep it that way.

Not that he'd confide all that to Tewkes.

"My 'attentions,' Tewkes," he said, "as you so quaintly put it, are only of the friendly kind, with thanks for all she has done for me. Besides, I'm hardly in a state to seduce anybody, not with my leg splinted and stiff as a fence post."

"It's said that you have always been an inventive gentleman with the ladies, my lord," Tewkes said with a fastidious sniff.

"And you are privy to none of my amatory inventions, you rogue," Harry said, laughing. "At least I hope you aren't. Now go see that Hollick has finished washing the dogs. I don't expect Gus to eat in the company of two dogs who have been rolling in the stable muck."

He wouldn't inflict an overly fragrant Patch and Potch on any lady, and he wouldn't subject a friend to them, either. His laughter faded to a smile as he thought of Gus. Yes, a friend. A friend who happened to be a lady. That was what she must be to him, and that was how he intended things to remain. A friend, and no more.

"*You know* I don't like repeating tattle, miss," said Mary as she twisted and pinned a resistant strand of Gus's hair into a curl. "But there's things being said in the servants' hall that you should know."

Gus sighed. This was one of the most difficult parts of managing servants. She couldn't forbid them from talking among themselves, but it was up to her to address the little rumors and misconceptions before they mushroomed into larger problems that unsettled the entire household. She also had to differentiate between a servant who came to her with a reasonable concern and one who was a troublemaker spreading ill-founded gossip. It wasn't always easy to tell the difference, especially being as young as she was, but Mary was one of the ones she could always trust.

"What is it, then?" she asked. "Are the footmen not

being respectful again? Or are the Italian gentlemen annoying the maids?"

"Oh, no, miss, it's not any of the staff, nor the Italian gentlemen, neither," Mary said quickly. "They've been charm itself, those three. No, it's what's being said about Miss Wetherby."

"My sister." Gus pulled her head free of Mary's hands and hairpins and twisted on the bench to face her. "What are they saying, Mary?"

Understanding the magnitude of the gossip she was about to repeat about her employer's older daughter, Mary stood at attention with the hairbrush in her hand.

"Hollick—that's the fellow who looks after his lordship's dogs—Hollick told us all over dinner that Miss Wetherby's broken from his lordship, and that there'll be no match between them," she said. "He said that everyone in London knows it, too, and that they all feel dreadfully sorry for his lordship, especially him being so hurt and all."

"Goodness," Gus said faintly. This was all the same sordid tale that Harry had told her as well, yet it seemed that his own dog-keeper had heard it first. She'd written earlier in the day to both Papa and Julia, begging for their side of the gossip, but of course she had not heard back. There was also the possibility that neither would reply; her family members were notoriously bad correspondents, especially when the subject was as complicated as this one. "I trust that is all you have heard repeated, Mary?"

"Most all, miss," Mary said, clearly determined to finish now that she'd begun. "They're also calling Miss Wetherby a—a jilt, saying she cast off poor Lord Hargreave on account of him being crippled, and that now she's set her cap on another gentleman, named Lord Southland."

This was worse than Gus had feared. Why was it that bad news, particularly bad news about someone else, always traveled so much faster than any good? She took a deep breath, deciding how best to respond. Once again, the truth would be safest, even if the truth was not very pleasant.

"What should we say here at the abbey, miss?" Mary asked, clearly worried by Gus's long silence. "I know we've all done our best not to let his lordship know Miss Wetherby is no longer at home, but—"

"That is no longer necessary, Mary," Gus said, unable to forget Harry's face when he'd showed her the magazine earlier with the dreadful item in it. "His lordship knows."

"Oh, the poor, poor gentleman!" exclaimed Mary with genuine sympathy. "But are these lies and slanders true, then, miss? What are we to say now to defend Miss Wetherby?"

"I shall tell you the same as I will tell the rest of the staff," Gus said evenly. "That my sister and his lordship have decided they no longer suit each other. They have agreed to part, and there will be no match between them."

Mary gasped. "But for her to leave his lordship when he's suffered so—forgive me, miss, but it's shameful, shameful, and there's no other word for it."

"There is no need for further words on the topic, Mary," Gus said, resolutely turning on the bench to face her looking glass again. "Recall that Miss Wetherby is my sister, and the elder lady of this house. Now, please, continue to do what you can with my hair."

"Oh, I'll do that, miss," Mary said, drawing the brush through Gus's hair with renewed purpose. "We must make you look as fine as possible, the better to cheer his poor lordship."

"Mary, I am dining with his lordship because he is a guest in my father's house," Gus said firmly, wanting to put an end to such speculation before it began. "Now that he no longer requires special foods, it only seems hospitable that I join him for supper. If he were not hindered by his leg, we would be at the table together in the dining room."

"Yes, miss," Mary said. "You always do make his lordship your father proud that way. There now, I've dressed your hair up higher in front, the way the ladies of quality are wearing it in London now, with curls pinned in back and one long one over your shoulder like a proper lovelock."

"A lovelock?" Gus repeated, dubious, as she studied the effect of the single fat curl trailing over her shoulder. She was accustomed to seeing her hair falling perfectly straight, or lightly crimped from plaiting. But she'd never seen it curl like this, and to her eyes it looked more like a pinned-on piece of borrowed hair than her own.

"Yes, miss," Mary said confidently. "Before Miss Wetherby left, her maid, Sarah, told me all about what the ladies of fashion were wearing, and showed me how they dressed their hair for day and for night. I've put a touch of sugar-water to that lovelock before I used the curling tongs, miss, so it will hold."

Tentatively Gus touched the curl, feeling how the sugar-water combined with the heat of the curling tongs had stiffened it into submission. Mary was right: It wasn't coming down.

"I'm not sure of this, Mary," she said to her reflection. "Though I suppose it won't matter once I've pinned on my cap."

"No, miss, no!" Mary exclaimed, scandalized. "No young ladies wear caps in the evening! Here, this is what I'm going to pin in instead, little baubles that your sister left behind."

In her palm were several little five-pointed stars, sparkling with cut brilliants, and backed with a curving tail.

"Hair springs," Mary said proudly. "Sarah says all the ladies wear them. Here, miss, I'll show you."

Deftly she tucked the stars in a cluster above Gus's right temple, turning each curving back until it held fast into her hair. Gus had to admit it was a pretty effect, like a tiny winking constellation in her hair.

"You do not think it is too bold?" she asked uncertainly, turning her head back and forth to make the stars twinkle. "It's only supper."

"It's supper with a peer, miss," Mary said confidently. "His lordship will take notice, you can be sure of that."

It wasn't that Gus feared Harry wouldn't take notice; she'd no doubt he would, Harry being Harry. What she dreaded was trying to dress too much like Julia, and having him think she believed she was a beauty, too.

Gus had no illusions about her appearance. She'd already suffered through her share of county balls and routs where she'd been cast so far back in Julia's glorious shadow as to be made invisible. She did not shine, especially not in company, and she knew that gentlemen always preferred a glowing beauty to her more humble attributes.

She had no illusions where Harry was concerned, either. He teased her because he was bored, and it amused him. He paid her compliments because he was a gallant at heart, and he appreciated and thanked her for all she'd done for him because he was well bred. He might like her as a friend, an acquaintance, a little sister, but it would never go beyond that. The last thing she wished was to make him think she was harboring false hopes for replacing Julia in his affections, and she feared that little stars in her hair might convey exactly that.

But she didn't want him to think she'd taken his invitation lightly, either. Even she knew that fashions that seemed excessive in Norwich would scarcely be noticed in London. Not only did the stars remain in Gus's hair, but she let Mary persuade her into wearing one of her silk gowns, a shimmering, deep red taffeta, and a strand of matching coral beads around her throat. She also left off her habitual kerchief around her shoulders, leaving the neckline of her gown uncovered. Having the top swell of her breasts visible above her whalebone-stiffened stays was, she knew, the proper style for evening, and quite modest by fashionable standards.

But for Gus, it felt daring, even brazen, and as she stood outside Harry's door, she had to fight the urge to run skittering back to her own room to change. Then the footman opened the door for her, and she entered, and there was no turning back.

"Good evening, Gus," Harry said warmly. "Pray forgive me for not rising to welcome you properly."

She hadn't expected this. The room that she'd thought she'd known so well had been transformed. Beside the bed was a beautifully set small table for two, with silver and crystal and linens borrowed from the dining room, and flowers in a porcelain bowl. The candles on the table and beside the bed had just been lit, their glow soft and inviting in the early-evening dusk.

"Look at this," she marveled. "How did you arrange all this, Harry, and in so short a time?"

"The credit goes largely to Tewkes," he admitted. "I had certain ideas, and he was resourceful in his arrangements, and in keeping them a surprise for you. Not an easy task when it's your household, either. Do you approve?"

"I do," she said, suddenly shy around him. She came to take her seat at the little table, with Tewkes stepping forward to ease in her chair for her. As soon as she sat, Harry's two dogs came to snuffle at her skirts, their tails whipping in welcome. "No one has ever done anything like this for me."

"Then it's past time someone did," Harry said. "Down, you two rascals. Leave the lady alone."

"I don't mind," she said quickly. She bent down to rub each one behind the ears in that velvety spot all dogs adored. "They're lovely dogs, Harry."

"They're damned wicked rogues," he said pleasantly, motioning for Tewkes to fill their glasses with wine. "I see they like you, however."

"They should," she said, "since I've broken one of Papa's cardinal rules by letting them stay here with you."

"Then that explains it," he said. "Being damned wicked rogues, they instinctively know to whom they should beg for mercy. But at least they're clean. I had Hollick wash them in your honor."

"I *am* honored," she said, looking up at him from the dogs. Harry, too, had made an extra effort for their supper. His nightshirt was fresh and pressed, the linen crisp and unmussed and the cuffs buttoned at his wrists, and he'd fastened the collar with a heart-shaped shirt buckle, gold set with topazes and diamonds, the same heavy gold of his onyx ring.

His jaw was so clean-shaven that the skin practically gleamed, and for the first time that she remembered, his hair was sleeked back into a neat queue and tied with a black silk ribbon. His broken leg had stopped grieving him, and without the constant tension of that pain, the rest of his body looked at ease again. He sat with his other leg bent at the knee, a much more relaxed and rakish posture. He finally resembled an earl, with all traces of his piratical self gone—all, that is, except when he smiled at her.

He raised his glass, and in response she raised hers, too.

"To friendship," he said, so short and simple a toast that she could happily agree.

"To friendship," she repeated, and drank. She was

careful to take only a few sips, while he, being a gentleman, drank deeply. She recognized the wine's label as being from her father's cellar, but she'd never tasted it herself, more usually drinking a lady's lighter wine or even abstaining entirely to be sure the meal ran smoothly. The wine was quite pleasing, and with no responsibilities, she permitted herself another few swallows. As soon as she set her glass back down on the cloth, Tewkes instantly stepped forward to fill it again with a promptness that she noted, and commended.

"Our supper should be here shortly," Harry said, "that is, if your cook is prompt."

"Mrs. Buchanan is never late sending her dishes to the table," Gus said, her taffeta skirts rustling around her as she settled into the armchair. "How she must be enjoying preparing a meal without me telling her what to do!"

"What she enjoyed was preparing something special as a surprise for you," he said, motioning for the footman to refill his wineglass. "You're very well liked by your staff. Most ladies can't say that of their household. But then, most ladies aren't as charming as you are."

She blushed and looked down at the wine in her glass. "You shouldn't say things like that, Harry."

"Why not?" he said easily. "I believe in telling the truth, Gus, and that is the truth. Here's more: You took my breath away when you entered just now. You're beyond all my imaginings."

She tried to smile as she sipped her wine, tried to turn his words around into a jest. "You mean you couldn't imagine me without an apron or a cap."

"No," he said, shaking his head a bit in disbelief, though he smiled still. "I meant that as well as I thought I knew your face and person, I was startled by how lovely you are when you're dressed as a lady. You *are* lovely, Gus."

She looked down again, squaring her thumbs around the base of the glass, unable to meet his gaze when he was saying such things.

"Please don't speak to me like that, Harry," she said softly. "You needn't. I don't expect it. I'm not Julia."

"It's a good thing you're not your sister," he said, "else neither of us would be here."

"I am serious, Harry," she said. "If you do not stop, I'll have to leave."

"You know I don't want that." He sighed with resignation and emptied his glass. "Very well. You have my word that no more truths of an uncomfortable nature will be spoken."

"Thank you," she said, forcing herself to look at him again. He wasn't exactly staring at her, but his blue eyes were watching her intensely, as if concentrating on remembering every detail of—of what? Her gown, the stars in her hair, the freckles on the bridge of her nose?

Unsettled, she swiftly looked away, her gaze landing on the flowers in the Chinese porcelain.

"Those roses are from my mother's garden," she said, determined to steer the conversation into safer waters. "The white ones were her favorites."

"I was told they were your favorites as well," he said. "I didn't know it was your mother's garden."

"She made things grow," Gus said, reaching to curl her palm around the nearest rose. It touched her that he'd bothered to ask about her favorite flowers, especially since the roses reminded her so deeply of her mother. "Roses, sweet herbs, children. Everything thrived in her care."

"She was your father's second wife?" he asked.

She nodded, smiling sadly as she thought of her mother. "She was. His first wife, poor lady, died bearing Julia, and Papa married my mother soon afterward. He always says it was the best decision he ever made, and I suppose it was. She loved Andrew and Julia just as much as she loved me, and she ran his household like clockwork for him. But then Julia's likely told you all that."

"She didn't," he said. "She told me next to nothing of your family. I didn't even know of your existence until your brother told me, the night I first arrived here."

"Truly?" she asked, surprised and a little hurt. As taxing as Julia could be, Gus had always thought of her as a sister in every way, but there were times when Julia didn't return the affection.

He smiled wryly. "You know how Julia can be. She's likely forgotten me entirely by now, too."

"If she has, Harry, then it's her loss," Gus said firmly, and took an emphatic drink of her never-diminishing wine.

"I tend to agree with you," he said, and sighed. "So I would guess you are much like your mother."

"I try to be," she said, "though that is very nice of you to say."

"More truth, that is all."

"It's a greater compliment than you'll ever understand," she said wistfully. "But tell me of your own family. Have you sisters and brothers, too?"

"Two brothers, no sisters," he said. "But I've also cousins who are more like brothers, so it feels like a larger family than it is. I also lost my mother too soon. She nursed three sons through the usual illnesses and accidents, then died herself from a simple quinsy after riding in an open carriage by night with my father. The quinsy turned putrid, and in three days she was gone."

"I'm sorry, Harry," Gus said, reaching out to rest her hand over his in sympathy. "Did you lose her recently?"

"Oh, no, over ten years ago," he said, turning his hand to claim hers. "My father took a second wife, a charming lady we all hold in the highest esteem. He's much happier now with her. But not a day goes by that I do not remember, and miss, my own mother as well."

"That is the same with me," she said softly, gazing down at their joined hands. She was always surprised by how small her fingers looked compared with his, and when he held her hand like this, she felt as if he were protecting her, rather than she comforting him.

Not, of course, that she'd any right to feel that way, or even to be holding his hand. She knew she should pull away, and yet once again she didn't. Perhaps it was the wine that was making her behave like this.

Or perhaps it was simply Harry himself. During Sir Randolph's last visit, Harry's leg had been freed from the fracture-box, and was now propped up with pillows, which gave him more freedom to move about the bed. He was sitting on the edge now, able to reach the table, and she was intensely aware of how close he was to her, so close that she could smell the spicy scent of the soap he'd used for shaving. She remembered how he'd stroked her arm yesterday, and simultaneously wished he'd do it again and prayed that he wouldn't.

"My father maintains that all men belong in the married state and are miserable otherwise," he continued, fortunately unaware of her thoughts. "Quite naturally, he's eager for me to marry and start siring sons of my own so he needn't worry about the dukedom. He's old enough himself that such matters concern him inordinately. Ah, here's our supper now, just as the clock strikes the hour."

She pulled away her hand as the door opened, not wishing to be observed by her servants. Earlier, she'd made a small speech belowstairs, repeating what she'd told Mary, and the last thing she needed was to have her words undermined by her own actions.

Led by Royce, the footmen brought in several dishes, presenting them to Harry, not her, before they set them on the table.

"Duck with oranges, my lord," Royce murmured. "Mushrooms in cream. Fricassee of veal with pickled barberries. Parsnip pie. Rice Florentine with braised leeks."

"Are you certain those are barberries, Royce?" Gus asked suspiciously, peering down at the plate. "I don't recall that Mrs. Buchanan had any in the larder. Please send Price down to speak with her, and make certain that—"

"Gus, my dear, you are not in charge tonight," Harry said mildly. "This evening I am the host, and the servants will answer to me, not you. All you must do is enjoy everything as my guest."

"But how can I enjoy it if I suspect Mrs. Buchanan has substituted a false ingredient, and then served—"

"Hush," he said. "You are my guest, Gus. No orders, no worries, no false ingredients."

She sighed deeply, considering the dish with the food arranged elegantly upon it. Everything did look very good, she decided as she picked up her fork, and it all smelled even better. And no matter where they'd come from, the pickled barberries looked exactly as they should.

It was a novelty to be a guest in her own house. There were, in fact, many novelties about this evening already, not the least of which was dining with a ridiculously handsome earl who was in his bed. And his dogs. She must not forget Harry's dogs, who were even now asleep on her feet. She sipped her wine, considering how wonderfully amusing all this was, and began to chuckle.

"Why are you laughing?" he asked, beginning to smile with her. "What's so funny?"

She touched her fingertips lightly to her lips, as if that would be enough to keep back her amusement.

"Everything," she said. "Nothing. Oh, Harry, I suppose I'm happy."

"So am I," he said, and laughed with her. "We are both of us extraordinarily happy."

"Yes," she said succinctly. "We are. Now, while I eat this excellent, excellent meal that you have ordered for me as your guest, I wish to hear you tell me more of your brothers. I wish that very, very much."

He laughed again, his eyes bright with pleasure and amusement. Yet still he did as she bid, and began to tell her tales of his childhood, of being the privileged oldest son of a duke, of his vast yet close family of cousins with more dukes sprinkled throughout. Most of all he told stories of the bond he shared with his two brothers. She learned that at present both were out of the country, one off in the distant East Indies, and the other in Naples with their father—which, to Gus's relief, explained why none of them had come to visit Harry. In fact he told her so much of those brothers, Rivers and Geoff, and the scrapes that they'd tumbled in and out of together, from London and Paris to Venice and Naples, that Gus soon felt as if she knew them herself.

In turn, Gus shared her past and family as well, from shrieking games of hide-and-seek through the abbey when she'd been little, to the raucous pantomimes that her mother had arranged and directed, and to the joy of learning to ride with her older brother, Andrew. She hadn't had anyone to talk with like this for years, and as she and Harry exchanged stories and laughter, she realized it wasn't just the wine. She truly was happy this night, happier than she'd been, really, since Mama had died.

Gradually the dusk outside the windows faded away to night and the footmen replaced the guttering stubs of candles for new ones, yet still she and Harry talked and talked. They drank, too, and by the time the lemon syllabub that was the meal's last sweet had appeared and the servants had been sent away, they were well into the third bottle of Papa's French wine.

"I have a confession to make, Gus," Harry said as he took the slender glass of syllabub in one hand. "While I was ill with the fever, I dreamed not of my sins, but of syllabub. Lemon-laced syllabub, exactly like this."

Dramatically he raised the flared glass as if it were another wineglass. "To syllabub, the supreme sweet of sweets!"

Gus grinned, and held her glass up, too. "To sweet, supreme, sweet, and silly-silly-syllabub!"

He frowned dramatically, lowering his glass. "I didn't say silly, Gus."

"No," she said, delicately dipping her silver teaspoon into the top layer of whipped froth in her glass. "But I believe it needed saying."

"You're right, clever Gus," he said. "It did need saying." He dug his spoon deep along the side of the glass, through the froth on the top and into the blush-colored liquid in the bottom. But he misjudged the force with which he pulled the spoon back, and the bowl flipped forward and catapulted a large blotch of the blush-colored cream onto the front of his nightshirt.

"Oh, no!" exclaimed Gus. "Look at you, Harry!"

At once she leaned forward with her napkin in her hand, ready to blot away the offending cream. She frowned with concentration, determined to tidy his shirt. Yet as she swayed toward him, she lifted her gaze from the front of his shirt. His smile faded as their eyes met, and he reached up to slip his fingers into her carefully pinned hair. Slowly he drew her forward and tipped his head to one side. His mouth found hers, and before she realized exactly how or what was happening, he was kissing her.

Gus didn't pull away, but the shock of being kissed made her go perfectly still. She had never been kissed before, not like this, and never, ever by a gentleman who was as accomplished at it as Harry. At least she decided he must be accomplished, because he took his time and didn't rush, gently wooing her with his lips, adding more pressure to make her relax.

Tentatively she began to press back, and discovered that the velvety friction of her lips against his was really very nice, and exciting, too, in a way she'd never expected. Without thinking, she rested her hands on his shoulders to keep herself steady, and he slanted his mouth over hers, coaxing her to part her lips. She did, only a little, yet to her surprise he thrust his tongue inside her mouth. She gasped, the sound caught vibrating between them as he deepened the kiss. He tasted of the wine, and the syllabub, and a certain indefinable quality that she recognized as purely male, and purely his. His tongue plunged deeper as his mouth ground over hers, so much that she almost feared he'd devour her.

Almost, but not quite: because the longer he kissed her, the more exciting she found it. Before this, she'd thought kissing was no more than the dry, dutiful pecks of pursed lips that she'd encountered beneath holiday mistletoe. But kissing Harry was like kissing fire, full of the heat and sensation that she now realized must be passion. She felt it through her entire body, making her knees grow wobbly and her heart race. She felt the heat coalesce low in her belly, a curious, delightful tension that made her only want to kiss him more.

When his hand left the back of her head to slide down her back and settle around her waist, she sighed with the pleasurable possession of it, of being desired by a gentleman. Because that was what it was, wasn't it? That was the reason he was kissing her, wasn't it? That he desired her?

It was a heady realization, made all the sweeter because she desired him, too. What a marvelous word that was—*desire*—to describe an even more marvelous feeling. She swayed unsteadily over the bed toward him and he pulled her closer, her breasts crushing shamelessly against his chest and directly onto the splotch of creamy syllabub. She didn't care, not one whit. She slipped her fingers into the black silk of his hair and back over his sleekly shaven jaw, relishing every second of being kissed by Harry, and kissing him in return.

When at last their mouths parted, she was almost dizzy with pleasure. It was an excellent thing that she had his shoulders for support, because she wouldn't have trusted her own legs to hold her. It pleased her no end that he seemed as affected as she was, his breathing ragged and his chest rising and falling beneath her.

"Goodness, Harry," she whispered, gazing rapturously into his blue eyes and trying hard to keep his face from spinning before her. "I've never done that before."

He smiled, and rubbed his thumb lightly across her cheek.

"Sweet Gus," he said. "I haven't, either."

She frowned, for as fuddled as she might be, she knew perfectly well that he'd likely kissed other women by the score.

"Don't tease me, Harry," she said as firmly as she could, striving to enunciate for emphasis. "I am as serious as serious—as *serious*—can be."

"So am I," he said. "I have never before kissed you, Gus. But I find I'd like to do it again."

"Oh, yes, Harry," she whispered. "If you please, yes."

But as she leaned forward to offer him her lips once more, she leaned too far. Slowly, slowly, she toppled to one side, slid from the edge of the bed, and landed on the carpet in an ignominious crush of silk petticoats.

CHAPTER
7

Under ordinary circumstances, Harry would have found the sight before him an enchanting one. A young woman sprawled on the carpet beside his bed, her skirts tossed up above her knees to display her neatly turned legs in pale blue stockings with rose-patterned red garters at the knee, and an enticing glimpse of her plump, pale thighs. From his spot on the bed above her, he also had an excellent view of her breasts, which now seemed to be spilling out of her red gown with more exuberance than he recalled from earlier in the evening. Her cheeks were flushed and her lips swollen and red from his kisses, and her hair was half unpinned and tumbling down around her shoulders.

In ordinary circumstances, he would have considered her the perfect picture of a young and willing wanton, and after a few seconds' admiration he would have been on the carpet with her to enjoy what she was so blatantly offering.

But these weren't ordinary circumstances. The young woman wasn't a wanton, but Gus. She wasn't blatantly offering anything, but sitting there dazed with inebriated astonishment while one of his dogs licked syllabub from her sleeve. And Harry wouldn't be joining her, as much as he wished to, because he couldn't, not with his infernal leg.

What he had done, however, was let them both drink too much, so much that they'd ended up kissing, and now—now he wasn't sure what was going to happen next.

"Are you unharmed, Gus?" he asked solicitously, even though he was sure that she was. Only sober people hurt themselves when they fell.

"Oh, yes," she said. She frowned down at her splayed legs, then swiftly yanked her skirts over them. She tried to stand by holding on to the chair, and when that didn't work, she scrambled over onto her hands and knees, her taffeta-covered backside turned up toward Harry.

Oh, if only these *were* ordinary circumstances . . .

"My lord," Tewkes said, cautiously entering the room. "Is everything well, my lord? I heard the crash, and—oh, Miss Augusta!"

He hurried forward to help her back to her feet.

"Miss Augusta has had a small mishap, Tewkes," Harry explained unnecessarily as he watched Gus's attempts to compose herself, smoothing her skirts and shoving the loose pins back into her hair. She didn't have much success, and Harry didn't care. He liked her like this, her usual tidiness a bit rumpled and disarrayed, and the more he studied her, the more he liked it.

The devil take him, but Gus really was a pretty creature. How had he not seen it before? He'd like to kiss her again; hell, he'd like to do a great many other things with her, too.

Still, as a gentleman, he knew what needed doing instead, and manfully he made himself say it.

"I believe Miss Augusta is ready to retire for the evening, Tewkes," he said. "Would you see her safely back to her rooms and into her maid's care?"

"You are mistaken, Harry," Gus said. "I am not ready to retire. You promised me music with our supper, and I mean to stay until I hear it."

Music. Harry had completely forgotten about that part of the evening, but now that he was reminded, he could see Vilotti and the others lurking in the hall with their instruments. If music was what she wished, then music she would have.

"Very well, my dear," he said grandly. "Tewkes, send in the musicians."

Gus beamed at him as the three Italians trooped into the room and took their chairs before the windows.

"Thank you, Harry," she said, her voice sweet and husky at the same time. "You always know how to please me."

He smiled back, his mind racing off into all manner of wicked directions. He was, he knew, in a most interesting state: not quite so foxed that he was numb to the pleasures of the flesh, but still sufficiently drunk that he could brush aside his conscience without too much difficulty, and see only the merits of pleasing Gus, exactly as she'd said. If he also pleased himself in the process, well, where was the harm in that?

"Help me with these pillows, Tewkes," he said, easing himself more into the center of the wide bed. Tewkes smoothed the sheets and plumped the pillows, arranging them behind Harry's back while Gus watched from her chair.

"You're looking very lonely, Gus, sitting by yourself," Harry said as soon as Tewkes was done. "Nearly as lonely as I am over here."

She blinked and looked at him curiously. "What would you suggest?"

He patted the space on the bed beside him. "That you join me here," he said as winningly as he could. "So we might listen to the music together."

He heard Tewkes make a strangled sound of disapproval in his throat.

Fortunately, Gus did not. She grinned and without hesitation came to climb onto the bed and sit beside him. She was on top of the coverlet and sheets, and he was beneath them, which offered some small degree of propriety. It was just as well, too, for kissing her had made his cock as hard as a ramrod beneath the covers, a sure way to frighten off any lady as innocent as Gus.

But it still didn't take Harry long to settle her back against the mounded pillows alongside him, and to ease his arm across her shoulders to draw her closer. By the time the musicians had begun to play, she was nestled neatly against him with her head resting on his shoulder and his arm curled around her. She was temptation incarnate, but as much as he wanted to kiss her—and a great deal more—he wouldn't, not before Tewkes and the musicians. He and Gus had already given them enough to talk about belowstairs, and for Gus's sake he wouldn't add any more. Blissfully unaware, Gus smiled up at him and sighed with drowsy contentment.

He understood that contentment, because he was feeling mightily contented, too. He hadn't realized until this moment how the broken leg had made him feel not only isolated and helpless, but lonely as well. Having Gus there beside him, warm and soft in her rustling silk gown, was the best cure for loneliness he could imagine.

He smiled, drowsy as well, letting the music wash over them. Thanks to the large meal and the wine, he was having a deuced hard time keeping awake himself. He let his hand drift lower across Gus's shoulder, his fingers grazing the swell of her bare breast as if by accident, and with a little sigh she turned and curled closer to him.

Damnation, she was asleep. He couldn't very well go on caressing her while she slept, or not the first time, anyway. Perhaps if he took a short nap himself, they'd both be more ardent later, when they woke.

He yawned at the thought, his eyes heavy. Yes, that

was exactly what he needed. A bit of sleep, a short rest. Gus deserved his best from him.

Dear, sweet, trusting Gus . . .

Gus didn't so much wake as drag herself back to consciousness. Her head throbbed, her mouth felt furry, and her side ached from where the whalebone had dug into her ribs. It was never a good idea to fall asleep in stays, and she shifted against the pillow, trying to find a more comfortable position. Why hadn't Mary undressed her properly before she'd gone to bed, anyway? It seemed odd that she'd gone to bed in her clothes, odder still that her hair was still bristling with pins that were jabbing at her head.

She opened her eyes a fraction, squinting against the brightness as she looked for her maid. The sun was just rising, slanting in through the windows directly into her face in a thoroughly unkind manner.

But those weren't her windows. This wasn't even her room. That was the mahogany tallboy from the best bedchamber, and those were the yellow silk curtains and hangings with the Chinese dragons.

Her eyes flew wide open, and she bolted upright. There were the three chairs that had been occupied by the musicians, the roses from her mother's garden in the porcelain bowl, and the small table beside the bed, still laid with the damask cloth from dinner.

With a sickening certainty that had nothing to do with her aching head, she forced herself to look down at the bed beside her. There, exactly as she'd known he'd be, lay Harry, soundly asleep. His hair was disheveled and pulled free of his queue, silky black against the white linen. He slept with one arm curled around the place where she'd lain, the impression of her body next to his still clear in the rumpled sheets.

Horrified, she covered her mouth with her hand to keep back her gasp. She could remember the supper, and drinking so much that she'd fallen over on the carpet, and Patch—or had it been Potch?—licking spilled syllabub from her sleeve. But most of all she remembered kissing Harry, here, on this bed. That was shameful enough, and she prayed she hadn't done anything further with him that she now couldn't recall. Oh, whatever had *possessed* her to behave like that with him?

Determined not to wake him, she eased from the bed as carefully as she could. She glanced at his watch, the gold cover sitting open on the bedside table: a quarter past five. If she hurried now, she could return to her own room, undress, and be in her bed for Mary to come wake her at the usual hour. If she hurried, that is, and was lucky, too.

She took one final glance at Harry. It didn't quite seem fair that he was such a handsome man, her heart making a little lurch of longing as she gazed down at him. He was back to his old piratical self, with the shadow of a night's beard fresh on his jaw, and snoring gently. His lashes were so long, feathered across his cheekbones as he slept, that he looked years younger than when he was awake. A boyish pirate, then, and far too irresistible, and she considered bending over to give him a whisper of a kiss before she left, then thought better of it. Heaven only knew what he'd remember when he woke, and she'd rather not be here when he did.

She slipped her feet from her slippers, and with the shoes in her hand she tiptoed from the room. At least with Papa and Julia still in London, she'd only the servants to avoid. To her surprise the footman who was usually standing by the door was not there; nor did she see any sign of faithful Tewkes. Perhaps she *would* escape without being seen, and in her stockinged feet she scurried down the long hall to her own room.

At last she reached her rooms, carefully unlatched the door, and slipped inside. She'd made it; she hadn't been caught, and she let out a long sigh of relief.

"Good evening, Miss Augusta," said Mary, trying to cover her yawn as she struggled to her feet to curtsey. She was wearing the same clothes as last night, and had obviously fallen asleep in the armchair while waiting up for Gus to return. Belatedly she noticed the rising sun through the windows, and corrected herself. "That is, good day, miss."

"Well, yes, good day, Mary," Gus said, blushing furiously with her slippers still in her hand. There was no use making excuses, especially not to Mary. Even a fool could see that Gus had spent the night away from her bedchamber and in the same clothes she'd left it last evening, and her lady's maid was no fool.

Mary looked her up and down, clearly drawing the obvious conclusion.

"Shall you be dressing for bed, miss," she said evenly, "or day?"

"For day," Gus said. She'd never felt so guilty in her life—but then, for the first time, she'd done something worthy of feeling guilty. "And please send word to the stable to have the carriage ready for me in an hour."

"Very good, miss," Mary said, heading briskly to the door to summon a footman. "Might I ask where you will be going, miss, so that I might lay out the proper clothes?"

"Norwich," Gus said, deciding on the spot. "I wish to visit the shops."

What she really wished to do was to go back to bed—*her* bed—and bury her throbbing head beneath the pillows. But she was in need of penance, and hers would be to be driven into Norwich to purchase a few necessary items for the house: upstairs candles, a larger copper wash-pot and fresh flannel for the laundry mangle, samples of broadcloth for new livery jackets for the footmen.

Besides, the fresh air would likely do her head more good than staying indoors—and most important, if she was on the Norwich road, she wouldn't have to see Harry.

"Shall I send to the kitchen for coffee, miss?" Mary asked. "Black coffee? I'm told it's a wonderful restorative in the morning after a, ah, rich supper, miss."

Gus looked at her sharply, her stomach roiling at the very thought of black coffee.

"Do I look so vastly sorrowful, Mary, as if I'm in need of a restorative?" she asked, then sighed as she sank onto the bench before her dressing table. "No, you needn't answer that. I'm sure I do. Send for the coffee, if you please, and some dry toast."

"A coddled egg will help, too, miss," Mary said, her voice finally showing a bit of sympathy. "Leastways that's always what Mr. Wetherby requests with the coffee after a night spent with friends."

"Thank you, Mary, I'll try that, too." She sighed again, striving to keep from groaning, and prayed her brother's remedy would help. She did feel wretched. The wine that Harry had chosen had been delightful to drink, but if this was the result of overindulgence, she could not imagine how anyone could become a confirmed drunkard. "If my brother and his friends recommend such a cure, then it must surely work."

"They say 'tis the price of friendly companionship, miss." Mary came to stand behind Gus and rapidly began pulling out the hairpins and tangles. "Among gentleman friends, that is."

Gus closed her eyes and did not answer. Of all the servants, Gus trusted Mary the most, and she knew no matter how much the others would beg her maid for more information, she wouldn't reveal that her lady had spent the night in a gentleman's bedchamber. But she also knew exactly where Mary was attempting to steer the conversation. There was only one gentleman friend that interested Mary at this moment, and that was the one who had been with her mistress last night. Gus was in no humor to discuss Harry, not with anyone, and she'd no notion of what she'd say even if she did. How could she, when she herself still wasn't exactly sure what had happened between them last night?

She let her neck relax as Mary pulled the brush through her hair, trying to sort out her feelings about Harry. She liked him. She liked him very much, which complicated things immeasurably. He had kissed her. She had kissed him in return, yes, but he'd started it. She still couldn't believe it had happened, that a gentleman like Harry had wanted to kiss *her*. She would be willing to dismiss the first time as an accident brought on by the wine, but then he'd said he wanted to kiss her again, and he had, and that had been even better. She'd felt alive, and she'd felt desired, heady, unknown sensations for her.

Most of all, that kiss had made her feel beautiful, and he'd never be able to understand what a rare gift that had been.

Nor had that been the end of it. After he'd kissed her, he'd wanted her to stay with him, too. He'd made room on the bed for her to sit with him, and while now the very thought of such familiarity made her blush, at the time it had simply seemed perfectly right. Lying with her head on his shoulder and his arm around her, listening to the music, had been magical. That wasn't a word that she'd ordinarily use to describe anything about her life, but because of Harry, it was.

But magical was last night, not this morning. She and Harry had agreed to be friends, nothing more, yet now—now that didn't seem possible. Because of that first kiss, everything between them was different, and was bound to change. Would he wish to kiss her again when she visited him in his room today? Would he now expect her to sit on his bed with him when she read to him? Was she a friend that now he kissed, or was she going to be something more?

And that, really, was her greatest worry: that something more. Harry was a man of the world, a gentleman of wealth and power, and by comparison she was a thoroughly insignificant country lady. He belonged with a brilliant, breathtaking beauty like her sister, a lady who would become his duchess and wear his mother's jewels, and make every man in the room stop and stare when she entered. Gus understood that. She had no illusions about her place in society, and she knew that Harry wouldn't, either. She would be at best a passing amusement to him, and destined to be swiftly forgotten as soon as he could return to his friends and family in London. He might even be done with her now.

All of which meant that there must be no more kissing or anything else between them. It would be painfully difficult, but for the sake of her future, she'd have to stand firm. As proud as she was that Papa trusted her to run Wetherby Abbey in his absence, this was one of those times that she wistfully wished he were here with her. Julia wasn't the only daughter who needed him. His presence would make everything honorable and respectable, and he'd make sure no one would ever question why Gus had spent so much time alone with Harry. She did dream of marrying someday, of having a family and house of her own, and the stolid country gentlemen that she'd likely attract would disapprove of any scandal in her past involving her and the fast and fashionable Earl of Hargreave. She might not have Julia's beauty, but she'd always had virtue, and she could not risk losing that for the sake of a few kisses, however sweet.

Her virtue, or her heart. Because as easy as it had been

to be kissed by Harry, it would be easier still to fall hopelessly, ruinously in love with him.

"*What in* blazes are you saying, Tewkes?" Harry demanded. "How can Lady Augusta not be at home? Where else would she be?"

"They say she has gone to Norwich for the day, my lord," Tewkes said, maddeningly unperturbed. "She is not expected to return until late this afternoon."

"Why would she wish to go to Norwich?" Harry continued to demand, his indignation rising. "What could she possibly want that is in *Norwich*?"

"Candles, my lord," Tewkes said. "They say she was intending to purchase candles."

"Candles," Harry repeated in disbelief. How could Gus go riding off to Norwich when he wanted—no, he needed—to speak with her?

He was angry that she wasn't here, but he was also worried. He truly hadn't intended to kiss her last night, but he had, and he knew damned well she'd kissed him back. Further, she'd curled up next to him, sweet as could be, and fallen asleep there beside him in the most companionable way possible. It had, hands down, been the best evening of his life in a good long while. So what reason could she have this morning for not just keeping away from him, but bolting from the very house?

No, he didn't have to ask that question. He knew the answer. *In vino veritas* was an old Latin saying he'd learned at school, but he'd always thought it should be *In vino amor*: in wine there is love. Wine—and they had drunk a great deal of wine, too—made everyone and everything agreeable.

But in the clear light of day, and doubtless with an aching head as an additional truth serum, Gus was bound to see things differently. To her he must appear an invalid, a cripple, an incomplete man. How could he not? She'd seen him at his very worst, delirious with fever and pain. Gus had more kindness and generosity than any other woman he'd known, but not even Gus would be able to forget what she'd seen, and think of him otherwise. He might have kissed her last night, but he'd also been incapable of helping her up from the floor when she'd fallen. He'd had to call Tewkes.

He couldn't fault her for having second thoughts, either. He'd assured her that all he'd sought was friendship, and to prove she believed him, she'd dressed like the lady she was. He'd told her she'd taken his breath away, and she had. She'd been a luminous, enchanting version of Gus, and so effortlessly desirable he'd been shocked by the intensity of it.

How had he responded? He'd betrayed her trust and lunged at her like some sottish tinker, and sullied the innocence of her kiss. He would ask her forgiveness, of course, and try to explain as best he could, but he didn't have much hope. She'd be justified in wanting nothing more to do with him, exactly as her sister had before her.

And he would be the loser. To be deprived of her company, her laughter, her wit, and her compassion—hell, even the adorable freckles scattered over her nose and cheeks—that would be his punishment.

He had survived the broken leg, survived the fever, survived being jilted by her sister. But he wasn't certain how he'd survive his days here without Gus in them.

Gus leaned back in the corner of the carriage's seat, her hat in her lap, as at last they turned off the Norwich road onto the one that curved through her father's land. Dusk had fallen, with murky shadows beneath the trees and mist already beginning to settle around the edges of their pond.

She had stayed in Norwich much longer than she'd intended. In the mercer's shop, she had met an old friend of hers, a friend who was so caught up with her new husband and newer baby that she'd asked only the most cursory questions about Julia and her father, and the unusual noble houseguest at the abbey.

With relief, Gus had listened eagerly to her friend's tales of this prodigious infant, and had accepted an invitation to tea so that she might view the baby for herself. The poor baby had not performed to his mother's standards, being cranky with colic, but Gus had been so happy to have anything to take her mind from Harry that she'd praised the baby to the skies, even after he'd spit up on the front of her habit, much to the mortification of his mother and nursemaid.

Now she was looking forward to a light supper in her own rooms and going straight to bed afterward. It was too late to see Harry now, and besides, that conversation could wait until the morning. She slowly walked up the front steps and into the house as Royce himself held the door open for her. She *was* late: A footman had just lit the oil in the large blue-glass night-lantern and was carefully raising it back into place.

"Good evening, Miss Augusta," Royce murmured.

"Good evening, Royce," she said, barely stifling a yawn as she headed up the staircase. "Please have Mrs. Buchanan send a light supper and tea up to my room."

"If you please, Miss Augusta," the butler said with uncharacteristic emphasis, "his lordship is expecting you to dine with him."

She paused on the top stair and looked back over the rail. "He is? In his bedchamber?"

"He is, Miss Augusta," Royce said. "If you wish, I shall convey your regrets to his lordship, but I can safely say he shall be disappointed to see me instead of you."

She bowed her head, struggling to decide what next to

do. Over the course of the day, she'd convinced herself that he would want nothing more to do with her after last night. Rejecting his further advances would be easy because there wouldn't be any to reject. She hadn't dreamed that he'd actually expect her to dine with him again, not after last night. Why didn't *he* have any remorse, anyway?

She sighed deeply. The conversation would be difficult, whether they had it tonight or tomorrow morning. He'd have to see her as she was now, though, in her plain gray woolen riding habit. She wasn't going to go through the rigmarole of dressing again, and she didn't plan on staying to dine with him, either. No, she had to stand firm.

She looked back to Royce, waiting expectantly for her reply. "I'll go to his lordship myself, Royce. But I still wish tea brought to my room in, oh, ten minutes."

"Very good, Miss Augusta." Royce smiled, more satisfied than he'd any right to be.

With another sigh, Augusta headed up the last steps and down the hall toward Harry's room. She paused to pull off her gloves and untie her hat, leaving them for now on one of the hall tables, and paused again to smooth her hair before one of the looking glasses.

She was stalling, and she knew it. She also knew she was being cowardly, but she did not want to see him. No, she must be honest: She didn't want this conversation because she *did* want to see him, very much, and she didn't trust herself to be strong and say what was necessary.

Be virtuous, she told herself with each trudging, reluctant step. *Be respectable, be honorable, be a lady. Do what is virtuous and* right.

But as soon as she passed the last footman and entered Harry's room, she knew that all the virtuous good intentions in the world weren't going to stand a chance against Harry himself.

He was sitting in the bed exactly as he had last night,

exactly as he had for weeks now. His dark hair was once again sleeked back from his face, his jaw shaven, his white linen nightshirt impeccable over his broad shoulders and chest. Once again, too, the room was ablaze with candles, their flickering light casting dancing shadows over the hard planes of his face. She never quite recalled what an impossibly handsome man he was, and each time she saw him again she was struck by it, a visceral blow against which she had no defense.

But this time, he wasn't smiling. His expression was serious, his blue eyes so dark and somber that she dreaded what might come next.

"Good evening, Gus," he said, his voice warm and welcoming, but reserved as well. Patch and Potch dragged themselves awake and lumbered to their feet, ambling over to greet Gus with their feathered tails wagging sleepily. "I'm honored that you decided to join me once again."

"I can't stay, Harry," she said quickly. She bent to pet the dogs, then straightened with determination, not so much clasping her hands before her as clutching them. "There are a few things I wish to say after last night, and then—and then I must go."

"I trust you'll stay long enough to hear what I've to say, too," he said. "Then you may decide if you wish to join me for supper again."

He gestured toward the table. Clearly he'd again planned a meal for her with the assistance of Mrs. Buchanan and the others. The table was even more beautifully set, with the Wetherby porcelain that her grandfather had had specially made in China and the Venetian blown-glass goblets that Andrew had brought home from his Grand Tour. Rising up from the center of the table like a delicate little tree was Mama's silver epergne, with a different, miniature fruit fashioned from marzipan poised on the end of each curving branch.

Gus blinked back a sudden wave of tears. If anyone

else had ransacked through her family's personal treasures while she'd been out, she would have been furious.

But Harry was different. He hadn't coerced her servants—in fact, they seemed like willing conspirators—and he hadn't ordered them to bring out these precious things for the sake of making an impressive show. He'd done it because he understood how much they meant to her, not as costly objects, but as extensions of her family. He understood family; she'd realized that when she'd heard him speak of his mother and father and his brothers. He'd assembled all these things on this little table just for her, a special kind of personal gift. Considering that he couldn't leave the bed, but had been forced to create this through others made it all the more meaningful.

Harry wasn't by nature a patient man, yet he'd waited here for her while she'd been purposefully staying away from him. No wonder seeing the little table like this charmed her, even as it made her feel guilty and selfish and utterly unworthy.

"This is beautiful, Harry," she said softly, at a loss for more words. All the arguments, all the careful reasoning that she'd rehearsed earlier in the carriage disappeared from her head. "Beautiful."

He nodded in acknowledgment but still didn't smile.

"You will note there is no wine on our table tonight," he said. "I want everything I have to say to be clear and unclouded."

"That is wise," she agreed quickly, relieved. "I welcome clarity, too."

Harry nodded, praying she couldn't tell how fast his heart was beating. He'd been waiting for her with everything ready for hours, listening for the sound of her carriage wheels on the gravel drive outside his window—not that he wished her to know that, either. This could be the last time he saw her like this, alone with him as she stood beside his bed, and he wanted to remember everything about her, in case memories were all he'd have left.

She was dressed in a sensible gray wool riding habit whose close-fitting, masculine jacket somehow made her seem more feminine by displaying her narrow waist. The dove-colored wool set off her pale complexion, and her once-severe hair had loosened during the day, with charming little wisps around her cheeks.

Her expression had been daunting when she'd first entered the room, her gray eyes as serious as storm clouds, but they had softened when she'd seen the table. He was glad, for it hadn't been easy to arrange everything through servants he didn't know, and he'd worried, too, that she might be angry at him for having them haul so much upstairs from the dining room. But it was clear she'd seen it exactly as he'd intended, and he let himself feel a tiny bit of hope that she might forgive him after all.

"I'm glad you approve, Gus," he said, hoping, too, that she'd soon approve of him as well. "I'll be a proper host and let you speak first."

"Me?" Her eyes widened, and her voice squeaked upward. "That is, I'd rather wait, Harry. You go first."

He hadn't expected that. "Will you at least sit?"

She hesitated briefly, then came and perched on the edge of the chair like a nervous little bird ready to fly away. She might do it, too, if he didn't say the right things.

He cleared his throat momentously, feeling as if he were making an important recitation in school, and one he didn't quite have by rote, either.

"Gus," he began. "Miss Augusta. I invited you here to dine with me last night in the guise of friendship. Unfortunately, what happened before the evening's end was not what I had planned, or what you deserved. I can fault my overindulgence, true, but most of the blame must lie on my own selfish and impulsive behavior, and I am heartily sorry for it."

"Oh, Harry," she said. "You needn't—"

"I do," he said bluntly. "I must. Because I know I'm on the thinnest of thin ice with you, Gus. I know how you must see me: not as a man, but as a cripple, an invalid, and an inconvenience. I'm your sister's wretched castoff."

She winced, which he didn't interpret as a good sign. Was he really so distasteful to her? So repulsive? He'd no choice now but to plunge onward, and say everything as he'd planned.

"You've been the one good thing to come into my life from this damnable mess, Gus," he said. "If I have shamed myself so grievously by my boorish behavior that you no longer wish my acquaintance, then I will understand. If you decide to shed me as your sister has, then I will understand that as well. I'll never forgive myself for driving you away, but I'll understand. I won't—"

"No more, Harry, no *more*!" She flew from the chair like the little bird he'd first thought her, but instead of flying away, she flew straight to stand beside the bed. "You are good and kind and brave and generous and if my sister cast you off, then she was a fool, and—and— oh, no more!"

Swiftly she bent forward and seized his face in her hands, her palms warm against his cheeks, and kissed him. Last night might have been her first kiss, but she'd clearly learned from the experience. She slanted her lips over his, pressing so deliciously that he'd no choice but to kiss her in return.

Choice, hell. This wasn't about a choice. This was about wanting to kiss her more than he wanted anything else in his life at that moment. He'd been so sure that he'd lost her, that he'd driven her away, and he hadn't, which made this kiss as full of joy as it was of passion. He forgot his well-prepared speech of contrition and apology, forgot his misgivings, forgot his worries, forgot his broken leg propped up on the pillow. All that mattered was kissing Gus.

He looped one arm around her waist and pulled her from her feet and onto the bed and against him. She came effortlessly, curling her hands over his shoulders and flexing her fingers as she kissed him. He thrust his fingers into the silk of her hair, pulling it free of the knot at the back of her head and scattering hairpins over the coverlet. He kissed her so deeply, with such hunger, that when their lips parted briefly, both of them were gasping for breath.

"Don't ever say such things, Harry," she said in a fierce whisper, resting her forehead against his as her hair streamed around them both. "Don't ever say things like that again, ever."

"I won't," he said, his hand sliding restlessly along the length of her back.

She nibbled lightly on his lips, sheer, teasing torment, then pulled back again, shifting away from him.

"Your leg," she said breathlessly. "I can't hurt your leg."

"You won't," he said, pulling her back into his arms to make her forget his leg and any other reason she might have for not kissing him.

"But what if I—"

His mouth swept down on hers again by way of an answer, and to silence her worries. He would never doubt her, not after this. Well, *never* might be too strong. At present his brain was incapable of considering the future, and focused entirely on kissing her in the present, and wondering how long it would take to undo the long row of buttons on the front of her habit's jacket. If only he could stand, he would have her freed of the entire rig— jacket, petticoats, shirt, stays, hoops, and shift—and have her naked in a matter of minutes.

Naked: no, as much as he wanted her, he couldn't think like that. Not yet, anyway. This wasn't a mistress.

This was Gus, and she was a lady. So why in blazes were they on each other now like stoats in the spring?

And why was he wasting time even thinking such thoughts when she was making the most wanton little moans into his mouth as he kissed her, when she—

"My lord Hargreave," called the voice on the other side of the bedroom door. "Miss Augusta. A word, if you please."

Gus tore her mouth away from Harry, and whipped around toward the door.

"That's Royce," she whispered breathlessly. "He wouldn't dare interrupt unless it was important."

"Go away, Royce," Harry called back over her shoulder at the closed door, not letting her go. "Miss Augusta and I are discussing the future of the Whig party in relation to the House of Lords, and cannot be disturbed."

Her eyes widened, and the ever-practical and serious Gus actually giggled, clapping her hand over her mouth to keep back the sound.

"I regret the intrusion, my lord," Royce said mournfully. "But this is a matter of importance. You have a visitor, my lord. His Grace the Duke of Sheffield, my lord."

"Your *cousin* the Duke of Sheffield?" Gus gasped with dismay. "Here? Now?"

Without waiting for an explanation, she wriggled free of Harry's embrace and scrambled from the bed. With the frantic efficiency of all women caught—or nearly caught—in the act of doing something they shouldn't, she smoothed her skirts and rebuttoned the two buttons on her jacket that Harry had undone.

"Why the devil should Sheffield be here?" Harry demanded, more frustrated than embarrassed.

Yet he could already hear his cousin's voice in the hallway, loudly inquiring why poor Royce didn't open the damned door. Gus had scarcely time to coil her hair back into a knot before Sheffield opened the door himself and came striding into the room.

"Harry, you rogue!" he exclaimed, beaming as he came forward to the bed. "Look at you here, as fine as a Turk!"

As unhappy as he was at being interrupted with Gus, Harry couldn't help but grin at Sheffield. Although technically a much-removed cousin, he was close enough in age to Harry that he'd always seemed more like a favorite older brother. They shared a physical resemblance, too, both being tall and dark with blue eyes, broad shoulders, and devastating smiles.

And, of course, they shared an obvious devotion to their dogs. If Harry was glad to see Sheffield, then Patch and Potch were equally delighted to see Sheffield's portly white bulldog, Fantôme, lumbering faithfully alongside him with his pink tongue lolling from his grinning mouth.

But while the dogs were busily sniffing and licking one another in joyful reunion, Harry saw at once that greeting his cousin was going to be much more complicated. Despite Sheffield's heartiness, his eyes betrayed him, and he was clearly shocked by Harry's appearance. That in turn worried Harry. Here he'd believed himself to be much improved, if not exactly back to his old self. Was he really as changed as that?

But for now that was far less important—and less complicated—than introducing Sheffield to Gus, who was hovering uncertainly and still fussing with her hair.

"Sheffield, may I present my hostess here at Wetherby Hall, Miss Augusta Wetherby," he said. "Miss Augusta, my cousin, His Grace the Duke of Sheffield."

"Welcome, Your Grace," she said, blushing prettily as she sank into the required deep curtsey for a duke. "You honor my father's house."

"Your servant, Miss Augusta," Sheffield said, bowing gallantly over her hand. "My family is most grateful to you for the generous hospitality you have shown Harry in his time of need. I can see he has been well looked after."

Trust Sheffield to know how to put a lady at ease, thought Harry. "'Looked after' sounds as if I'm some mongrel dog found by the crossroads, given a bone and an old blanket in a box near the fire," he said. "The pure truth is that Miss Augusta saved my life."

Her blush deepened. "Oh, Harr—that is, my lord," she stammered, not nearly as adept as the men were at this polite game. "I fear you're exaggerating my role."

Harry smiled, striving to reassure her even as she stood out of his reach. "It's no exaggeration, not at all."

"You were feverish, my lord," she said. "I venture that you misremember. Your Grace, I hope that you will join Harr—his lordship and me for supper, and be my father's guest here at the abbey."

Sheffield bowed. "I accept both invitations, Miss Augusta."

"My family is honored, Your Grace," Gus said. "If you will excuse me, I will go speak to my cook, and make the other arrangements for rooms for you."

She curtseyed and backed from the room. Harry could sense how relieved she was to have this excuse for her escape, but he still couldn't help missing her acutely the instant the door closed after her.

"So tell me of your leg, Harry," Sheffield said, settling into the armchair beside the bed that Harry regarded as Gus's. "I've come clear from Paris to hear your version of the tale."

"I was thrown by a horse and broke my leg," Harry said. "This is a fine season for Paris. How are Diana and the children?"

"Diana is as beautiful as ever, the children are thriving, and Paris was most agreeable," Sheffield said. Fantôme whined at his feet, and with a grunt he hoisted the dog onto his lap. "Or at least it would have been if I hadn't returned to discover most of London discussing your hapless adventures. Sir Randolph will be joining us here tomorrow, so there'll be no gilding of the truth."

Harry sighed, leaning back against the pillows so that he stared up at the pleated canopy overhead, and not at his cousin. He might as well tell Sheffield the truth, or at least most of it. His cousin likely knew the majority of it already, anyway.

"Very well, then," he said. "The ungilded truth is that I came to this house last month intending to ask for the hand of the Honorable Miss Julia Wetherby."

"A lady who'd tempt any man," Sheffield said, rubbing Fantôme's pointed ears and making the dog drool with happiness. "Alas, she knows it, too."

"I learned that," Harry said. "Unfortunately, I had to be tossed by her father's hellish horse first. She discovered that her love for me did not include me with a broken leg, and she . . . left me for the more flourishing pastures in London."

Sheffield frowned down at the top of Fantôme's head. "You do know that it's expected she'll now marry Southland?"

Harry shrugged, and tried to sound cavalier. "Southland is welcome to her. I consider myself to have made a fortuitous escape."

"Yet you haven't, Harry," Sheffield said. "You're still here in her family's house, which must be a damned uncomfortable place for you to be."

"It's not at all," Harry said. "Gus looks after me most excellently."

Sheffield looked up at him over Fantôme's wrinkled forehead. "I assume that *Gus* is a familiar endearment for Lady Augusta?"

"It is," Harry said, feeling his face grow warm. He'd marched right into that one, hadn't he? "But it is not an, ah, exclusive endearment. She is widely known as such by her family and close friends."

"Indeed," Sheffield said, his voice purposefully bland. He leaned forward and plucked one of Gus's hairpins from Harry's coverlet. "Broken leg or not, I can imagine how excellently she is looking after you."

"Stop there, Sheffield," Harry said sharply. "It's not like that."

Sheffield smiled and leaned back in the chair, gently running his palm along the dog's side. "So you intend to marry the lady?"

"Damnation, it's not like that, either," Harry said, his happiness at seeing his cousin rapidly fading. "Once you come to know Gus better, you'll understand."

"What I understand, Harry," Sheffield said, "is that if her father weren't such a doting, empty-headed ass about Lady Julia, he'd already be outraged by how familiar Miss Augusta is with your bedchamber. She is a viscount's daughter, not a scullery maid. If you're not careful, you'll have Wetherby here with the banns all read and a musket at your back."

He found another of Gus's errant hairpins and held it up to Harry. "Unless, that is, having been spared one Wetherby daughter, you will be content with the other."

Harry grabbed the hairpin and tossed it on the nearby table. It wasn't that he didn't want to marry Gus specifically. In his present state, he didn't want to marry anyone. No woman would want a bridegroom who was a prisoner of his bed, and not in an interesting way, either. How could he even consider marriage when he wasn't able to stand before a minister?

"What will make me content, Sheffield," Harry said, scowling darkly, "is to have you mind your own affairs."

Sheffield smiled, refusing to fan Harry's temper.

"You needn't listen to me, Harry," he said evenly. "But I understand your father is on his way back to England as fast as his passage can be arranged, and I am certain he will have his own ideas about your situation."

"From Naples?" Harry asked, stunned. He hadn't requested his father's return, and he wasn't sure he wanted it. It wasn't that he didn't wish to see his father—they got along much better than many fathers and sons—but he could imagine all too well Father's humor after being interrupted on his leisurely pleasure-tour of Italy to hurry home because Harry had toppled from a horse. Hell, he'd never hear the end of it.

"From Naples," Sheffield said.

"But that could take weeks," Harry said, for once hoping for a long passage for his father. "Months, depending on the winds and seas."

"That doesn't matter," Sheffield said. "The sooner we can remove you from here and take you back to London, the better. Tomorrow, after Sir Randolph's visit, would be ideal. You're welcome to stay with us, if you wish. Diana would love being able to fuss over you, and the children would regard it as the greatest fun imaginable."

Harry didn't say anything. He had a sudden, nightmarish vision of what recuperating at Sheffield House would be like, with his cousin's ever-cheerful wife never leaving him alone, and his two small sons swarming over his bed with their toy soldiers and animals.

"I'm sure she'd do her best to keep you entertained," Sheffield continued blithely. "Sir Randolph will call on you daily to tend to your leg, your friends can visit to cheer you, and you can put the inconsequential Miss Augusta from your thoughts for good."

At once Harry was ready to defend Gus. "I'll thank you not to refer to Miss Augusta in that fashion."

Sheffield sighed. "I'm sorry, that was a bit harsh," he said. "But be rational. Your predilection for fair-haired beauties with large breasts is no secret. If you were to come across Miss Augusta in the company of your past conquests, you would not so much as notice her."

Harry couldn't deny that past full of lushly endowed blond ladies. They'd been his weakness for as long as he'd taken notice of women, and they of him. But Gus was different—not that he seemed able to describe how to Sheffield.

"It's likely circumstances that have drawn you and the lady together," Sheffield said with more generosity. "She has shown you great kindness while you have been here, and it's natural to feel gratitude in return. But you'll see the shift in your attachment as soon as you're parted. It will be for your own good, and hers as well. Once we have you safely back in London, then—"

"That's enough, Sheffield," Harry said curtly. "Enough. Gus will be back any moment. I'm not discussing this further with you."

But Sheffield simply smiled, his hand resting on the now-sleeping dog's broad back.

"We will, Harry," he said. "And I don't intend to leave this house without you."

CHAPTER
8

The next morning, Gus sat in the little folly near her mother's rose garden. The folly was meant to look like an undersized Roman temple, with a ring of cushioned benches inside. Papa had had it built for her mother as a wedding present, a gift that Gus had always found terribly romantic. Her mother had retreated here often with her sewing or a book, and Gus had joined her with a doll, or handwork of her own. With the fragrance of rose on the breeze, it was one of the places in the house where Gus could still feel her mother's presence, and as she sat on the bench, her knitting in her hands, she longed more than ever for her mother's good sense and counsel.

She wished that Papa were here, too. Entertaining both an earl and a duke on her own was a sizable responsibility, and as blustery as Papa could be, he would have eased some of the more awkward moments with His Grace.

And the longer Papa remained in London, the harder it became for Gus to deny that his trust also had a tinge of neglect to it. His letters to her were brief and apologetic, ending with paternal promises of love and devotion, but no mention of when he'd return home. Gus was sure that Julia did take considerable watching, but she also suspected that Papa was having every bit as good a time as Julia was, drinking and dining with his friends, going to cockfights and horse races. He never would have dared leave Julia alone with Harry, even with a broken leg. With Julia, such unattended proximity would have been unthinkable and scandalous, yet clearly not even their own father could imagine Harry taking an inappropriate interest in Gus.

But he had. He *had*.

She glanced up from her needles, past the folly's stone columns and back to the house. The windows on the west corner belonged to Harry's room, and she could just make out the curtains fluttering at the open casements. She could imagine him there, sitting in the bed and holding court with his visitors. Both Sir Randolph and Dr. Leslie were there with him now, consulting together on the state of Harry's leg and offering their combined opinions to his cousin, who was there, too.

She had pointedly not been included. There was, of course, no real reason she should have been. She was not a member of Harry's family, she was not a surgeon, and, most of all, she was not male. The simple fact that she had been at his bedside, holding his hand, from the beginning did not matter, especially not to His Grace the Duke of Sheffield.

Because His Grace did not approve of her. He'd done his best to charm her last night as the three of them had dined awkwardly together: he'd praised Mrs. Buchanan's meal and told Harry again and again how, if he'd had to fall off his horse, he'd be fortunate to do so where Miss Augusta could find him.

But as flattering as all this was, she sensed that, deep down, he found her wanting. She could tell by how he'd look at Harry with genuine fondness, and concern as well, and then how his gaze would cool when he looked at her, as if he couldn't imagine the two of them together. It wounded her, that coolness, because she understood it entirely. He was simply thinking the same thing that everyone else did, and he believed that Harry needed rescuing from her unworthy self. As the evening had worn on, she'd said less and less, and she'd felt herself shrinking shyly into the shadows, not eating, not drinking, not laughing, not enjoying the performance the musicians had given after supper, almost as if she was determined to prove she deserved His Grace's low estimation.

For his part, Harry could not have been more loyal or attentive, striving to include her and asking her opinions. But it was painfully clear to Gus that the world he and his cousin inhabited was a far different place from her own, and if their London had been on a faraway star, it could not have been more removed from her own little world here in Norfolk. Just as she felt herself vanishing, Harry, too, was slipping away from her, back to the family and friends who so clearly adored him, and where he belonged.

She bowed her head over her knitting, struggling to find peace in the rhythm of making perfectly looped stitches slide from one needle to the other. Since the moment she'd seen Harry weeks ago, lying pale and in pain in last summer's leaves, she'd fought the temptation he'd presented, and she'd resolutely told herself over and over that he could never be hers.

Last night, when he'd told her she was the best thing to come into his life, her hopes had soared to giddy heights, and she'd shoved aside the guard she'd so cautiously built around her dreams and set them free. He'd said glorious things to her, things only he could say and only she could hear. She'd kissed him and he'd kissed her, and she'd imagined herself in his arms forever, and it had been perfect.

But it wasn't, because His Grace had come, and that . . . had been that.

She tried to focus on her work, on the yarn slipping over her finger and around the needle, dip and catch and slip a new stitch, again and again and again. Her mother had taught her that there was peace to be found in the repetition of needlework, that by keeping her hands busy, her thoughts would settle on their own.

"Miss Augusta?"

As much as she'd believed her mind had been wandering, she started at the footman's interruption. "Yes, Price, what is it?"

"If you please, miss," he said, "his lordship and the others wish you to come join them."

She was up in an instant, stuffing the half-knitted stocking into her workbag as she hurried along the garden path and into the house. She tried not to run, but she couldn't help it, and by the time she reached Harry's room, she was breathless and her heart was racing wildly.

The scene was exactly as she'd expected. Harry was sitting in the middle of the bed, holding court as usual. The two surgeons and their assistants stood on one side of the bed, near Harry's splinted leg, while Sheffield stood on the other, with Tewkes hovering nearby. The only surprise was that Harry was wearing a dark blue silk brocade dressing gown over his nightshirt, which she supposed Tewkes must have insisted upon in deference to all the company in the room.

"Thank you for joining us, Miss Augusta," the duke said gravely. "I had rather hoped this conversation would be taking a different turn today, but the medical gentlemen have another idea."

Immediately Gus feared the worst. Swiftly she glanced from one male face to the next, eager for any hint of what was coming, and found none.

"Is there something amiss, Your Grace?" she asked anxiously, looking not at him, but at Harry, who wasn't betraying any more than the others. "A complication, or a setback?"

"We must do what is best for his lordship, Miss Augusta," Sir Randolph intoned. "That remains of utmost importance, and we must—"

"Everything is fine, Gus," Harry said, at last breaking into an enormous grin. Excitement and the blue silk made his eyes even brighter. "My infernal leg is healing better than either of these learned gentlemen thought it would. I've been given leave to begin lifting and working it, with the hope of standing—standing, Gus!—a week from today."

"That is excellent news, my lord," Gus said, not wishing to rejoice too exuberantly before His Grace. "When I saw such long faces, I feared otherwise."

"It is not all good news, Miss Augusta," the duke said, his disappointment clear. "I'd hoped to relieve you of my cousin's care and take him with me back to London, but according to these gentlemen, he is still not fit for a journey."

"The jostling of a carriage could undo everything," Sir Randolph said. "I believe in a cautious approach. Great care must still be taken, and his lordship must not let his enthusiasm overcome that caution."

"Hang caution," Harry said. He threw back the coverlet with all the pride of a conjurer revealing his latest trick. "Look, Gus. They've changed that ghastly fence post of a splint for this more modest version."

There was in fact a new, smaller splint bound to his leg, the twin leather pieces now stopping short of his knee. But with more of his leg revealed, what struck Gus was how wasted the limb itself had become. In the weeks he'd been bedridden, he'd lost considerable flesh and muscle, and she knew from having seen others cope with similar wounds that his recovery was not going to be an easy one.

"I've been granted permission to sit on the edge of the bed with my knee bent," he said with unabashed excitement. "I wanted you here to see the momentous event.

True, it's only my first effort, but mark it now, Gus, so you can remember it when I'm dancing again under the stars at Vauxhall Gardens."

Gus smiled, keeping her misgivings to herself. She understood the silk dressing gown now: He'd had Tewkes prepare him for this brief venture upright, even though it was, really, no more than a first step in a long recovery. His eagerness to reach so small a goal was almost unbearably poignant to her. Dancing at Vauxhall was a long, long way in the future, if it ever did happen again, but for his sake she'd smile, and pray he proved them all wrong.

She wasn't the only one. Sheffield rested his hand gently on his cousin's shoulder.

"There's no need to prove anything to us, Harry," he said. "Time enough for talk of dancing."

But Harry only smiled, his eyes bright with determination. "I've done nothing but lie about for weeks, Sheffield. Now is as good a time to begin as any."

He meant it, too, pushing himself over to the edge of the bed. The surgeons and their two assistants both hurried over, ready to assist, and Gus retreated out of their way.

But Harry wanted no help, and waved them away. He managed to swing his good leg over the side of the bed, and paused, marshaling his strength for the real challenge.

"I don't need help," he said. He was already breathing hard from that simple exertion. "I can do this myself."

"You can't, my lord," Sir Randolph said quietly, coming to stand directly before Harry. "Not the first time. The muscles around your knee will be too stiff from disuse. Pray permit me to help."

Harry muttered something that was likely an oath, then nodded curtly. Bracing himself on his arms, he slowly began to pull his healing leg from the bed. Sir Randolph slipped his linked hands beneath Harry's knee while his assistant supported the leg, holding it out straight as it had been these last weeks.

"There, my lord," Sir Randolph said softly. "Whenever you give me leave, I will attempt to bend your leg at the knee, and I apologize in advance for the discomfort I will cause. The pressure shall be slow and steady, my lord, and it will be easier to bear if you can breathe easily, and refrain from holding your breath."

Harry might not be holding his breath, but Gus was holding hers, her fingers pressed lightly to her lips. She remembered all too well what both surgeons had said after the accident, how they'd worried that there'd been more damage inside Harry's leg beyond the broken bones—muscles and tendons torn and never to mend.

They'd said then that only time would tell if he'd ever regain true use of his leg. That time had now come. Did Harry know it, too? Was he aware of how significant this simple exercise might be?

"Please try to relax, my lord," Sir Randolph said. "I'll begin whenever you wish. Steadiness, not haste, will best answer the task."

Harry nodded, his expression full of resolve. He took three deep breaths to steel himself. "As you wish, Peterson."

"Thank you, my lord." With almost imperceptible pressure, Sir Randolph began to bend Harry's knee for him at the joint, taking care to put no stress near the break.

Harry grimaced and swore, clearly surprised by both the effort and the pain. At once Sir Randolph stopped.

"If it's too much to bear, my lord—"

"It is not," Harry said firmly, taking another deep breath. "Proceed, if you please."

This time Sir Randolph continued slowly bending the knee until it formed a right angle, and then just as slowly once again straightened it. As he did, Harry closed his eyes, his face tense and hard as he fought against the pain, his fingers digging deep into the mattress.

"Well done, my lord," Sir Randolph said after he'd repeated the process three times. "That's sufficient for the first day."

"No, it's not," Harry growled. Beads of sweat clustered along his hairline, and he swiped his sleeve over his forehead to wipe them away. "Not at all."

"Harry, please," Sheffield said with concern. "Listen to Peterson. You can't rush this. You've nothing to prove to anyone in this room."

"Damnation, I must prove it to myself," Harry said. He looked up, past Sheffield to find Gus. "Gus, here, give me your hand."

She stepped forward and he seized her hand, his fingers linking instantly into hers. There wasn't a question of her giving him her hand; he claimed it for his own, holding on as tightly as a drowning man might. Perhaps in a way he was that desperate. When she gazed down at him, she could see the mix of emotions behind his eyes, determination and suffering and fear of the future all mingled together.

In response she quickly curled her fingers more closely into his, forgetting all the others around them. He flashed a quick, small smile of gratitude and understanding, just for her, then looked back to Sir Randolph.

"I am ready, Peterson," he said. "I'll ask you to remove your hand, and let me try the knee myself."

Sir Randolph frowned. "Oh, my lord, I do not know if that is wise."

"Is there any chance that I could injure myself further by performing the same motion that you just did for me?"

"It will be extremely taxing, my lord," Sir Randolph said, "and there is the chance that—"

"That if I cannot do it now, I may never be able to do

so on my own again?" Harry said. "That's what you're not saying, isn't it?"

Sir Randolph sighed, nearly a groan. "Yes, my lord," he admitted unhappily. "There is that unfortunate possibility."

"Then I would rather know now," Harry said firmly, "than continue to grasp at an empty hope. I'll ask you to take your hand from my knee, Peterson, so the test is a fair one."

"My assistant must remain to support your lower leg, my lord," protested the surgeon. "A sudden movement could still disrupt the healing."

"I do not believe I could make a sudden movement with that leg if my very life depended on it," Harry said. "But I shall take care."

Sir Randolph shook his head. "You will do this against my advice, my lord," he warned. "Nor will I be responsible if the results are not what you desire."

Harry smiled, but this smile had little humor to it.

"I won't fault you, Peterson," he said. "I've spent most of my life going against the sound advice of others, and I see no reason to change my ways now. Your hand from my knee, if you please."

Reluctantly the surgeon removed it, taking the place of the assistant supporting Harry's lower leg.

Harry nodded and glanced up one last time to his cousin. "A small wager, Sheffield?" he asked. "A hundred guineas says I can bend my own knee."

"You're daft," Sheffield said. "I won't bet against you."

Harry smiled, but no one else did. It occurred to Gus, there in the middle of all these men, that turning this into a kind of challenge, a test, was a peculiarly male thing to do. Peculiarly male, and peculiarly Harry as well. Only she knew that despite his bravado, his palm was damp against hers and his heart was racing. He'd orchestrated this moment for himself to combat his own apprehensions, and now it was up to him either to follow through, or to back down.

Gus didn't doubt for a moment which he'd do.

"Be brave, Harry," she whispered, leaning close so the others wouldn't hear, "and try. You can do no better than that."

He smiled at her one last time. Then he stared down at his knee, clearly concentrating, and his fingers tightened again around Gus's. His thigh trembled from the effort, but slowly, slowly he was able to bend his knee on his own, not as far as Sir Randolph had been able to take it, but enough. Enough to prove he hadn't lost the ability, enough to make his point, enough to make the others in the room break into spontaneous applause.

But it was to Gus that he turned.

"There," he said, breathing as hard as if he'd run a race. "I did it, Gus. You saw, didn't you? I did it."

She nodded, not trusting her voice. She didn't know why she felt so close to tears. She should be happy for him, overjoyed by what he'd proved he could do. Besides, the last thing she wished to do was weep before His Grace and the others.

"Pray excuse me, Miss Augusta," Sir Randolph said firmly, "but it would be best for his lordship to rest now."

He didn't wait for Gus to reply, but immediately began to guide Harry to the center of the bed. Her hand slipped free of his, and she stepped back, out of the way of Sir Randolph and his assistant.

Harry didn't fight the surgeon, either, gratefully sinking against the pillows. Clearly he'd marshaled all his limited strength for that single effort, and now he was markedly pale, his face taut with exhaustion. He listened, but barely replied as Sheffield congratulated him on his progress before he left the room, and as Sir Randolph and Dr. Leslie did the same. Gus hung back, waiting for the time they were all gone and she could be alone with Harry.

Finally only Tewkes remained, but not for long. "Should I draw the curtains, my lord?"

"Leave them as they are," Harry said wearily, "and leave us as well. I wish to speak with Gus alone."

She drew the familiar armchair close to the bed, leaning forward so their faces were level.

"I shouldn't stay long, Harry," she said. "You need to rest, and don't say you don't."

He sighed, and smiled. "I won't, because I do," he admitted. "Ahh, Gus, that did not go as I'd planned. Not at all."

She'd known he was tired, but still she'd expected to see more of triumph in his eyes, rather than the unmistakable despair that she found there now.

"I do not know what you were planning, Harry, to be so disappointed," she said softly. "What I saw you do was something close to a miracle. You were determined, and extraordinarily brave."

"That was hardly a miracle," he said with a disparaging sniff. "A miracle would have had me hop from the bed and stride about the room."

"And I say it was a miracle," she insisted. "Harry, I'm sure Sir Randolph told you the same as he told me, that there was a distinct possibility more of your leg was damaged, beyond the bones alone, and that you would never walk unassisted again. You proved that wasn't the case."

"Sir Randolph always exaggerates," he said. "That's how he can command more sizable fees."

"He wasn't exaggerating," she said bluntly. "I saw your leg when they cut away your riding boot, and I watched Dr. Leslie set it. If Sir Randolph had been here then, I believe he would have taken your leg off and been done with it, and we wouldn't be quarreling about this now."

He frowned, his expression so dark that she wasn't sure if he'd heard or not. "This isn't quarreling."

She sighed, not wanting to upset him. "Very well, then," she said. "We're not quarreling."

"Not at all," he said, and she was startled by the depth of sadness in those words. "I thought today would be easier. I thought that once I had the smaller splint, my leg would feel more like it used to. And it doesn't. Not at all."

"But this is only the first day, Harry," she said gently, once again taking his hand. "You were grievously hurt, and healing takes time. It will not be easy, no, but if you are as determined as you were today, then you will succeed."

He raised her hand to his lips and lightly kissed the back of it, as if in gratitude. "My cousin desires me to return to London with him."

"But Sir Randolph forbids it," she said quickly. "I heard him say so."

"Sheffield has reluctantly agreed to abide by Sir Randolph's orders, yes," Harry said. "But his reasons for wishing me to leave here had more to do with you than with the woeful state of my leg."

Gus's heart sank. "I'd guessed as much from his manner. He does not care for me, does he? He finds me lacking."

"Quite the contrary," he said. "He cares for you a great deal. He reminded me of your station, that you are an unmarried lady with an immaculate reputation. He said that for your sake, it's not right for me to remain here as your guest at Wetherby Abbey."

"It's not," Gus agreed wistfully. "Especially not with us alone together except for the servants. If you'd been able to travel, you would have been gone from here ages ago."

Harry sighed his impatience. "Don't be willfully blind," he said gruffly. "You've given me every reason in the world to stay."

She tried to pull her hand from him, but he held it fast.

"Listen to me, Gus," he said, his gaze so intense that she couldn't look away. "All my life, everything has been exactly as I've wanted. For better or worse, it's part of who I am, what I was raised to be. I've never been denied or refused in any significant way. Until now, and this infernal leg. Now nothing is right, and it has been . . . humbling. Nothing is how I wish it to be. Except for you, Gus. Except for you."

"Please, Harry," she whispered, her heart beating wildly. "You shouldn't be saying such things to me. *Please*."

"I know I shouldn't," he said, his voice low and harsh with urgency. "I won't dishonor you, Gus, and I won't disgrace you. I've sworn that to Sheffield, and more important, I owe that to you. Besides, in my present state, I'm not exactly worthy of your regard in return."

"That's not true," she protested. She left her chair to sit on the edge of the bed, needing to be closer to him. "I've never once thought that, let alone spoken it to you."

"You don't have to," he said. "That little demonstration of my infirmity earlier was sufficient to put an end to even my misguided optimism."

"You're wrong," she said firmly. "What you see as weakness, I saw only as strength and courage."

He shifted restlessly against the pillow. "Now you are the one who is exaggerating, Gus."

"No, I am not," she insisted. "Exaggeration is not in my nature, Harry. I should have thought by now you would see that I am hopelessly practical. Next week you will leave this bed, and you'll dress like a civilized gentleman, exactly as you said. That alone will make you feel better. The more you work your leg, the stronger it will become, and the stronger *you* will become. I won't pretend your recovery will be easy, for it won't, but I shall be there with you for encouragement, if you wish it."

"Of course I wish it," he said, apparently indignant that she'd even suggest otherwise. "You were there from the beginning. I expect you to see it through to the end."

She drew back. "Goodness, Harry. Is that more of you being noble and expecting to have whatever you want?"

He sighed, chagrined. "I suppose it is," he said. "But I cannot imagine this recovery without you at my side. May I have the honor of your presence, Miss Augusta, as I swear and stagger my way through these next weeks?"

"Yes, my lord," she said succinctly. "I do not quit in the middle of a task, and I don't believe you do, either."

"Ever the optimist." He smiled wearily. "All of which is exactly why you have become so important to me. Dear Gus! What's to be done with us, eh? Where are we bound?"

She looked down at her hand clasped in his, wanting to choose her words with care without the distraction of his blue eyes watching her. She had never been half of an "us," especially not one as complicated as this, and she'd never been faced with the choice that now stood unavoidably before her.

She could consider her reputation and her virtue, and put an end to this nebulous "us" before the rest of the world began whispering about it, too. Harry might not be able to leave with his cousin, but she could certainly ask His Grace for a place for herself in his carriage to London. There she could take refuge in her aunt's house with her father's protection until Harry was sufficiently recovered to leave Wetherby Abbey. Then he could return to his old life, and she to hers, and that would be a tidy end to that.

Or she could remain here with Harry.

She could stay, and be completely reckless and irresponsible for the first, and perhaps the only, time in her life. She could relish this time with Harry, likely the only man she'd ever know who possessed this devastating degree of charm, handsomeness, and pure manly manliness. She knew that wasn't a very elegant turn of phrase, but that was how she thought of it in her head: Harry's manly manliness, and how it could reduce her to blithering, incoherent bliss. It was part of the reason that her feelings of friendship had already slipped halfway to being in love with him. She'd only to look up at him now to be reminded of it, and the power of his kisses and whatever other wonderful wickedness might come from them.

Most of all, staying here with Harry was a two-headed gamble. First, she'd gamble on herself, that as the plain second daughter of a viscount, no one in London would bother to gossip about her. And second, she'd gamble on Harry himself: that all his talk of what she meant to him might actually promise something lasting between them, that being halfway in love could blossom into a glorious entirety.

She understood now why her eyes had filled when he'd been able to bend his knee. It meant he was on his way to being healed, on his way to not needing her, on his way to leaving forever.

It was all part of the gamble. A gamble, yes, but one that in the end she was willing to take.

"I'm no sibyl, Harry, able to see into the future," she said slowly, "and I cannot begin to guess what will happen with us. But I will venture that perhaps we are worrying overmuch about what is proper and what is not, what is friendship, or—or a different regard."

"'A different regard,'" he repeated ruefully. "I suppose that is the genteel way of saying I want nothing more than to pull you down beside me and kiss you senseless."

She blushed, imagining him doing exactly that. "Perhaps instead we should concentrate on making your leg—your *infernal* leg—better, and simply accept each day as it comes to us, and let it lead us where it may."

His dark brows came together. "Meaning exactly what?"

"Meaning that I will stay here with you, and you with me," she said, "and that whatever else happens between us will simply . . . happen."

He smiled with obvious relief, raising her hand to kiss it again.

"How did you come to be so wise, tucked away here in the backwaters of Norfolk?" he teased. "No wonder I've become so deuced fond of you."

She smiled, willing to tease him back. "It's because I've always lived in Norfolk, not in spite of it. If I had been reared in London, I'd be as great a fool as everyone else there."

"Meaning me, of course." He chuckled, reaching up to thread his fingers into her hair. "Then if you are wise, and I am not, would you explain to me why after all my resolutions to be entirely honorable where you are concerned, I still can think of little beyond kissing you."

"Even a simpleton can answer that," she said, letting him draw her down. "Because kissing can be honorable, and—and I wish to kiss you, too."

"Most excellent wisdom," he murmured, feathering small kisses along her jaw. "You know, I do believe kissing will help my leg improve as well."

She chuckled softly, with pleasure and anticipation.

"Then I suppose you must kiss me as often as you please," she whispered. "Because I intend to see you dance under the stars, exactly as you promised."

Sheffield left the next morning, alone, and although Harry was sorry to see him go, he was also pleased to once again have Gus to himself. But while he'd hoped that, now his recovery had fairly begun, it would progress with ease, he swiftly learned how wrong that hope was, even with Gus at his side.

The next weeks were every bit the challenge that everyone had predicted, and more, too, since those doing the predicting weren't the ones suffering through it. Each day seemed to bring both a small accomplishment, yet with it a fresh reminder of how far he'd still to go.

He'd eagerly anticipated being finally freed from his bed and his nightshirt, to be permitted to dress like a regular gentleman and sit in a chair. But even with Tewkes and a sturdy footman to help him, the once-simple process of dressing had become painfully complicated.

Tewkes had already thoughtfully enlarged the cuff in a pair of his breeches to allow for his splint, but the opening still wasn't large enough. The seam had had to be entirely split, with the two halves left trailing open in a disreputable fashion. Even so, wrestling the breeches up over the ungainly splint had been so lengthy an exercise that he'd been nearly exhausted by the time it was done.

There had been even more surprises from the rest of his clothes. Harry had always prided himself on having his clothes perfectly tailored to his body. His coats and jackets were cut to display his broad shoulders and chest and fit precisely around his well-muscled arms, and he liked to wear his breeches so shamelessly close that he often caught even the haughtiest of ladies stealing a look, to his considerable amusement.

But now his very clothes seemed determined to betray him. He hadn't realized how much flesh and muscle he'd lost while he'd been ill, not until Tewkes had fastened the long row of buttons up the front of his favorite embroidered waistcoat. The silk no longer fit snugly across his chest the way it once had. Instead it sagged forward, pulling away from his diminished body by the weight of the silk embroidery. The coat was even worse. Not only did it hang loosely from his shoulders, but because he'd lost so much of the muscles in his arms from inactivity, the sleeves were too long, falling over his hands. It all made him feel like a frail old man in borrowed clothes.

"No matter, my lord, no matter," Tewkes had said loyally, trying to pull and smooth the too-big clothes into place. "I'll send for Mr. Venable to come directly. A tuck here, a stitch there, and he'll have you looking handsome as ever, my lord."

Before the week was over, the tailor had come down from London and altered his clothes to fit. It had been gratifying, if predictable, that Mr. Venable had also made a fuss about how the adjustments were not permanent. They could be reversed as soon as "his lordship is back to his old self."

His old self: Not an hour passed that Harry wondered if such a creature had even existed. At least the tailor's pinning and stitching had been familiar, fragments of his former life. He could not say the same about the man who brought his newly ordered crutches. While Sir Randolph had taken Harry's measurements, the crutch maker had brought the finished products to Wetherby Hall himself, not only to trim them if necessary, but to instruct Harry in their use.

Harry had scoffed at such instruction. How hard could it be to master a pair of wooden sticks? Yet he'd learned soon enough that the answer was very hard, very hard indeed. The crutches made him feel like a baby learning to walk all over again, and his clumsy, tripod self lurched unsteadily along the abbey's galleries and halls with a rhythmic thump that he came to loathe. In the beginning, he'd shamefully required a pair of footmen to catch him if he lost his balance and collapsed like an ill-built house of cards, but with practice he became more adept, albeit no more graceful.

He was encouraged to straighten his still-splinted leg, and to put as much weight as he could bear upon it, which to his chagrin was pitifully little. Sir Randolph assured him that no matter what he accomplished, any exercise could only help the healing. With no other course to follow, Harry persevered with the crutches each day as long as he could, pushing himself until his good leg shook and his shoulders ached, and suffered through the torturous stretching that the recovering leg required. But each day, too, he could last a little longer, and go a little farther, as his strength gradually began to return.

He swallowed his pride and let himself be helped down the stairs, so that he could make his way through the gardens and down the long drive and back. As clumsy as the crutches were, they gave him independence, and though he remained a cripple, at least he was no longer a rebarbative invalid.

It was, he thought cynically, simply one more example of degrees and rank.

He had never worked so hard at anything as he had learning to maneuver on the crutches, but then he'd never had such a grand goal before him, either. What he'd tell anyone who asked was that he wished to dance once again beneath the stars at Vauxhall Gardens. This had been his first goal, and because it made others smile, he fell into offering it so often that it became pat, an amusing and convenient response to a difficult question.

But he kept his real goal to himself, buried deep within somewhere near to his heart, and he shared this goal with no one—not even the one person for whom it was intended.

He wanted to be worthy of Gus.

For her, he wanted to be whole, without flaw, for that was what she deserved. The fact that she accepted him as he was, as damaged goods, was unbearable to him. He wanted to be able to take her hand and proudly lead her into a room. He wanted to help her into his carriage, and give her lovely bottom a surreptitious pat as he did. He wanted to chase after her laughing through the garden, and climb the steps to the little temple beyond the roses and hide away with her there until they missed dinner, and supper, too, if they pleased. He wanted to sweep her into his arms and carry her to his bed, and make passionate, perfect love to her, until she cried out his name with joy and promised to love him forever.

That was what he wanted.

What he did not want was to be her burden, her inconvenience, the halting, shambling man whose needs must always be considered. When they went out to the opera or the playhouse, he wanted people to marvel at her, as she deserved, and not crane their necks for a glimpse of the unfortunate crippled Earl of Hargreave. He wanted the world to know that he loved her for who she was and not because she was the only one who'd have him.

And he did love Gus. He wasn't exactly sure when that had happened, but it had, and he now understood what his father had always told him about love changing everything. It did. He felt a little jolt in his chest each time he looked at her. The time he spent in her company flew by, and the hours they were apart dragged like an anchor in sand. The oddest part was how he felt her to be another part of himself that he'd never realized was missing, a charming addition of wry humor and practicality and kindness. Just as the poets claimed, she made him feel complete.

What made him feel like an utter fool, of course, was that he'd spent so much time and effort settling on the perfect bride, and had decided upon Julia, who would have been a complete disaster of a wife. Meanwhile, he hadn't considered Gus at all—hell, he hadn't even realized she existed—and yet here he was, ridiculously in love with her and determined to claim her as his wife.

It was difficult, keeping such a goal to himself. They were together every day, and well into every night, too. She dined with him, and read to him, and walked beside him as he lumbered along on his crutches. She helped him each morning with the exercises to stretch his leg and keep the muscles limber while the bones healed. For this, she'd replaced Tewkes, who'd been too afraid of hurting him. Gus wasn't, and seemed to sense exactly how far she could push him for his own good, ignoring his oaths in the process.

She laughed with him, but never at him, not even the time when Patch had tangled around his good foot and nearly sent him crashing into the carp pond. She wrapped the heads of his crutches with lambs' wool to cushion them, and knitted a special giant sock of scarlet wool to fit over his foot and splint. It was the first thing that anyone had made specifically for him as a gift, and as peculiar as it was, he cherished it because it had come from her.

But the most difficult part of each day came at the end of it, after they'd dined together, when they sat together to listen to the music played just for them, exactly as it was now.

Nine weeks had passed since he'd broken his leg, nine weeks that he'd been here at Wetherby. He had improved; even he couldn't deny it, and Venable had been summoned twice to let out his clothes, exactly as he'd predicted. While Peterson still cautiously kept a splint in place on his leg, it was now more of a light brace for support than to hold the broken bones together. Each day he managed to put a bit more weight on it through his hobbling gait, but at least now he could wear a stocking and shoe on the foot like a gentleman. He'd also grown strong enough to rely on a single crutch, which did feel like progress.

Summer was in full flower, with the warmth of the long,

bright days lingering past sunset. With the windows in his corner bedchamber thrown open, the evening air was filled with things that never entered a London night: the sounds of crickets and nightingales, the luminous silvery light of a full moon, the honey-sweet fragrance of the woodbine. In sympathy, the Signor Vilotti chose pieces by Scarlatti, Vivaldi, and Corelli that combined both the sweetness and the sensual indolence of summer, music that sang seductively through the summer night.

Harry sat on the cushioned settee with Gus curled beside him. Because of the evening's warmth, he had left off his coat and his neckcloth, and carelessly rolled back the sleeves of his shirt over his forearms. Gus, too, had pared down her dress on account of the heat, wearing her light linen gown without hoops or a kerchief around the neck, and no cap to hide her hair. Her head rested against his chest, his arm around her waist.

For him, it was absolute torture.

She was soft and warm against him, her body fitting neatly against his. He'd only to glance down a fraction for the most splendid view of her breasts, raised up enticingly by her stays. Lovely breasts, he thought with despair, high and plump, the skin luminous and dusted lightly with freckles, and practically begging for his caress. A tiny trickle of sweat had gathered between them, there at the edge of her shift, and as he watched it slide slowly downward, over one curve and into the shadows.

Choking back a groan, he forced himself to look away, but only as far as her skirts. Without hoops, the soft linen was crumpled and limp, draping and accentuating the shape of her hips and legs beneath it. She'd kicked off her shoes and curled her feet on the settee, not bothering to cover them with her skirts. In pink lisle stockings, her feet were delicate, her ankles neat, and he couldn't help but imagine the rest, her garters and the white thighs above them, and finally the heaven that lay between them.

He struggled to rein in his thoughts, trying to focus on the music instead of Gus. He wasn't exactly a hard-bitten rake, but he wasn't a saint, either, and since he'd left school and come to town he'd kept a succession of mistresses, the way most gentlemen did. When he'd thought he was going to propose to Julia, he had ended things with the last one, sending her off happy with a generous settlement and a few pieces of jewelry.

But that had been over three months ago. Broken leg or not, three months was a painfully long time for him to be without a woman. The fact that the nearest one was also the one he desired more than all the others combined only made his suffering more acute. All Gus would have to do was look down at the front of his breeches.

He was sweating with the effort of not embarrassing himself, and still it wasn't enough. He had to think of something other than Gus, and from the dustiest corner of his brain he abruptly seized onto the Latin declensions he'd memorized—mostly—in school.

First declension singular: aqua, aquae, aquae, aquam, aqua.

That was so dry and dull that it was actually working. He took a deep breath and marched his thoughts briskly to the plurals.

First declension plural: aquae, aquarum, aquis, aquas, aquis.

Second declension singular: servus, servi, servo—

Unaware of his Latin fortifications, Gus burrowed more closely against his chest with a contented small sigh. Her breasts were pressing against his side, the womanly scent of her body mingling with the fragrance of the honeysuckle, and all of it was enough to make him weep. Then as she settled, her hand brushed innocently across his thigh, her fingers only inches away from his doom.

He swore, jerking against the back of the settee. Startled, she sat upright, and the musicians stopped abruptly, too.

"Oh, Harry, I've hurt you, haven't I?" she said, distress all over her face. "I shouldn't have crowded you on the settee like that, I know, and now I've bumped your leg, and—"

"No, no, it's fine," he said quickly, recovering. "None of it's your fault, sweet. I'm, ah, I'm tired, that is all. Signore Vilotti, I thank you, but that will be all for this evening."

The musicians gathered their instruments to leave, and as Harry stood, Gus bent down to retrieve her shoes from beneath the settee, presenting Harry with one final, wickedly tempting sight of her upturned bottom.

"I hope you sleep well, Harry," she said with concern, resting her hand lightly on his arm as the musicians left. "I pray I didn't make you walk too far today. I wouldn't want to—"

"Don't worry," he said softly, and kissed her, partly to reassure her, but mostly because he very much wanted to. He'd become remarkably skilled at kissing her while he balanced against his crutch. He kissed her hungrily, wanting her to know how much he desired her and how much he cared for her. He hadn't told her yet that he loved her—that had to wait until he could ask her to marry him—but he hoped that, after kisses like this one, it wouldn't come as a great surprise. He took his time, too, relishing the response of her velvety warm mouth.

"Goodness, Harry," she murmured as at last they separated. Her eyes were heavy-lidded and her lips were wet and swollen, and when she smiled she looked almost dazed with pleasure. "That was rather—rather extraordinary."

"You inspire me, sweet," he said, the simple truth.

He brushed his thumb over her lower lip and she drew it into her mouth with a playful little nip that nearly finished him, then and there.

"You do that and more for me, Harry," she said, her voice husky with longing. He recognized that longing even if she didn't, and if he didn't send her on her way now, it would be too late for them both.

He yawned dramatically, striving to stick to his story of exhaustion. "Good night, Gus."

She smiled with obvious regret, and kissed him quickly once again. "Good night, Harry."

He hated watching her leave, her shoes in her hand as she blew him a last kiss from the doorway. Every night it was harder to part from her, and he wasn't sure how much longer he—or she—would be able to keep his noble, confounding promise to respect her virtue.

He swore softly from frustration as Tewkes helped him undress for bed. Before he doused the candle for the night, he opened the drawer in the table beside the bed and pulled out the curved box with his mother's ring. He tipped it this way and that, making the diamonds dance in the candle's light, and he imagined the ring on Gus's finger as the memory of their kiss still lingered.

Soon, he thought. Soon. Because Gus believed in him, he would dance under the stars at Vauxhall Gardens, exactly as he'd vowed. And when he did, he'd make sure she danced with him, as his wife, his countess, his love.

CHAPTER
9

Without question this was the most perfect and most perfectly blissful summer of Gus's life, and her only regret was knowing that it could not last. Later, when she thought back over those magical weeks with Harry at the abbey, she could see exactly when everything had changed, and the end had begun.

It was the day the chamber horse was delivered.

For the first time in a fortnight, the weather had kept her and Harry inside the house. After thunderstorms at dawn, the air had remained heavy and still, with dark clouds low in the sky and thunder continuing to rumble ominously close. Instead of walking in the garden as they usually did in the morning, they'd retreated to the back drawing room. Gus was sitting at her desk reviewing household accounts, while Harry read in an armchair near the window, his dogs sprawled sleeping at his feet. The dogs were the first to hear the wagon in the drive, rising drowsily to go to the window to investigate. Gus followed, equally curious.

"What are you expecting today, Harry?" she asked. By now she'd grown accustomed to Harry's various orders arriving from London, whether books, wine, delicacies, clothes, or musicians, and because the wagon that was drawing up in the backyard wasn't one of the usual Norwich purveyors, she guessed this must be another. "Whatever it is, it's large and mysterious."

"Mysterious?" he asked, putting aside his book. "What makes it mysterious? Wizard's markings and flying monkeys?"

"Not mysterious like that, Harry," she said. "But it is a sizable crate, much larger than your usual books and oranges. Ah, there's Mr. Royce, ready to investigate. He's suspicious, Harry. He's scowling, and whatever it is, he's not letting the men unload it. Perhaps it is your flying monkeys after all."

When Royce appeared in the drawing room, his explanation was equally exotic.

"The men say it's a chamber horse, miss," he said with undisguised skepticism. "They wish to bring it into the house."

"A chamber horse?" Gus repeated dubiously, again looking through the window down to the crate. "That sounds like something my father might have ordered, some new accoutrements for the stables. I should think it belongs there, rather than in the house."

"No, it does belong in the house, Royce," Harry said, coming to stand beside her at the window. "It's for me. The last time Peterson was here, he mentioned he would be sending a chamber horse for my use, but I'd forgotten entirely. I suppose this must be it."

"But what exactly is it, Harry?" Gus asked, bemused. She imagined an oversized hobbyhorse, with Harry sitting astride. "Some manner of nursery plaything?"

"Not at all," he said. "It's a kind of chair for exercise, that's supposed to mimic the motion of riding a horse. I've heard of them, but never seen one myself."

"Truly?" Gus asked, her eyes widening. "Have the men bring it inside, Royce. I suppose it should be taken to his lordship's room, for his convenience."

With considerable effort, the crate was wrestled up

the stairs and the chamber horse installed in one corner of Harry's increasingly crowded bedchamber. To Gus's disappointment, it didn't resemble a real horse at all, but a curious contraption of mahogany and leather from a cabinetmaker's shop.

The top part of the horse looked like an oversized chair that could have belonged in any dining room, with an elegantly carved back and arms. The seat of the chair, however, was attached not to the back and arms, but to a tall leather box, pleated like bellows, that was raised up nearly three feet from the floor by a sturdy platform. The platform had a step that pulled out like a drawer.

Gus studied the horse, unconvinced. "It's a foolish-looking thing, Harry," she said finally. "How is that supposed to be of use to you?"

"Peterson says I'm not to think of it as a replacement for riding," he said, also sounding unconvinced, "but as a way to strengthen my leg without the stress of a real horse beneath me."

He pressed his palm on the leather seat and pushed down. "You see, there are metal springs inside. I'm supposed to sit here, and push myself up and down. He says that once I can do that for a quarter of an hour at a time, putting more of my weight on my leg, then I'll be ready to try standing."

"I suppose if Sir Randolph says it will be of benefit to you, then it must be," Gus said, trying to visualize Harry performing such an exercise.

Harry nodded and sighed glumly. "All I can think of is some stout old codger jostling up and down and convincing himself he's taking exercise."

"You're neither old nor stout," she said firmly, "and there's definitely nothing codger-like about you. If the chamber horse will make your leg stronger, then it's worth trying."

"You are right and wise, as always." He sighed again

and resolutely took off his coat. Handing Gus his crutch, he hopped onto the horse's step. "Off to the races."

Gingerly he lowered himself onto the horse's leather seat. With a great *woosh,* the springs sank down, and Harry did, too. He pressed his feet on the step and his hands on the armrests, and immediately sprang up again with another *woosh.* He did it again, faster this time. He looked both startled and delighted, like a small boy who'd discovered some wicked new trick.

Gus laughed, unable to help herself, and he laughed with her.

"Is it that much fun?" she asked.

"It is," he declared. "You must try it."

She wrinkled her nose and shook her head. It was one thing to watch Harry ride the chamber horse, but quite another to picture herself bouncing up and down with her skirts flying around her legs.

"Come along," he said. "Here, sit with me. It's quite big enough for both of us."

"I don't know, Harry," she demurred. "Sir Randolph didn't advise me to use it."

"He's not here to see you do it, either," he said. "There are no witnesses of any sort. Come along, Gus. You're braver than that. Don't be a spoilsport."

She narrowed her eyes. He knew exactly how to bait her, and it worked, too.

"Very well, then," she said, bunching her skirts to one side. "And don't you ever again call me a spoilsport, my lord."

She climbed up onto the little step, and then onto the horse, squeezing beside him on the wide leather seat. Harry, however, had other plans. He took her by the waist and pulled her directly onto his lap, swinging her legs sideways over one arm of the horse. Unbalanced, she gasped, and grabbed his shoulders to catch herself.

"There," he said, with a satisfied grin. "That's much better. Are you ready?"

He didn't wait for her to answer but pulled down with his arms, then up with his legs. The springs did the rest, bouncing them both upward. Gus squealed with surprise, then laughed, and hung on to Harry to keep from flying off the horse. Over and over he bounced them up and down, both of them laughing uproariously with sheer giddy foolishness. The motion was rather like riding a horse, if the horse was badly trained, and the saddle was like Harry's lap.

Which, Gus was rapidly realizing, it wasn't. Not at all. The up-and-down motions of the horse's springs were making her bottom slide back and forth over the hard muscles of his thighs in a way that was becoming increasingly exciting. It was the same as when he kissed her, a heat and a tightness coiling low in her belly and between her legs that was exceedingly pleasant, and that she'd no wish to stop, because Harry himself was the reason.

She was, in short, feeling . . . *amorous*. Her heart was beating faster and her hair was falling down and her breath quickening, and the more she laughed and bounced and wriggled across the Harry's lap, the more intense the feelings became. She suspected Harry was feeling the same, for his face was flushed and his eyes had the look that she'd come to recognize as *that* look, and when abruptly he stopped the horse, she reached up to kiss him just as he bent toward her.

She loved when he kissed her like this, hard and demanding with his tongue deep in her mouth, and she dug her fingers into his shoulders, holding tight and taking in more of his raw energy. With her eyes closed, she gave herself over to the sensations kissing him always aroused, now coupled with the feelings that had come from being bounced against his leg.

He tipped her back into the crook of his arm, and she

went gladly, feeling the springs quivering lightly beneath them. She was so lost in kissing him that she didn't notice he was pulling out the pins that closed the bodice of her gown, pushing the sides apart. Deftly he scooped her breasts above the edge of her stays and pushed down the neck of her shift to bare them entirely.

He bent his head to suckle her nipples, one at a time, licking and nipping and teasing them to stiff, rosy points. She sighed restlessly, arching her back, and threaded her fingers through the black silk of his hair. It was all so very good, making her almost dizzy with longing for something that she couldn't define, and when he shoved aside her skirts to run his hand along her leg, she only pointed her toe, eager for more.

His hand moved higher, past the top of her stocking, past her garter, over the heated skin of her thigh and higher still, to the place where she ached most for him. At last he touched her there, stroking her lightly to coax her to open for him, and with shameless ease she parted her legs and moaned into his mouth. He caressed her with winning little circles full of shimmering sensations, sensations that made her feel ripe and wet and alive. When his teasing finger slipped inside her passage, she cried out and shuddered with the pleasure of it, arching her hips up for more.

"You're so hot, Gus," he whispered raggedly, his own breath coming in great gulps. "You're so damned hot and wet and ready, and the devil take me now, I want you even more."

He pulled his hand away and she whimpered in protest, already missing his touch. He seized her hand and pushed it down to the front of his breeches, forcing her to feel the thick length of his cock. She had glimpsed men's members before, when they'd pulled them out to piss against a wall or tree, and from Julia she had learned how those same cocks wanted nothing more than to serve women.

But this was Harry, and Harry's cock, and even as she was shocked by the size and hardness of it, she couldn't help but be fascinated, too, her fingers closing around it through the linen of his pants. He groaned, bucking against her hand in much the same way she'd done for him.

"That's because of you, Gus," he growled. His face was fixed in a contorted grimace, his eyes dark. "That's what you do to me."

In some foggy corner of her head, she knew exactly what he wanted, and if she agreed, she would be ruined. Her maidenhead would be gone and her virtuous reputation with it. Worse, he could leave her with a bastard child. The whole world would know her shame, her weakness, and no other man would ever want her.

But no other man was like Harry, and no other man ever could be. If he wanted her, then she wanted him, too, and the throbbing need between her legs made her forget everything else.

"I want you, too, Harry," she whispered fervently, and she felt his cock press harder as if rejoicing. "Every moment since I met you has been leading to this, and I want you too much to wait any longer."

"The bed," he said, his urgency too great for more words. "Damnation, where's my crutch?"

"Lean on me instead," she said, sliding from his lap. "It's only a few feet."

He reached for her and pulled her back, his kiss so raw and demanding that she felt light-headed with desire. He slipped his arm around her shoulder and hopped forward, a lurching progress where he was half leaning against her, and half dragging her the short distance across the room. She wasn't sure if one of them pulled the other onto the bed, or if they simply fell together, and it didn't matter.

What did was that she was lying on her back on the

dragon-patterned yellow silk, and Harry was kissing her again, kissing her hard, even as he was bunching her skirts around her waist.

"You're so beautiful, Gus," he said hoarsely. "So beautiful, and I've never wanted any woman more."

"Oh, Harry," she whispered, staring up into his blue eyes. No man had ever called her beautiful, and to hear it from a man as beautiful as Harry himself made her smile wobble with wonder. "I think I've always wanted you."

"And now you have me," he said, and kissed her again, thrusting his tongue into her mouth and being piratical and dark and thoroughly Harry about doing it. She'd a fleeting moment of misgiving as she thought of how she must look, and then he was parting her, stroking her again, making her think of nothing beyond how much she wanted him.

He muttered a random oath, misplaced enough that she opened her eyes again.

"It's my infernal leg," he muttered, his face tense with frustration, "and the infernal brace that's tangled in your petticoats."

"Then tear them," she said, wishing all problems were so readily solved. "I don't care. It's you I want, Harry, not my infernal petticoats."

She heard the rip of cloth, and she grinned, pulling him back down to her. She was feeling reckless and abandoned, sufficiently reckless and abandoned that she reached for the buttons on the fall of his breeches.

He grunted as her fingers blindly found him, circling velvety, hot male flesh instead of cloth. Goodness, he was large, she thought, as he sprang forward against her hand.

"Damnation, Gus, don't," he said, sucking in his breath. "I'm too primed already."

She didn't understand, but she didn't have to, either, not when he kissed her again. He slipped two fingers inside her, easing and widening her and sleeking inside her at the same time. Impatiently she raised her hips to welcome him farther, craving more, and suddenly it wasn't his fingers at her opening, but his cock, pressing into her. She started and twisted as he pushed harder, surprised by the fullness and the little sting that she realized must have been her maidenhead.

He paused, panting, and gazed down at her. "I'm sorry, sweetheart," he said gruffly. "Trust me that it will be better."

She nodded, her own breathing ragged, and reached up to cradle his handsome face in her hands. She'd followed him this far. Why would she stop trusting him now?

But when he slowly began to move inside of her, she gasped and her eyes widened, startled by his cock stroking her from deep within while his linen shirt grazed her bare nipples. With her hands on his shoulders, she tentatively began to move with him, trying to answer his rhythm. She raised her legs to push against him, and he groaned, which she'd already learned was a good sign. She lifted her legs higher, wrapping them around his hips, and groaned herself when his cock slipped even deeper into her.

"That's it, Gus," he said, grinding against her. "You have all I can give."

Ordinarily that would have made her smile with joy, but she was beyond smiling now. The heat that he'd been building within her was like a wildfire now, and each time he withdrew and plunged back in only made her burn hotter still. She slid her hands beneath his shirt to find his bare back, her nails digging deep into his muscles as she rocked with him.

Everything was building now, higher and higher until with a suddenness that stunned her, she soared free, her body releasing and convulsing around him. With a long groan, he came, too, pounding into her again and again before, exhausted, he dropped on the bed beside her.

She felt his cock slide from her passage, with a little

gush of their mingled spendings, and when he reached for her, pulling her close, she smiled and curled into him. Only now did she realize how, in their haste, they hadn't even kicked off their shoes, and with misguided guilt she thought of how Father would be furious if he ever saw shoes on the best bedchamber counterpane.

Foolish, foolish, she thought, drowsy and sated and safe. Oh, she'd never felt as safe as she did now with his arm around her. No, better than safe: She felt cherished. He'd promised her he'd make this better, but she'd never expected, never imagined, never dreamed it would be like this.

She felt as if this coupling had somehow bound their souls together as well, as if all the kissing and teasing and laughing that had served to draw them closer this summer had only been a prelude to the intimacy of this moment. She was his now, and he was hers. It was as simple, and as complicated, as that.

He brushed her hair aside to kiss her nape. "My own Gus," he murmured. "Are you all right?"

"Of course," she said, smiling that he'd show such concern. "I'm with you."

He grunted and pulled her closer. She thought of asking after his leg, but then decided not to. If they'd done anything to hurt it, she would have known by now, and it was better if she let him think she'd forgotten about it entirely. Which, really, she had.

She smiled, drifting a little closer to sleep.

"I'm sorry, sweetheart," he said softly, so softly she wasn't sure at first that she'd even heard it. But then he said it again, and she couldn't pretend she hadn't. "I'm sorry, sorry for all of this."

She had to answer, and she twisted around to face him. "Why should you be sorry for anything, Harry?"

He did look sorry, his blue eyes melancholy. "Because it wasn't supposed to be like this," he said. "I rucked up your petticoats and tumbled you like some common tavern wench, and I'll never—"

"Hush," she said gently, pressing her fingers across his lips to silence him. "That's nonsense, Harry. That *was* perfect, because it was with you. Why would you wish it any differently?"

"Because I love you, Gus," he said gruffly. "There, I've said it, and I hadn't meant to do that, either. I love you."

She stared at him, forgetting to breathe. She'd never doubted that she loved him, but to hear the same words from him now, here, after what they'd just done, was almost too much for her.

"I love you," he said again, more forcefully. "You needn't stare at me like I've grown another head, Gus. I love you, and I'd rather hoped that you—what the devil?"

"Miss Augusta?" That was Mr. Royce, knocking and addressing her from the other side of the bedchamber door. "Are you within, Miss Augusta?"

"She's occupied, Royce," Harry called. "Go away."

"You can't say that to him," Gus said, sitting up. "It must be important for him to come here. What is it, Mr. Royce?"

"I am sorry to disturb you, Miss Augusta," the butler said through the door, "but there is a footman waiting in the front hall, sent in advance of His Grace the Duke of Breconridge. His Grace should be arriving here shortly, and I thought you would wish to be advised."

"My father." Harry pushed himself upright, stunned. Here he'd been in the middle of the most important conversation of his life with the most important woman in it, only to have his father interrupt. It was the one sure thing for which his family could be counted upon—no matter how far away they might be, they would still always appear at the most inopportune moment possible.

"Your *father*!" Gus wailed. "Your father here *now*!"

She flew off the bed before Harry could stop her, frantically shaking and smoothing her skirts and tugging her shift and stays back over her bare breasts.

"He's not here yet," Harry said, hating to see her covering herself again so soon. He'd spent weeks speculating what her breasts were like, and the reality had so far exceeded his speculation that he could have happily enjoyed them the rest of the day. "It's only the running footman he's sent ahead. We still have a little more time."

"But His Grace will be here soon enough, and I must be downstairs to greet him," she said, her anxiety like a palpable, growing force in the room. "I want to make a better start with him than I did with His Grace your cousin."

"You were fine with my cousin." With a sigh of regret, he began putting his own clothes to rights, buttoning the fall on his breeches. He still had so much he wished to say to her, but there was no point in even trying when she was like this, and again he groaned over his father's exquisite timing. "Sheffield found you most charming."

"He couldn't have found me anything, Harry, because I scarcely said a word in his company," she said, trying to pin her gaping bodice closed with the few pins that remained. "I found him *daunting*. Oh, look at me! Do you have any notion where the pins went when you pulled them out?"

"I dropped them," he said honestly. "At the time, I'd other things to consider."

She was standing before him with an odd, self-conscious look on her face. "Forgive me, Harry, but I believe I must make use of your washstand. Turn around, if you please, and don't watch."

Dutifully he turned around. It seemed peculiar that after all they'd just shared—and what she'd freely let him see—she'd turn suddenly modest when it came to washing herself. But then, this would all be new to her, and he smiled to think that he'd been her first lover, and if he had anything to say about it, her only one, too.

"I don't want you to be daunted by my father," he said, raising his voice as he still sat on the bed with his back to her. "He wouldn't want that, either. He may be a duke, but he's really quite ordinary."

"He's not ordinary at all," she said with despair. "He's not even an ordinary duke. He's the Duke of Breconridge, and he has royal blood, and he's vastly wealthy and powerful *and* he's friends with His Majesty."

"You can say most of that about me as well, Gus," he said, "and you manage not to be daunted by me."

"You're different because you're you," she said with succinct, if not exactly comprehensible, logic. "Am I presentable now, Harry?"

He turned back around and felt that now-familiar little jounce when he saw her. She wasn't a beauty in the tedious, predictable way of regular features and a classical profile, but to him she was the most beautiful woman in the world. She stole his breath away; there was no other way to describe it. He loved her round face and her freckled nose, her wide, pale gray eyes and her pink mouth like a rosebud, because he loved her.

He especially loved how she looked at this moment, a little ruffled and rumpled, with her hair disarrayed and her skirts mussed, because he was responsible for it. But with her mouth still swollen from his kisses and her eyes with that heavy-lidded satiety of a well-pleasured woman, there was also no doubt what she'd been doing, and the way her skirts were creased mostly in the front, where he'd pushed them up and crushed them, was the final telltale sign.

His father would see it in an instant, too.

"You look lovely," he assured her, which was true. "Absolutely lovely. My father will be enchanted."

"Truly?" she asked, self-consciously smoothing her hair again.

"Truly," he said, touched by her insecurity about meeting his father. It was hard to believe that the same Gus who briskly oversaw a houseful of servants could be so intimidated at the prospect of his family. "I should warn you that if he's come racing all the way back from Naples, he's going to be much more concerned with my leg than with you, at least in the beginning."

"That's why you must be spruced up as well." She picked up his coat from the floor, critically brushing some invisible dust from the dark wool before she held it out for him to put his arms in the sleeves. "I want him to see that I've taken excellent care of you. You're his heir. You're important to him. Likely he already blames my family for you being hurt in the first place, and I want him to know that I've done my best to—to—oh, Harry, why am I being so *foolish*?"

Her face crumpled, and she bowed her head into her hands. At once he took her into his arms, the most natural of all things for him to do, and held her close. He liked holding her, comforting her like this. She'd done so much for him that it felt good to be able to do the same for her. He felt responsible for her, the way a man was supposed to.

"You're not foolish, Gus," he said. "Not at all."

She snuffled against his shoulder, doubtless leaving a few tears for his sharp-eyed father to spot. He fished in his pocket for his handkerchief and handed it to her.

"It's natural for you to feel a bit, ah, unsettled, under the circumstances," he continued, hoping he was sounding manly and consoling. This was new territory for him as well. In the past, his customary response to weeping young women was to depart as quickly as possible. But this was Gus. This was different. "But you're never foolish."

She lifted her head and blew her nose noisily into his handkerchief. "Nor am I a spoilsport."

"No," he agreed, though he'd forgotten all about that. Even the chamber horse seemed like eons ago. "I'm not sure I'd love you if you were."

At last she smiled through her tears, like the sun breaking through the clouds, or at least the sun if it had acquired a red nose. He couldn't help but smile back.

"I do love you, you know," he said, and with his fingers beneath her chin he lifted her head to kiss her, lightly, sweetly, because that seemed right, too.

But what wasn't right was having Royce again at the door, informing them that His Grace's carriage had been spotted on the upper road. There was no denying Father's imminent arrival after that, and as swiftly as they could, he and Gus made their way downstairs to the front hall, with Gus rushing briefly belowstairs to address the servants in regard to the house's latest guests.

Gus had suggested that Harry wait in the nearest drawing room where he could sit in a chair, but he'd insisted on being here in the hall. He hadn't seen Father for nearly a year, and despite the duke's inconvenient arrival, Harry was looking forward to the reunion. He wanted to see Father as soon as he arrived, and as a matter of pride Harry also wanted to greet him not as an invalid, but upright and on the mend, albeit with the support of the crutch.

But his main reason for being here now was to be at Gus's side, exactly where he belonged, and where she needed him to be.

She came bustling from the servants' hall just as Father's carriage drew up before the door. She stood beside Harry, so close that her skirts brushed against his legs. Addressing the servants had obviously helped her with her nervousness. She once again appeared the composed mistress of the house, and Harry didn't miss how she'd paused long enough to clip her silver chatelaine to her waist, the dangling keys a badge of her role in the household. He was inordinately proud of her, his own dear Gus, and he was determined to show her to best advantage to his father so he'd feel the same about her.

He saw how she purposefully raised her chin and swallowed, the little ripple of anxiety along her throat. He would have taken her hand in his to reassure her, but she'd already clasped her hands before her, another of her no-nonsense ways of bolstering her confidence. Instead he leaned over, whispering in her ear so no one else could hear.

"Remember that I love you," he said. "Whatever else may come, remember that."

She turned toward him quickly, her flash of a smile bright and endearing. "I love you, too, Harry."

She loves me: There it was, the first time she'd said it to him, and he couldn't help but grin in return. She loved him! He hadn't doubted it, not really, but to hear her speak the words aloud was like the most magical incantation, a spell that sealed his happiness.

And then suddenly, in the middle of his unabashedly lovesick reverie, appeared his father.

"Harry, let me look at you!" he exclaimed before he was even in the door. Father was tall and straight, an imposingly handsome gentleman even as he neared fifty, and the very picture of what a duke should be. Beneath his powdered wig, his face was brown from the voyage from Italy, and as always he was dressed elegantly in the French manner, in a burgundy-red coat, costly lace dripping from the cuffs of his shirt, and silver braid on his black beaver hat.

But to Harry, he was simply Father, and while Harry bowed as best he could with the crutch, Father embraced him heartily, and with an open affection that he hadn't shown Harry for years, not since he'd been a schoolboy.

That alone told Harry how worried Father had been for him, but the uneasy mixture of shock and relief in his eyes above that beaming smile told him the rest.

"So Peterson still has you splinted, yes?" he said, stepping back to stare down at Harry's leg. "But I see you can't put much weight on the leg yet. You require those sticks to support you. That surprises me."

"I'll be rid of it all soon enough, Father," Harry said confidently. "But both bones were broken, and Peterson is being cautious."

Father nodded, yet clapped his hand on Harry's shoulder as if he couldn't bear to be separated.

"I met with Peterson in London, before I came here," he said. "We'll speak later of what he told me. Have you any lingering aches or discomforts?"

"No, no, Father, I'm vastly improved," Harry said, striving to put the best face on his injury even as he worried uneasily about what Peterson had told the duke. "You should have seen me the week it happened."

"I'm rather glad we didn't, Harry," said his stepmother, Celia, gliding forward to kiss Harry's cheek. How had he missed seeing her, Harry wondered with chagrin. Like Father, she was impossible to overlook, in silk, furs, jewels, and an oversized plumed hat, a beauty still though she must be over forty, and a lady who'd brought Father nothing but joy when they'd wed four years ago. She, too, couldn't quite hide her concern as she smiled. "It would have broken my heart to see you in such an unfortunate state. But your poor father—he was in such a froth to return to you that he made everyone thoroughly miserable on our voyage."

Harry could well imagine that. Father did not like to be crossed, even by the wind and sea.

"But I am much better, Celia," he said. "Infinitely better, and all on account of the great kindness and skill of this lady."

He slipped his hand through Gus's arm. Just as she'd done with Sheffield, she had somehow inexplicably faded into the background, and he had to physically bring her forward.

"Father, Celia," he said, "I am honored to present to you Lady Augusta Wetherby. Lady Augusta, my father, the Duke of Breconridge, and my stepmother, the Duchess of Breconridge. I do not exaggerate when I tell you that I would not have survived without her care."

Gus curtseyed deeply, and with more grace than he expected given how terrified he knew her to be. As she bowed her head, he'd a glimpse of a long piece of loose hair trailing down her nape, escaped and unpinned, that made him smile fondly all over again.

"Miss Augusta," Father said, taking her hand to raise her up. "We've heard much of you and your good works on my son's behalf. I cannot thank you enough, and I shall always be in your debt for preserving him."

For the first time Gus smiled. "Thank you, Your Grace," she murmured. "His lordship was my father's guest, and I was honored to do it."

"I'd say Harry was the honored one, to have the good fortune to have landed in your safekeeping," Father said, smiling back at her. "I understand you were also responsible for plucking him from the leaves and muck."

"Not myself, I didn't, Your Grace," she said, nervousness making her literal. "His lordship is rather too large for that."

Father laughed, and she smiled again, encouraged, which encouraged Harry as well.

"But I did find his lordship after his fall, yes," she said, clearly feeling braver. "I do not know what Sir Randolph has told you, Your Grace, but your son was in a most grievous condition and in much pain, yet he bore his sufferings from that time until now with great courage and fortitude."

"Heavens, Harry," exclaimed Celia with amusement. "It would seem that you have not only a savior in Miss Augusta, but a champion as well."

Gus flushed. "Forgive me, Your Grace, I did not intend to draw attention to myself, but rather to praise his lordship's fortitude."

"Which you did most admirably, my dear," Father said, his smile indulgent and warm. "Now, having come so far, I would like to speak with my son in private."

"Of course, Your Grace," Gus said, flustered. "Forgive me for not offering that convenience to you sooner. I trust the front drawing room, here, off this hall, will be agreeable. Is there anything else you require? Tea, wine, chocolate, or barley water?"

"Would you please walk with me in your garden, Miss Augusta?" Celia asked. "I've been so long in that stuffy carriage that a stroll among flowers seems like the pleasantest diversion possible."

"Show Celia your mother's roses," Harry urged. "She'll enjoy them."

"I would indeed," Celia said, retying the silk bow of her hat. "Roses are my favorite flower of them all."

"Very well, Your Grace, I'll be delighted," Gus said quickly, curtseying again to the duke before she turned to lead Celia to the garden. "I hope you will both agree to be my father's guests in this house for as long as you wish. I have already had rooms prepared for you."

"You are too kind, Lady Augusta," Celia said, following Gus. "The duke and I will be honored to stay here as your guests."

"Well, now, Harry, that leaves us together," Father said as the two women left the hall. "What is the state of Wetherby's cellar? Does he have a brandy worth drinking?"

Harry smiled. "No need to throw yourself on Wetherby's mercy, Father. I've arranged regular deliveries from Berry Brothers while I've been here, and I can offer an excellent Madeira for us."

"Here I thought you were at death's very door," Father said wryly, "and yet you still had the presence to have your wine sent from London."

"I'm your son through and through, Father," Harry said. He sent one of the footmen off for the wine and led the way into the drawing room as two footmen held the double doors open. He tried not to feel self-conscious about the crutch, or be aware of how closely Father was watching him and how he moved. He could hardly chide Gus for being uneasy around his father if he himself was, too. What was the word she'd used? Daunted?

They sat in two chairs near an open window, with Harry making sure his good leg was extended and the crutches tucked behind the back of the chair. He was expecting news about his brothers and cousins, tales of the voyage from Italy, and a certain amount of raillery about having fallen from Wetherby's horse in the first place.

But Father had different plans.

"I understand from Sheffield that you nearly died, Harry," he said bluntly. "Would you agree with that estimation?"

Harry hesitated only a moment. "I would agree," he said. "But I didn't die."

"I'm glad of it," Father said, his voice softening. "Your brother would have made a wretched duke in your stead."

He glanced down at Harry's healing leg. "I'm glad you kept your limb, too. A gentleman should have two legs, as God intended."

"That was Miss Augusta's doing," Harry said. "I've little memory of the events, but Tewkes assures me she fought Peterson tooth and nail on my behalf. Rather, on behalf of my leg."

"Sheffield told me that, too," Father said, taking the

glass of brandy that the footman offered on a silver charger. "He'd only the highest praise for Lady Augusta."

"Did he?" Harry grinned, unable to help it. "And here she thought Sheffield didn't like her."

"Oh, he liked her very much," Father said. "And I agree with him that, even after a few moments in her company, I can see that she has far more merit than that silly sister of hers. If you'd wed Miss Wetherby, we would have accepted her into the family as your choice, but in my estimation, her inner qualities are no match for her beauty."

"No, Father," Harry said heartily—perhaps, he realized later, a bit too heartily. "I consider myself fortunately delivered from that match. There's no comparison between the two sisters."

"None at all, that I can see," Father said. He paused, again watching Harry closely. "Have you found Miss Augusta as agreeable in your bed?"

Harry gulped. "Father, I don't believe that the lady deserves—"

"No more, Harry, no more," Father said with obvious disgust. "Don't make it worse by lying to me. I saw it as soon as I entered this house. The way you two looked at each other made your entanglement so painfully obvious that I was ashamed for you. You know I've never interfered in your *petite amours,* but when you take advantage of an unattended and innocent lady—"

"It's not like that, Father, not at all," Harry said defensively.

Father stared at him over the Madeira, incredulous. "Then, pray, tell me, what is it like? Did you ravish the lady outright? Take her against the wall, or over a bench?"

"*No.*" Harry was appalled that his father would suggest such things of him—and worse, of Gus. He knew what his father's reputation had been before he'd remarried, knew that he'd been a regular patron of the most exclusive brothels in town, knew that he'd always kept a mistress. Objectively Harry knew all of this, because he was his father's son, and his own past was much the same. But hearing Father now speak of Gus in the same way he'd speak of some Covent Garden doxie was intolerable.

"Don't make Gus sound like one of your whores," he said, his voice clipped and his hands bunching into fists at his sides. "I love her, Father, and when my leg has healed, I intend to ask her to marry me."

"Perhaps you should have first informed your cock," Father said irritably. "It appears to be the best-functioning portion of your anatomy at present."

"Enough, Father," Harry said curtly. "I won't listen to you speak of Gus in this—"

"Oh, get down from your high horse, Harry," Father said. "At least you care sufficiently about the lady to defend her. How long has this been going on? A week? A month?"

"Not long," Harry said, hedging. How could he explain to Father that it had really only been a matter of hours? "Not that it is any of your affair."

"Long enough, then," Father said grimly. "And it *is* my affair, Harry. You will marry Lady Augusta, and as soon as it can be arranged. Today is Tuesday. Saturday should be time enough to procure a special license and make other arrangements, and to make sure her bumbling father is at last at her side to give her away."

"Saturday? This Saturday?"

"Exactly," Father said, drumming his fingers on the arm of the chair with impatience. "My concern is not entirely for Miss Augusta and her reputation, Harry. There may well be a third party to consider. You are my heir, and will be the next Duke of Breconridge. If you have already managed to fill Miss Augusta's belly with your seed, then that child, too, may one day be a duke. And I will not have any scandal or suspicion attached to his birth, nothing that will bring any disgrace to him or this family. Do you understand?"

Harry nodded, his head spinning from the suddenness of it. While he didn't regret making love to Gus—not at all—for her sake he did regret the circumstances. Now it appeared that he'd deprived her not only of a proper seduction, but of a proper wedding as well.

And a child, a baby, the all-too-tangible proof of their coupling. His heir. How had he become so caught up in loving Gus that he'd forgotten that very distinct possibility?

"Of course I understand, Father," he said slowly, his thoughts racing on to imagine himself with not only a wife, but a baby as well, and he was stunned by exactly how pleasurable those thoughts were. "I will be proud and honored to marry Gus—that is, Lady Augusta."

Father lowered his chin and glowered. " 'Gus'?" he repeated, the single syllable rolling with dismay. "You call the woman who will be the next Duchess of Breconridge *Gus*?"

"I do indeed, Father." Harry smiled wickedly. In the midst of this serious conversation, her nickname seemed such a ludicrously insubstantial objection that it was a relief. "Though I promise not to have her presented to His Majesty by that name."

"Gus," Father repeated, sighing with resignation. "I cannot fathom why you call such a winsome little lady by such an appalling name."

"Because she's always been called that," Harry said, an obvious explanation to him, "and I cannot imagine calling her anything else. She's my own dear Gus."

"Gus," Father said again, but more thoughtfully this time. "Lady Gus. No. You will not insist that I call her so?"

"You may call her whatever you wish," Harry said, as firmly as he dared to Father, "and whatever she agrees to."

Slowly Father smiled, too, leaning back in the chair. "You do love her, then."

"I do," Harry said, thinking of all that those words meant to him now. "After these last weeks, I cannot fathom my life without her in it."

Father nodded. "Forgive me for paternal crowing, but I did tell you that that is how it should be with a wife. Honor her, protect her, respect her, indulge her, but do it all because you love her, not because it's a duty or obligation. That's the path to lasting happiness."

"I do recall you saying that, Father," Harry said, willing to humble himself a bit for the sake of the peace. "But I was a headstrong ass and didn't believe you. Now I do, so you may crow at will."

Father chuckled, motioning to the servant to refill his glass. "I'm glad you're finally showing some sense, Harry. Better later than never. Shall we ask the ladies to join us, so we might begin making plans for your wedding?"

Harry leaned forward, his smile gone. "Don't, Father, I beg you. Let me ask her to marry me first. I don't want her thinking she's being forced into this."

Father's brows rose. "Have you any doubts as to her answer? What lady would refuse you?"

"She won't," Harry said. He knew what Father meant: that no lady would refuse his fortune and his title, with the likelihood of a dukedom in time. Plenty of ladies married doddering old men and blithering idiots for less of a prize. Gus wasn't one of them. If—no, *when*—she married him, it would be for himself, hobbled and imperfect though that might be, and not the wealth and power and grand houses that came with his name.

"Then why not settle this among us now?" Father said. "If that fool Wetherby were here, watching after her as he should, then we'd be making the settlements while you two watched."

"Father, please," Harry said. "Let me speak to her alone first. I want to give her Mother's ring."

Father smiled, almost wistfully. "You have your mother's ring here?"

Harry nodded, already picturing the flower of diamonds on Gus's finger. "When you see it on Gus's hand, you'll know she's accepted me."

Father finished the wine and stood, holding his hand to help Harry rise, too.

"Very well, then, Harry," he said. "Do it your way. But mind you, don't waste time about it. The wedding will be Saturday, whether you've made your pretty proposal or not."

CHAPTER
10

Gus hurried up the back steps from the servants' hall, reviewing all the things she'd already done, and what still needed doing. Having Harry's parents appear unexpectedly like this presented an enormous number of tasks for her and for the household, and she doubted Harry himself, being male, had any notion of even half of them.

She had first met with Mrs. Buchanan to see what could be contrived for a suitable dinner for His and Her Grace. There was no time to send for more provisions from Norwich; Mrs. Buchanan would have to make do with what was on hand in the pantry and larder, and she was not happy about it. Next Gus met with Mr. Royce to review which members of the staff could be pressed into helping with the service, as well as how the table was to be laid and arranged, and which wines should be brought up from the cellar.

Then there was the question of where everyone should sleep. By rights, the duke and duchess should have the best bedchamber with the yellow silk hangings, but Harry was so firmly entrenched there that he couldn't be moved, not even for his father. Fortunately, Her Grace had told Gus that, unlike most noble couples, she and duke preferred to share a single bedchamber, which made it easier for Gus to have the second-best one readied. But they had also brought personal servants as well as the driver and footmen connected with their carriage, and these all had to be fed and housed as well. It was a giant puzzle for Gus, fitting so many pieces together, but one she welcomed—not only for the challenge itself, but because it made her think of something other than Harry.

Harry. At once he filled her thoughts; she couldn't help it. His handsome face, his laughter, the way he'd kissed her and caressed her and brought her to pleasure she'd never dreamed possible. Even the heady memory of what they'd done made her blush, and resolutely she shoved the thoughts aside for what must be the thousandth time. She'd barely time to make herself ready for dinner, and she didn't need Mary guessing her thoughts as she arranged Gus's hair and helped her dress.

To her relief, Mary must have been pressed into other preparation belowstairs, and was not waiting for Gus in her bedchamber. Swiftly Gus undressed herself, thankful to be alone. As she'd feared, there were telltale stains on her petticoats from their lovemaking, with a long rip along one side from where she'd ordered him to tear it away. She wadded up the garments and stuffed them beneath her mattress, hiding them from Mary for now, and then at last rang for the maid to join her.

For once Mary did not pry, but instead chattered on excitedly about what she'd seen and heard from the other servants about the duke and duchess. Ordinarily Gus would have hushed her, not wishing servants to gossip about guests, but this evening Mary's words simply washed over her unheard. As she sat on the bench at her dressing table, she could think of nothing but Harry.

He'd told her he loved her, and they'd been the most glorious words she'd ever heard. But then he'd said other words that had not been quite as glorious.

It wasn't supposed to be like this . . .

Those words had drummed over and over in her head, driving doubts where there had been none before. Did he regret what they'd done? Had his passion been so fleeting that he'd wished it away? She'd given her maidenhead to him willingly, but she wasn't so blindly lovesick that she'd forget the consequences of that gift.

Because now she was *ruined,* another fearsome word, one that unmarried ladies like her were only supposed to whisper with dread. In romantic books, if the gentleman truly loved the lady he'd ruined, he'd behave honorably and marry her. But what if that was only in books, and not in life? What if Harry was feeling trapped instead of honorable, and she'd become no more than an embarrassment, an encumbrance?

How much she wanted to trust Harry, wanted to trust him in everything. But those words kept coming back to her, jabbing at her trust like anxious little fists of doubt.

It wasn't supposed to be like this . . .

While they'd walked in the garden, Her Grace had told her that she and the duke didn't intend to remain at Wetherby Abbey long, only a few days at most. She'd meant it generously, understanding the inconvenience that their visit had caused to Gus and the house, and wanting to lessen the imposition. But Her Grace had also said that they intended to take Harry with them back to London.

And then, just like that, he'd be gone.

It wasn't supposed to be like this . . .

Oh, she'd so little experience, and no one to ask! When Harry had first told her he loved her, those other words had made her hold back, wanting to protect that last little bit of her heart. But when he'd stood by her side in the hall with the sun falling all around him and told her again that he loved her, she'd wanted so much to believe him that she'd told him the same, her heart spilling out with the words. Because she did love him, loved him more than she'd ever thought possible.

And because, for her, it *was* supposed to be like this.

"Are you well, miss?" Mary asked with concern. "You're looking pale."

With effort Gus pulled herself back to the present. Mary was right: Her reflection in the looking glass before her was pale, her freckles more pronounced across her cheeks and the bridge of her nose. Yet it wasn't just the pallor that made her face seem unfamiliar, or the fashionable London style that Mary had coaxed her reluctant hair to assume. She wasn't the same woman who'd begun the summer, or even the day. Loving Harry had changed her forever, and the proof was there in her own features.

"I'm fine, Mary," she said, hooking her pearl drop earrings into her ears. "I suppose I'm a little weary, that is all. There's been so much to do with the duke and duchess here."

"Yes, miss," Mary said, giving Gus's hair one final pat. "It's a pity your father isn't here to see how well you've arranged everything so successful. He'd be so proud of you, miss, sitting at dinner with a duke and a duchess!"

Gus's smile was small and tight as she turned away from the looking glass.

"Let us survive dinner tonight before you speak of successes, Mary," she said, standing and smoothing her skirts over her hoops. "I'm terrified that one of the footmen will drop a tureen full of soup to splatter on Her Grace's gown, or that some stray mouse will go racing through the dining room beside His Grace's chair."

"I wouldn't worry, miss, not at all," Mary declared, and pressed her hands together. "Don't you look fine, miss, and fit for London society! You'll have His Grace and his lordship squabbling over who'll take you in to dine, that's for certain, and the poor duchess left behind."

Gus smiled, more at Mary's loyalty than the compliment itself. She was wearing her best silk damask gown, deep blue with a pattern of silver pomegranates embroidered around the neckline and on the cuffs, and she knew it suited her. But the gown had been stitched by a Norwich mantua maker, not a fashionable one in London with a French name, and she knew that in comparison with the golden-haired and elegantly stylish duchess, she'd be a poor second.

"I do not believe Her Grace will worry overmuch about competing with me, Mary," she said wryly. "If Julia were here, then things might be different, but—ah, there's someone at the door, Mary. Would you please answer, and if it's one of the maids from Mrs. Buchanan, tell her I'll be there directly."

Hurriedly she reached for her folded fan from her dressing table and tucked it into her pocket for later. *There,* she thought, *that should be all,* and she turned, ready to head downstairs to the kitchen for one last conversation to reassure Mrs. Buchanan.

But the servant at her bedchamber door wasn't one of the scullery maids from the kitchen. It was Tewkes.

He bowed before her, holding out a small silver salver with a letter on it.

"From his lordship, Miss Augusta," he said, holding the salver out to her. "His lordship desires that you read it and reply at once."

Gus took the letter, her heart racing. Only her full name—*Lady Augusta Wetherby*—was written across the front. It was strange to realize she'd never seen his handwriting, not once, and yet somehow she was sure she would have recognized it anywhere, bold and slashing and masculine. She turned it over in her hands, her finger slipping beneath the seal. That, at least, was achingly familiar to her, the armorial figure from his intaglio ring pressed into the wax reminding her of all the times she'd held his hand while his leg had pained him.

He'd written only a few lines on the heavy cream

stock—a few lines that could mean everything, or nothing.

> My own Dear Lady,
>   Please honor me with your presence, & join me now in the rose garden.
>   With Much Love & Affection,
>   Yr. Ob't. S'v't.
>   Hargreave

"I must go to him," she said aloud without realizing it, then with a little shake she turned back toward the servants. "Mary, please tell Mrs. Buchanan that I will come to her in a quarter hour, no more. Tewkes, you need not tell his lordship that I'll attend him, because I am going to him directly."

She truly did have only a quarter hour, because a quarter hour after that the duke and duchess would appear downstairs for dinner. She prayed that whatever Harry wished to say to her could be said in fifteen minutes' time, but beyond that she didn't dare hope.

She knew exactly where to find him in the rose garden, a curving stone bench beneath the arbor, because they'd often stopped there to rest his leg. Twilight had just begun to fall for the summer night, with the first stars beginning to show overhead and a silvery crescent moon rising over the tops of the trees. The birds were singing their last songs for the day, settling to roost, and the glowworms were beginning to show in the hedges around the garden. The kitchen doors were thrown open to catch the cooler evening air, and from them came the distant sounds of clanging pans and crockery, and Mrs. Buchanan calling orders to her staff as the last preparations for dinner were made.

Aware she hadn't much time, Gus walked briskly along the familiar paths, her shoes crunching on the gravel and her silk skirts rustling around her ankles. Her heart was racing and her breath quick as she turned around the last tall hedge, and there he was.

Harry was sitting on the bench, a lantern with a thick candle inside hooked to the arbor's post. He, too, was dressed for dinner, more formally than she'd ever seen him. His suit was a soft blue-gray, almost as if it had been cut from the twilight sky, with curling silk embroidery dotted with gold paillettes that winked in the candlelight. The buttons on his coat and waistcoat sparkled as well with cut stones that might have been paste, or might just as well have been diamonds, and there were more cut stones on the buckles of his shoes. As soon as he saw her, he smiled and began to stand.

"Don't rise on my account, Harry," she said, coming forward to take his hand as she bent to kiss him lightly, a greeting more than a passionate lover's embrace.

"Thank you for coming, Gus," he said, his eyes dark in the half-light. "I'd almost persuaded myself that you wouldn't."

"Of course I would," she said, more breathlessly than she wished. She sat on the bench beside him, sweeping her skirts to one side. "But I haven't much time, and neither do you. Your father will be—"

"I know we don't have time," he said firmly, "and I don't want to squander what we have discussing my father. What happened today—"

"I know," she said quickly, saying the words before he'd say them himself. "It—it wasn't how you wanted it to be."

"Not at all," he said, agreeing far too fast. "It wasn't right."

She looked down at their clasped hands, rubbing her thumb lightly over his, and she blinked, struggling to keep back the tears. She'd guessed right. This was how it would end, then, with an agreement that everything had been an impulsive mistake.

"No," she whispered miserably. "Oh, Harry, I'm sorry."

"You've nothing to be sorry for, Gus," he said. "I'm the one who should be down on my knees, begging your forgiveness in every way I can. But I can't. Damnation, I can't. But I can do the one thing I should have done long ago."

He reached into the pocket of his coat, fumbling a bit, before he drew out the little plush-covered box. Of course she recognized it. Of course she knew what it was, but knowing still didn't keep her from gasping, her hand fluttering to her mouth.

"Dearest Gus," he said, opening the box to take out the ring. "Would you do me the greatest honor in the world, and be my wife, my love, my life?"

The ring was even more magnificent than she remembered, the large round stone surrounded by smaller ones, like an icy white flower blooming with diamonds. She swallowed hard, her head spinning as she willed herself not to faint. What kind of useless woman fainted when the man she loved asked her to marry him?

"Oh, Harry," she said, blurting out the first thing that came to her. "That's—that's the ring you brought for my sister."

He stared at her. "It's my mother's ring," he said. "I brought it with me to Wetherby, yes, but it never came near your sister's hand. *This* is where it belongs."

He took her hand and gently, easily, slipped the ring onto her finger.

She stared down at it in wonder, hoping he didn't notice how her hand was shaking. "It fits me," she said. "It wouldn't have fit Julia."

He laughed, delighted. "Julia wouldn't have fit me, either. I was just too much of a blockhead to see it at first.

You're the one I love, Gus, and the one who was meant for me. The only one."

"Harry," she whispered, overwhelmed. "When you said this afternoon that things hadn't happened as you'd wished, I thought you had regrets about—about what we'd done, and wished to be free."

He stared at her, incredulous. "Why in blazes would I ever think that, Gus? Why would I regret loving you?"

She shook her head, unable to answer. So far she'd said everything wrong that she could, babbling on about Julia and telling him she'd doubted him. She looked up from the ring to his face, letting herself tumble into the infinite love she found in his eyes.

"Oh, goodness, Harry," she said, faltering. "I—I don't know what to say."

"You could say yes," he said. "That would do."

"Yes," she said, never realizing how magical a word it could be. "Yes, Harry, I'll marry you, and—and oh, I do love you so much, and—"

But whatever else she'd intended to say was lost between them as he pulled her from the bench and into his arms and kissed her. He kissed her exactly the way that she liked, impetuous and demanding and rather masterful, turning her breathless and mussing her clothes and hair and generally making her think only very wicked, wanton thoughts with him as the centerpiece. She was sure that no other man could ever kiss her like this, despite having no kissing experience where other men were concerned—which, considering she now was going to forsake all others and be Harry's wife, was perfectly, perfectly fine.

When at last they separated, he was breathing hard, and even by the lantern's light she could see that he was flushed, and that his forehead, right where his hair fell forward, was glistening with a tiny beading of sweat. True, the evening was warm, but she was certain that she'd done that to him, just by kissing him. She'd *aroused* the Earl of Hargreave, and she grinned, unable to help herself.

"Don't you smile at me like that, Gus," he warned. "Because when you do, I forget entirely about going in to dinner with Father and Celia and think about other things that I'd rather be doing with you. Here. Now. On this bench."

"Ooh," she said, blushing but intrigued. "If we're thinking of the same things, then you are making me forget about dinner, too. I'm not sure, however, that a stone bench would be the most comfortable of places on which to lie."

"One does not necessarily need to lie anywhere, Gus," he said. "Your ignorance is appalling. Your husband will have his work cut out for him, teaching you everything you need to know."

"My husband." She ran her hand lightly down his chest in wonder, her smile wobbling. The ring on her hand was beautiful, the weight unfamiliar, and yet so full of sparkling promise for their shared future. "My husband, Harry."

"My wife, Gus." He raised her hand and kissed the back, then turned it and kissed her palm, giving it a seductive little nip that sent chills rippling up her spine. "But if we don't go into the house soon, Father will hunt us down. You must trust me that that would not be an experience you would enjoy."

She laughed softly and leaned forward to kiss him again. "Can we tell them? About getting married?"

He wasn't entirely paying attention to what she was asking as he trailed his fingers over the tops of her breasts. "We can, and we will. I do not wish for a long engagement."

She sighed, surprised by exactly how pleasurable that grazing little touch was. "I don't suppose I might come to your room again this evening?"

"What, for another round on the chamber horse?" he said, more to her breasts than to her. "As much as I wish it, no. I suspect that this may in fact be the last time we'll be allowed alone together. Father feels your father has been negligent in guarding your virtue."

"Father trusts me," she said defensively.

"Yes, he did, didn't he," Harry said drily. "He trusted me with you as well, and we both know how that has turned out. Not that I would wish it otherwise, mind you. But my father is here to see that propriety reigns once again, no matter the hour of the day or night."

Gus sighed with regret. It was sobering to realize that while Father had followed Julia to London to make sure she didn't misbehave with gentlemen, she had been the one who'd leaped headfirst into mischief with Harry. So while she could understand the duke's reasons for wanting a show of propriety, the wicked part of her—a part she hadn't known she possessed, and the part of her that was even now arching her back so that his fingers could dip into the front of her gown and under her stays and shift to find her breasts—argued differently. They were going to be married and they'd already made love once, so where was the harm in doing it again?

But his mention of the hour did remind her of her promise to Mrs. Buchanan. That quarter hour she'd allotted to Harry must nearly be done by now.

"What is the time?" she asked.

He pulled out his gold watch, flipping the lid open with his thumb. "Nearly eight thirty. Later than I'd thought, though I'll grant it is nearly dark now, isn't it?"

"Eight thirty!" cried Gus, stunned. "Harry, we were to sit at the table at eight!"

To her horror, he actually shrugged his silk-covered shoulders. "Father won't care, once we tell him the reason."

"But I've kept Mrs. Buchanan waiting, Harry," she

said, slipping from the bench and tugging her bodice back into place. "She's been working herself and the staff into an absolute frenzy all day to make a meal worthy of your father, and now I will have spoiled it."

"*We* spoiled it," he said mildly, though he did reach for his crutch. "And I'd do it again, too, given the choice."

"Oh, yes, and lose the best cook in Norfolk," Gus said. "You go explain to your father and Her Grace. I'll join you as soon as I've done my best to placate Mrs. Buchanan."

"Gus, wait," he said, standing, and finally he looked as concerned as she did. "Don't tell the servants about us before we tell Father. You can't do that."

"It will serve you right if I do," she said, only half teasing. "I will see you in the drawing room with your father and stepmother."

"Gus, please," he said softly. "Please."

He reached out to take her hand, which she knew was as much to keep her from leaving without him as it was from fondness. But she was willing to pretend she didn't, because she was fond of him as well.

"Please listen to me, Gus," he said, his voice an interesting mixture of male reason and humbled pleading. "If your cook is the marvel you claim, then she will have devised a way to keep everything simmering in your absence. No doubt she has done it before, and will do it again. She will cope. You, however, will have but one chance to walk into that drawing room by my side, ready to announce that we will be man and wife. Only one, Gus. My own dear, dear Gus."

She sighed, unable to resist him when he called her that. She kissed him again, unable to resist that as well.

"Very well, then, Harry," she said. "I'll concede, and go with you, instead of downstairs. But if the pudding is dry or the joint too done, you cannot say a word. Not a single word, not over so much as one burned crumb."

vicar about my request for an hour for the service, I'm sure he will accommodate us. You two will be wed on Saturday, no mistake of that."

"But I've only just accepted Harry's proposal, not three hours ago, and we told you in less than two," Gus said, perplexed. "Forgive me, Your Grace, but these preparations you've made do not seem possible."

At once Harry reached out to place his hand over hers, mentally blasting his father's thoughtlessness. This was exactly what he didn't wish to happen, and now it had.

"You agreed that a long betrothal would not suit us, Gus," he said, hoping she'd focus on their shared future, and not consider too closely what his father had just said. "I love you so much that I've no wish to wait a day longer than I must."

"But that's only four days, Harry," she said with a plaintiveness that struck straight to Harry's heart. "That's no time to make preparations."

"It's plenty of time for whatever preparations need doing," Father said with such heartiness that Harry wished he could throttle him. "It's a wedding, not a coronation."

Gus glanced at Harry, making it silently clear that, to her, their wedding was every bit as important as any coronation.

"If you please, Your Grace," she countered bravely, "I should rather like a new gown to wear to my wedding, but four days—"

"Plenty of time, my dear," Father declared, sweeping aside her objections with a wave of his hand, his jeweled rings catching the candlelight. "Celia, what is the name of your mantua maker? That charming woman I tithe to? We'll have her and her seamstresses brought up here tomorrow, and make whatever fancy Augusta desires."

"Mistress Wilkerson, in Bond Street," Celia said. "Brecon, pray be aware that she will send you an astounding bill for her services. Mantua makers are not like ordinary trades-men. They do not like to be hauled about on male whims, and she will expect to be paid accordingly."

"If you please, Your Grace," Gus said hesitantly. "I would prefer my mantua maker in Norwich, a most agree-able woman who has made all my gowns and my sister's, too, and she might be persuaded to—"

"But this Mistress Wilkerson dresses not only Celia, but every other lady of rank in London," Father said, basking in his generosity. "You're going to be a countess, my dear, and a duchess in time. Harry will expect you to dress like one, not make do with some woman in Norwich."

"Brecon, please," Celia said, her voice full of gentle warning. "The bride is always right, and Augusta's wishes must be obeyed. Pray forgive Brecon's ignorance, Augusta. He likes to arrange things, it's simply his way."

Arranging things was a nice way of putting it, thought Harry grimly. *Interfering* and *meddling* might be closer to the point. For the sake of keeping the dinner rela-tively pleasant, he wouldn't say anything—not yet.

"But Brecon is correct in one regard," Celia contin-ued. "You should have a most splendid gown for your wedding, the very best that your woman can contrive, with pearls and brilliants and lace. Not only will you wear it to your wedding, but also when you are pre-sented at court."

Harry glanced at Gus with growing concern. She was visibly fading away and growing more and more quiet as his Father and Celia made plans for her wedding and her dress. They meant only the best, but Gus didn't know that, and all the confidence she'd shown earlier had vanished, just as it had when Sheffield had visited.

"I want you to be pleased, Gus," he said, gently turn-ing her hand over on the table so their fingers were inter-twined. "As far as I'm concerned, you can have your gown made by your own mantua maker in Norwich, and it will be exactly as you wish."

"Be reasonable, Harry," Father said impatiently. "We're doing her a favor so she will be properly attired for court, not—"

"She's not part of our family yet, Father, not until she marries me," Harry said firmly. "If Gus wishes her gown for the wedding to be made to her own taste and by this other woman, then that's what she should have. God knows she'll have plenty of other clothes and nonsense made in the future."

Gus smiled at him, her fingers curling more tightly into his. It was hardly the first time he'd stood up to Father— they were far too much alike for it to be otherwise—but it was the first time he'd done it defending Gus, and her smile made him feel as if he'd just slain a dragon. Hell, a dozen dragons.

"Harry's right, Brecon," murmured Celia, understanding. "It is the bride's day, not ours."

Father frowned and shook his head. "Very well, then, very well. But next week, Celia, when we're all back in London, I trust you and the other ladies will take Augusta about to your shops and make her known."

"In London?" asked Gus, her smile gone again. "London?"

"To my house," Harry said. He was certain he must have mentioned it to her before, an agreeable house on Grosvenor Square that had come to him through his mother's estate. "We'll go there directly after the wedding, in my carriage."

"But what of your leg?" she asked anxiously. "Sir Randolph hasn't said you can travel yet."

"Peterson gave Harry leave to travel a fortnight ago," Father said. "He told me so himself yesterday in London."

She frowned with confusion. "Is this true, Harry?"

"It is," he said, again wishing Father had kept this news to himself. "I could leave, but I haven't."

"He's been dawdling here because of you, Augusta," Father said, stating the obvious. "I'll grant that you are a very pretty reason for staying here in Norfolk, but he needs to return to town, to tend to his affairs and show himself about. And you as his new countess, too, of course."

"But why so soon?" she implored. "What is the need for such haste in all of this?"

Father's expression turned solemn.

"Because of the circumstances of my son's dalliance with you, my dear," he said. "A swift marriage is the best preventive for scandal."

Gus flushed and whipped around to face Harry again, her eyes full of shock and hurt. There weren't any dragons being slain now: instead he'd become the unfortunate dragon himself, and if he'd felt proud of himself before, now he felt like the lowest creature in Creation. Without a word she pulled her hand free of Harry's and shoved her chair back from the table.

"Pray excuse me, Your Grace, Your Grace," she said as she rose, "but I—I am not well."

"Gus, please stay," Harry said, holding his hand out to stop her. "Please."

But she slipped out of his reach, and without looking at him, ran swiftly from the room.

"Well, go after her, Harry," Father said. "You can't let her run off in tears like this."

"She wouldn't have run off, Father, if you hadn't insulted her," Harry said, furious. He pushed back his chair, knocking his crutch to the floor, and to his humiliation one of the footmen retrieved it for him. Finally he hobbled out to the hall, determined to find Gus.

He didn't have far to look. She'd only gotten as far as the front staircase, sitting on the second step and crying inconsolably with her face in her hands. He lowered himself onto the step beside her, and as he raised his arm to slip it around her shoulders, she scuttled away from him to the far side of the step. He sighed; this was not going to be as easy as his father had thought.

"Here now, Gus, don't cry," he began. "My father had no right to say that to you, I know, but he—"

"You shouldn't have *told* him, Harry," she said, lifting her tear-streaked face. "Not about—about us!"

"I didn't have to tell him, sweetheart," he said. He liked being able to call her that, because at last she truly was his sweetheart. "He figured it out for himself. It wasn't that difficult, not with the state of our clothing at the time."

"Not—not that, Harry," she said, her eyes brimming with tears. "Though that was shameful enough. You—you told him we were going to marry even before you asked me. That's what—what isn't *right*."

"Oh, Gus," Harry said, the safest thing he could think to say under the circumstances. He'd hoped she never would have realized this, but thanks to Father's interference, it wasn't much of a secret. The last thing he wished was for her to believe he'd been pressured into marrying her, and now, clearly, that was exactly what she did believe.

"Is that all you can say?" she said, her face flushing with misery. " 'Oh, Gus,' as if I were a child? As if that—that's any manner of explanation?"

She looked down at the diamond betrothal ring on her hand, and began to tug at it fiercely.

"If that is all I am to you, my lord," she said, struggling to pull the ring from her finger, "then perhaps we do not belong together. If I mean no more to you than 'oh, Gus,' then perhaps I shouldn't marry you at all."

"Don't, Gus," he said as calmly as he could, placing his hand over hers. "Please."

She looked at him defiantly through her tears, her hands

still fighting with the ring under his. "Why should I listen to you, Harry?"

An excellent question, thought Harry, and if he offered the wrong answer, he had a distinct feeling that she might leave him. But what was the right thing to say? What excuse could he possibly offer that would make her stay?

The truth, came a small voice in his head. *Trust her, and tell her the truth.*

He was glad the small voice was so confident, because the rest of him certainly wasn't. Truth telling was not a familiar gambit for him where ladies were concerned. But this was Gus, and the truth seemed to be the best he had to offer her.

"Because I love you," he said slowly, truthfully, "and because I always will love you. I think in a way I've loved you since I opened my eyes to find you looking down at me all serious and worried for my sorry, broken self."

Her hands stilled beneath his fingers. "You *were* sorry."

"I was," he agreed. "And you saved me. I wouldn't be here now without you."

She gave a deep, shuddering sigh. "Then why did you tell your father we were going to marry before you'd asked me?"

"Because Father informed me of it first," he said, keeping to the truth. "Before he even asked after my leg, he told me that I must preserve your honor by marrying you."

Her face began to crumple with misery, and he quickly continued. "But that's not why I proposed to you, Gus. If you love me, you know that. If I'd any brain at all, I would have asked for you weeks ago. Months. I've known it that long."

Unable to resist, he slipped his arm around her shoulders and pulled her close. She came, but her body was still stiff, resisting, not trusting. Clearly more truth was needed, no matter how humbling it might be.

"You do know me, Gus, better than the rest of the world," he continued. "Which means you should know by now that no one, not even my father, could make me do anything as important as marrying if I didn't want to."

She made a little hiccuping sound, which he took to be encouraging.

"That is true," she admitted. "You are wickedly stubborn."

"Indeed I am," he said, "and so is Father. I come by my stubbornness through him. We both like to have our own ways. No, we expect it. He wants to think that our marriage is his idea, while I know it wasn't. You should know it, too."

She twisted beneath his arm to gaze up at him. It was a good thing that he was sticking to the truth, because there was no conceivable way he could have done otherwise faced with those wide gray eyes, red-rimmed because he'd made her cry. If he wasn't careful, he could drown in eyes like that.

"If you've known for so long that I was the one you wished to marry," she asked slowly, "then why did you wait until today to ask?"

"Why," he repeated. This was going to be the hardest truth to confess, but he knew he had to do it. He looked down at the step. Her slippers were pale blue silk with some sort of darker blue pouf of feminine foolishness above the toe, and neat curving heels, her feet impossibly small and dainty beside his huge, clumping, man's foot. He adored her little feet. Hell, he adored all of her, a realization that gave him the last bit of courage he needed for truth telling.

"Why," he said again, and for what he hoped would be the final time. "Because I wanted to wait until my leg was as it should be again, and I didn't have to rely on a piece of wood to prop myself upright. I wanted to be able to stand before you the way a man should, and not be some sort of pitiful cripple that you'd pity. That was why I was waiting, Gus."

He took a deep breath. "And, damn it, because I was afraid you'd turn me down on account of my leg. There. That's why."

She stared at him with patent disbelief. "You would think that of me, Harry? That I would be so shallow as that?"

"It's not being shallow," he said, the logic clear to him. "It's being practical. No woman would wish to be shackled to a cripple. Consider your own sister."

"Your leg is not the sum of who you are," she said firmly, "and I am not Julia. What if your leg hadn't improved? What if it doesn't progress further? Sir Randolph has never offered you any unqualified assurances."

"My leg will grow stronger, Gus," he said with equal conviction. He had to believe it would; he refused to consider any other possibility. "It already has. I need more time, that is all."

She eased closer to him, her body softening against the hollows of his own. "It wouldn't have mattered, Harry," she said softly. "I still would have said yes."

He kissed her then, unable not to, her mouth warm and yielding. Kissing her also meant he wasn't required to speak any more uncomfortable truths—though there was one more that likely needed saying.

"I'll speak to Father about being so heavy-handed, sweetheart," he said, the words landing somewhere into her hair over her left ear. "God knows marrying in such haste isn't what either of us wished, but I want you to enjoy it as much as you can."

She smiled wistfully. "I'd marry you this minute if it meant we could stay here together, just the two of us."

"I wish it could be like that as well, sweet," he said,

thinking of how if they were already married, she'd be in his bed tonight. "But I'm afraid our days alone together here are done."

Watching Gus with Father and Celia had been something of a revelation to him. She'd really no idea what she was getting into by marrying him. His life—and now her life with him—was crowded with people in London, and wherever they went, they would be noticed, remarked on, discussed. Because it had always been that way with his family, he'd never given it much real thought, but for a quiet, country-bred soul like Gus, becoming the Countess of Hargreave was not going to be easy, not for either of them.

"Whatever may happen, Gus, you know I'll look after you," he said with a fresh seriousness. "I'll always be by your side when you need me. You'll be my love, my wife, my countess."

She made a breathy little chuckle of happiness, endearing and seductive as hell, because she didn't realize it. "I'll look after you as well, Harry. That's what husbands and wives do for each other."

"Yes," he said, the new responsibility of all this pressing heavily upon him. "I suppose they do."

He drew his arm more protectively around her. He liked that she trusted him as well as loved him. He liked that very much. That was how a wife should be. He loved her more than he'd thought possible, and he'd no regrets for anything. But at that moment, he felt at once very young, and very old.

CHAPTER
11

The next three days passed in an excited blur to Gus, and she was the center of it, an unusual place for her to be. In addition to having a gown made and fitted for the wedding and as well an elegant merino riding habit suitable for traveling to London, there were prodigious assaults on the ladies' shops of Norwich with the duchess—who had now given Gus leave to call her by her first name—in command, for shoes and hats and gloves and handkerchiefs and every other garment and gewgaw of silk and lace that a lady-bride of her rank would require.

There were meetings with the minister who was to marry her and Harry, and more meetings with Mr. Royce and Mrs. Buchanan to settle all the ledgers and household accounts before she gave up running the house and left. There were preparations for a wedding tea and a lavish bride's cake to follow the ceremony. There were long walks in the garden with the duchess, who kindly explained what sorts of new responsibilities Gus would have as Countess of Hargreave, and offering sage, if daunting, advice about how best to take her new place in London society. There were calls to receive from well-wishers around the county, who showed as much curiosity about Gus's husband-to-be as they did wishing her well. There was, of course, the sizable challenge of lodging and feeding two such important guests as His and Her Grace.

But there was, sadly, very little time spent with Harry himself. Although Gus knew that this enforced separation was likely for the respectable best, she still longed for the old freedom she and Harry had when it had been just the two of them, and they'd done as they pleased about the house and garden. Since the night she'd accepted his offer of marriage, she had only seen Harry over the white damask cloth of a formal dining table, and never alone. The duke saw to that. The kiss they'd shared on the stairs had been the last.

It didn't seem fair, not at all, and she could see the frustration building in Harry to match her own. But then she'd remind herself that after Saturday, they'd be together always, and it made these few days of forced separation easier to bear. Not easy, but easier.

And then, on Friday afternoon, the day before the wedding itself, everything changed again.

She was in her bedchamber with Mary, sitting on the floor amid open trunks and boxes as she tried to decide which of her belongings to take with her for her new life, and which to leave behind. It was untidy work. Her hair was tucked up under a plain cap, and she wore an old gingham apron over an older petticoat.

"What of these slippers, Miss Augusta?" Mary said, handing her a pair of embroidered silk shoes. "Surely you'll have use for these in London, and there's no wear at all to them."

"They have no wear because I only wore them once, to the Roxbys' Christmas ball," Gus said, running her fingers along the embroidery. However pretty the shoes might be, they brought back dismal memories of sitting unwanted and unnoticed in an uncomfortable chair beside the wall while she'd watched Julia and the others on the dance floor. The shoes had no wear because she hadn't danced that night, not once. Of course that had been long before Harry, but it was still a time she'd no wish to revisit or remember, not even with a pair of shoes. She was determined that her future with him would be different, and she resolutely put the shoes aside.

"I believe I'll leave them behind, Mary," she said, putting them in the discard box. She sat back on her heels, listening. "There's a carriage in the drive. Oh, heavens, who could possibly appear now, when we're in the middle of this mess?"

"You don't have to receive them, miss," Mary said. "Mr. Royce can tell them you're not at home."

"Let me see who it might be," Gus said, wiping her hands on her apron as she went to the window. "If it's a friend, then of course I'll—oh, Mary, it's Papa, come home at last! Send word to His Grace and his lordship!"

She ran down the front staircase, her skirts flying, out the front door and down those steps as well, reaching the drive just as the footmen were opening the carriage door. She flung herself at her father as soon as he stepped from the carriage steps, her arms unable to reach all around his girth in the most familiar way imaginable.

"Here you are, Gus," he said, laughing happily. "Come now, let me look at you. It's been weeks since I've seen you, daughter."

"Months, Papa," she said, as she stepped back as he'd asked. She couldn't keep from grinning as she straightened her cap. "You've been gone since the end of April."

He laughed and blotted at his forehead with his handkerchief, not in the least upset that she'd pointed out his error. "Not that you've minded one jot, have you? Little minx! You've spared me the cost of tricking you out for a season in London by doing your husband-hunting at home. You always were the clever lass, Gus, and what a prize you've claimed for yourself!"

She wrinkled her nose. "Oh, Papa, don't," she said,

blushing furiously. "I didn't set out to do anything of the sort. Harry and I simply fell in love."

His broad face softened. "That is what I wanted most to hear, Gus. That this rascal loves you as you deserve."

"He does, Papa," she said, smiling so hard that she was nearly crying, or perhaps that was from happiness. "But you mustn't call him a rascal, at least not in His Grace's hearing. His Grace is very particular about such things."

Papa puffed out his cheeks with jovial bluster to show exactly how much he cared for His Grace's particulars. "His lordship's a rascal until he proves to me he's worthy of my sweet little Gus."

He pulled off his black cocked hat and settled it on Gus's head, crushing her cap beneath it, the way he'd done since she was a little girl. It fit her no better now, and, laughing with delight, she had to shove the oversized hat back on her head to be able to see.

The first thing she saw was Julia, daintily stepping from the carriage with a footman holding each hand. She wore a wide-brimmed hat covered in striped silk with several nodding ostrich plumes, a close-fitting red jacket and matching petticoat—but then, everything Julia wore was close-fitting—and an enormous white swan's-down muff.

"Gus!" she exclaimed, sweeping forward. "Dearest sister!"

She didn't embrace Gus, nor did she wish it, instead presenting her cheek to be kissed. Gus wasn't surprised—it was usual with Julia, who didn't like being disarranged—and she dutifully kissed the offered cheek, with its familiar whiff of bergamot, face powder, and hair pomade.

"Gus, Gus, little Gus," she said. "So much has changed since last we saw each other!"

"Yes, it has," Gus said proudly, lifting her chin so she could peek out from beneath the brim of Papa's hat. "How very fine of you to return home for my wedding to Lord Hargreave."

"Oh, but look, Gus," she said. "You see I am now betrothed, too."

She pulled her left hand from inside the muff and waggled her fingers. Her ring was pretty enough, a sizable yellow topaz surrounded by diamonds, but it couldn't compare to the ring that Harry had given Gus.

Gus knew that she shouldn't be vain, and it was never wise to compete with Julia in any matter. But she'd stood in her sister's shadow for so long that, just this once, she couldn't help herself.

Slowly she held out her own hand, the cluster of diamonds sparkling brilliantly in the sunlight.

"This is from Harry," she said shyly. "It was his mother's."

"Very handsome," Julia said with a little moue of annoyance, and swiftly turned back to the carriage. "*Here* is my beloved himself! Lord Southland, my sister, Augusta. Gus, the most gloriously perfect gentleman in London, Lord Southland."

Possessively Julia seized his arm to draw him forward. Gus curtseyed, looking at him with interest, not only because he'd won Julia and would now be part of their family, but also because she'd heard Harry mention his name as being a London acquaintance. He was tall and blond, his face ruddy and weathered from much time out-of-doors, with heavy-lidded pale eyes and full lips. The warm day must have made him fall asleep in the carriage, because he looked scarcely awake now, yawning widely to show his teeth and cricking his neck to one side as Julia hung on his arm.

"So you're Julia's sister, are you?" he asked, looking her up and down and taking in her worn apron and her father's hat. He blinked drowsily, sticking two fingers beneath the band of his hat to scratch his head. "You cannot be the one who's to wed Hargreave."

"I am, my lord, on both counts," Gus said, determined to be agreeable even if he was not. Now she remembered how Harry had dismissed Southland as amiable if vacuous, a younger son with no ambition to clutter his thoughts, and she had to agree. No wonder Julia thought he was perfect.

"I never should have guessed you were sisters," he said, and yawned again. "Should I, Julia?"

"Not at all, my darling Southland," Julia said, gazing up at him with adoration. "You are scarcely the first who cannot believe we are sisters."

"Where in blazes is Hargreave, anyway?" Southland asked, gazing about as if expecting Harry to pop up from beneath the steps. "I should drink to his health and happiness and all that."

"Yes, yes," Papa said, winking at Gus as he plucked his hat back from her head. "High time I spoke with his lordship and asked his intentions regarding you, eh, Gus?"

"Papa, please," she said. Harry would understand Papa's humor, but she worried about how the duke—who already held her father in very low esteem—was going to respond. "Let's go inside so you can refresh yourself, and then we'll all meet for tea."

"For tea, hah," Papa said, climbing the steps. "Gentlemen want something stronger than that, Gus."

"Hear, hear, Wetherby," echoed Southland, eagerly following him up the steps. "Nothing like the dusty road to give a gentleman a raging thirst."

"Isn't Southland a perfect Adonis?" Julia whispered to Gus. "He's *so* strong, Gus, and so manly, too. I vow that if he weren't the son of the Marquess of Otley, he could be a blacksmith, he's that strong. Wouldn't you agree?"

"I suppose he is," Gus said, preoccupied with figuring out which bedchamber would do for Adonis. "Though I should wish rather more from a husband than the ability to make horseshoes."

Julia made her expression solemn. "Oh, of course you'd say that, Gus," she said as they walked through the door. "Forgive me for being thoughtless. What else *can* you say, under the circumstances?"

It made no sense to Gus, but then that wasn't unusual with Julia. Besides, the only circumstances that concerned her now were the immediate ones, here in the hall. Harry was waiting there with the duke and duchess beside him, all of them ready to greet her father, for which she was grateful and relieved. As handsome as ever, Harry was standing as straight and tall as he could on his good leg, barely using the crutch for balance at all, a skill she knew he'd practiced, and she was touched and proud of him for making the considerable effort.

Julia was welcome to her empty-headed Adonis. She'd take her Harry any day, who was far stronger than Julia would ever understand.

But while Gus couldn't look away from Harry, her father was focused on something else entirely. Lolling on the floor at Harry's feet as usual were Patch and Potch, and they were all that Papa could see.

"Gus, why are there dogs in my house?" he asked, stunned into a frozen state of disbelief and disapproval. "Dogs. *Dogs.* In *my* house."

"Papa, please," Gus said quickly, grabbing him by the arm. "Your Graces, my lord, I believe you know my father, Viscount Wetherby. Lord Southland, and my sister, Miss Julia Wetherby."

The duke nodded curtly, not exactly the picture of cordiality. "Good day, Wetherby. I am glad your affairs permitted you to return home for your daughter's marriage to our son."

Oh, this wasn't good, thought Gus with dismay, praying that Papa would manage to say something civilized in return.

For once, miraculously, he did. "Your Graces, my lord," he said, lifting his hat and bowing. "I'm honored to have you as guests here at Wetherby, and for such a fine reason, too. I wouldn't have missed my daughter's wedding to his lordship for all the tea in China."

The duke smiled. "Indeed. My wife and I have much to discuss with you before our children are wed tomorrow, Wetherby. Have you a place where we could retire?"

"My library will serve," Papa said, bowing again as he indicated the way for them to follow. "Gus, will you have Mrs. B. send up some sort of little somethings for us?"

"You're looking well, Julia," Harry said once the parents had left. "London must agree with you more than the country air."

"Thank you, my lord," Julia said, making languishing eyes even as she clung to Southland's arm. "I only wish I could say the same to you."

"Julia!" Gus exclaimed, appalled. "I cannot believe even you would say something so—so *barbarous*."

"Your sister's entitled to her opinion, Gus, however ludicrous," Harry said, outwardly mild, though the glint in his eyes showed something far different. "One cannot change a leopard's spots."

Gus remembered this mood well from when he'd first hurt his leg, dark and dangerous with frustration and anger, too. Even his blue eyes turned darker and more ominous. She'd been wary of the signs then, and she was now as well.

But clearly Julia was not. "His lordship understands me, Gus, even if you do not," Julia said blithely. "I'm only speaking the truth. If he were well, then he wouldn't be a cripple."

"How is the old leg, Hargreave?" Southland asked.

"Must be the very devil, having to hop about like an old crow."

"I manage," Harry said, his voice clipped, the two words razor-sharp.

Not that Southland seemed to notice, either. "You know we're to become brothers," he said, slipping his arm familiarly around Julia's waist. "This lovely creature has finally agreed to marry me."

"Congratulations," Harry said, his gaze not leaving Julia. "A small word of advice, Southland, one that you'll do well to take. Never go riding with the lady."

"I cannot fathom why not," Southland said, mystified. "She's as fine a rider as any lady I know."

"Yes, I am," Julia said with more than a touch of belligerence. "At least I manage to stay seated on my horse."

Gus seized her by the arm to turn her away from Harry, and what she feared would be certain disaster.

"Come, Julia, you must see my gown for the wedding," she said with forced cheerfulness. "The mantua maker made the final fittings just this morning."

"Gus, don't," Julia said, trying to pull free. "I'd rather stay with Southland."

"I'm certain the gentlemen will be much happier without us for a while," Gus said, half dragging her sister with her from the hall and up the stairs. "Besides, I wish you to see my gown. It's so grand, even you shall approve."

But as soon as they reached Gus's dressing room, where the gown was hanging on pegs in readiness for tomorrow along with the rest of her new wedding clothes, Gus swiftly closed the door and turned to confront her sister.

"I do not know what your intention may be, Julia," she said with uncharacteristic ferocity, "and I don't know all that happened between you and Harry. Nor, to be honest, do I wish to know. But I will not have you vexing him or disturbing our wedding."

Julia's eyes widened, and she stepped back with mock horror.

"My word, Gus, I've never seen you like this," she said. "Quite the little lioness, aren't you?"

"You're jealous of me, aren't you?" Gus said, the first time in their lives that she'd been able to say that to her sister. "You could have married Harry yourself, and you cast him off, and now you can't bear the idea that *I'm* the one marrying him instead."

"You're only half right, Gus," Julia said. "I did wish to marry Harry and become a countess and a duchess. But I did not wish to marry a man who was crippled and needy, and thus you are quite, quite welcome to him and his crutch."

"You are cruel, to speak so of him!"

Julia smiled. "The truth can be cruel, Gus, and I've said nothing that wasn't true."

"Your venomous version of the truth!" Gus exclaimed. Julia was right: she never had talked back to her quite like this, but then she'd never had Harry to defend, either.

"You couldn't bring yourself to visit Harry when he was ill," she continued, "yet now you *dare* to make light of his suffering with your—your *foolishness*!"

Julia sniffed and turned away. "Did he tell you what happened that day in the woods?"

"I know he didn't fall from Hercules," Gus said staunchly. "He was thrown, and I suspect you had something to do with it."

"But you do not *know*," Julia said, pouncing on the truth. Considering how foolish she could be, Julia was often surprisingly adept in a quarrel, employing any misstep that Gus made against her. "Not for certain. I doubt Harry does, either, for all that he tried to slander me just now. He should take care. Southland won't like that, and he'll defend me, too."

"I wouldn't test Harry's memory, Julia," Gus said. "Not unless you wish an unpleasant surprise if he recalls more than you want."

Julia smiled with maddening indulgence and began walking slowly about the small room, critically eyeing Gus's new belongings as if she were browsing the goods of an inferior shop.

"I'm unconcerned, Gus," she said. "The talk in London is that Harry's not at all the gentleman he once was. Now that I've seen him, I'd say the talk is right. He's not only crippled, he's . . . different. No wonder the duke came racing clear from Italy to see for himself."

Doggedly Gus followed Julia around the room, her hands knotted in fists at her sides. "If that was His Grace's reason for coming here," she said, "then at least he's seen for himself that there is nothing wrong with Harry's wits."

Julia shrugged carelessly. "Perhaps," she said. "But he did get his main wish. He's found a wife for his oldest son. You already know all of Harry's weaknesses, and you aren't particular about them. That's much better than having another potential bride or her family ask difficult questions about Harry's health, and embarrass His Grace."

Gus gasped. "That is absolute rubbish, Julia, the worst kind of speculation and gossip! His Grace wanted Harry to marry me swiftly because he discovered we'd—"

She broke off abruptly, realizing too late that she'd nearly revealed the truth to Julia. She turned around to face the window, wanting to hide the guilt that was surely on her face from Julia, but her sister had already seen enough.

"He—Harry—he ravished you," Julia whispered behind her, her voice filled with genuine shock. "That's it, isn't it? He took your maidenhead, and the duke learned of it and is forcing him to marry you. Oh, Gus, that is it, isn't it?"

"No, it's not," Gus said bravely, turning back to face her sister. "He didn't ravish me. I wanted to—to lie with him as much as he desired me. We're lovers, Julia. We love each other, and we wish to wed so that we may be together for the rest of our lives. There, *that* is the truth, and I swear by everything holy that it is so."

She'd never seen Julia so stunned, and certainly not by anything she herself had said. The customary well-practiced archness was gone from her face, and beneath the elaborate hat and plumes she looked confused, even baffled.

"Harry loves you like that, Gus?" she asked. "You?"

Gus nodded. "He does," she said, "and I love him the same way in return."

"You remind me of Mama when you say that," Julia said slowly. "How she always said true love would find a way."

Gus smiled wistfully, thinking of Mama, too. "With Harry, I did find true love."

"Did you." Julia tried to smile, her eyes watery with tears as she pulled out a lace-edged handkerchief. "He never loved me like that."

"Oh, Julia," Gus said softly. "You weren't right for each other, that is all."

Julia shook her head, shaking away Gus's consoling words. "What I said about Harry being different—that's true. When he looks at me now, I'm only one more lady. But when he looks at you, his eyes burn for you. I've never had that, either."

"But you will, Julia," Gus said, close to tears herself. "You have Southland."

"Southland." Julia smiled through her tears, and looked down at the ring on her hand. "I do have him, the great, handsome ninny. He'll suit me a thousand times better than Harry ever could, anyway."

She laughed, and Gus laughed, too, and they hugged and cried and hugged again.

"I hope that you and Harry will be vastly, vastly happy," Julia said when they separated for the last time. "Considering how you love each other, it cannot be any other way, can it?"

"And I hope that Southland comes to love you the same way," Gus said fervently. "You deserve nothing less."

"He will," Julia said, smiling. "He may not know it yet, but I shall make sure that he *will*."

"More brandy, Harry?" asked Father, pushing the bottle across the table toward him. "The night is young, lad, and tomorrow you become a married man."

Harry glanced up at the case clock in the corner. The night wasn't young; it was very old, nearly half past eleven. He'd been sitting here with his father and Gus's father and that damned fool Southland for hours and hours, ever since the ladies had retired after supper.

Despite the best efforts of the older men to get him as drunk as they were, he wasn't, not by half. The evening would have been much more enjoyable if he had been. As it was, he'd had to sit through one garrulous story after another of wedding-night mishaps, of brides both terrified and as lustful as March hares, of grooms bold and shy and bedsteads that had collapsed outright. None of it had seemed very funny to Harry, but then, nothing had seemed very funny to him today.

It had begun when he'd seen Julia Wetherby walk through the door this afternoon. He'd known he would have to see her again, one way or another. She was, after all, his future wife's only sister. Not that he harbored any regrets or unfulfilled longings for her, anyway; his main thought in regard to Julia was that he'd been lucky to escape.

Yet the moment she'd stepped into the house, the plumes on her ridiculous hat bobbing in the summer sun, that other morning had come rushing back to him, and every blasted detail that he'd mercifully forgotten had returned with it.

He remembered her upturned face as she'd popped from the bush, whooping like a Bedlamite, and the plume on her riding hat quivering and the skirts of her habit flapping around like a flag in the fog. He remembered how the horse had bucked and flailed in terror, and how he'd fought back, barely managing to wrench the animal to one side and away from Julia before he'd been thrown. He remembered hurtling through the air and landing hard, and leaves that had smelled of mold and decay. He remembered Julia abandoning him, disappearing completely, and more pain than he'd thought a man could endure.

And then he remembered Gus, coming to him like an angel: his salvation, his dearest love, and the woman whom tomorrow he'd make his wife.

He should be the happiest of men, with the happiest of reasons. Yet ever since he'd seen Julia and remembered too much, he'd felt nothing but anger for what had happened to him. Though a great deal was Julia's fault, he did not blame her. He'd been every bit as foolhardy as she had, accepting a mount that was clearly unaccustomed to new riders and then riding that horse pell-mell into the mist-filled woods, simply because a pretty girl had dared him.

Because of those rash and reckless choices, he would not be able to stride down the aisle tomorrow with Gus, or help her into their carriage, bedecked with flowers from the wedding, or, when they finally reached London and home, sweep her into his arms and carry her over the threshold. No matter what the surgeons promised, he knew he'd never be the same again, and all the self-doubt and disappointment that he'd thought he put behind him came rushing back, with more besides.

He'd been a rash, headstrong, careless fool, and now he'd pay for it the rest of his life. Worst of all was realizing that Gus would now have to pay for it with him. She'd never have the husband she deserved, and it was all his own damned fault.

He'd never forgive himself.

All through the afternoon and evening he'd tried to put the memories and the anger away and focus instead on tomorrow, tried and failed. Instead he'd been ill mannered and curt to those who did not deserve it and surly when he should have been joyful, while his thoughts had churned and his guts had twisted with emotions he could not control.

He pushed his chair back from the table, reached for his crutch, and stood. "Pray excuse me, gentlemen," he said, bowing. "I'll bid you good night now, and leave you to drink on in my name."

"Harry, good Harry, you cannot leave us yet," protested Wetherby, his broad smile as lopsided as his wig. "We've yet to have a good song. A wedding song for the bridegroom, heigh-ho!"

"Forgive me, but I am weary," Harry said, wishing he could make the words less curt. "Tomorrow shall be a long day."

"We'll let you go, son," Father said, smiling indulgently. "Tomorrow may be a long day, but tomorrow night will be even longer, and we want you to show your mettle, eh?"

The others roared, but Harry merely nodded and retreated to the hall as fast as he could. Despite what he'd just said, he knew that sleep would be impossible, and instead of going directly to his bedchamber, he headed to the rear of the house and the garden door, hoping that a bit of evening air might do him good. He could see the gardens through the windows, the hedges and paths crisp in the moonlight, and in the distance the slatted top of the arbor where he'd proposed.

He would miss this house. Not because it was extraordinary in itself, but the time he'd spent here, falling in love with Gus, had made it so. There'd been no expectations from others, no prying eyes, no gossipy items in the scandal sheets reporting their whereabouts and doings. Here at the abbey, there had only been the two of them, and it had been magic.

No wonder he wasn't looking forward to returning to London. London would be filled with judgments; he'd known that even before Father had warned him of what people were already saying. His time here away from town had made him come to realize exactly how harsh London could be. From experience he knew it was a fine place if you were young and beautiful, strong and rich. He'd be considered weak now, fit for whispers and ridicule, and he knew, too, that all the young ladies and their mamas that he'd passed by would now have their daggers ready for poor Gus. He'd no doubt that the two of them would persevere, but it would not be easy, not for either of them.

Most of the house was already asleep for the night, with the night-lanterns offering their wavering light through the silent halls. He heard voices rising from the back stairs and the distant clatter of pans from the kitchen; doubtless the poor scullery maids were there still, striving to stay awake and praying the great lords upstairs would finally go to bed. Weary footsteps came up the stairs, and he melted back into the shadows, not wanting to frighten whichever hapless girl it might be on her way to her bed beneath the eaves.

She carried a candlestick before her, the pale light washing irregularly before her as she came up the winding steps. Yet instead of following the turning to the next landing, she stepped out into the hall, a small, pale figure. She wore slippers on her bare feet, a shawl wrapped over her nightgown, and her long braid swung like a pendulum between her shoulder blades.

He'd know her anywhere.

"Gus," he said, calling to her softly. "Here."

"Harry?" She came to him slowly, as if she didn't trust it to be him. Her face was ghostly by the candlelight, her eyes enormous. "Why are you here? Why aren't you with the other gentlemen?"

"Because I'd had enough," he said. "Why were you downstairs?"

"Oh, it was nothing," she said. "There was a question of missing silver spoons and forks after the washing-up, but it turned out to be a simple matter of miscounting, and hardly worth the fuss and accusations."

She set the candlestick on a nearby table and raised both hands to smooth her hair neatly back from her center part. His gaze dropped down to watch her breasts rise with the motion, and press against the white linen of her nightgown. He'd never seen them so clearly without stays, uncrushed by whalebone and buckram, and the way they swayed, round and firm beneath the thin linen, was mesmerizing. It was the first time they'd been alone together all week, and her nearness was heady and potent.

"They're all so on edge with the wedding tomorrow," she continued. "One would think they were the ones being married instead of us."

Her smile was shy, almost uncertain. He knew that that uncertainty was his fault, a reaction to how uncivil he'd been at supper. He hated himself for making her doubt, even as he doubted himself. He could have apologized for everything and asked her to forgive him.

Instead he pulled her into his arms and dragged her back with him, using the wall for support. His mouth crushed down on hers as if he were famished, kissing her with a demanding and ruthless intensity. Desperation drove him, and he wanted—no, needed—to lose himself in her and forget everything else.

He thrust his tongue deep in her mouth, wanting to become part of her any way he could. With an eagerness he hadn't expected, she gave of herself and molded against him, looping her arms around the back of his neck to steady herself. He shoved the shawl from her shoulders, letting it drop to the floor, and now there was no more than a thin layer of linen over her body and beneath his hands.

His hands: damnation, he could not keep his hands from her. He could feel the heat of her skin through the linen, and the way her soft flesh filled his palms as she pressed against him. He pulled her tight against the front of his breeches so she could feel his hard cock and how much he desired her.

"This is how much I want you, Gus, how much I need you," he said roughly, moving against her. "This is how hard you make me every time I'm near you."

"Yes," she whispered, a breathy sigh against his ear. "I've missed you, Harry. I've missed *all* of you."

She shimmied against him wantonly, and he kissed her hard again, what little control he had left fraying by the second.

"Then come upstairs with me," he whispered urgently. "Now, to my bedchamber. No one will know."

She looked at him, her eyes heavy-lidded with desire, yet still shook her head.

"I shouldn't, Harry," she said reluctantly. "Tomorrow's the wedding, and I promised I'd behave until then."

"Damnation, this isn't about *behaving*, Gus," he said roughly, and kissed her again. How else could he make her understand? To have her with him now, tonight, was exactly what he needed most, and blindly he yanked at the drawstring closing her nightgown's neck, pulling it open and down. He cupped his hand around her breast and tugged gently at the nipple. At once it tightened into a furled bud beneath his fingers. He tugged harder, caressing her breast at the same time, and she whimpered into his mouth and arched her back, shamelessly pressing her breast against his hand for more.

Suddenly a wedge of candlelight cut across the floor not far from where they stood. He heard Wetherby's voice, singing some lewd doggerel verse, and his own father's laughter, all coming closer by the second.

Gus heard it, too. She gasped with alarm, pushed herself free of him, and bent to pick up her shawl while he swore with frustration. Once they were wed, he'd make sure that every single room in his house had a lock so that he could enjoy his wife any time and way he chose without any meddlesome interfering.

She seized the candlestick and darted forward, around the corner, to intercept the others.

"Is that you, Gus?" Wetherby asked as he and Father came into the hall. "What are you doing about at this hour?"

"There was a small fuss in the kitchen that needed my attention," she said. "It's all resolved now."

Harry stood in the shadows, breathing hard. He should be the one defending her, not skulking here like a powerless coward. Yet if he stepped forward now, she'd be the one shamed before their fathers, leaving Harry no choice but to remain where he was. He could see her from the back, the very picture of bridal innocence, her head slightly bowed, her shawl wrapped tightly around her shoulders, and the candlestick in her hand. The nightgown revealed just a hint of her delectably round bottom, and he barely stifled a groan of frustration.

"Trust you to make certain everything's settled for the night," Wetherby said proudly, "and the day before your own wedding, too. Ah, Gus, what shall I do without you? I hope that young Harry understands the prize I'm giving up to him."

"I believe he does, Papa," she said. "But to me, Harry's the real prize."

Her father sighed deeply. "Then he's the most fortunate gentleman in England, Gus. Come, then, let me see you to your room for the last time. Hah, how I hate to say that!"

She joined him, the light from her candle fading away as together they walked up the stairs.

Harry stood against the wall until he was sure they were gone, letting the darkness settle around him. Then, finally, he took his crutch and made his slow way to his own room, with only his thoughts and despair for company.

"*I know* they say that every bride's a beauty on her wedding day," Julia said, watching as Gus stood before her looking glass for the last time. "But you truly *are* beautiful today, Gus, and I vow I never thought I'd say that."

Gus smiled, for she'd never thought she'd hear her sister say that, either. But Julia was right: today she was beautiful, and not even she could find fault with herself. Her gown was breathtaking, white silk with gold and silver embroidery that sparkled in the morning sunlight. Over the widest hoops she'd ever worn, the gown's spreading skirts were trimmed with silver silk ribbons and little puffs of golden gauze, centered with white silk flowers, and deep flounces of lace fell gracefully below her elbows. Even the duchess had had to admit that the mantua maker from Norwich had done better than anyone had expected.

She wore her mother's pearl earrings, a gift this morning from Papa that had made her cry, and around her throat and wrists were the diamonds that Harry had had delivered to her this morning, another gift that had made her weep. The necklace and twin bracelets were magnificent pieces that truly were worthy of a peeress, but what had touched Gus far more was the card he'd enclosed, telling her the pieces had belonged to his mother, and how honored she'd be to see them now on her new daughter-in-law. That made Gus feel as if the two mothers, though gone, would be with her in church, and what better blessing could she have than that?

"How odd it is to think that by noon I shall have to call you 'my lady,' " Julia said. "Lady Augusta Fitzroy, Countess of Hargreave!"

"It sounds very grand, doesn't it?" Gus said, trying to swallow her nervousness. She knew that as a bride, she was supposed to be the center of attention, but she wasn't comfortable with it, and she longed for the day to be done so she could simply be alone with Harry.

"Someday—though not too soon, I pray!—you'll be the Duchess of Breconridge, too," the current duchess said. "Then the only other woman in Britain that you'll have to curtsey to will be Her Majesty herself."

That was far too much for Gus to consider now. "Has anyone seen Harry this morning?" she asked anxiously. "Is he ready, too?"

"I have," Julia said. "He's already left for the church, looking solemn and handsome as sin itself, though perhaps a bit pale. I'd wager he's nervous."

"What cause for nervousness could he possibly have?" the duchess asked. "He loves Augusta, and she loves him, and there's no better grounds for a happy marriage. If he's pale, it's likely because the other gentlemen poured far too much liquor down his throat last night in the name of bachelor sport."

Gus nodded. Harry hadn't seemed drunk at all when she'd seen him last night in the hall. But the curious humor that had plagued him all afternoon and evening had remained, a dark, possessive, almost angry mood that seemed to have no reason or cause. She wished he were happier for their wedding, but perhaps it was simply the way he showed his nervousness—though Harry had always seemed so self-assured that she'd a difficult time imagining him being nervous about anything, even their wedding. If how he'd kissed her last night was any indication, he certainly wasn't nervous about their wedding night.

"There's the carriage," Julia said, gazing out the window, "and Papa's down there as well, already giving orders to the poor driver. Oh, how fine the footmen look, Gus! Every one of them has a white flower pinned to his livery coat and another to his hat, and even the driver has a white bow on his whip, all in your honor. If you're ready, we should go down."

"I'm ready," Gus said as firmly as she could, as much to convince herself as anyone else. She took her bouquet from Mary, praying that no one else could see how the flowers—roses from Mama's garden—trembled in her hands.

Her heart was racing so fast that she felt nearly lightheaded, and it didn't calm as she walked down the stairs and into her father's carriage for the final time as Miss Augusta Wetherby. It raced still as they drove to the little church on the edge of the abbey's lands, and as she walked down the aisle she was sure she would have toppled if she hadn't had Papa's support. Only the two families were gathered to witness the service, yet even their familiar faces were a blur to her.

Then Harry took her hand. Harry, her Harry, solemn and impossibly handsome, his blue eyes bright with love and desire.

He leaned down to her, whispering so that no one else heard.

"My own dear Gus," he said. "I thought I couldn't possibly love you more, but I do."

She smiled, the joy swelling up within her to take away every doubt and fear. His hand was her lifeline, the same as hers had been to him, and she clung to it, never wanting to lose him or his support.

The rest passed with a speed that astonished her. The ceremony, the new gold ring on her finger, the toasts and the bride cake, the tears and hugs as they said good-bye, the servants standing in a line on the drive to wish her farewell as she and Harry were driven away in his carriage, and her last glimpse of the only home she'd ever known.

She sat back against the pale leather seats and looked down at her hand, still holding tightly to his. She was Harry's wife now, and he was her husband, for better or worse, for richer or poorer, in sickness and in health, as long as they both shall live. They were *married*. There was no turning back now, and with a tremulous smile she raised her lips to kiss him.

CHAPTER
12

"Here we are," Harry said as the carriage slowed before the inn. "About damned time, too."

Under ordinary circumstances, he would have driven straight through to London, stopping only for fresh horses and meals. But because this was his wedding night and, for Gus's sake, he'd decided not to spend it in a lurching coach. He'd made arrangements for them to stop for the night in Mildenhall, about thirty miles and six hours into their journey.

The Ox & Plough was a tolerable inn on the market cross, and while it was hardly the most romantic of places, the innkeeper was a forthright fellow—and, more important, his wife was a stern taskmistress. The beds would be fresh and the food acceptable, which was the best one could ever hope for on a public road. Besides, Harry expected that he and Gus would be so enamored with each other that the amenities wouldn't really matter.

But he hadn't counted on the toll that thirty miles and six hours of riding in a coach—even his well-appointed coach—would take on his leg. As the afternoon had worn on, the jostling of the road had made the barely healed bones ache as badly as they had weeks ago, with each bump and jar reminding him yet again of how disappointing a husband he must be. He had tried to continue as usual with Gus, but he'd been relieved when she'd fallen asleep against his shoulder and he'd no longer had to pretend.

"Where are we?" she asked, groggy, as she slowly sat upright.

"Mildenhall," he said. "We're stopping here for the night."

"Good," she said, reaching for her hat from the seat beside her. "I never thought I'd be so weary from simply sitting in a carriage all afternoon. How is your leg?"

"Perfectly fine," he lied, not wanting her sympathy, not today. "I'm looking forward to supper. Among other things."

She smiled and blushed. "It's our first time among strangers as husband and wife. Do you think anyone will know we're just married?"

"They will," he said as the carriage stopped in the inn's yard, "because they're expecting us. You're a Fitzroy now, Gus, and you'll soon learn we don't do anything halfway."

Already the inn's stablemen were hurrying toward the carriage, and Greene, the innkeeper, was striding out to greet them, too, the green apron that marked both his trade and his name flapping in the breeze, while other guests appeared at windows and doors to gape at the titled newcomers. There was nothing like a carriage with gilding on the wheels and a noble crest painted on the door to draw attention in a stable yard, and he wanted Gus to enjoy the attention that her new status brought her.

But right now she did not appear to be enjoying it at all. "Goodness," she murmured, her eyes round and serious. "All those people wish to see us?"

"It's you they wish to see," he said proudly. "They know you're the new Countess of Hargreave. Everyone loves a new bride."

"I hope they will not be disappointed when they see

me," she said, her voice small as she sat back against the squabs and away from the window.

"Of course they won't be disappointed," he said, surprised she'd say such a thing. To his eyes, she had never looked more lovely or stylish than she had today, first in that golden gown for the wedding, and now in her traveling habit, a brilliant plum merino that made her gray eyes sparkle like silver, and that fitted her curving figure in such a way as to make her waist very small and her breasts temptingly full. He completely approved.

Her hat reminded him of some Frenchified confection, covered with white silk bows like whipped cream, and large amethyst and diamond earrings—another of his wedding gifts to her—hung from her ears. Earlier her hair had been crimped into tight, stylish curls, doubtless by her well-meaning lady's maid, but while they traveled the elaborate curls had fallen, and her hair was simply straight and a little mussed, the way he liked it best.

All in all, he thought she looked charming and utterly delectable, and as happy as he was to show her off, he couldn't wait until they were at last alone, and he'd have her to himself.

"You must believe me, Gus," he said firmly as the footmen began unlatching the carriage door and folding down the steps. "I will be the envy of every man here."

She smiled, a tentative smile, but a smile nonetheless, and leaned forward to kiss him quickly. "I love you, Harry."

He kissed her back and winked. "I love you, too, sweetheart."

The door opened, footmen in livery standing on either side, and a crowd of expectant faces beyond them. Damnation, he'd been so busy reassuring Gus that he'd forgotten the trial he'd now face himself. He must step down from the carriage ahead of her, turn, and hand her down, too. It was one of the simplest routines of good manners, and one he'd done for so long with the ladies in his family that he gave it no thought.

But it was simple when he'd had two good legs, not one, nor relying on a crutch at that. Of course his footmen would be there to keep him from falling flat on his face, but that was humiliating in itself, having to be helped down like a doddering graybeard.

And blast it, Gus knew it, too, better than anyone else.

"Would you like me to go first?" she asked gently. "Then you can lean on me to settle your balance."

"Thank you, no," he said curtly, his pride winning over his gratitude. "I shall manage."

He took a deep breath and stood, bracing himself on the frame of the carriage's door. The folding steps were small and narrow, never the most stable of arrangements. He reached behind him for the crutch from the seat, and she handed it to him, making sure he'd a firm grip before she let go. He felt as if every person in the yard was holding their breath, waiting for him to fail, and fall.

Every person but his wife.

"Go on, Harry," she said quietly behind him. "You're the bravest man I know, and you'll be fine."

He could do this. Blast it, he *could*. He took another deep breath, placed the end of the crutch on the first step, and hopped down one step, then two, and then he was safely on the ground. Then he turned, and as gallantly as he could, held his hand out to Gus.

She was frozen on the step, her expression fixed and tight with trepidation beneath the frothy hat. He took her hand, giving it a gentle squeeze.

"Courage, Countess," he said softly. "I didn't fall in love with a coward."

She glanced down at him sharply, and for one dreadful moment he wondered if he'd teased too hard. Then she grinned at him, her entire face lighting up like sunshine. She smiled, and everyone in the crowd smiled as well. She stepped lightly down the steps then, deftly managing her skirts and hoops as if she'd been doing this all her life.

A small girl in a snow-white cap and apron was pushed to the front of the crowd. In one hand was a large bouquet of flowers tied with white ribbons, a bouquet that wobbled dangerously toward the ground as the girl made a quick, jerky curtsey in front of Gus.

"My lady," she said, thrusting the bouquet upward. "For you, my lady, with our regards and best wishes upon your marriage."

Harry smiled, delighted by the tribute for Gus's sake. He expected her to take the bouquet and move on, as most ladies would. But instead she crouched down to the child's level, heedless of her silk petticoats in the yard's dust.

"Thank you so much, lamb," she said, her smile warm as she accepted the bouquet. "What is your name?"

The little girl glanced back over her shoulder, clearly seeking the approval of some adult in the crowd before she replied.

"Ann Greene, my lady," she said finally.

"I am most honored to make your acquaintance, Miss Ann Greene, and very grateful for the flowers," Gus said. She drew the largest flower from the bouquet, and handed it to Ann. "Will you please keep this, and think of me on your own wedding day?"

Ann nodded and took the flower gingerly by the stem. Then she curtseyed again and fled back into the crowd. As Gus rose, those nearest chuckled with pleasure and began to applaud the new countess, and soon a swell of cheers was added. Gus smiled and blushed, and took Harry's arm once again.

"Well done, sweetheart, well done," he said to her, proud of her in a thousand ways. "You couldn't have been better. I believe that was the innkeeper's daughter, too."

"I hope I didn't frighten the child," she said with concern. "If a countess had spoken to me when I was that age, I would have perished from fright."

"Then I'm grateful no countesses ventured into your young life, or you wouldn't be here now," he said, steering her toward the inn's door. After nearly a week of keeping apart from her, he relished being able to touch her again, even in little ways, a hand curling around her waist, a palm gently placed on the small of her back. "Come, I'm famished. I recall they have a respectable bill of fare here."

"Good day, my lord, and welcome," said the innkeeper, hurrying to bow before them as soon as they stepped inside. "May I offer my congratulations to you both on this happy day?"

"Thank you," Gus said. "Your daughter is charming."

"I thank you for saying so, my lady, I thank you very much," Greene said, bowing again. "She's a good girl, she is. Now, my lord, regarding your rooms. Everything is in readiness, exactly as you wished. Our very best bedchamber, on the west corner and overlooking the churchyard for a most peaceable night, connecting to a small parlor useful for receiving visitors."

"Excellent," Harry said, eager to be done with this talking and alone with Gus. "We'll take possession of them directly. Our servants should be arriving shortly with the baggage, and I'll ask you to show them upstairs as well."

"Very well, my lord," Greene said, clearly hesitating. "Pray forgive me, my lord, but I wish to accommodate you and her ladyship in a way that is most agreeable to you. When you requested the corner bedchamber, I thought only of obliging your wishes. However, my lord, now that I see the extent of your, ah, your infirmity, why, I—"

"My 'infirmity'?" Harry repeated, instantly on edge.

"Yes, my lord," Greene said, pointedly staring down at Harry's leg. "I only wish to make things easy for you, my lord, and when I see how you labor, why, I cannot recommend the original rooms on account of the stairs and the distance—"

"I do not *labor*," Harry said. He could feel his face flush and his voice grow louder and more angry, things he did not wish to do but seemed incapable of stopping. Yet he felt convinced that everyone within the tavern, porters and serving maids and guests as well, was staring at his leg and the crutch, just as they'd done when he'd been outside, and it unsettled him. "Your presumptions regarding my injury are not welcome, Mr. Greene."

Greene ducked his head, still determined to please. "Forgive me, my lord, I meant no insult," he said. "But if you wish to keep the corner rooms, I can arrange for a chair to be carried up the stairs, and—"

"No chair," Harry said, horrified by the image of being lugged up the stairs like an old trunk. "Damnation, man, I am not some infernal *cripple*!"

Gus lay her little gloved hand on his arm. "Harry, please," she said. "He means no insult to you. He's only trying—"

"I know what he's trying to do," he said, "and he needn't do it any longer. He should show us to our rooms directly, or we'll find lodgings elsewhere."

"Forgive me, my lord, but that will not be necessary," Greene said, bowing his head with defeat. "This way, if you please, my lady, my lord."

He led them down a short hall to the staircase—a long, steep staircase, far steeper than any he'd climbed at Wetherby. Harry stared up it, realizing the enormity of the task he'd just set for himself.

"It's pure stubbornness, you know," Gus said mildly

beside him. "You can change your mind, and no one will fault you for it."

"It's confidence, Gus, not stubbornness." He was, of course, being stubborn, but he would not admit it, and now he'd no choice but to climb the damned stairs.

"Very well," she said. "May I walk with you, or will you insist on making your martyr's climb alone?"

"Please yourself," he said, ignoring the part about being a martyr. "I'll not stop you."

Greene had paused on the steps, patiently waiting for them to follow. Harry didn't want anyone waiting for him, ever, and resolutely he began up the stairs. It was hard work, even harder than he'd anticipated, and he hated how he had to lurch and hop up each step like a lopsided crab, hanging to the rail. Even worse was how others in a greater hurry, up and down, were forced to squeeze past him with muttered apologies.

Only Gus followed. He didn't look back to see her, but he knew she was there, silently measuring her steps to match his. He hated that, too: not that she followed him, but that he was limiting her, holding her back, when the two of them should be laughing and racing up these stairs together to their bedchamber. His frustration and resentment built with each step, and by the time he finally reached the top landing, he was breathing as hard as if he'd truly climbed a mountain. Beneath his coat, his shirt was plastered with sweat to his back.

"This way, my lord," said Greene, waiting at the landing, his face so full of pity that Harry longed to strike him with his crutch. "Only a bit farther, my lord."

Harry bit back an oath and followed, doing better now that they were done with the stairs. At least Greene hadn't been exaggerating to make him feel better: their rooms were only a short distance more, and the innkeeper unlocked the door and opened it with a flourish.

"Our best rooms, my lady, my lord," he said proudly. "I hope they suit?"

"Oh, yes, thank you, Mr. Greene," Gus said, beaming. "This is splendid. And the flowers! Surely those are your wife's doing. Please thank her for me."

The room was exactly as Harry had hoped, airy and pleasant for an inn, and most of all tidy and clean, with bare floors well swept and a sizable bed filling much of the room. In honor of their newlywed status, there was a large pitcher filled with flowers in the center of the table. It was awkwardly arranged, but since Gus was pleased, he was grudgingly pleased as well. At least the flowers made the place smell sweet.

"Thank you, my lady," Greene said with obvious relief. "Is there anything else?"

"We would like supper sent up directly," Gus said briskly, tugging off her gloves and unpinning her hat. "His lordship would like two beef chops, browned but not overcooked, with a pot of mustard besides. As for the rest, I shall trust you to bring the very best of your day's fare with the very best of your wines, and as swiftly as possible. My husband is quite hungry after our journey."

The innkeeper bowed and hurried off, and as soon as the door was closed behind him Gus came and slipped her arms inside Harry's coat and around his waist.

"Here we are, husband," she said playfully. "Alone together in the best room of an inn. It makes me feel vastly wicked."

"That was what it was supposed to do," Harry said, then sighed and eased free of her, dropping heavily into a nearby armchair.

Gus frowned. "Did I overstep by ordering your supper? Was there something you'd rather have had than the chops?"

"Why should I object?" he said. "You know my tastes as well as anyone by now."

He took off his hat and tossed it onto the bed, wiping his sleeve across his brow. The trial on the stairs had left him weary and disgusted with himself, and in no humor to play a proper bridegroom. He wished to wash and change his clothes, requiring his servant, who was inconveniently not there.

"What the devil is keeping Tewkes?" he asked, struggling to pull his arms from the sleeves of his coat while sitting. "They should have been close behind us."

"Perhaps he and Mary ran off together to Calais," she said, helping him pull his coat off the rest of the way and folding it neatly, as neatly as Tewkes himself would have done. "I'm sure they'll be here as soon as they can. Your carriage was much the faster without the baggage."

"*Our* carriage," he corrected, knowing he should thank her but feeling so out of sorts that he didn't, which made him feel worse. "It's yours, too, considering you're now my wife."

"However could I forget?" she asked, leaning over to kiss him, lightly brushing her lips over his.

He hadn't believed he was in the mood for kissing, but she was both irresistible and persistent. He also hadn't realized how exciting it could be to have her kissing him, and he let himself enjoy it, letting her coax his lips apart and deepen the kiss until he couldn't help himself, and reached up to rest his hand on her waist. She took that as invitation enough to sit on the arm of his chair, which then led naturally to her sliding a little farther down and onto his lap, and a much more favorable position for kissing.

Until, that is, the knock on the door interrupted them, and she quickly—too quickly—hopped up.

"That must be supper," she said cheerfully. "Enter."

To Harry's dismay, three servants marched in carrying

trays with sufficient food and drink to feed an entire household.

"You didn't have to let them in, you know," Harry said as the servants began setting the table with supper. "You could have sent them away."

"I could have," Gus said serenely, sitting across from him at the table, "but then I recalled that you are famished, and I did not wish you disappointed or unhappy."

"Oh, no," he said, thinking of how much he'd liked having her kiss him. "I'm not that."

But he would have to admit—not that he did—he was indeed hungry, and the food was much better than he'd expected. The chops in particular were exactly as he liked them, even down to the mustard on the side, and he silently marveled over how she'd achieved that precise way of bringing him such comfort. By the time the meal was done and the servants had cleared away everything but the wine, he found she'd made him forget everything that had spoiled this afternoon, and remember only how much he loved her. No wonder he also found his mood much improved.

Apparently so did she.

"You must be unfamished now," she said, sitting across from him with a half-drunk glass of wine in her hand. Even by the candlelight, her cheeks were pink, charmingly so, and her eyes were bright and silvery. He suspected the cause was the wine, but he also hoped at least a fraction of it was due to him.

"Altogether unfamished," he said, "but not sated."

She chuckled, a deep, throaty chuckle that he didn't think he'd heard from her before, but found thoroughly enticing. It couldn't all be the wine, could it?

"Sated," she repeated, pronouncing it with relish. "That always sounds like such a wicked word, when all it really means is satisfied."

"Everything seems wicked to you this evening," he said, teasing. "First this room, and now mere words."

"But inns do seem wicked," she protested. "People coming and going at all hours, using false names, embarking on mysterious business and liaisons."

"What manner of inns does your father frequent?" he said, laughing. "All the ones where I've stayed have been very dull and respectable affairs by comparison."

She ducked her chin and sipped her wine, her amethyst earrings bobbing against her cheeks.

"Perhaps I exaggerate a little," she admitted. "I do not know for certain about false names and mysterious business. But once when Father had taken us down to London, we stayed in a room next to an amorous couple who were very noisy, thumping the bedstead against the wall and moaning and crying out all the night long. Papa was incensed, and banged against the wall to try to shame them into stopping. When they didn't, he made Julia and me wrap scarves around our heads so our maiden ears wouldn't hear the racketing."

"But you did hear," he said, intrigued.

"Of course we did." She leaned over the table toward him and lowered her voice to a completely unnecessary confidential whisper. "Julia fell asleep, but I slipped the scarf away from my ears so I could listen. I'd no real notion of what exactly the people were doing, but I could tell they were enjoying themselves. The sounds they made were *exciting*."

"Indeed," he said, amused and aroused by the thought of her eavesdropping on some anonymous couple's lovemaking. "You say that as if you're excited now from remembering."

It didn't take much perception to make that guess, but the way she grinned and pressed her hand briefly over her mouth showed exactly how good a guess it had been.

"There's only one thing to be done, then," he said,

pushing his chair back from the table. "We must try making some noises of our own."

She pushed her chair back, too, and came toward him, stopping just out of his reach.

"Because Mary has not yet arrived," she said, beginning to unbutton the neat row of buttons on her habit's jacket, "I fear I must undress myself. I trust you will not mind it."

"I'll overlook it this time." Damnation, he was already hard in his breeches, and all she'd shown him was the white linen blouse, cut like a man's shirt, beneath her jacket. She shrugged it off her shoulders, turning the sleeves right-side out and beginning to match the seams to fold it.

"Drop it," he ordered. "To the floor. A truly wicked minx wouldn't bother with folding."

She looked momentarily surprised, then did as he asked and dropped the jacket, the metal buttons clinking lightly on the floorboards.

"You called me a minx," she said as she unbuttoned the cuffs of her blouse. "Is that what you think I am?"

"Most times I'll think of you as my wife," he said, "but tonight I believe you're a minx. A wicked, wicked minx."

She laughed, pulling the shirt free of her waistband and then, in a single sweeping move, drawing it over her head and letting it float to the floor. Next she untied the petticoat that went with her habit, and the one beneath, and let them fall into a ring of crushed silk around her ankles. Daintily she stepped free, now clad only in her shift, her stays, and her hoops.

He sighed. She would be absolutely captivating if she weren't wearing the hoops, ugly rings of linen-covered cane that hung like drums around her waist.

"Hoops," he said. "Why the devil do ladies insist on wearing those things?"

"To support our skirts to the fashionable width," she said promptly. "Julia says I'll be scorned as a dowdy if I don't wear them all the time in London."

He sighed again. London would come soon enough, and he'd no wish to think of it just yet.

"Since I do not wish you scorned in any way," he said, "feel free to wear them in public. But at home with me, I would be heartily grateful if I never saw them around your waist again."

"Agreed," she said, untying the hoops and tossing them onto the pile of her other clothes. "I don't like wearing them, either. They make me feel clumsy and ungainly."

"Not you," he murmured, distracted. He didn't like hoops, but he did like stays, especially the ones she was wearing now. Covered in some sort of flowery dark red silk, they raised her breasts up for his approval, and narrowed her waist. Beneath them she wore only a knee-length shift of linen so fine that it revealed the darker hair at the juncture of her thighs, with her legs in pale blue stockings and red garters, and little shoes on curving heels.

For the first time she stepped close to him. She turned around to present her back and the zigzagging lacing of her stays, as well as her delightfully rounded bottom.

"I'm sorry to have to ask you to unlace me," she said, "and I don't know if, being a gentleman, you'll even know how to undo the lacing knots."

"I'll try," he said, seeing little use in revealing exactly how much experience he had in unlacing stays, and quickly, too. "But I believe the light will be better on the other side of the room."

She twisted about to look over her shoulder. "Nearer to the bed?"

"Exactly," he said, standing. "And you doubted you were a minx."

It took him a while to reach the bed, not because of

his leg, but because in the course of crossing the room she managed to divest him of his neckcloth and waistcoat, and to untuck his shirt from his breeches as well. When at last he sat on the edge of the bed, she insisted on taking off his shoes and his stockings, and had untied his splinted brace as well.

"There," she said, kicking off her own shoes. "Now we're almost even."

"Not quite," he said, pulling her closer between his knees and turning her around. "Not until you're rid of this."

Deftly he undid the knot in the lacing, then took his time drawing it through the eyelets to torment her. At last the lace pulled free and her stays slipped forward, away from her chest. She shrugged them forward from her shoulders to drop heavily to the floor, and as she did he reached forward to cup her breasts in his hands.

She gasped, then sighed with pleasure, swaying back toward him as he teased her nipples into stiff little peaks. He kissed her nape before he trailed more kisses along the side of her throat to the sensitive place behind her ear. She shuddered with delight, her lips parted and her breathing ragged.

"Are you feeling wicked yet, sweetheart?" he whispered into her ear.

"Oh, yes," she said, the words barely audible.

"Good," he said, tugging a little harder on her nipples as he caressed her breasts. "Now take down your hair for me."

She gave an impatient small shake to her head. "Now, Harry?"

"Now," he said. "Or else I'll stop."

Quickly she raised her hands to her hair and began to pull the pins that held it in place, letting them, too, drop and scatter to the floor. Finally her hair tumbled down, and she shook it free around her shoulders, a shining curtain of hair that smelled of lavender, a scent he always now associated with her.

"There," she said, turning around to face him. "Now it shall be my turn to order you about, Harry. You're still wearing far too many clothes for my tastes, beginning with this shirt."

She unfastened the buttons at his throat and the diamond shirt buckle besides, and the buttons on each cuff in turn. He loved how serious her expression had become, how determined she was even as she looked as wanton as a woman could, her hair loose and her shift pulled down beneath her breasts. God help him, he'd never tire of her breasts, and he reached for her again.

"Not yet," she said, chuckling and wriggling free. "I told you, it's my turn now."

She slipped her hands beneath the hem of his billowing shirt and up his torso, her palms sliding across his belly and up his chest. He loved seeing the look of delight on her face as she explored him, and he loved even more how she touched him, her little hands eager and curious. Laughing, she finally pulled the shirt up and over his head, and he loved the greedy expression on her face, too, just before she kissed him.

But what she began as a playful kiss soon turned into something more urgent, more raw. His kissed her hard, his mouth desperate for the tenderness of her lips. He swept his tongue deep into her mouth, his first possession of her, and felt how in response she clung to him, pressing her body against his, her breasts against his bare chest, skin against skin. That was enough for him; they'd dallied too long, and his need was too demanding to wait any longer.

"My turn," he said, his voice rough with wanting, and before she could protest he swept her shift over her head and off as well. He drew in his breath, stunned by how beautiful and desirable she was, far beyond his imaginings. Her full, ripe breasts rose and fell with her rapid breath, and he'd bruised her lips to ruddy fullness with his kissing. She was dusted with freckles everywhere on her pale skin, and her cheeks and chest were flushed with her arousal. She tossed her hair back over her shoulders and restlessly shifted her thighs together, seeking ease from the longing he'd built between her legs. He understood: His cock was like iron in his breeches, his balls taut with need.

She smiled, suddenly shy, and curled her hair behind her ear, an unconsciously seductive gesture that drove him wild.

"All you've left me with now are my stockings and garters," she protested, her voice husky and low, "whilst you still have your breeches."

"Not for long," he said, tearing the buttons open and shoving his breeches from his hips.

His cock sprang free, hard and ready and done being patient. He hooked his arm around her waist and pulled her up onto the bed. She fell back with a gasp of surprise, her hair fanning out on the sheets and her breasts bouncing. She pushed herself back up on her elbows to watch him climb onto the bed with her.

"I still have my stockings," she said, raising one leg to begin untying her garters.

"Leave them," he ordered. "I like them as they are."

He did like them, the bright scarlet ribbons tied below her knees, red against white skin. She hadn't yet lowered her leg entirely and he caught it, kissing the inside of her knee above the garter as he knelt between her legs.

Watching him, she shivered and wrinkled her nose. "That tickles, Harry."

"Does it now?" he said, unable to resist giving her one last little nip. "Bend your knees and spread them for me, and I'll show you something that doesn't."

She obeyed instantly, her eyes heavy-lidded with anticipation, and he couldn't resist kissing her again, his mouth grinding over hers. He took her by the hips and pulled her closer so that he was settled between her wide-spread thighs. She was rosy and wet with arousal, the proof that all their little games had been as exciting for her as they'd been for him. He rubbed the head of his cock along her opening and she sighed, her eyes widening at the sensation. Restlessly she canted her hips up, sliding along his length in invitation with a whimper of longing.

"You're so damned hot, Gus," he growled, pulling her closer and setting his cock at her opening. "I want to stop and enjoy this, but I can't hold back, not when you're like this."

He grasped her firmly by the thighs, opening her wider, and settled his cock between her lips. She was wet and hot, weeping for him, and this time when he thrust into her, she gasped with only pleasure. Three quick strokes and he was buried deep, and there was no other place in Creation he wished to be.

He kissed her hungrily, and she responded, her hands moving up and down along his back.

"Oh, please, Harry, don't stop," she whispered, her expression feverish as she spurred him onward. "Please, please, don't ever stop!"

It was encouragement he didn't need, not with her. He slipped her thighs over his arms and she curled her legs over his back, the silk of her stockings rasping seductively against his skin. Relentlessly he drove into her, nearly pulling out with each thrust, only to plunge back into her depths. She writhed beneath him, her breasts jolting and her hips rocking up to meet him. With each thrust she let out a breathy little cry of abandoned joy that was the most intoxicating sound he'd ever heard.

"My God, Gus, you're good," he muttered, grunting with each thrust. "So good."

"Don't—don't stop," she pleaded, panting as she clung to his shoulders. "Oh, Harry, *please.*"

He could feel his cods tightening as he came close to spending, and he drove her harder, faster, as her cries came louder in his ear. The blood pounded in his head, and every muscle in his body strained. Everything narrowed to only Gus, and his desperation to lose himself in her. In a frenzy he pushed harder, and as he did, he felt her convulse around his cock.

She cried out one last time as release swept her away, her fingers digging into his back as she arched and shuddered with the force of it. With that, his own crisis exploded as well, and with a roar, he emptied himself into her, pumping hard, until at last he sank down beside her, burying his face in her lavender-scented hair. He was spent, exhausted, as winded as if he'd just run from Norwich himself. He didn't care. He'd found Heaven, and he was in no hurry to leave.

Still breathing hard, he pushed himself up to gaze down on her face. Her eyes were closed, her lashes feathering over her rounded cheeks, and her own breath only now beginning to calm. He kissed the bridge of her nose, just to remind her he was there with her. Her eyes fluttered open and she smiled, a blissful, slightly crooked smile.

"Oh, Harry," she said, her voice a delightful croak. "I have no words."

"You don't need any," he said, kissing her forehead, her cheeks, her chin. Her skin tasted salty; he thought it was delicious. "Not now."

Wanting to relieve his weight on her, he rolled onto his back, pulling her with him to lie on his chest. That made her laugh, and she sprawled shameless over him, letting her legs tangle with his.

"Happy?" he asked.

"Umm," she said, the picture of contentment, and idly traced her fingertip along his jaw. "I am *sated.*"

He chuckled, spreading his fingers to curve comfortably around her bottom. "Sated and spent, I'd wager. I'd also wager that if we'd any neighbors in the next room, they'd have heard you the same as you heard those other lovers years ago."

"Hah, they'll have heard you, too," she said. "But it doesn't matter, Harry. We're married."

"Because we're married, it matters very much," he said. He took her wandering fingertip and kissed it. "Few husbands are as fortunate as I am."

She smiled down at him, her smile wobbling, and he reached up to brush the first tear that trickled down her cheek. "What, because you married a minx?"

"No, Gus," he said softly, drawing her down to kiss. "Because I married the one woman in the world that I love the most."

CHAPTER
13

It was long past nightfall when their carriage finally rumbled into Grosvenor Square, and with anticipation and a little trepidation Gus looked from the window for her first glimpse of her new home.

They had tarried an extra two days longer than planned at the inn in Mildenhall, for the simple but excellent reason that they'd been unable to tear themselves from the bed. For those three nights and two days, they'd done nothing but make love, with a smattering of eating and sleeping. It had been the most glorious way to begin their married life together, and Gus had been very sorry when they'd finally left early this morning. She'd been even more sorry as the day and their journey had dragged on. The closer they drew to London, the more crowded the roads became and the slower their progress had become. Harry's mood and conversation also declined precipitously as the day went on, and by the time they'd finally reached the city, he was nearly silent. She knew it was all due to his leg, and the strain of the long day in the carriage—not that he'd admit it, not even to her—but she'd enough butterflies of her own that she wistfully wished he'd been able to offer her even a little reassurance.

She had only been in London three times before, the last time being four years ago. She remembered it as being enormous, with street after street of houses, churches, and other fine buildings, noisy, and so filled with an astonishing number of people that she'd been relieved to return to her quiet home in Norfolk.

Now London would be her home. She and Harry would also be expected to spend several months of the year at Breconridge Hall, his father's home in Hampshire, but this house in Grosvenor Square belonged entirely to Harry.

And now to her as well.

"It's the second house, there, with the white stone front," Harry said beside her. "Does it suit you?"

"How could it not, Harry?" she said, staring up at the house as the tired horses stopped before it. The house was larger than she'd expected—much larger than Aunt Agatha's, the only other London house she'd visited—four stories in height with three bays of windows, and a handsome doorway with an oversized arched entryway. By the light of the lanterns outside, it seemed elegant but severe, almost chilly, and a far cry from the cheerfully old-fashioned abbey. "But it does seem large for just you."

"It was always intended for only one person," he said, looking over her shoulder. "Father built it as a dower house for my mother, intending it for her when he died. But because she died first, he leased it until I came of age, and then he gave it to me. Now it's ours. Come, let's go inside. I've had enough of this damned carriage."

The front hall of the house was tall and narrow and very grand, with a sweeping stair and a floor of black-and-white-patterned marble. At the top of the first landing was an arched alcove, and in it stood a white marble statue of an ancient goddess, like some ghostly stone sentinel.

The servants were waiting for them in a row to greet them: butler, cook, three footmen, and two maids. Harry presented them with such haste and disinterest that Gus couldn't begin to catch their names. But she smiled as warmly as she could at their bows and curtseys, and resolved that tomorrow there'd be plenty of time to learn names and duties, as well as begin reviewing accounts.

She could tell she'd have her work cut out for her. Seven servants were not nearly sufficient staff for a house of this size, and she could already see a dozen warning signs, from dust rolling beneath the hall chairs to woodwork in need of polishing. It was clear that the bachelor master had let things slide, and she couldn't wait to make the changes to improve Harry's house for him. *That* she knew how to do.

"There's one parlor in there," Harry said, waving a hand toward one tall set of double doors, "and another behind it, plus the dining room and the library on this floor. Upstairs there's a gallery, a ballroom, and the usual bedchambers. I'll show you all tomorrow, when we're both not so wicked tired. Besides, it all looks much more agreeable in the daylight."

He was already making his way up the stairs, one step at a time. Although he wasn't complaining—he never did—she could tell by the way he grimaced at each step how much his leg was bothering him after they'd spent nearly fifteen hours traveling. She knew better than to say anything about it, however, and in silence she climbed beside him, measuring her steps to match his.

At the landing he stopped in front of the marble goddess, nearly out of breath, and pointed to the left. Though she stood directly in front of him, he pointedly looked past her.

"The countess's bedchamber and rooms are at the end of that hallway," he said. "Your maid should have already arranged your things for the night."

Gus frowned, not liking the way this was heading. "And where, pray, is the earl's bedchamber?"

He turned to look in the opposite direction. "Down there."

"That would seem to me to be an unconscionable distance apart," she said, setting her hands on her hips. "I would not expect you to share my dressing room with my clothing and things strewn all about, but no husband and wife should be so far removed from each other each night."

"It is the most common arrangement in town," he said, pulling his hat a little lower over his eyes. He wasn't exactly being stubborn, but rather thick-headed and *dense,* and she could not fathom why. "It is the custom. We may still visit each other's beds at any time, of course."

"My lord Hargreave," she said, her voice taut with wounded anger. "I do not give a tinker's damn for what the custom of the *town* may be. Whilst we are in our house, our home, we may sleep together on the middle of the dining table for all the *town* will ever know of it."

He frowned, still avoiding meeting her eyes. "Gus, please."

" 'Gus, please'?" she cried, her voice now breaking with emotion. "That is all you can say? 'Gus, please'? Have these last three nights meant nothing to you? Did you take no pleasure in what we did?"

"We were in an inn," he said. "We weren't here."

"What does it matter, when I am your *wife*?"

"Because, damnation, it wasn't supposed to be like this!" he said, his distant reserve suddenly snapping. "As soon as I stepped through that door, I remembered how I was when I left, how I was whole, and now I cannot even walk up my own *stairs*!"

Something snapped inside her, too, all the anxiety and strain and fears for him that she'd kept bottled tight within.

"Who knows how anything is *supposed* to be, Harry?" she demanded. "I am no Cassandra, able to peer into the future, and neither are you. You don't know what may happen tomorrow, or next year, or even a minute from now. The past is done, over, and cannot be changed, and the future will unfold in its own time. All we truly have is this moment, here, now, with that wretched statue watching us, and I won't let you—"

But what she wouldn't do didn't matter, because he was kissing her, one arm around her waist to jerk her close against him. All the emotion and tension that had been building between them roared into that kiss, his mouth bruising and possessive against hers. She pushed her hands inside his coat to cling to his back, wanting to be closer still. Her hat fell to the floor, and he thrust his fingers in her hair, tangling it. He was kissing her with such ferocity, such desperation, that it made her dizzy with the force of it. She could feel the hard heat of his cock grinding against her, and more, she felt her own body tightening in response as well.

He groaned into her mouth, an impossibly male sound, and when he finally broke his mouth from hers, he still could not look away from her face, staring into her eyes as if she held every secret in the world.

"I have far more than this moment, Gus," he said roughly. "I have you."

And she knew there'd be no more talk of her sleeping in the distant room at the end of the hall.

"I thought I'd never see you in a carriage again after Tuesday," Gus said as she settled on the squabs beside him. "Yet here we are, only three days later. I am stunned, Harry, truly stunned."

Harry laughed, something he'd done a great deal with her these last three days. Of course he'd been doing a great deal of some other things with her as well, wonderfully wanton and voluptuous things, that had gone far toward making him forget the tedious trip to London. They had kept to his bed and ignored the rest of the world, and let the cards of well-wishers who had called pile up on the salver beside the front door. He had sent his regrets and canceled appointments with his agent, Mr. Arnold; Sir Ralph; his tailor, Mr. Venable; and several old friends at his club, while Gus had put aside all her grand plans for remaking his household. Being in bed—his own bed—with Gus had been entirely worth it, and if he'd had his wishes, he would have preferred they continue in this fashion forever.

But to do so would have been unfair to Gus. Not that she would have objected to remaining in bed with him; far from it. Yet if she was to be accepted into London society as his wife and countess, it was time they were seen together in public. Riding in their carriage through Hyde Park today would be their first appearance, and later this evening he'd take her to his box at the playhouse. That ever-growing stack of cards in the hall was proof of how curious society was to meet his new wife, and he was proud to oblige.

Gus, however, was not nearly as confident. "Do I look well enough, Harry?" she asked anxiously, fiddling with her hat. "Julia says that Hyde Park is where all the people of fashion go to ogle one another, and I don't wish to embarrass you."

"How could you embarrass me?" he asked. "You look beautiful. You *are* beautiful."

She was wearing the plum merino habit and the ribbon-covered hat, and she did look beautiful. He'd have to ask Celia to take her to her London mantua maker now that they were in town, and have Gus order as many others as she wanted. As charming as she looked, he didn't want anyone saying she had only one habit, or accusing him of being a less-than-indulgent husband.

She sighed, unconvinced. "Are you sure I'll do, Harry?"

"Of course you'll do," he assured her, linking his hand into hers. "All that's required of you today is to sit beside me and smile and nod. No one makes real conversation in the park, because no one stops, and most of them can't ride and be witty at the same time."

"That is good," she fretted. "Because I'm not witty even when I'm sitting still."

"Hush," he said gently. "You're the Countess of Hargreave. You're my wife, and I love you beyond measure."

At last she smiled. "I love you, too, Harry."

He ducked beneath the sweeping brim of her hat to kiss her.

"Today we'll ride about the park," he said. "Then the playhouse tonight. Tomorrow Sir Randolph is coming to inspect my infernal leg."

"He doesn't inspect you, Harry," she said. "He examines you. I'm sure he'll only be pleased with your progress, too."

"There's been damned little progress that I can tell," Harry said. "Not of late."

"Now you should be the one who needs hushing," she said. "Each day you're getting stronger. I can see it, even if you refuse to. I would not be surprised if he finally gives you leave to put weight on your leg."

"We'll see," he said, noncommittal. He refused to get his hopes up. It was his leg, after all, and while Gus was set on being cheerful about it, he didn't share her optimism.

"In any event," he continued, changing the subject back to their newlywed obligations, "after Peterson is done with me, we must begin our wedding calls. I saw that Celia left us a list of all the lady grandees who must be honored with our presence. They all live here in the

West End, so I figure we can make four or five at a time. We'll begin with the duchesses."

"Duchesses," she murmured faintly. "Goodness. Are there that many?"

"No more than a dozen are in town at present," he said. Most new husbands didn't make wedding calls with their wives, but he wanted to make sure that Gus was properly launched, and he was determined to protect her as much as he could from any casual social cruelty. "Remember that one day you'll be a duchess, too, so you must not be intimidated. Four of them are in the family, anyway. There's Celia, of course, and then her daughters—Diana, Charlotte, and Lizzie—who are married to my father's cousins. I expect you'll all be great friends."

"I hope so," she said faintly.

"You will," he said. He knew the kind of social warfare that diverted London ladies, and he understood why Gus felt uneasy about plunging into those treacherous waters. "The ladies of our family are a formidable force, sweetheart, and as one of them, you'll never have better allies. And next week, of course, is the Queen's Drawing-Room."

She let out a long, worried sigh, and pulled her hand away from his to clasp hers tightly in her lap. "Could not we go to a later drawing room, Harry? Her Grace said that Her Majesty holds them every month. Could not we wait a bit later, when I feel more—more at ease with society?"

"You can't send regrets to Her Majesty, Gus," he said, placing his hand gently over her tightly knotted fingers. "She knows we're married, and she'll be expecting me to present you to her."

"But surely there are other ladies she wishes to see more," she said, a quiver of panic in her voice. "Surely Her Majesty would not notice if I were not there."

"I fear she would," he said, "and others would notice

our absence as well. We must appear at court, Gus. It's expected of us, the responsibility and allegiance that comes along with our titles. I assure you that a great many days I'd rather be anywhere than listening to the drones in the House of Lords, but I sit there because it's my duty."

She sighed mightily. "When you explain it in such a fashion, then of course we must go," she said. "But the thought of curtseying before all those people terrifies me. What if I stumble? What if I fall, there before Her Majesty?"

"Then you will hardly be the first to do so," he said. "It's not such a fearsome ordeal. You'll wear your silver and gold gown from our wedding and stick tall white feathers in your hair like all the other ladies. We'll walk up to where the queen sits, I'll present you, and you'll curtsey. That's it. The queen won't expect any wit from you, and besides, her own English is still so atrocious that she wouldn't notice if you said the cleverest thing imaginable."

Still she looked miserably uncertain, and he covered her hand with his for reassurance. "I know you'll be a success, Gus. Be who you are. The ladies who'll wish you to be otherwise aren't worth knowing. That's all you need remember. I can assure you that it's a great deal easier than running an estate like Wetherby Abbey."

She sighed. "Truly, Harry?"

"Truly." He leaned forward and kissed her lightly on the cheek, taking care not to knock her hat askew. "Besides, I shall be with you through it all."

"Will you swear to that?" she asked.

"Of course," he said. He would, too. He'd do anything she asked of him. "I'll swear by anything you wish."

At last she smiled. "I won't make you swear any terrible oaths, Harry. That would scarcely be wifely of me."

He smiled, too, but his words remained serious. "You

were with me when I needed you most, Gus. The very least I can do is steer you through the rigmarole of calls and court. Ah, here we are at the park now."

"Look, Harry, look," she said, turning toward the window. "I've never seen so many people parading about!"

The day was a sunny one, and the park was crowded. Carriages of every description, some open, some closed, filled with ladies in extravagant hats, drove slowly up and down Rotten Row. Gentlemen and a few more ladies in riding habits rode on horseback, while a smattering of officers seemed determined to display both their scarlet coats and their spirited mounts.

"Oh, Harry, people are waving at us!" Gus said, flustered. "What shall I do? How do I reply?"

"You smile and wave in return," Harry said. "There's no other trick to it. They recognize the carriage, and they're eager to see you."

"Me," she said in wonder, her eyes wide. "I still cannot conceive of anyone taking that much interest in me."

"I fear it's the curse of becoming my wife," he explained, even as he hoped she wouldn't come to think of their marriage in that way. "Ah, here are several of my acquaintances."

Three gentlemen and a lady rode close to the carriage, clearly peering in at Gus as they nodded in greeting.

"Good day, my lady," called one of the gentlemen as they passed by. "So good to have you back among us, my lord!"

"That *was* easy," Gus said with such genuine surprise that Harry laughed again.

"By sunset the entire town will be praising you to the veritable skies," he promised. "Your beauty, your gentility, the quality of your dress."

"Goodness," she exclaimed again, but she was smiling now, and as other carriages and riders passed them by she enthusiastically waved and returned their salutes.

By the time they'd driven back and forth along the King's Way three times, he was quite sure he'd never enjoyed an afternoon in Hyde Park as much as he did with Gus.

"One last pass, sweetheart," he said, "and then home. We needn't begin dressing for evening until five or so, which should leave us time for a swift, ah, interlude, if you can be persuaded."

She blushed and chuckled. "How exactly do you mean to persuade me, Harry?" she said, sliding her hand along the inside of his thigh. "If it's the same way that you—"

"By all that's holy, it *is* Hargreave!" exclaimed a young man on horseback, his leering face suddenly filling the window, with his friend behind him. "Risen from your Norfolk grave to return among the living?"

"Cobham!" Harry said, delighted to see so old an acquaintance, both from school and as a more recent partner in many late-night adventures, even as he regretted how quickly Gus's hand had retreated from his leg. "Sweetheart, this is Lord Cobham, a very old friend, and there behind him is Lord Walford. My wife, Lady Hargreave."

"Most honored, Lady Hargreave," Cobham said, his gaze boldly wandering across Gus's breasts—a bit too boldly for Harry's tastes. Gus wasn't another of their casual lady-bird conquests; she was his *wife*. "I say, Hargreave, we've heard such fatal things of you, that you're quite the wreck. Happy to see they're false."

"Base exaggerations from the mouths of rogues and dogs," Harry declared, striving for the same old familiar bravado. He was thankful he'd stowed his crutch below the seat, away from view, and that his leg with the brace was hidden by Gus's voluminous skirts.

"Do you know there's even a betting book open on you at the club?" Cobham said, as if this were the best jest in the world. "Greatest odds were that you'd knocked your head and lost your wits, and had been committed to an asylum in the north. Second greatest was that the surgeon had taken your leg outright and that you'd have a peg leg when you came back to town for entertaining the whor—ah, for walking."

He glanced uneasily at Gus, mindful of what he'd just nearly said. *A peg leg*, thought Harry with disgust. At least the reality wasn't that bad, but trust a dolt like Cobham to only see the lubricious possibilities.

"I suppose no one expected me to return with a wife," Harry said, purposefully taking Gus's hand.

"Not at all," Cobham said soundly. "After Miss Wetherby returned without you and took up with Southland, we all believed you were done."

"I did not lose my senses," Harry said lightly. Apparently Cobham hadn't heard that Julia and Gus were sisters, more fool he, and the longer Cobham lingered, the more he wondered how he'd ever been friends with the man. "I came to them, and chose the right sister to marry."

"Oh, indeed," Cobham said, embarrassed by the show of affection. "Tell me, Harry. Would you be up for sport on Wednesday? There's a small wager involving some of the usual fellows, to see how fast we can cross the west corner of Hampstead Heath. You've always been the very devil in the saddle. Are you game?"

Harry's smile stiffened. He hadn't expected this today, not as long as he kept safely in the carriage. Yet the word would be out soon enough. He might as well put the truth out with it, too.

"I fear not," he confessed. "Truth is, my leg still vexes me too much to ride."

"Does it now?" Cobham said, craning his neck to try to see for himself. "Sorry to hear it, very sorry indeed. You know Harper at the club thought he saw you put down at Mildenhall, and said you were a proper gimp now. Never knew he'd be right."

"Forgive me, Lord Cobham," Gus said sharply, the

first words she'd spoken. "But I am surprised one gentleman would describe another as a 'gimp.'"

At once Harry put his hand on her sleeve, even as Cobham's words sliced through his good mood like a knife.

"It's well enough, Gus," he said, praying she'd understand and say no more. "I *am* a gimp, a cripple, whatever Cobham wishes to call me."

"I meant no harm nor disrespect, my lady," Cobham said contritely. "It's only to hear such unfortunate news of a fellow who once led us all—well, it's a damned shame."

"It is," Harry said curtly. "If you'll excuse us, Cobham."

"Yes, of course," Cobham said, wheeling his horse away from the carriage. "Good day, my lady."

"Why did you tolerate that, Harry, when he so clearly insulted you?" Gus demanded furiously as soon as Cobham was out of hearing. "How can he pretend to be your friend and speak to you so?"

"Because Cobham can be an ass," Harry said bluntly, then took a deep breath, struggling with both his temper and his frustration. "If you did not care for how he addressed me, then I did not care for how he looked at you. I have known him for years, but perhaps the time has come that our acquaintance will be, ah, of less importance to me than it once was."

"I would never want you to break with a friend because of me, Harry," Gus said, her eyes wide with concern. "If you wish to join him at that race, or whatever it was, you should go, and not worry about—"

"I have no wish to go," he said, surprising himself. Only a few months ago, he would have been the first on the heath with Cobham and the others. Now their company held little appeal, and even if he could have ridden with them, he realized he would not have gone. He had been blaming the changes in himself on his injured leg, but perhaps he'd been wrong. Perhaps it was love that had changed him, and for the better, too.

Love, and Gus.

"I've no wish to join them in the least," he said, more firmly. "I find I'd much prefer the company of my wife."

"You are certain?" Gus asked warily. "I refuse to be one of those dreadful scolds who tries to dictate her husband's affairs."

"I cannot imagine you ever becoming a henpecking scold," he said, smiling. "You're my love, my wife, my countess, my champion, but never my scold."

She lowered her chin, peeking out at him from beneath the ribbon-covered brim of her hat. "I am also your minx," she said. "You mustn't forget that."

"I don't, not for a minute." He yawned dramatically. "I find I am weary of the park, wife, so weary that all I can think of is our bed."

She grinned. "Then take me home, husband," she said, her voice low and husky. "Take me home, and to bed."

With a sigh of pure happiness, Gus sank back against her chair in the theater box as the performers took their final bows, and finally left the stage. People in the other boxes were already rising from their seats and gathering their belongings to leave, but she wanted the magic to last just a little longer.

"That was *perfect,* Harry," she said. "Poor Prince Hamlet! I knew from the beginning that he was cursed, and doomed to die, yet still I'd dared to hope he'd somehow be saved."

Beside her, Harry smiled, sharing her pleasure. "I'm afraid old Hamlet never will be saved, sweetheart," he said. "Not even Mr. Garrick would dare change Shakespeare's ending, especially one that's been popular for so long."

"I suppose not," she said, considering, as she tapped her fan on her knee. "But if it were left to me, I would have kept both Prince Hamlet and Lady Ophelia alive, so they could have wed."

He laughed. "*Hamlet* was never meant to be a love story, Gus."

"I know that!" she said, swatting his arm with her fan even as she laughed with him. "But it's not just the play that has been perfect, Harry. It's—it's been everything about this entire evening."

Her laughter faded to a smile as she gazed at Harry. He promised that they'd come to the theater as often as she liked when they were in London, but this first time would always be special in her memory. The candlelit playhouse, the music, the brilliance of the audience, and the wonder of the play had made it that way, but best of all had been having him beside her, her handsome, perfect love of a husband. Impulsively she leaned forward and kissed him, a long and leisurely kiss, by way of a thank-you.

Afterward he smiled, so wickedly that she couldn't wait for them to be home again.

"That will give the gossips something to share tomorrow over breakfast, sweetheart," he said. "Who would have guessed that *Hamlet* would make you so amorous?"

"Oh, yes, what could be more scandalous than a wife kissing her husband?" she teased, even as she knew he was right.

At every intermission, their box had been visited by well-wishers, friends and acquaintances of Harry's who had come to meet her and welcome him back to town, and even during the play, she'd been acutely aware of how many faces in the audience had been turned their way, all eager for a glimpse of the new Countess of Hargreave. At first she'd felt shy and uncomfortable under so much scrutiny, as if she and Harry were some new display in a shop window.

But as the evening had progressed, she'd grown more relaxed, and had even come to enjoy the attention, laughing and chatting with Harry's friends as if she were still at the abbey and not in a private box at the Theatre Royal. Harry had made it easy, exactly as he'd promised, prompting her with names, reminding her of a story, simply slipping his arm affectionately around her shoulders for everyone to see. Whenever she thought she could not possibly love him any more, he managed to prove her wrong, simply by being Harry.

"I love you, Harry," she said, unable to keep from telling him yet again.

"And I love you, too, Gus," he said fondly, and gave her another quick kiss. Then with a sigh, he reached for his crutch, and slowly stood. "I'd say the worst of the crush has left by now, and it won't be too great an ordeal to find our carriage. High time we left for home, my lady."

He looked genuinely tired, and with concern Gus quickly rose at his side. This must have been a long night for him, making his way through the theater's crowds as well as climbing the stairs to the box.

"I saw a bench in the lobby where we can wait for the carriage," she said, taking his arm.

"A *bench*," he said, mustering suitable scorn as he brushed aside her worries. "What manner of husband waits on a bench?"

"A sensible manner of husband, if his leg is bothering him," she said promptly. "*My* husband, if he has sufficient sense to—"

"Lord Hargreave, good evening." The doorway to their box was suddenly filled by an imposing older lady, glittering with jewels. Behind her hovered several attendants, one holding the lady's small dog. "I have come to greet your bride."

"Lady Tolliver, we are honored," Harry said, immediately managing the closest thing to a bow that Gus had seen from him in months. "May I present my wife, Lady Hargreave? Augusta, the Dowager Marchioness of Tolliver."

His expression was so uncharacteristically respectful that Gus realized at once that Lady Tolliver must be one of the "lady grandees," as he called them, the important noble ladies of London society. Immediately she sank into a curtsey beside him, staying down until Lady Tolliver flicked her fan for her to rise.

"Let me see you, Lady Hargreave," she said, and obediently Gus looked up into the candlelight. Lady Tolliver scowled with concentration as she studied her, her powdered hair towering over her equally powdered and rouged face. Although Gus felt her cheeks growing warm, she forced herself to meet the older woman's sharp-eyed gaze. She couldn't be cowardly; she needed to be confident, poised, the way the Countess of Hargreave should be.

"Have you no voice, Lady Hargreave?" the marchioness said. "Or has Hargreave wed you because you are mute, and will never be able to speak back to him?"

Shocked, Gus could of course think of nothing to say in her defense. Instead her mouth hung open as if she truly were bereft of speech, her curtsey wilting into an awkward crouch of crumpled silk.

The marchioness scowled, her disgust clear. "This is shameful, Hargreave," she said as if Gus were unable to hear as well as speak. "How can you expect this pitiful creature to act as your countess? Or worse, how can she ever assume the title of Duchess of Breconridge?"

"Because she is my wife, Lady Tolliver," Harry said firmly. He took Gus's hand, linking his fingers tightly into hers, and raised her back up to stand, slipping his arm over her shoulders to draw her close. "I married her because I love her, but also because I believe she will be an exceptional peeress. She already is."

Gus squeezed his hand in gratitude, and love, too. If the marchioness weren't looming before them, she would have thrown her arms around Harry's shoulders and kissed him, then and there in the playhouse.

But the marchioness *was* still there, and still looming.

"How, Hargreave?" she demanded, making a disparaging little puff of disapproval. "Explain it to me. How could this girl possibly be of any use to you?"

"Because I am very useful, Lady Tolliver," Gus said. Harry's confidence in her and his arm around her shoulder gave her the courage to answer for herself, and once she'd begun, she bravely continued. "I have maintained my father's household for him since my dear mother's death six years ago, and I did so with the same thrift and efficiency with which I am now addressing my husband's establishment."

"Quite true, Lady Tolliver," Harry said. "She is doing her best to correct my sorry bachelor housekeeping. I was apparently the most lax master imaginable."

Lady Tolliver raised a single skeptical brow, still focused on Gus. "Your father's establishment in Norfolk," she said. "Is it of a notable size?"

Gus nodded. "We've fourteen servants in the house, and a dozen more in the stables," she said proudly. "I also kept the housekeeping books, and managed the purchases and accountings as well."

At last Lady Tolliver nodded, her painted cheeks crackling as she slowly smiled.

"Commendable," she said. "I am glad to see you show a clear and honest face, with pride in your industry, unlike these young trollops who glory in their indolence. You appear to be a sensible lady, Lady Hargreave. Is that true?"

"Yes, Lady Tolliver," Gus said. Belatedly she remembered how Harry had advised her to be herself, and at least this was one accomplishment she could claim with perfect confidence. "I am very sensible."

"Sensible *and* useful," Harry said helpfully.

Lady Tolliver ignored him. "I was also given to understand, Lady Hargreave, that you tended to Hargreave's broken limb with more success than that pompous fool Peterson."

"I did what was necessary, Lady Tolliver," Gus said, hoping the marchioness hadn't heard anything else about Harry's stay at their house. "Lord Hargreave suffered most grievously, and I did what I could to ease his recovery."

"Such becoming modesty, and far better accomplishments to your credit than painting posies on vases," Lady Tolliver said, finally granting her approval. "A sensible young lady indeed. You've chosen well, Lord Hargreave."

"Thank you, Lady Tolliver," he said. "I am amazed that Augusta would have me."

"You should be, you impudent rogue," she said, cackling. "Your grandmother would scarce believe it."

She turned back to Gus. "You may call on me, Lady Hargreave," she said. "I should like to hear more of how you restored Lord Hargreave to such vigorous health."

"Thank you, Lady Tolliver," Gus said with a quick curtsey. "Good evening, Lady Tolliver."

"Good evening to you, too, Lord Hargreave," the marchioness said as she began to withdraw. "Guard your new wife well, Harry. She is a prize beyond measure."

He bowed, and as soon as the marchioness left, he turned to Gus, striking his palm to his chest and making a google-eyed face of amazement.

"What a feat!" he exclaimed. "You have made a conquest of the formidable Lady Tolliver, simply the most fearsome dragon of all noble London."

"Only because you helped me, Harry," Gus said. "I would have sunk completely to the floor in a silent puddle if you hadn't."

"Nonsense," he said, laughing happily. "*I* am neither useful nor sensible, but only an impudent rogue. You heard her yourself."

"You were most useful to me," Gus said, laughing with him more from relief than amusement. "I wouldn't have been able to speak a single word if you hadn't been beside me."

"No, sweetheart," he insisted. "It was all your own doing. Your success in Society is now assured, you know. You can tell she'd absolutely given me up as a lost cause, for all that she was my grandmother's dearest friend."

"Truly, Harry?" she asked, "I was hardly brilliant or witty, and I blushed like a ninny. All I did was speak to her of servants and keeping house."

"But that was more than enough to win her complete approbation," Harry said proudly. "It's exactly as I told you. Be your own shining self, and the world will be at your feet. Now come, let's take ourselves home to celebrate."

Slowly they made their way through the passage and down the stairs to the lobby, for while much of the audience had already left, a great many people were still taking their time leaving the theater. Of course, too, after they'd finally reached the bottom of the stairs, Harry steadfastly refused to sit on the lobby bench to rest while their footman found their carriage. By the time the carriage finally appeared before the theater's door he'd become quiet and drawn with exhaustion, leaning heavily on his crutch. With concern Gus shepherded him into the street, and soon they were standing before the open carriage door when a small group of revelers called Harry's name.

"Hargreave, is that you?" The man's voice was slurred with drink, and while from his dress it was clear that both he and the other man with him were gentlemen, it was likewise clear to Gus that the young women with them were most definitely not ladies. "Finally returned to town, have you?"

Harry turned, staring to make out their faces by the wavering street lights. "Is that you, McCray?"

"It is, by all that's holy," the man said as one of the women curled lasciviously around him. "But I'd hardly know you, Harry. My God, what a transformation! What's become of you, Harry? You're dragging your leg like a Southwark beggar!"

The four laughed raucously, and Gus felt Harry tense beside her.

"Ignore them," she said softly, her hand tightening on his arm. "Please. They're drunk, and mean nothing."

He drew in his breath, and slowly let it out. Finally he nodded and began to turn back to the carriage.

"Pity the old cripple-man, kind sir!" McCray continued, mimicking the wheedling plea of a beggar to the roaring laughter of his friends. "Spare a ha'-penny for the old cripple-man, would you?"

"Ignore them," Gus said urgently, already in the carriage. "Please, Harry."

His face rigid, he climbed into the carriage, frustration and exhaustion making him more clumsy than usual. Before the footman closed the door, a handful of coins rained on the carriage, ringing against the painted side. One landed inside the carriage, at Harry's foot. He snatched it up, and furiously hurled it back out the window.

"Home," he said curtly to the footman. *"Home."*

CHAPTER
14

Sir Randolph has arrived, my lord," Wilton said.

"I will see him at once," Harry said. "Show him here directly."

He was sitting in the library, wearing his banyan over his shirt and breeches. It was only nine, but he had already been there since before the sun rose, exhausted but unable to sleep, and the coffee he'd been drinking since he'd come downstairs hadn't helped, either. His mood was as black as the coffee, his melancholy unshakable. How could it be otherwise, when last night's shameful little scene in the street before the theater kept playing itself over and over in his head?

"Have a fresh pot of coffee and another cup brought for Sir Randolph, Wilton," Gus said. Of course she was here with him. Of course she'd wish to hear Peterson's judgment. Now that they were married, she deserved to know in exactly what circumstances she'd found herself, saddled with a crippled husband. But there'd been no conversation between them, no cheerful banter, because he hadn't wanted any. He'd rebuffed her with single-word replies to her questions and a curtness she did not deserve. He hated himself for doing so, which made his humor blacker still.

Peterson was shown in, wearing what appeared to be exactly the same suit he'd worn for every visit to the abbey, and he did exactly the same things he'd been doing for weeks now, too. He flexed Harry's knee and ankle joints, and ran his hand along his shin, feeling for where the break had been. But this time, when he was done, he did not restore the brace, but put it to one side.

"I wish you to try standing, my lord," he said, "without the splinted brace to support you. I wish to see you straighten your leg and put your full weight upon it."

"You are sure, Sir Randolph?" Gus asked anxiously. "The bone is ready to bear such a test?"

"I believe it is, my lady," Sir Randolph said. "However, it is his lordship's decision. If he is content with conditions as they are, then he need not do it. But if he does not choose to try the leg now, then the time for doing so may be irrevocably lost."

"Damnation, I'll do it," Harry said. His heart racing, he stood first with the crutch. Slowly he straightened his injured leg, touching his foot flat to the carpet for the first time. He took a deep breath, and gradually shifted his full weight to the now-unprotected leg.

It held, and did not give way as he now realized he'd feared. He smiled in triumph at the surgeon.

"Do not abandon the crutch, my lord," Peterson cautioned. "That is still necessary, and will be for some time. But I wish you to try a step, even two."

Harry nodded with determination. His leg felt bare without the wooden support around it, weak and exposed. Awkwardly he swung his foot forward, his first real step in months, and then took another. It was difficult, and it was painful, but he did it, and that was what mattered.

He felt exhilarated, beyond mere joy to something higher. Automatically he looked to Gus. She had her palms pressed to her cheeks, and she was crying.

"Look at you, Harry," she said. "*Look* at what you've done!"

But Sir Randolph was frowning. "Are you conscious

of the difference, my lord?" he asked with concern. "The break and scarring have shortened your leg by at least an inch. Are you aware of it, my lord?"

Now that he'd been told, Harry could feel it, an off-balance hitch as he stood. He tried to square his shoulders, straighten his spine, balance his legs. He stepped again, and realized the truth of what the surgeon was saying. What he'd attributed to stiffness and the brace was really the difference between his two legs, the lopsided lurch that had marked those first steps.

"That will correct itself over time, yes?" he asked, desperation in his voice. "As it heals further, the difference will go away?"

He already knew the answer from the surgeon's face.

"I am very sorry, my lord," he said, "but I fear the change is permanent, an inevitable result of the healing. In time and with practice you may one day learn to walk with the use of a cane instead of the crutch, but I do not believe there will ever be a time that your balance, or lack thereof, will permit you to walk unassisted."

"So I shall never run again," Harry said slowly. "Or dance. Or fight with a sword, or with fists. Or sail. Or walk along a sandy beach. In short, many of the things that I have considered ordinary pleasures are now forever beyond me, and I shall always be considered a hobbling, halting cripple."

"I would, my lord, dare to hold out a possibility of riding," Sir Randolph said, striving to be hopeful. "Perhaps within the year, if your favorable progress continues."

"What, on the meekest of little ponies?" Harry asked cynically. His hopes plummeted and crashed as swiftly as they'd just risen. "With a groom to hold the bridle?"

"Forgive me, my lord, but you are far too hard on yourself," the surgeon said, trying to put the best face on things, exactly as Gus did. "You have made considerable and exceptional progress. Much more than I would have thought possible when I first attended you, and saw the damage to the limb."

But Harry did not want to hear it, not a single word. He realized now that he hadn't truly been realistic. He'd told himself that he'd been preparing for the worst, but instead he'd been nurturing a fool's hope for a complete recovery and a return to what he'd once been. He'd let himself be distracted by Gus, and by their marriage, and his father, and coming back to London, but he couldn't ignore the hard truth any longer. A fool: That was what he was, a fool for the fall in the first place, and a fool for believing it could ever be undone. That realization made the truth about his future unbearable.

"Forgive *me*, Peterson," he said, the words little more than a snarl full of bitterness. "But to hell with your progress, and to hell with my damned leg."

He lurched from the room, not caring about anything beyond nurturing his misery, and intending on doing so in his own room, locked away from the rest of the world.

"Harry, please," Gus said, rising from her chair. She looked from Harry, leaving the room as fast as he could, to Sir Randolph, standing abandoned in the middle of the library. "Sir Randolph, I am sorry this happened, but his lordship's disappointment may have, ah, affected his temper."

Sir Randolph smiled sadly. "There is no need to apologize, Lady Hargreave. I understand his lordship's distress entirely. I have observed it before in similar cases. His lordship is a young gentleman, still in impulsive youth. He cannot see beyond what he has lost, and be grateful for what was spared. I can only pray that, with time, he comes to understand the difference."

Gus nodded and bowed her head, her hands clasped tightly before her.

"Go to him, my lady," Sir Randolph said. "I can find my own way out, and I believe his lordship needs your solace far more than I do."

"Thank you, Sir Randolph," Gus said, running up the stairs after Harry.

She found him in his bedchamber, staring out the window with his back to her, his head bowed and his chest heaving with anger. There had once been several porcelain candlesticks and a decorative Chinese bowl on the mantel of his room. Now there was nothing but shards of smashed porcelain in the grate and a chair tipped over as well. It was clear enough to Gus what had happened, and she nodded to Tewkes, hovering uncertainly in the doorway to the dressing room, to send him away. This was the sort of challenge that wives were supposed to address, though she hadn't the faintest idea of how it was done.

"Harry," she called softly.

"Leave me, Gus," he said without turning. "I wish to be alone."

An angry Harry was never good, but in her experience a stubborn Harry was even more difficult. How had things gone so badly so fast? To be sure, the jeering man tossing the coins at them last night had been unspeakably cruel, but why had he been worse than Cobham calling him a gimp? Lately Harry had seemed to be so much better, so much more accepting of his limitations. He should have been pleased by Sir Randolph's assessment, and no longer having to wear the brace on his leg. Instead he'd become inexplicably furious, and now she felt as if they were both back to the beginning, with him lying angry and frustrated in his bed at the abbey.

"What will being alone solve, pray?" she asked. "The destruction of more porcelain and chairs?"

"It is what I wish," he said, his voice distant. "This has nothing to do with you, Gus."

She sighed. "We are expected to sup with your father and Celia at their house in an hour."

"You may go without me if it pleases you."

"It does not please me, not at all." She hated talking to his back like this. "If you will not accompany me, then I shall send word that we are unable to attend."

"Tell them anything you damned well please," he said. "I am not going."

"Very well." She took a deep breath, unsure of what to do next. "I shall send our regrets."

He didn't answer, and he didn't turn. She sighed again, and crossed the room to stand behind him. Gently she slipped her hands around his waist, and pressed her cheek against his back. He tensed his shoulders beneath her touch but did not acknowledge her.

"I love you, Harry," she said softly. "No matter what, I'll always love you."

He could say all he wanted that this wasn't about her, but when he ignored her, then it became about her, too, whether he wished it so or not. And it hurt, having him reject her like this. It *hurt*.

She reached up and kissed the side of his jaw, rough beneath her lips. Then she slipped away from him, and left him, as he'd asked. What choice, really, did she have?

She hoped he'd send for her so they could dine together, and when he didn't she ate in her room, or more accurately, she had tea and toast, all she could stomach. She sat alone and tried to distract herself by reviewing the household accounts, and failed, the numbers unable to combat the loneliness. Without asking, Mary prepared her bed—the countess's bed in the countess's bedchamber—and sadly Gus knew that the servants must already be discussing the first quarrel between her and his lordship.

Except that it wasn't a quarrel, because a quarrel could be made up with apologies and kisses. This black mood of Harry's frightened her, because it made her feel helpless.

She couldn't sleep in that cold, empty bed, and she wouldn't. As soon as Mary left her, she took her candlestick and in bare feet padded down the long hallway to Harry's darkened bedchamber. He was sound asleep, his breathing regular. How he could sleep while she was wide awake because of him seemed beastly unfair, but it also gave her courage.

She pulled off her robe and nightgown and slid into the bed beside him, her naked body pressed close to his. At once he rolled over toward her, unconsciously seeking her in his sleep, his arm curling protectively around her waist as he drew her close. It was all she needed, and at last she was finally able to fall asleep.

The next morning she awoke to him making love to her, and she dared to hope his brooding, black mood had lifted. But to her dismay she found nothing had really changed. He refused to leave his rooms, and though he tolerated her company, he seemed to take no pleasure or enjoyment in it.

The only time that a glimpse of his old self—and how she despaired of thinking of this as his "old" self, as if it was a thing of the past and gone forever!—returned was when they were together in bed, but even that felt tarnished, mere soulless coupling without the joy of love to gild it. Still she said nothing, not wishing to aggravate him further, and praying that he would find peace on his own.

For four days they went on like this, but on the fifth Gus could bear no more. After a near-silent breakfast where he sat across from her engrossed—or pretending to be engrossed—with the morning paper, she finally spoke.

"Harry," she said as firmly as she could, which wasn't very firm at all. "Harry, I have tried to be understanding, and obey your wishes, but we cannot continue in this fashion."

He looked up from the paper, his coffee cup in his hand. Because it was another warm day, he was wearing a yellow silk banyan and nothing else, and she'd tantalizing glimpses of his bare chest as he moved.

"I told you before, sweetheart," he said. "This has nothing to do with you."

"But it does," she said. "We can't keep hiding away in the house like a pair of recluses. What of those wedding calls we must make, and the suppers and parties we've rejected? What of Lady Tolliver's invitation?"

He set the cup down carefully. "I thought you'd prefer it that way, Gus. You've made it clear enough that you've no real taste for society."

"But it's not about society, or even my wishes," she said, her hands twisting in her apron, below the table where he couldn't see them. "You've told me so yourself. What of our obligations, our responsibilities? What of the Queen's Drawing-Room today?"

"Send our regrets," he said. "Her Majesty will survive the disappointment."

"It's more than that, Harry," she said, persisting. "Your friends must be wondering what's become of you, and your family's concerned. People call every day, yet we receive no one."

"Why should they be concerned?" He reached for another piece of toast and began to butter it methodically, crust to crust. "We're newlyweds, in our honeymoon-month. We're supposed to want no other company but our own."

"I wish that a—a surfeit of honeymoon passion were the reason, Harry," she said, unable to keep the sadness from her voice. "I know that you'd wished for better news from Sir Randolph. I know you were disappointed.

But there are many men who have suffered far worse wounds and injuries and yet continue to lead—"

"No." He swore, and tossed the butter knife onto the plate with a clatter. "It's not the scars. It's *how* it happened that torments me, Gus, night and day and every hour in between, and knowing how one moment of my own unthinking idiocy could have so completely changed my life. Having those fools taunt me the other night, then hearing Peterson—it's all come back, Gus, as keen as a blade between my ribs."

She drew in her breath. "I didn't think you remembered anything, not after you struck your head."

"I didn't at first," he said. "I do now. Seeing your sister brought it back."

Now she remembered the last time his mood had darkened like this, when Julia and her father had returned to Wetherby the day before the wedding. She hadn't understood at the time, but it made sense now.

"It was Julia, wasn't it?" she asked uneasily. "She never would tell me, but it's easy enough to guess, knowing her. She did something to make you fall, didn't she?"

"It wasn't her fault, Gus," he said, the now-familiar bitterness welling up in his voice. "It was mine."

He shoved his chair back from the table and rose, unable to keep still. "Everything I did that morning was wrong, Gus. I should never have agreed to ride out with her on such a wet morning. I should have refused your father's horse, and not been too proud to admit that the beast was unrideable. I shouldn't have raced after Julia into a wooded place that was unknown to me, and I should have been expecting her to jump out before me."

"Then she *did* do something," Gus said. She wasn't surprised, but it still upset her that Julia had, once again, behaved irresponsibly and dangerously, and yet had escaped any consequences. "You could have been killed, Harry."

"I don't blame her." He paced back and forth as if driven by the memory, the yellow silk billowing out behind him.

Gus didn't miss the terrible irony of this: that while he fought with himself over remembering how he'd broken his leg, he seemed to forget entirely how uneven his gait had become as he lurched back and forth with his pacing.

"I should have known she'd do something like that," he continued. "I was the one who should have shown good judgment, and not agreed to her ridiculous game. But I didn't, and now I'm left with knowing one moment of sheer idiocy has changed my life forever. My *God*, what I would give to go back and undo every blasted thing about that morning!"

"Not everything was bad about that morning, Harry," Gus said slowly.

He stopped abruptly, staring at her in disbelief. "How in blazes can you say that to me?"

"I can because it's true," she said, her voice trembling with emotion. "Because if you hadn't fallen and been hurt, you would never have fallen in love with me."

She didn't know what she expected him to say, if she'd hoped that he'd tell her she was worth more than any crooked leg.

But he didn't. He didn't say anything. He just stood there, staring at her, the expression in his blue eyes as unchanged as if she hadn't spoken at all.

She couldn't stay, not after that. She turned and ran from the room, her hand pressed over her mouth to keep from sobbing before the servants.

She'd gambled, daring to say aloud what she'd been keeping inside for days. She'd gambled, and now she had lost. She curled on her bed in a tight knot of despair, letting the tears stream down her face.

"Forgive me for intruding, my lady," said Mary softly,

finding her. "But Mr. Wilton said I was to come tell you that Her Grace the Duchess of Breconridge is below asking for you, my lady. He says that Her Grace doesn't believe you're not at home, my lady."

Gus heaved a deep, shuddering sigh, struggling to fight back her tears. She'd no choice but to see Celia; if she didn't, she'd no doubt that the duchess herself would come upstairs to find her. Besides, if she hid in her rooms, she'd be absolutely no better than Harry.

"Tell Mr. Wilton to show Her Grace to the green parlor, Mary," she said, pulling out her handkerchief to blot her eyes. "I shall be down directly."

She paused before one of the looking glasses in the hall to pat her hair, then hurried down the stairs to greet Celia.

"My dear Gus," the duchess said warmly, embracing Gus. "I knew you'd be home. I came to offer my assistance regarding the drawing room at the palace this afternoon. You should be dressing already if you wish to be on time. Is your maid sufficient? You wish your plumes to be securely in place, you know, so they don't wander when you curtsey. Should I send my hairdresser here to you, just to be sure?"

"We shall not be attending," Gus said. "Harry is indisposed."

"Or more accurately, Harry doesn't want to go, just as he hasn't wished to go anywhere these last few days." Gracefully Celia spread her skirts as she sat on the edge of the settee, patting the seat for Gus to join her. "We've all noticed, you know. Have you any notion as to why?"

Gus sat beside her, her hands tightly clasped in her lap and her diamond betrothal ring winking slyly up at her. She did not wish to be disloyal to Harry, but confiding in his stepmother would not be like telling his secrets to a friend her own age.

"When Sir Randolph came to the house this week to

examine Harry, he finally let Harry put his full weight on the damaged leg," she said. "Harry did so well, too, walking clear across the room and back. Oh, Celia, I was proud of him!"

"As well you should be," the duchess said. "You have seen him through his entire recovery, and that he can walk again is a miracle of your doing as much as his."

Gus shook her head. "To us it seems a miracle, but not to Harry. He was terribly discouraged because his leg isn't perfect, and according to Sir Randolph, it never will be again. He'll always need some sort of support, a cane or stick if not the crutch. He did not wish to hear that, and stormed from the room. It was very—very ill mannered of him."

"Or childish," Celia said succinctly. "But pray continue."

"I believed his black mood came from not wanting people to stare at him, or make comments," Gus said, her shoulders sagging and her voice forlorn. "He hates the pity that people feel for him, and will fly into a rage over next to nothing, as he did with Sir Randolph. But just now he told me that wasn't the reason. He is blaming himself for breaking his leg in the first place, Celia, and it has made him so angry and discontented that there is no living with him. When he is like this, I wonder if we would be better off not married at all."

She was crying again, fat tears of unhappiness sliding down her cheeks. She felt in her pocket for her already-soggy handkerchief, but Celia handed Gus her own instead, fine linen with the Breconridge ducal crest.

"Here, here," Celia said gently, sliding closer to put her arm around Gus's quaking shoulders. "We'll have no more of that talk. I have been married to two excellent gentlemen, and I was widowed for eighteen years in between, and I can assure you that being married to an excellent gentleman—such as your Harry—is far, far more agreeable than being alone."

Despondent, Gus shook her head. "But when I finally told him what I'd been thinking all along—that some good did come from his fall, for without it, we would never have fallen in love—he did not wish to hear it. He didn't care at *all*."

"Oh, he cares, Gus," Celia assured her. "It's obvious to everyone that he's deeply in love with you. He would not behave as he has if he weren't."

"It's a wicked unfortunate way for him to show it!"

"Yes, it is," the duchess agreed. "But I can assure you that Harry is equally perplexed. All his life he has been cosseted and praised as his father's heir, and because of it, he has always been conscious of being first. When his two brothers return, and you see how he is with them, then you'll understand how seriously he takes his place as the eldest son. He always strives to be the best at anything he attempts, and the most perfect in every way. And now, because of his broken leg, he's not. He's flawed, and I suspect he feels he's somehow let all of us down. Most especially you."

Agitated, Gus slipped free of Celia's arm and rose, and unconsciously began to walk back and forth across the floral-patterned carpet exactly as Harry had done.

"But Harry hasn't failed any of us," she protested. "He's been brave and determined, and I love him all the more because of it."

"That's why he loves you, too, Gus," Celia said, opening her fan. "He and his father are so much alike. They long to be heroes. They want to protect those they love, and will move Heaven and earth to do so. Consider how Brecon raced across the sea as soon as he learned that Harry was hurt, and how many mountains he willingly shoved aside to make certain you married him."

Gus stopped pacing before Celia, thinking. What the

duchess said was right. Harry did want to protect her. He didn't exactly slay dragons, but he'd always been there to support her whenever she needed him, or when she faltered.

"You understand," Celia said, nodding as she smoothed the backs of her gloves. "I can tell by your expression. That will, I think, be the secret of drawing Harry from his doldrums. You must contrive a way to make him believe you need him to rescue you."

"Rescue me?" Gus asked, mystified. "Forgive me, Celia, but I'm hardly a damsel locked in a tower, any more than Harry's a knight errant on a white charger."

"Heavens, no," Celia said, standing to leave. "We live in modern times, and a good thing, too. But I am certain you can contrive some little way to achieve it, and in time to salvage your first drawing room this afternoon as well."

"But how, Celia?" Gus begged. "What should I do?"

Celia smiled. "You're the lady who married him, not I," she said. "You love him, and he loves you. You'll find a way. I shall send my hairdresser to you at once to help you prepare, and we shall all be waiting for you at the palace. Good day, Gus, and the very best luck as well. I pray we'll see you this afternoon."

Harry stared out his bedchamber window, something he'd done a great deal of lately, and saw no more of the walled garden with the neatly clipped boxwood hedges and the two cherry trees now than he had all week. Perhaps even less, for his thoughts were in such a shambles it was unlikely he'd see anything set before him.

He had just done the one thing he'd never wanted to do, the one thing he'd never believed possible. He'd hurt Gus, wounded her with callous words as surely and sharply as if he'd used a sword against her. Her beautiful eyes had filled with pain and tears, and she'd been too upset to fight back the way she usually did. Instead she'd fled and left him, exactly as he deserved.

And what excuse had she given him for hurting her like this? She'd simply told the truth.

The truth. He'd been so damned focused on himself and his own misery that he'd completely overlooked the truth that she'd presented to him, shining bright in its purity.

If he hadn't fallen from his horse, he would never have fallen in love with Gus.

Was there ever a greater truth than that? Over and over these last weeks he had thought of how much the fall had changed and narrowed his life for the worse, but not once had he paused to consider what would have become of that same life of his if he'd managed to stay on Hercules's back. He would have proposed to Julia Wetherby, and she would have accepted. He would have married her. They would have become the most fashionable young couple in London. He would, within a matter of months, have become completely, absolutely bored with her.

He never would have fallen in love with Gus because, lunk-headed churl that he'd been, he would never have seen her. She would always have been in the shadows, outshone by her sister the way the moon fades and vanishes before the sun. He would never have discovered the sweetness of her kiss, her kindness, her generosity, or her passion. He never would have learned where all her freckles were, or felt the warmth of her smile when it was meant just for him. He would never have known the joy of loving, and being loved by, Gus.

His wife.

He could hobble through life with his leg the way it was, but he could not begin to imagine it without her by his side. And yet by his words he had just done his best to drive her away forever.

He threw open the door and charged down the hall toward her room, determined to apologize to her and beg for forgiveness and give her anything, anything at all, that she wanted in order to win her back. He didn't pause to knock at her door or wait for a footman to open it for him.

Two startled maidservants, brooms in hands, stared at him and dropped in immediate curtseys.

"Where is her ladyship?" he demanded. "Why isn't she here?"

The younger maid looked ready to burst into tears. "Forgive me, my lord, we do not know. She has not been here this last hour."

He wheeled around, desperate to find her. Damnation, it was his own house. She had to be here somewhere. Unless she'd already left, both the house and him, and he was too late, and—

"Whatever are you doing, Harry?" Gus asked mildly, coming up the stairs. "You're huffing and racing about like the town bull up there. You'll terrify the servants behaving like that, you know."

She smiled up at him. There were no signs of tears, no distress in her face now. The change was so complete that it threw him off balance.

"Where did you go?" he asked.

"Oh, I was downstairs," she answered vaguely. "Look what arrived with the morning mail: the latest issue of *The London Observer*. Do you remember how I read aloud to you when you were first recovering?"

"I do," he said, and he did, remembering how her eyes would widen at the outrageous tattle, thinly veiled against libel with initials in place of proper names.

"I thought it might amuse you if we did that again," she said, her face upturned as she paused on the step below him. "Would you find that diverting?"

He nodded, and she smiled, joining him to walk back to his rooms.

"I'm sure it's all the most dreadful scandal and foolishness," she said cheerfully, flipping through the pages. "But you can tell me how wrong everything is, the way you did before."

How in blazes was he supposed to apologize when she was acting as if nothing had ever happened? How could he beg for forgiveness when there didn't seem to be anything to apologize for?

She touched her hand to the silver coffeepot. "Still warm," she said with satisfaction. "Here, let me pour you a fresh cup."

She filled his cup and added the exact amount of sugar that he liked. "The toast, however, is quite cold. Should I send for more from the kitchen?"

"No, I am fine," he said, sitting once again in his chair across the small table from her. This was very odd, as if their morning was beginning all over again to wipe away his outburst. He was always saying how he'd wished to turn back time, but now that it seemed as if it were happening, he wasn't sure he liked it.

"Here we are, 'Notes of the Town,'" she said, smoothing the page open. "That's the part with the scandal."

She cleared her throat momentously, and began to read.

We hear that Lady G—t—n has of late displayed a most particular Fondness for the lemonade sold by a certain Confectionary in Covent Garden. Her Ladyship vows this lemonade has become her Nectar of Youth, and ascribes her Glowing Beauty to its miraculous properties. It is whispered, however, that her Vitality and Fresh Complexion may be more the result of the Amorous Ministrations of the handsome French confectioner himself, and another Variety of Restorative Elixir of which he is the sole manufacturer.

Gus laughed gleefully. "Oh, Harry, is that as wicked as I think it is? Are they saying that this lady is conducting an intrigue with a French confectioner?"

"I can't imagine another interpretation," he said, smiling himself. Gus was looking so charmingly wicked herself that he was tempted to toss her back upon the bed for a bit of intriguing of his own. But he told himself he could not do so until he'd found the opportunity to apologize. It would be a kind of penance, and motivation, too. "Of course they mean Lady Gunston. Everyone knows she dallies with her footmen and grooms, so why not with her French confectioner as well?"

"Particularly if he is handsome," Gus said with relish. "Oh, here's one about another bride!

We do love the Aura of New-Wedded Bliss and Contentment that surrounds a freshly married husband and wife, and there are few things more Sweet than to witness the Joy of the Honey-moon state. So is the situation of the newly married Lord H—g—e, returned to London after a lengthy stay of recuperation in the Country.

"Oh, Harry, that's you!" she said excitedly. "That *H—g—e* has to be Hargreave."

"I suppose so," he said, instantly wary. "Perhaps you shouldn't read on, Gus."

"Of course I'm going to read on," she said. "I want to see what they say of you. If I learn you are visiting a Frenchwoman making lemonade, then I shall be very cross indeed."

She held the page up, reading more loudly.

We were most pleased to see His Lordship driving once again along Rotten Row, and rejoice both in his recovery and in the return of his Gallantry to Town. However, we were less than Impressed by the Lady he has chosen as his Bride, the former Miss W—y, a plain country Miss with a freckled visage and no particular Air of Gentility.

Gus's voice faltered as she read the cruel words, and Harry reached across the table to try to snatch the paper from her hands.

"I warned you not to read it, Gus," he said. "It's hateful slander, that is all, and means nothing."

But to his dismay she pulled from his reach, continuing to read aloud to the bitterest of ends.

We have heard that this Lady was his nursemaid, addressing his needs whilst he was Ill. But though we applaud her Tenderness, we cannot help but ponder why His Lordship felt to reward such an ordinary lady with Marriage. It is widely remarked that this unfortunate Pair have not been seen about Town of late, provoking whispers that perhaps His Lordship has already suffered a Change of Heart regarding his ill-favored Bride.

"Damnation, Gus, I told you not to read that!" This time Harry grabbed the magazine from her hands and hurled it directly into the grate and onto the fire, where the flames at once curled and licked through the pages. "It's rubbish, every word, and signifies nothing."

But Gus sat across from him with her head bowed, pale and sadly wilted with misery.

"Oh, Harry," she said with a little catch to her voice. "Is that truly why you've no wish to leave the house? You are ashamed of me?"

"How can you ever think such a thing of me?" he asked, appalled. "I love you more than any man has ever loved his wife, Gus, and no vile words scribbled by an anonymous coward will ever change that."

"You didn't marry me because I looked after you, did you?"

"Of course not!" he declared fiercely, his temper rising. "I married you because I loved you, and love you still, and will love you as long as I've a breath in my body."

"Oh, Harry," she said softly. "I love you, too."

He was glad to hear that, of course, but he would not let himself be distracted. The more he thought of what had been written of her, the more furious he became.

"I'll prove how much I love you, Gus," he said, striking his fist for emphasis on the table. "I'll take the bastard who wrote this to court for slander, and have him put in jail for printing lies about you. I'll make sure he and the rest of his verminous pack never dare mention you on their pages again. They'll learn the hard way not to slander my wife."

"You needn't do that, Harry," she said uneasily. "You've told me yourself that it's impossible to fight the scandal sheets. Better that I should learn not to be so tender, and ignore them. Besides, there must be so many other people who believe this as well about why we've not gone out, and you cannot go raging about London trying to make your point to them, too."

"Oh, yes, I can, Gus," he declared, full of bravado for her sake. "I can show them all how much I love you, and how honored I am to have you as my wife and countess. We shall go to the queen's infernal drawing room today, and we'll show them all."

Gus gasped, her hand fluttering to her mouth. "Are you certain you wish to do this, Harry? You know that everyone will look at us, and there will be a great deal of walking for you."

"I'll manage," he said, sweeping aside her objection. Hell, for her sake he'd drag himself the entire length of the palace and back again. "I'll want them all to look at us, and see me with you."

He pushed himself to his feet and went to the chest of drawers, pulling out a round-sided leather box. He placed it on the table before her.

"Here," he said. "I had that brought out for you."

She glanced up at him, questioning, then slowly unfastened the hooks and opened the box. To Harry's satisfaction, she gasped again, exactly as she should have. This wasn't quite the same as the apology she deserved, but it was a good start.

"That's my mother's tiara," he said. "I want you to wear it this afternoon, as well as the necklace and bracelets I gave you at our wedding."

Carefully she lifted the tiara from the box. In her hands, it was even more magnificent than he'd remembered, a small half crown of swirling diamonds that sparkled brilliantly in the sun shining through the window.

"Oh, Harry," she said. "You spoil me."

"Not nearly enough," he said proudly. "You wear that on your head, and that gold-and-silver gown you wore to our wedding, and I swear you'll be the most beautiful lady there. I want every man there to envy me, and every lady to wish she were you. We'll prove to them that no fool's slander can hurt us."

But to his surprise, she didn't smile, and she didn't look up. Most ladies would have been overjoyed to have a fortune in diamonds dropped into their laps, but then he'd long ago learned that Gus wasn't like most ladies. Most of the time, he was glad of it, and then there were other times, like now, when he'd no notion at all of what she was thinking. She could mystify him that way.

"Gus," he said softly, once again sitting across from her so their faces were level. "What is it? Do you not wish to go after all?"

She shook her head, still bowed to avoid meeting his

eyes. Clearly something was bothering her, but damnation, why was she making it so difficult?

"Do you not care for the tiara?" he asked carefully. "I'll grant that it's a bit old-fashioned, but after today we can have the stones reset if that is what you wish, so that—"

"No!" She looked up quickly, appalled. "I would never do that! The tiara was your mother's, and I will be honored to wear it today, just as I will be honored to be at your side."

"Very well, then," he said, sitting back. He could sense that there was more that she hadn't said, something that was plaguing her still. But knowing Gus, no amount of guesses or prodding would make her speak until she was ready. He'd simply have to let her choose the time to say whatever it was, if indeed it needed saying after all. "I'll be equally honored to be with you. We'll show them all, won't we? We'll do that, Gus, the two of us together."

Finally she smiled, more brilliant than all the diamonds in her hand, and enough to make his heart lurch with joy.

"Yes, we will, Harry," she said. "Together we *will*."

"*Look at* the crush of carriages, Harry," Gus said, pressing as close to their own carriage window as she could without disturbing her hair. "Who would have guessed there were so many in London?"

Harry smiled, and Gus could not help but smile back. He was gloriously handsome across from her, dressed in a dark blue suit thick with embroidered gold thread, his eyes a sunny blue and his dark hair powdered fashionably gray. Best of all, his entire self had changed, as completely as night into day. Celia had been entirely right about how he needed to feel he was protecting her, though Gus herself was mystified by how conveniently that particular cruel item had appeared in the magazine today. Who would have guessed that *The London Observer* would, combined with love, bring Harry back?

"All the fine folk and their carriages come out from hiding for a drawing room at the palace," he said. "Cast the bread crumbs on the pond, and all the goldfish rise gobbling to the surface."

Gus looked back over her shoulder at Harry. "That's a silly comparison," she said. "No sensible goldfish would ever dress like this in the middle of the day. I'm terrified I'll bend too far when I curtsey and lose my plumes."

"You won't," he assured her. "I saw the armaments that hairdresser employed to secure the plumes to the tiara and the tiara to your hair. That rig may never come out."

"Don't say that," Gus scolded, touching her head lightly once again for good measure. She might not be a slippery goldfish but, dressed as she was, she did feel like a fancy wooden doll, too stiff to move. She'd never worn such elaborate and formal clothing, or any that was so uncomfortable, either.

Beneath her glittering gown, she wore an extra two petticoats as well as her hoops to make her skirts suitably wide for court, and additional lace flounces pinned to her sleeves to give grace to her gestures. Her gown now occupied so much space that she was forced to sit across from Harry, alone on her seat in solitary splendor so her skirts would not be crushed. The diamond necklace and bracelets were heavy around her throat and wrists, and the coronet and the pins that held it pressed into her head.

Most challenging of all, however, were the plumes pinned into the front of her coronet, three white ostrich feathers that signified she was now a married woman, and that towered, nodding, nearly two feet above her head. As foolish and awkward as the plumes were, every woman of rank was required to wear them to court. Even now Gus had to sit leaning slightly forward so that the plumes wouldn't break against the roof of the carriage.

"You look exactly as you should, sweetheart," Harry said.

She wrinkled her nose. "Meaning that I do not look exactly *good*."

"No," Harry admitted. "No lady looks good with her hair powdered gray and feathers on her head, and you already know my feelings in regard to the hoops. But I am glad you held firm against the paint."

She grinned. "I shocked the hairdresser by refusing it."

"You'll likely shock a good many more people besides him," Harry said. "But because I love you, I have always loved your freckles, and I will happily present them with the rest of you before the queen. Besides, it's always disconcerting to see a lady's painted cheeks crackle when she smiles. Here we are, our turn at last."

Amid a flurry of footmen around their carriage, Harry stepped out first, then turned to help Gus. They were better at it now, the choreography becoming more automatic between them, even as Gus had to turn sideways like a crab to maneuver both her hoops and her plumes through the carriage door.

Her heart was racing, and she'd only a moment to spare to look up at the front of St. James's Palace. She'd heard the complaints about how St. James's was an inconvenient, old-fashioned pile, but it seemed very grand to her, and filled with richly dressed gentlemen and ladies. As they slowly made their way through the door, down the long hall, and into the last antechamber before the drawing room itself, she felt the too-familiar nervousness and doubts begin to settle in.

Harry squeezed her hand. "You'll do fine, sweetheart," he said, sensing her anxiety. "In my eyes, not one lady in this entire place can hold a candle to you."

She smiled tentatively at him. "But I'm to be presented to Her Majesty, Harry. The *queen*."

"She'll be delighted with you, Gus," he said. "All you must do when your name is called is curtsey as low as you can, kiss her hand, and retreat. Most likely the queen won't say a word, and neither will you. Remember, too, that she's not some fearsome creature, but a lady not so much older than yourself."

"Not daunting?" Gus said, though deep down she did not believe it.

"Not at all," Harry said, and winked at her.

But she'd noticed something else. "You're walking on both legs, Harry."

"Three legs," he said wryly, "one being wooden, if you count the crutch."

She knew the effort this cost him. He'd only just begun to walk like this, and it was still an awkward, halting lurch of a walk. But the most difficult part for him must have been the attention he was drawing, from curious glances to out-and-out stares. Others pointedly—and rudely, she thought—had walked around them, as if Harry's slower pace was intolerable. The fact that he could make a jest of it all now showed how hard he was trying, and she wished she could have made those others simply treat him as they had before.

"I'd say two legs, not three," she said. "You're doing so well, Harry."

"I wish it were better for your sake, Gus," he said. "I want everyone to look at you, not me, and thus I have vowed to do my best to be as unobtrusive as possible."

That made her grin despite her nervousness. The thought of her tall, smiling, wickedly handsome husband in his gold-laced suit ever being unobtrusive, crutch or not, was preposterous. And yet Harry had put aside his own worries to ease hers, which only made her love him all the more.

"I am serious, my love," he said, leaning close so only she could hear him in the crowded hall. "You *inspire* me."

She shook her head, the plumes wafting over her brow.

"No, Harry, it's the other way around," she said, choosing her words with care. "You worry that you're not worthy of me because of your leg, that somehow you've failed me, when instead you've done everything for me, Harry, absolutely everything, and oh, I can't *begin* to tell you how much!"

He smiled crookedly. "It's a deuced odd time for you to tell me any of it, sweetheart."

"I can't help myself, Harry." He was right: it *was* a deuced odd time. They were surrounded by strangers, an Austrian ambassador in the line ahead of them and a merchant's wife and her daughters behind them. It was crowded and stuffy and noisy, the narrow hallway filled with the scent of smokey candles and too much scent trying—and failing—to cover the nervousness of too many overdressed people.

But now that Gus had started to tell Harry her true feelings, she wasn't going to stop. She couldn't, and in a rush all the words she'd been keeping bottled up within her spilled out.

"Whenever I'm shy or anxious or unsure," she said, "you've been there to reassure me, and take care that I don't make a complete ninny of myself. With your father, and at the inn in Mendenhall, and at the playhouse when Lady Tolliver came to our box—you were always there beside me, Harry, as strong and as sure as any husband could be, and not once—not *once*—did it have anything to do with your leg."

She gulped, with emotion and with the need for a deep breath. She hadn't dared to say all that before, fearing she'd only upset Harry more, but now that she finally had spoken, she felt almost light-headed with relief.

But he hadn't answered, not a word. Instead he was simply staring at her, his brows drawn together. At least he didn't look angry. He looked thoughtful, which was much more encouraging.

"It's because I love you, Gus," he said, as if it all were obvious. "I didn't want to see you hurt. I wanted things to be right for you. It doesn't have anything to do with my leg."

"Not at all," she said. "Your leg doesn't matter to me, not a bit. I don't care if you never dance with me. You'll always be perfect to me, Harry, because I love you, and you love me, and that's perfect, too."

"No, Gus," he said slowly, pausing just long enough for her to feel a little lurch of uncertainty. "It's you who's perfect. You understand me better than I do myself. I needed you to show me what was truly important, Gus, because I was clearly too thick-witted and stubborn to see it for myself. I could break my other leg and both my arms as well—"

"Hush, don't say such things!" she exclaimed anxiously. "Don't tempt Fate!"

"Why shouldn't I, when Fate has already dealt me the best hand of cards ever given to a man?" He raised her hand, kissing the back of it lightly, his gaze never leaving her face. "Fate put me on that infernal horse, and threw me from it as well, but Fate also brought me you. And that's what matters most. You, Gus."

She was speechless, but in the best possible way, because it meant that there was, for once, nothing left to say. He'd said everything. She longed to kiss him, there in the line of other peers waiting for admission, and she'd already arched up toward him with her lips parted when she thought better of it. He did not, and kissed her anyway.

"There," he said. "That's for luck. Not that my wife requires it, but just in case."

She laughed softly and blushed, aware of the disapproval of others waiting around them. She didn't care. Harry was her husband and her love, and there could never be anything wrong with kissing him.

Yet as they reached the doorway to the drawing room, her bravado faded. The room was large and very warm, with the summer sun streaming in through the tall windows, hung in red, along one wall. Throngs of courtiers lined the walls, watching the presentations, and somewhere among them would be Brecon and Celia and the rest of Harry's large family. At the far end, beneath a small red canopy, sat Her Majesty in an elaborate armchair, her attendants clustered around her.

"It's much farther than I thought it would be," Gus whispered with trepidation as their turn came closer.

"Be brave," he whispered back, and though he smiled, she saw he was anxious, too. Of course he'd be: this walk would be far more of a trial for him than it ever would for her.

She smiled back, as warmly as she could. "You be brave, too."

"Together," he said. "We'll be brave together."

She nodded and took a step apart from him, letting him hold her left hand slightly raised, the way that was required. Then, at last, they began to walk toward the queen.

Gus held her head high, mindful of her plumes, and stared straight ahead. She tried not to think of the dozens of important people watching her, or of the queen waiting at the other end of the room, and she tried, too, not to clutch too tightly to Harry's hand. She measured her steps to match his, something that came naturally to her now, as it should.

"I'm sorry, Gus," he said softly, startling her.

She glanced at him sharply. He was still looking straight ahead as they were supposed to, reminder enough to jerk her eyes back forward as well.

"That's the rest of what I needed to say," he continued, so softly that no one else would guess that he'd spoken at all. "I'm sorry for everything I've done or said to hurt you. Forgive me, if you can."

They were nearly to the queen, close enough that she must answer him now, or not at all.

"Yes," she whispered. "Always."

She wanted to say more, much more, to tell him how much she loved him in a thousand different ways, but the queen was directly before her, looking up at her expectantly.

"The Countess of Hargreave," announced a slightly bored male voice.

Harry's fingers tightened briefly around hers and then released her. She was on her own now, and as gracefully as she could, she curtseyed deeply, her hoops and stays creaking and her skirts crumpling around her on the floor. With her head bowed, she saw the queen's hand, plump and white and not unlike her own, before her. She bent and briefly kissed the back of it, and then rose, her head still bowed. Now all she must do was retreat backward to rejoin Harry, and relief swept over her. She hadn't fallen. Her tiara hadn't tumbled from her head. She hadn't embarrassed herself or Harry. She'd survived, and she was done.

Her Majesty, however, had other ideas.

"You are the new country bride of Lord Hargreave, yes?" she asked in heavily accented English.

Startled, Gus looked up. Harry had assured her there'd be no conversation, and here the queen was speaking to her.

"Ye-yes, Your Majesty," she stammered.

The queen smiled. She wasn't very pretty, with a broad face and flaring nostrils, but to Gus she looked kind.

"We have heard the story of your courtship," she said. "We are pleased by your devotion to Lord Hargreave whilst he was ill. You are improved, Lord Hargreave?"

"Yes, thank you, Your Majesty," Harry said behind her. "Because of my wife, I am."

"We are glad of it," the queen said. "Such love and devotion are to be praised. We trust we will see more of you both at court."

She nodded, dismissing Gus, who was at last free to retreat as the next name was called. Harry took her hand, and solemnly they backed away the required number of paces, before, at last, they could slip among the bystanders. She was vaguely aware of people praising and congratulating her for doing so well and receiving the queen's favor, but all that mattered to her was Harry. He pulled her to the back of the crowd, into an alcove by a window.

"You did it, Gus," he said. "You were perfect."

"*We* did it," she said breathlessly. "We showed them, didn't we? We showed them *all*, and—and—oh, Harry, I love you so much!"

He pulled her close and kissed her, heedless of how many people were watching or her plumes or his crutch or anything else, because nothing mattered except that they were together.

Together.

EPILOGUE

*Vauxhall Gardens, Kennington, near London
June 1769*

The evening was warm for June, with countless stars in the cloudless night sky reflected in the silvery surface of the Thames. But for the Londoners who'd been rowed across the river that night, the stars and moon couldn't begin to compare with the excitement they found at the pleasure garden at Vauxhall. Whether in the gaily-painted supper boxes or simply strolling the wide paths beneath the trees, the throngs of merry-makers laughed and flirted and drank and danced, every one of them enthused to be able to enjoy themselves in so delightful a spot.

Harry and Gus were among them. They had come to Vauxhall with his father the duke, Celia, and several other members of the family, claiming the very best supper-box: close enough to the orchestra pavilion to enjoy the music, but not so close as to make conversation impossible. Their supper was long done and cleared away, and the rest of their party had gone to stroll through the gardens' walks, leaving Harry and Gus alone together on a cushioned bench in the box.

"Was there ever so lovely a night, Harry?" asked Gus, her head pillowed against his shoulder. "I do not know which shines more brightly: the stars in the sky, or the fairy-lights in the trees. I do love the fairy-lights."

"An excellent guess, sweetheart," Harry said. "But fairy-lights in the trees are not my surprise."

"Oh, you and your confounded surprise!" Gus sighed and turned around to face him. "Honestly, Harry, I have heard so much tonight of this great surprise that when it actually occurs, I shall be so weary of the subject I will take no notice."

In Gus's mind, there could be no better way to pass the summer evening than lying lazily against her husband's chest as the music drifted around them, tucked back into the shadowy corners of the supper-box. A surprise seemed entirely unnecessary.

"I thought you liked surprises," Harry said, curling his arm protectively around her waist, or where her waist once had been. She was five months' gone with their first child, and the soft swell of her growing belly had begun to show beneath her silk skirts. "I thought they amused you."

"They do," she said, running her fingers lightly along his jaw. "If they didn't, I would never have survived being married to you, Harry."

He chuckled. "But you must admit you are never bored."

"Not at all," she said, "nor do I wish you to change, not ever. Which is why I find your insistence on the significance of this particular surprise particularly vexing."

He sighed dramatically. "Clearly you have waited long enough," he said. "Come, on your feet. Time for your surprise."

Reluctantly she rose, and he stood beside her, linking his hand fondly into hers to lead her down from the box, leaning on the ebony cane that had finally replaced the crutches. They slowly made their way through the crowd toward the music, a footman in their livery walking respectfully behind them. After nearly a year of being the Countess of Hargreave, Gus was now accustomed to the attention that followed her and Harry wherever they went. They'd become a popular couple in London society, and the love they shared was so obvious that they made even strangers smile.

"So what *is* this surprise, Harry?" Gus asked. She was curious now; she wouldn't deny it. "Is it a musical surprise?"

"In part," he said. "Here, this way, toward the front."

She hung back, watching the two rows of dancers skipping and hopping through a raucous country dance. "Wait until they're done, Harry," she said. "I've no wish to be trod upon."

"I cannot promise, sweetheart," he said. "I'm sadly out of practice."

She frowned, the music ending and the dancers scattering. "Practice for what, Harry?"

"For dancing." He handed his cane to the footman and bowed to Gus. His expression was solemn, but his blue eyes sparkled as he reached out to take her hand. "Will you honor me with this dance, my lady?"

She caught her breath, her hand fluttering to her mouth. She noticed now how none of the other dancers had returned to the floor; instead they crowded around its edges, watching and smiling with anticipation. She saw, too, how Harry's father and Celia and the others from their party were there now as well. Even the orchestra's conductor was smiling, beaming down at them from his stand.

"Oh, Harry," she said, torn between being immensely flattered, and fearing that he was making an equally immense misjudgment. He managed about the house without his cane, but she hadn't seen him trust his leg like that anywhere else, let alone dance upon it. "Are you certain you wish to do this?"

"I promised you last summer I'd dance with you beneath the stars at Vauxhall," he said. "True, it has taken me longer than I'd hoped, but tonight I will keep my promise to you, Gus. If you'll accept."

He lifted her hand to his lips, his gaze never leaving hers, and it was more than enough to make her heart skip.

"Then yes, my lord," she said, letting him lead her forward. "I will dance with you."

"A good thing you accepted," he said to a smattering of applause around them. "I would have felt like a deuced idiot if you hadn't."

"You know I can never refuse you anything, Harry," she said, standing across from him. "Not even this."

"Especially not this," he said, and winked. "My first dance with you. Catch me if I stumble, sweetheart."

She gasped, not even wanting to consider that possibility, but the music had already begun, and now it was too late to stop. The dance was an old, familiar piece, with the conductor slowing the rhythm to a pace that was almost stately. Back and forward, turn, turn, and back again: The steps came effortlessly to her, and to Harry, too. It was not perfect, but it didn't need to be, and when the last note rang out over the trees, Harry pulled her close and held her tight, there with all of Vauxhall cheering.

"Were you surprised, sweetheart?" he said, his voice low by her ear for only her to hear. "Wasn't it worth it?"

"Oh, yes," she said, so happy that tears stung her eyes. "You kept your promise, exactly as you said you would."

"I always will for you, Gus," he said. "It's part of loving you as much as I do."

"Then promise you'll always love me as much as I do you," she said, reaching up to kiss him.

"Forever," he said, just before his lips met hers. "Forever."

Read on for an exciting preview
of Isabella Bradford's
next Breconridge Brothers novel

A SINFUL DECEPTION

He knew in an instant that she was different from every other woman in the ballroom.

Lord Geoffrey Fitzroy watched the lady as she paused in the arched doorway, a figure of perfect, self-contained calm beyond all the others with their whirling spangled silks and too-bright laughter. She didn't fidget or preen, the way women usually did while they were waiting to be announced to the company. She simply *stood*, and made standing look more elegantly fascinating than Geoffrey had ever dreamed possible.

"Who is that divine lady?" he asked his brother Harry, the Earl of Hargreave, who was beside him at the far end of the ballroom with the other gentlemen who'd rather drink than dance.

"Which lady, Geoffrey?" Harry asked as he reached for a fresh glass of wine from the tray of a passing footman. "The room is filled with ladies."

"The one in blue," Geoffrey said, amazed that his brother needed more description. To him there was clearly only one lady among the scores in attendance who could be called divine, a term he had not carelessly. Even at this distance, she was exceptionally beautiful, but not conventionally so, with pale skin and gleaming dark hair that she wore without powder. "There, in the doorway."

"That's Miss Serena Carew." Harry turned towards Geoffrey, one brow raised with bemusement. "I cannot believe you don't know her. Or rather, *of* her. No gentleman truly *knows* the distant Miss Serena Carew. None of us poor sots are worthy of her acquaintance."

Geoffrey emptied his glass, setting it on a nearby sideboard. "Then that's only because she has yet to know me," he said confidently, smoothing his sleeves to spruce his already immaculate evening coat. "A lack I intend to remedy at once."

"I thought you kept clear of unmarried ladies," Harry said. "I recall you being quite firm on the subject of remaining a bachelor as long as was humanly possible."

Geoffrey shrugged, his gaze still intent on the lady. "I'm not intending matrimony, Harry. I'm fully aware of how far I can go before her family begins demanding the banns be called. *Exactly* how far."

"A moment, Geoffrey." Harry took him by the arm to hold him back. "Take care. You should know the lady's story before you begin the chase. She's old Allwyn's granddaughter, and he guards her like a hawk with a favorite chick. That's his sister Lady Morley with her now."

"What of it?" Geoffrey smiled, nonchalant. It didn't matter to him that she was the granddaughter of the Marquis of Allwyn, not when he himself was the son of the Duke of Breconridge. "That's hardly enough to put me off."

"There's more," Harry said. "Her father was employed by the East India Company, and she was born and spent her childhood in India."

"Truly?" Geoffrey studied her with ever-growing interest. "Where? With all the other English in Calcutta?"

"At first, yes," Harry said, tapping his ebony cane lightly on the floor. "But the father had a falling out with the Company after his wife died. Turned Turk, as they say, and went off to make his own fortune trading jewels and living like a pagan in the hills, complete with a harem of Hindi mistresses. I don't know all the details—I doubt Allwyn himself does—but you'll see soon enough how it has marked Miss Carew."

Geoffrey's curiosity—and his interest—grew as he continued to watch Miss Carew and her aunt. They had been announced to the company and were slowly making their way through the room, the older woman smiling and nodding and greeting friends. Miss Carew simply followed. It was if she'd removed herself to another place entirely, a place she preferred far more than the gaiety and music of this ballroom. Geoffrey was not only attracted; he was intrigued. What could be more fascinating than a beauty with a mysterious past?

Not, of course, that he'd confess any of this to his brother.

"I cannot believe you'd call a lovely creature like that 'marked'," he said instead. "Surely you exaggerate, Harry."

But Harry shook his head. "Judge the lady for yourself, and decide if I exaggerate. You'll see soon enough that she is not at ease in company—*any* company."

Geoffrey grinned. "Fifty guineas says that she'll dance with me."

"Fifty?" Harry said, chuckling. "I'll say a hundred, the surest wager I've ever made. I've never once seen that particular lady dance with anyone."

"One hundred it is, then," Geoffrey said, patting Harry on the shoulder. "Watch me proceed, brother, and be astonished. I'll be collecting those guineas before the late supper."

Geoffrey plunged into the crowd, determined to win

both the wager and the lady. Based on experience, he'd every reason to be confidant, too. He was tall and handsome, with an easy, infallible charm that women of every age and rank found nearly impossible to ignore or resist. He'd begun beguiling his nursery-maids in the cradle even before he could speak, and since then the results had been the same with every other female he encountered.

It was simply a fact: he liked women, and they liked him, very much. Why should Miss Carew be any different? In his estimation, Serena Carew was the most interesting and beautiful young lady in the room. It only made sense that she should be dancing with him.

There was, of course, the faint possibility that she would reject him outright, the way his brother had predicted. Some ladies did insist on the nicety of a proper introduction, even in a crush like this, but he'd risk it for the chance to speak to her first, without the aunt or anyone else interfering. Besides, he never tired of the intoxicating challenge of pursuit, the first step towards flirtation, passion, even seduction. Anything was possible.

She was turned away from him now, her back to him as he drew closer. Her shining dark hair set her apart from all the powdered heads around her, with the pale nape of her neck an elegant, vulnerable curve above the blue silk of her gown. She wore drop earrings and a necklace of diamonds and sapphires so large that on any other woman her age, the stones would surely have been paste. Yet on Serena Carew, Geoffrey knew they were genuine; nothing about her would be so blatantly false.

"Miss Carew," he said when he was at last close enough that she'd hear him.

She did, and turned to face him in a single fluid movement. From a distance he'd seen she was a beauty, but he wasn't prepared for the impact of that beauty with only a few feet between them. Her pale skin was golden ivory, her mouth full and red, her nose regal and her brows perfectly arched, but it was her eyes that stunned him: almond-shaped and the color of clearest amber, deep-set and shadowed with mystery, and perhaps melancholy as well. Geoffrey wasn't sure. Blast, he wasn't sure of anything when he stared into eyes like that.

But to his chagrin, he clearly had not affected her the same way. There wasn't a flicker of warmth in those golden eyes, nor encouragement, either.

"I do not know you, sir," she said, a simple declaration.

He smiled his most winning smile, determined to thaw her chill, and not just because he knew his brother was watching, either.

"Lord Geoffrey Fitzroy," he said with as much of a bow and flourish as he could manage in the crowd around them. "Your servant in every way, Miss Carew."

She did not smile in return, nor did she so much as dip her head in acknowledgement of his higher rank. Instead she regarded him impassively, her expression not changing even a fraction.

"Indeed, sir," she said. "If you are in truth the nobleman whom you profess to be, than you cannot be my servant. It is impossible for you to be both."

"But I am," he said, smiling still. With a different inflection, her words might have been banter, teasing and intimate, but she was making it clear enough that they weren't meant to be anything but discouraging. Damnation, could she have somehow learned of the wager he'd just made with his brother? What other reason could there be for her to be behaving so coldly towards him?

"My name and title are mine through birth," he said, "but you, Miss Carew, are the sole reason for my devoted servitude, and I—"

"Lord Geoffrey, good evening!" exclaimed Lady Morley, joining them. "Why, Serena, my dear, I see you have already met one of the most notable gentlemen in the room."

Lady Morley beamed at Geoffrey, her dark eyes sharp beneath her oversized, frizzled wig. Clearly she'd overheard, and clearly, too, she was determined to repair matters as best she could.

"Such a splendid gathering, Lord Geoffrey," she continued. "I trust you are enjoying yourself?"

"I am, Lady Morley," he said. He didn't usually consider chaperones as allies, but in this case, he'd take any help that was offered. "Especially now that I am in the company of two such lovely ladies."

Lady Morley chuckled happily and fluttered her fan. It was the response that Geoffrey had hoped to win from Miss Carew, who continued to regard him with the same degree of dispassionate interest that she'd display towards a lower order of insect.

"Lord Geoffrey is the son of His Grace the Duke of Breconridge, Serena," Lady Morley said, a not-very-subtle explanation for the younger woman, "and he is the younger brother of the Earl of Hargreave. His charm, of course, is all his own."

Geoffrey smiled, charmingly. He'd heard this kind of explanation from mothers and aunts and older sisters so many times that he could interpret its true meaning perfectly: *This handsome fellow is only a second son, Serena, but he's one with his own fortune and therefore well worth your attention, and while the older brother may be married, his wife has only given him daughters, so there's still a chance for you to become a duchess.*

Geoffrey could only hope Miss Carew interpreted the message, too. "I see the musicians are returning to their chairs," he said, bowing towards her, "and the next set of dances will be beginning shortly. Will you honor me with the pleasure of a dance, Miss Carew?"

"Of course she would," Lady Morley swiftly answered for her. "Serena, dance with Lord Geoffrey."

"*No!*" protested Miss Carew with haste, and almost alarm. "That is, you know I do not dance, Aunt, and I—"

"Nonsense," Lady Morley said briskly, the merest hint of admonition in the word. "You dance like an angel, my dear. I insist. Go, take your place with Lord Geoffrey among the other couples whilst room remains on the floor."

Still Miss Carew hesitated, her unexpected reluctance an unflattering challenge to Geoffrey. Perhaps she truly did dance like a goose. A beautiful face was no guarantee she'd be light on her toes. But for the sake of that beautiful face, as well as for the wager—he could practically feel his brother's gaze in the middle of his back—he was determined to persevere.

"One dance, that is all," he said softly, coaxing, and holding his hand out to her. "I ask for nothing beyond that."

"Very well." With a sigh she looked down, avoiding his gaze, and carefully placed her hand in his palm. "One dance and no more."

"One dance, then," he repeated. He closed his fingers around hers to lead her towards the floor. Her hand was cool and soft, as reserved as the rest of her, which did not surprise him.

"I must apologize for my aunt, Lord Geoffrey," she said. "She can be unconscionably forward where I am concerned. Pray do not feel any obligation to dance with me."

"There is no obligation, Miss Carew," he said firmly, and just as firmly pulled her along until they stood facing one another, waiting for the other dancers to take their places in line. "When we are better acquainted, you will realize that I seldom, if ever, do anything I don't wish to do. I'm stubborn that way. I wished to dance with you, and now I am, and I only hope that you will come to find the experience enjoyable as well."

Before she could answer, the gentleman at the head of the line loudly announced the dance's name: *Lady Randolph's Frolic.* At once the musicians began to play, and Geoffrey had no choice but to bow and begin leading Miss Carew through the steps. The dance was a rollicking country reel that was complicated to follow, and offered no opportunity for further conversation. All that Geoffrey could do was smile, and admire Miss Carew as she danced.

It was impossible not to. She was dressed in much the same fashion as the other ladies, and it was clear that beneath her blue silk gown, her slender figure wore the whalebone-stiffened stays and hoops that were required for every proper English lady.

But she didn't dance like an English lady. Not at all. Oh, she followed every step with a precision that would make her dancing-master proud, her back straight and her head held high. Yet there was a sinuous grace to her movements that could never be learned in any London drawing-room, nor would it be entirely proper there, either. Her amber eyes lost their sadness and sparkled, and her lips parted and gradually began to smile with pleasure. The slight dip and sway to her hips, the arch to her wrists and arms, the way she unconsciously framed the rising swell of her breasts with every gesture—all of it was innately seductive, and the fact that she seemed entirely innocent of the effect she was creating only made it all the more enticing.

Geoffrey couldn't look away, and neither could any of the other men around them. He couldn't recall a dance that was over and done so swiftly, nor another that he'd wished would never end.

"Mercy," she said breathlessly, pulling free of Geoffrey's hand to draw her fan from her pocket. She spread the blades with a single sweep and began to fan her still-flushed cheeks. Belatedly she remembered to curtsey, her fan still in her hand.

"I thank you, Lord Geoffrey," she said as she rose. "If you please, I should like to return to my aunt now."

He'd won his wager with his brother. He'd had his dance with Miss Carew. He'd made every other man in the room envious. He'd no reason not to do what she asked, and lead her back to her aunt's side. But instead he stood before her, oddly off balance and incapable of doing what he should or what was expected.

"If you please, Lord Geoffrey," she said again, uneasily this time. She was already composing herself, withdrawing back into being that proper English lady.

And he did not want to let her go.

"Another dance," he said, reaching for her hand.

She pulled away, shaking her head. "I agreed to only the one dance, Lord Geoffrey."

"You can't deny that you enjoyed yourself," he said. "You do indeed dance like an angel."

She shook her head again and closed her fan. "If you'll excuse me, Lord Geoffrey—"

"Then come walk with me in the garden," he said with all the charm he possessed. "The moon is full and the stars are bright."

She blushed, gathering her skirts with one hand. "Forgive me, but I must return to my aunt directly."

"*Kāyara*," he said, smiling still as he called her a coward in Hindi. He hadn't planned to say that; it simply came out.

But it worked. She stopped abruptly, frozen in place.

"What did you say, Lord Geoffrey?"

His smile widened. "*Mairh āpakō ēka kāyara bulāyā.*" *I called you a coward.*

She raised her chin, striving to be aloof. "I am an English lady, Lord Geoffrey. You should not address me in Hindi."

"Yet you understood me, Miss Carew," he said easily. "And you *are* being something of a coward."

She blushed again and frowned. "Come with me, Lord Geoffrey," she said, turning away with a rustle of silk. "We must speak, alone, where no one else will hear."

She didn't look back to see if he followed, assuming he would. He did, of course. Hadn't he been the one who'd suggested they step outside in the first place?

He followed her from the ballroom, through the tall, arched door, and onto the stone terrace above the garden. There were a few lanterns here to light the steps down to the paths below, but most of the terrace was cast in welcoming darkness beneath the trees. Several couples lingered in the deeper shadows to take advantage of the privacy, the women's silk gowns faintly luminous and their little sighs of pleasure clear.

Steadfastly Miss Carew walked past them, not looking as she led Geoffrey to the farthest end of the terrace. At last she turned and faced him, her arms folded over her breasts with discouraging determination. Moonlight spilled over her face and throat like a caress, and emphasized the dusky cleft between her breasts. Clearly she'd no idea of how delectable she looked, her eyes golden and her skin velvety pale. Geoffrey certainly did, and with the memory of her sensuous dancing still fresh in his mind, it was requiring all his willpower not to take her immediately into his arms.

"Now, Lord Geoffrey," she said, her voice both low and fierce. "Tell me why you addressed me in that—that ridiculous manner."

"It was hardly ridiculous, Miss Carew." He wasn't accustomed to wasting perfectly good moonlight in mere conversation, but if that was what it would take to win her, then he'd oblige. "You were in fact being quite cow-ardly."

She sighed impatiently. "I didn't mean *what* you said. It was *how* you said it, in—in a foreign language. Why did you speak so?"

"To amuse you," he said easily, shifting closer to her. "I knew you were from India, and I thought you would find it entertaining."

"What could you know of India, Lord Geoffrey?" she demanded, much more warmly than he'd expected.

"Not nearly as much as I wish to," he said. Even when she was trying to be stern, her voice enchanted him, husky and mellifluous with a hint of an exotic accent. "When I visited India, I found it the most fascinating and beautiful place on earth."

She nodded, quick little jerks of her chin. "So that is it. You are but one more younger son turned nabob."

"Like your father?" he asked, unable to resist.

"No," she said firmly. "My father was a gentleman of honor, an officer in the East India Company. He was no rapacious English nabob, rushing across the sea to grasp at opportunity and make his fortune however he could."

"But I didn't go to make my fortune, either, Miss Carew," Geoffrey said. "I went for pleasure."

She raised her brows in disbelief. "I'm not a fool, Lord Geoffrey. No English gentleman goes out to India for pleasure."

"I assure you I did," he said. "When I was done with school, my father wished me to travel across the Continent to complete my education in Paris and Rome. I re-fused, and insisted on India instead. I've always been fascinated by the east, you see."

With her mouth set, she searched his face, clearly de-ciding whether to accept his answer or not. She should have; it was the truth, every word.

"Do you truly speak Hindi," she said quickly, shifting

to that language once again, *"or did you recite those few words by rote like a trained parrot?"*

He laughed, as much at her bravado as at the words themselves, and answered her back in Hindi as proof. *"I speak it well enough to know how gravely you have insulted me."*

She drew in her breath sharply, surprised by his response.

"Then we shall consider it even between us," she said in English. "My father was the bravest European in the Company's Territories—as brave as any lion!—and he would not have taken kindly to hearing his daughter called a coward."

"Then please forgive me, Miss Carew," he said, bowing. "You've already proven your bravery by joining me here. I'll admit I made a sorry jest, but I intended it without malice."

"It no longer matters, Lord Geoffrey." She dropped her arms to her sides, as if the brief exchange had knocked the fight from her. "You startled me, that was all. It was the first time I'd heard Hindi spoken in years."

He lowered his voice, liking the idea of a confidential secret language they could share. *"Mairh khuśī sē, yaha āpa kē sātha bāta karēngē."*

I'd happily speak it with you.

"No, Lord Geoffrey," she said in English, the words turning brittle and sharp. "I am an English lady, and I intend to speak like one. I must be more . . . more careful."

"Careful, Miss Carew?" he asked, puzzled. "Careful of what? Surely not of me?"

But she only shook her head, raising her small chin with fresh resolve. "If you were so enamored of India, why did you leave? You are a gentleman of rank and wealth. You may do as you please with your life. Why are you not there still?"

"Because I was called back on account of my older brother," he said. "I had no choice."

"No choice, Lord Geoffrey?" she asked curiously. "Your brother holds such sway over you?"

"Not in the way you imply," he said. He did not like telling this story, for it brought back a time of dread and uneasiness; he had never felt so helpless as he had on that long, bleak voyage back to England. "I received a letter—a letter many months old—that informed me that my brother had suffered a grievous accident, and was not expected to live. Even though I feared I would most certainly be too late, I sailed for home at once."

"Oh, no," she said softly, resting her hand on his sleeve. "Such a loss! I am so sorry, Lord Geoffrey."

"You needn't be." He smiled crookedly, liking her touch on his arm. "Harry survived, the devil, and recovered to greet me on my return, and with a new wife as well. So while all my cynical acquaintances were ready to congratulate me on taking my brother's place, the story had a far happier ending, and a good thing it was."

Her eyes widened with shock. "But—but how could you ever replace your brother?"

"Only as my father's heir," he said quickly, wanting to reassure her. "That's all that's required of second sons, you know, to be another male in constant readiness. I could never replace Harry in any other way, nor would I wish to become Duke of Breconridge at such a price."

He knew he'd said too much. He couldn't help it. He always did when he spoke of Harry's accident, and though he'd come to realize it was only his way of dealing with such a near-tragedy, it still made him feel a bit foolish.

"I didn't intend to rattle on like that, Miss Carew," he said, "but if you had a brother or sister, then you would understand."

"But I do understand." The melancholy that he'd first

glimpsed in her eyes was now there in her voice. "Such a loss would have been intolerable for you to bear. Indeed, how fortunate for you both that the story had a happier ending."

Of course she'd understand loss. She was an orphan, the only survivor of her family in India. Instinctively he slipped his hand over hers, linking their fingers together.

"Again I find I must apologize to you," he said gently. "I'd no intention of raising old sorrows."

She glanced down at their joined hands, and slowly curled her fingers into his.

"Why should you be so kind to me?" she asked wistfully. "I've done nothing that would make me deserve that from you."

"But you did," he insisted. "I spoke without thought, and I was wrong."

She looked up, her smile small and bittersweet. "And I say you are being kind to me, and generous as well. You are not what I expected, Lord Geoffrey, not at all."

"Nor are you, Miss Carew." He used their linked hands to pull her close, gambling that she wouldn't reject him. "The gossips do you great injustice."

"I'd rather not imagine what they say of me." She came to him effortlessly, as if she belonged in his arms. "But I must be careful in all things, you see, and especially cautious in whom I trust."

"I'm eminently trustworthy," he said, though as soon as he'd spoken he realized how hollow his words must sound, given that he'd just slipped his arm around her waist.

She knew it, too. But while her smile turned wry, she still didn't pull away. "You did not come here into the moonlight to make empty declarations like that one, Lord Geoffrey. I would rather guess that your intention was to seduce me."

"Ahh," he said gruffly, chagrined. Of course that had

been exactly what he'd intended, more or less, but he hadn't expected her to acknowledge it quite so bluntly, and especially not after such a somber conversation. "You are very direct, Miss Carew."

"It's the truth, isn't it?" Her sapphire earrings bobbed against her cheeks as she rested her open palm lightly on his chest. "That is the reason all gentlemen—no, all *men*—pursue women. It is no great secret. I may be a lady, Lord Geoffrey, but I am not a fool."

"I never thought you were, sweet," he said softly, grazing the back of his fingers over her cheek. If she were going to be so deuced frank, then he saw no reason not to show her that he, too, knew what was supposed to happen in the moonlight. "You strike me as being remarkably clever."

"Oh, I am, Lord Geoffrey," she said. "You've no notion of how clever I can be."

"Then you must educate me," he murmured, no longer really paying much attention to what she was saying. She fit neatly against him, her waist charmingly small. He liked how she was gazing up at him, how her amber eyes were filled with warmth, and he liked her scent, an exotic mix of sandalwood and roses. "I'll enjoy that."

"So shall I." She hesitated for a long moment before continuing, tracing her fingers absently over the silk embroidered scrolls along the front of his coat. "Have you heard of *kismet*, Lord Geoffrey? It is a Persian word, not Hindi, but it was much used in India. Do you know its meaning?"

His Persian was nonexistent, but that was one word he knew, just as he knew the trouble it could bring him.

"One moment now, Miss Carew," he said, his well-practiced bachelor instincts instantly turning wary. "I don't believe in love at first sight, no matter the language."

"Love?" she repeated, astonished. "I said nothing of

love, Lord Geoffrey. I spoke of kismet. Of fate, or destiny, or fortune. Of how our lives are pre-ordained, and we are helpless to make them otherwise. I spoke nothing of love."

He frowned and drew back from her a fraction. "But what other destiny is there for a beautiful lady than love?"

"Not for me," she said softly, sadly. "Never for me."

He was accustomed to arch beauties who pretended to scorn the men around them as unworthy of their love, but never a lady who described herself in this way. The sorrowful conviction in her voice made no sense, even as it touched him.

"Don't say such grim things, Miss Carew," he said, striving to cheer her as once again he drew her into his arms. "You simply haven't found the proper man, that is all."

She shook her head, watching her hand settle over the front of his coat, over his heart.

"When first I took notice of you," she said, her voice barely above a whisper, "I believed you were no better than any of the other foolish young gentlemen my aunt has presented to me. Yet as soon as you spoke, I sensed you were not like the others. How, or why, or in what fashion, I cannot yet tell, but you are. You were sent to me for a purpose. That was what I meant by kismet. And though I wish with all my heart that it were not so, I feel the pull of kismet, and of you."

Kismet. He realized with dismay that there was absolutely no way that he could kiss her now. She was still as beautiful, still eminently desirable, but she'd changed everything with her belief in fate, in destiny, in kismet.

Because in some devilish way he couldn't begin to understand, he believed it, too.

"I must go," she said, suddenly slipping free of his embrace with the same sinuous grace that she'd shown while dancing. "This is wrong. I can't be alone with you any longer."

He reached out, determined to capture her, but her blue silk gown was already disappearing into the shadows.

"A moment, Miss Carew," he called, following swiftly after her. "Don't go just yet. What of fate, of kismet?"

She paused, her head bent, before finally glancing back at him over one pale shoulder. "Each day I ride in Hyde Park at half-past two."

Then she fled, nearly running, her slippered feet silent on the stone.

Geoffrey stopped, staring after her as he raked his fingers back through his hair. She could run as fast as she pleased, but she couldn't escape, not from him, and not from herself, either. He'd played this game before. He knew how it would end. No matter how deuced mysterious she tried to be, he'd solve her puzzle in the end. He nodded, reassuring himself. Of course he'd win. He always did where ladies were concerned.

Yet even as he sauntered back into the brightly-lit ballroom, he could not put Serena Carew from his thoughts, or that single word she'd whispered to him.

Kismet.